RICHES UNTOLD

Book One
THE CHRONICLES OF THE GOLDEN FRONTIER

Riches Untold

~

GILBERT MORRIS
and
J. LANDON FERGUSON

CROSSWAY BOOKS • WHEATON, ILLINOIS
A DIVISION OF GOOD NEWS PUBLISHERS

Riches Untold

Published by Crossway Books
           A division of Good News Publishers
           1300 Crescent Street
           Wheaton, Illinois 60187

Cover illustration: Tony Meers
Cover design: Cindy Kiple

First printing, 1998

Printed in the United States of America

Library of Congress Cataloging-in-Publication Data
Morris, Gilbert.
    Riches untold / Gilbert Morris and J. Landon Ferguson.
        p.   cm. — (The Chronicles of the golden frontier ; bk. #1)
    ISBN 1-58134-014-1 (pbk. : alk. paper)
    I. Ferguson, J. Landon, 1952- . II. Title. III. Series: Morris,
Gilbert. Chronicles of the golden frontier ; bk. #1.
PS3563.08742R53 1998   813'.54—DC21
                                              98-17250

06		05		04		03		02		01		00		99	
15	14	13	12	11	10	9	8	7	6	5	4	3	2		

Especially for my beloved wife, Rebecca.

J. Landon Ferguson

CONTENTS

PART ONE

New Orleans

Swept Away

A balmy breeze stirred Jennifer Hamilton's wavy auburn hair as she watched a storm roll across the hazy distance, moving above the Gulf with its solid sheets of rain, just as it did almost every afternoon. As she strolled through the French Quarter with its heavy fragrances, she observed the changing world, her green eyes sharp with anger at the imposing presence of the Union soldiers occupying New Orleans. According to the New Orleans *Picayune*, the war was almost over, but that wouldn't bring her father back. A sergeant in Stonewall Jackson's corps, he had died in the battle of Fredericksburg.

Making her way out of the shadows, Jennifer moved quickly to a sunny river wharf. Ignoring the dull-faced people passing by, she made her way along the solid planks, her footsteps echoing loudly. The shrill of a steamboat whistle pierced the damp air as she glanced out upon the Mississippi, a river now ruled by Union ironclads and wooden gunboats. Her hatred for the Union alternated with feelings of depression and defeat. She slumped slightly as if a great weight rested on her finely pointed shoulders. At the age of seventeen, life had already shown her its rough ways.

It had seemed like a good idea, she reminded herself, to put on a new dress and take a walk, hoping to boost her spirits. She had smiled at her reflection in the mirror, her fair-skinned face bright with enthusiasm as the blue dress, tight at her waist, revealed her blossoming figure. As she now gazed into the muddy river, its agitation matched her own inner turmoil. Her only outlet had been the romance novels she was ashamed to read, though the books brought relief from the unyielding discipline and self-denial that had been forced upon her.

Jennifer moved slowly back along the wharf, unmindful of the busy world around her as she let the rippling water hold her attention. At one spot the rail was missing, but she took no notice, mesmerized by the reflection of sparkling sunlight. Almost losing her footing, she quickly stepped back in an attempt to regain her balance.

Just at that moment a tall man in a Union uniform came rushing by, his mind occupied with other things as Jennifer backed into his path. The abruptness of the collision sent Jennifer screaming over the edge and into the shallow water along the muddy bank. Immediately the man jumped from the pier, splashing into the water to help her. He pulled her up by the arms, the mud sucking at their feet as they moved safely to the bank. A chuckling crowd peered from above as the lieutenant tried futilely to brush the sticky brown mud from her dress.

"You . . . you . . . !" Jennifer, so terrified and angry she could hardly speak, gasped for breath. "You idiot!"

"I'm sorry, miss! I didn't mean to push you into the river. Are you all right?"

Jennifer pushed her clinging hair out of her face and spat the earthy-tasting river water from her mouth. "How dare you!" she moaned, dabbing ineffectually at her ruined dress, then really looking at the man for the first time. The Union uniform and the foreboding it caused in her contrasted with his countenance. His dark blue eyes seemed genuinely sensitive. A thin mustache accented his aristocratic face, and sincerity resonated in his calm voice.

"At least let me help you get out of the river," he said courteously as he pulled her up the bank and onto dry land. "I'm Lieutenant Drake DeSpain. May I give you a ride home? My carriage is nearby." His sharp eyes were filled with self-assurance as he held her arm tightly.

Jerking her arm free, Jennifer glared angrily at the tall soldier. She wanted to lash out at him, but he truly seemed apologetic, though the way his blue eyes followed the curves of her wet dress did make her uncomfortable. She pinched the water out of her stringy hair, self-conscious about her drenched appearance and the stench from the river mud. "You could at least do that much!" she snapped, angered by her embarrassment as much as anything else.

After climbing into the carriage, Drake gave her a blanket for warmth as the horses' hooves clopped briskly down the busy street. "I really am sorry," the soldier said, his voice smooth and easy, his face friendly. "May I ask your name?"

Struck by his politeness, the full pout she'd been wearing vanished. "Jennifer Hamilton."

"A lovely name," he murmured with a slight smile on his lips as he sat there in his mud-stained, soaked uniform. "I'm not laughing at you, Miss Hamilton. I'm laughing at myself. That was the dumbest thing I ever did!"

Noting her shyness, DeSpain took the burden of the conversation. He was a handsome man, and Jennifer felt her cheeks warm with color as she turned her face to look the other way.

Following her directions, they soon arrived at a rather drab one-story house in a war-weary neighborhood. Jennifer quickly left the carriage and ran up the steps to the front porch, which was supported with four small, faded columns. Hurriedly she opened the front door. Moving swiftly, Drake stood right behind her, apparently eager to be of further assistance. A small woman with worried features met them at the door, her light brown hair swept up and her blue eyes stern with concern.

"What happened to you?" she questioned, staring at Jennifer's disheveled appearance. "And who are you?" she demanded of the tall man who stood awkwardly in a soaking wet Union uniform.

"Well . . . oh, nothing happened, Mother!" Jennifer exclaimed quickly. "This—this is Lieutenant Drake DeSpain. He pulled me out of the river after I . . ."

The small woman turned to the man standing quietly before her, her eyes as cold as polar ice.

"I'm afraid it was my fault, Mrs. Hamilton," the officer offered quickly. "I was rushing along the pier and accidentally knocked your daughter into the water. If there is anything I can do to help or to compensate for . . ."

Cora Hamilton gave him a skeptical appraisal. Since as far as she was concerned all Union soldiers were villains, she slammed the door in his face. She turned impatiently to Jennifer, still standing there wrapped in a blanket, looking bewildered. "How dare you associate with the likes of him!"

Jennifer hesitated, her eyes wide and alive, a mischievous smile tugging at the corners of her mouth. "Mother . . . he's the best-looking man I've ever seen."

Her mother's face twisted with disgust. "He's a *Yankee!*" She quickly collapsed in a nearby chair, feeling faint. The excitement was too much for her poor health.

~

The next morning, still wearing her nightgown, Jennifer sat in a big bay window holding her longhaired yellow cat, Salome. The animal purred with contentment as Jennifer dreamed of the man who had so awkwardly run into her the day before. He was a Union officer, and she detested everything Union! And yet, he seemed so charming and romantic, so absolutely handsome! Her mind and her heart were in conflict, but her heart seemed to be winning the battle.

A loud knock boomed at the front door, and Jennifer lowered Salome to the floor, then slipped into a long robe. She fluffed her hair as she crossed the front room, a slight hope evident in her green eyes as she opened the door. A well-dressed black porter stood there holding a spray of red roses.

"M-mornin', m-ma'am," the round-faced black man stuttered. "Are you Miss Jennifer Hamilton?"

Jennifer drew back slightly. "Yes, I am."

"Fo' you, Miss Hamilton," the black man said, bowing as he handed her the fragrant flowers. He turned and stepped away, waiting with his hands behind his back as he gazed into the distance.

Jennifer took the vase and set the flowers on a table. She quickly plucked a white card out of the arrangement and opened it.

Dear Miss Hamilton,

It would be my greatest pleasure if you would find the grace to accompany me to dinner tonight.

Most Sincerely,
Drake DeSpain

Flustered, Jennifer thought, *I can't say yes to a man I met only yesterday. On the other hand, if I say no, I may never hear from him again.* She turned back to the open door and the waiting porter. "Tell him I accept."

The porter showed his big white teeth in an encouraging smile and tipped his derby hat in agreement. "Yes, ma'am. He say he will be here at six o'clock, if dat be all right with you."

"That'll be fine," Jennifer said quickly and eased the door closed. She watched the Negro in black boots board the carriage and snap the reins as the horse jerked the carriage away.

Spinning around, Jennifer took a deep breath, heady with the fragrance of the red roses. She smiled as she read the note again, enjoying the artistic curves of DeSpain's graceful handwriting. Concern about socializing with a Union officer was far from her mind. A handsome man wanted to spend time with her!

～

Promptly at six o'clock the same carriage arrived back at Jennifer's house. Drake DeSpain emerged and walked confidently toward the door.

Quickly shutting the curtain she was peeking through, Jennifer smiled at her reflection in the mirror one last time, her heart racing as she arranged her auburn hair that she wore up, with a few strands curling beside her oval face. She wished she didn't have such a plain face, although she'd been told she was pretty.

Her mother, dressed in black, approached, almost beside herself. "Jennifer, I thoroughly disapprove of . . . of your dating a Yankee!

Must I remind you that they killed your father? And this man," she said scornfully, turning her head toward the knock at the door, "I just know he's no good! There's something about him . . ."

"Oh, Mother!" Jennifer responded pleasantly. "*He* didn't kill Papa—he's a gentleman." She simply would not class this man with the Yankees she so detested! Certainly such a kind man was nothing like those who had killed her father or put New Orleans under their stern domination. She'd wondered whether he had Christian faith like she and her mother, but that would have to be considered at a later date. Moving quickly to the door, she paused and took a deep breath as she undid the latch. Mrs. Hamilton followed, her arms folded in front of her.

Opening the door, Jennifer's eyes gleamed as she smiled invitingly. "Hello, Mr. DeSpain. Please come in."

Drake entered, handsome and tall in his best parade uniform. In his confident voice he said, "Good evening, Mrs. Hamilton. How are you? Miss Jennifer, you look mighty nice. Shall we go?"

Jennifer turned to her mother, who had not spoken a word. "Don't wait up for me, Mother. You don't need to worry."

"I am worried," Mrs. Hamilton replied with a scowl.

Smiling and ignoring her mother's concern, Jennifer pulled the door closed behind her. She and her new friend strolled down the walk to the carriage, Drake holding her arm gently. The porter opened the carriage doors for them, then climbed up to his seat. He shouted "Shoo" to get the horse moving.

"That's a lovely red gown," Drake complimented, his eyes sparkling in the late afternoon light. "I hope I didn't ruin the dress you were wearing yesterday." He laughed as he said, "I had to throw away my uniform. It was ruined."

Jennifer laughed with him, then answered, "My dress is fine." Uncertain of what she must and must not say to remain proper in the eyes of this intriguing man, she chose to remain quiet.

The ride through the cool evening shadows and the rain-washed streets of the New Orleans French Quarter was pleasant. The unmistakable sound of brass horns echoed with their animated rhythm as the sound of occasional laughter drifted to the coach, the nocturnal personality of a city that had learned to thrive despite affliction. The coach halted in front of Antoine's, a well-respected establishment known for its fine cuisine. Jennifer thought she would burst with excitement but contained herself, a slight smile accenting her young and innocent face.

Once inside, Drake pulled her chair out and seated her at a lavishly decorated table with a white tablecloth, gleaming silver, and fresh-cut azaleas. Deeply impressed, Jennifer watched Drake, his wavy brown hair combed carefully above the short-cropped sides, his sensitive face appealing and romantic, his deep blue eyes fixed on her.

"Would you like some wine before dinner?" he asked as he nimbly waved for the waiter.

"I'm sorry, but I don't drink," Jennifer said evenly. "Our family has strong Christian roots, and we never have wine or liquor in our home."

"You don't mind if I indulge, do you?" Drake asked politely.

"Not at all, as long as you don't drink too much." Her tolerant answer hid her inner misgivings.

"A hearty red Beaujolais will be fine," he told the waiter and then returned his attention to Jennifer. "You seem quiet tonight. I wouldn't have guessed you were the quiet type yesterday."

She bashfully glanced away, maintaining her pleasant smile. "I was rather upset yesterday."

"And rightly so." He smiled. "It probably isn't every day you get dunked in the river by a clumsy oaf like me."

Jennifer laughed faintly as the waiter returned and observed the wine serving tradition, Drake sampling and approving the wine before his glass was filled.

To Drake, the soft light of the restaurant paled around Jennifer's bright green eyes and her wide smile. Drake drank in her beauty—her long curling lashes and straight English nose, her thick auburn hair that formed a widow's peak above an oval, fair-skinned face. *Such a lovely beauty*, he thought, trying not to stare. *I'll have to be careful with this one—I don't want to get too committed.*

"What do you do in the army?" Jennifer asked. "Have you ever been in any skirmishes?"

"Me? Heavens no! I've never fired a shot. I work on General Butler's staff, far away from any battles."

"I might have guessed," Jennifer said, softening, relieved at the accuracy of her earlier assumptions about this man. He seemed very well-to-do. "What do you do when you're not soldiering?"

"Oh, a little of this and a little of that. I keep myself busy in a variety of ways. I recently won a large pot in a poker game, and I couldn't wait to spend it on you." His eyes sparkled as he spoke.

Color filled her cheeks. *He seems so real and sincere, so important,* she mused, admiring the long, dark face of a man who was clearly accustomed to the finer things in life. *He's so handsome, so relaxed and easygoing.* But a nagging concern ate at her: he was a gambler, and his wine-drinking and gambling were not what she wanted in a suitor. She silenced her thoughts by telling herself, *He's a soldier—that's just the way such men are. If he weren't in the army, he'd be a different person.* Within herself she knew she needed to guard her admiration for Drake because of the irreconcilable spiritual differences between them, but she refused to face those differences directly. Not tonight.

A light dinner of fresh-boiled shrimp, followed by a creamy soufflé, delighted Jennifer as she idly gazed at Drake.

He folded his white napkin and placed it carefully on the table. "They're playing a song even I can dance to, a slow one. Shall we?" he asked as he stood and held his hand out to her.

"I'd love to," Jennifer responded, taking his hand and following him toward a group of people dancing to the accompaniment of a violin.

He led her across the floor, his rhythm and movements precise and easy. "You dance well," he whispered in her ear.

For a moment Jennifer felt light-headed. She had finally found a real man who cared about her. She wanted to tell him that she had been waiting a long time for someone like him, but she dared not—not yet. Certainly such a good man had made his way into her life by divine providence. "You lead well," she whispered back, enjoying the comfort of being held.

The evening drifted into the late hours all too quickly for Jennifer. Drake generously spent his money, obtaining the finest services from the smiling restaurant staff. He handled himself like a perfect gentleman. But the evening soon waned, and the crowd dwindled.

"I wish this night could last forever," Drake said softly, his face close to hers, "but we must be going." He took her arm as he escorted her outside, where a porter hailed their carriage in the damp and cool French Quarter night air.

They sat close together during the ride, the dark sky brightened by a gleaming tiara of stars. Huge water oaks draped heavily with Spanish moss made an occasional dark canopy overhead as they traveled along, noticing only each other. Once at her house, he escorted her up to the front porch, where they paused in the soft glow of yellow light from a front window.

Drake clutched her hands in his, pulling her nearer. "I want to share a poem with you."

Jennifer, overcome with longing, could only gaze into his deep blue eyes.

He recited the poem softly.

> I cast my eyes to the heavens above
> And a star broke loose.
> The falling star was you, my love.
> And I could not refuse
> To be with you forever—
> Until my life I lose.

Her eyes shone as Drake held her tightly. At first she resisted but then relaxed, and he kissed her gently, bringing her excitement and joy. She gently pushed away. "Please . . . I don't know . . ." she said, though she continued to let herself be held in his long arms. "That was a lovely poem. Who wrote it?" she asked, hoping to distract Drake from further physical affection.

"I wrote it just for you," he murmured.

Jennifer felt helpless in his arms. She wanted the scene to end, and yet . . . "Is that how you really feel?"

"Yes, Jennifer, it is." He relaxed his hold on her, letting her move toward the door. His lips formed a gentle smile. "Good night. I'll call on you tomorrow."

Jennifer returned his smile, not wanting him to stay but not wanting him to leave. She desired to say so much more, but Drake turned to depart. He paused and looked back at her. "Jennifer, you are very special," he said, then stepped off the porch into the darkness.

Once inside, Jennifer took a deep breath, shaking her head in dismay. *I can't believe I let him kiss me!* She paused a moment in the light of a kerosene lamp. *I'm too taken with his feelings for me! I don't even know if he's a Christian.*

~

Two weeks later a shaft of morning sunlight shone on Jennifer as she sat in her room and wrote in her diary. Salome sat on the bed next to her, licking his paws. Jennifer held a pen near her mouth, thinking, then continued writing.

> Drake is all I can think about. He's taken me to nice places every night—he must have spent a fortune! But it's more than that—he's everything I could want in a man, so kind and so thoughtful, so funny and always laughing—and he's SO handsome! When he kissed me the other night I felt helpless.
>
> There's no denying it: for the first time in my life I'M IN LOVE! It's so exciting that I can't find the words to describe it. I think Drake loves me, he sure acts like he does; but not knowing for certain is more than I can bear. If he asked, I'd probably marry him. Mother would never approve, but it's *my* life. I don't know for sure if he shares my faith in Christ, but then again, would God bring such a good-hearted man into my life if He didn't intend for me to have a relationship with him? At times I feel great anguish about this, but at other times I have peace. All I know is, this is all so wonderful, I can hardly believe it's happening to me!

≈

That evening Drake took Jennifer to a romantic little sidewalk cafe overlooking the French Quarter. A sweet olive bush bloomed nearby, filling the warm air with its delightful fragrance. Jennifer enjoyed being in Drake's presence, but this evening his usual slight smile was missing as he sat quietly gazing into the shadows.

"Drake, is something wrong?" Jennifer asked.

He turned, his look steady, a hint of helpless pleading in his eyes. "Jennifer . . . I believe something has happened to me, something that has never happened before." He paused, running his hand across his square chin. He reached for her hand and held it firmly. "I've fallen in love with you." He glanced away quickly, then reached in his pocket to produce a small gift box. "Here," he said and handed it to her.

Jennifer opened it to see a diamond ring of exceptionally fine quality. She stared at Drake in disbelief.

"Will you marry me?" he asked, tightening his grip on her small hand.

Unable to contain her emotions, tears welled up in Jennifer's eyes and trickled down her cheeks as a nervous smile spread across her face. She'd hoped and dreamed of this, having convinced herself that she could surely persuade Drake to become a Christian soon after they married. *I'll be able to get him into church, and he'll be saved there—I just know it*, she thought. "Drake," she said, her voice shaky, "yes, I'll marry you."

Leaning over the small table, Drake kissed her forcefully as she placed her arms around his neck and held him close. When he sat back, his smile returned. The people sitting at nearby tables held up their drinks in a toast.

Dabbing at her eyes with a napkin, Jennifer regained her composure before she spoke. "Drake, this is so wonderful—I've never been so happy."

≈

The next morning Jennifer came into the kitchen to find her mother cleaning dishes at the sink. Reluctantly she moved around a small table and stood behind her mother, waiting, dreading the response her news would elicit. "Mother, I—I have something to tell you."

Mrs. Hamilton slammed down a pot and whirled around to meet her daughter's expression. "And I know what it is—you're going to marry that Yankee! You've been out with him every night since you met him!" Mrs. Hamilton was small but intimidating in her anger, her eyes bright and glaring.

"But, Mother," Jennifer pleaded, "please understand, I love him!"

"I'm sure you do!" her mother snapped. "Any young girl's first love is 'true love,' but it will pass, Jennifer—believe me, it will pass."

Jennifer dropped her eyes sorrowfully, keeping her hand on the back of a chair to steady herself. "I want to marry him, Mother. I can't live without him."

"Jennifer, I know about men like him! He has no character—I can tell!"

Jennifer turned away, tears flowing down her cheeks, her lips quivering. "But, Mother, I love him, and I know he loves me!"

"You will indeed marry him," her mother said quietly, her voice low with resentment, "but it will be behind my back and without my blessing."

～

Drake planned the elopement so he could pick up Jennifer when her mother was away. It was a beautiful spring day, and the bright sun made pronounced shadows on the ground as Drake loaded the last of Jennifer's things onto the carriage. She cuddled Salome as she climbed on board, the fresh smell of the new life of spring scenting the humid air as they made their way across town.

She had left a note for her mother on the dining room table.

Dear Mother,

    I've eloped. I shall not be far away, and in time perhaps we can visit. I pray that you will find it in your heart to forgive me.

                                    Love,
                                      Jennifer

"I've invited a few of my friends." Drake smiled as he sat close to Jennifer, his head nodding in rhythm with the movement of the carriage. His uniform was parade dress, complete with a polished saber, and his dashing appearance matched his optimistic smile.

Wearing her best Sunday dress, which though stylish was far less than a wedding gown, Jennifer had expected a brief ceremony in front of a preacher at a small church. She hadn't expected any guests except for one of Drake's friends who had agreed to be best man. "If I'd known you were going to invite your friends, I might have invited a few of mine," she whispered with disappointment.

"Don't worry, sweetheart," Drake insisted, "it's not going to be a big affair. It's only right that my friends attend and bless our marriage, then celebrate with us." He put his arm around her and pulled her to him, giving her a quick kiss on the cheek.

"Did you find a place for us to stay?" Jennifer asked, a slight uncertainty in her voice.

"Only the best for you, my love. We'll start off by staying in the finest hotel with the best service," Drake bragged as the carriage scurried along under the shade of massive live oaks. "Nothing is too good for you, just wait and see!"

Jennifer smiled, her green eyes twinkling, delighted that she was marrying such a fine man. God had been so good to her.

They arrived at a small church on the outskirts of the city where about a dozen men stood outside waiting. Dressed in full Union regalia and wearing sabers, they cheered as Drake and Jennifer approached, one burly, bearded man instantly grabbing Jennifer's hand to help her step from the carriage.

"Hey, Drake," he observed a bit boisterously, "you pick 'em mighty young, but she's a beauty! Sergeant McDonnell at your service, ma'am!" He took a deep bow.

The rest of the men laughed heartily. Jennifer noticed the smell of alcohol on the man's breath. Apparently they had already begun their celebrating.

Inside the small church, tall stained-glass windows shone bright as the preacher, an old minister who had conducted hundreds of weddings, took his place in front of the couple. For a moment

Jennifer thought she might cry, the uncertainty and excitement both tugging mercilessly at her emotions. Drake stood tall and erect next to her, wearing the slight smile to which she'd grown accustomed.

"I do," Jennifer answered at the appropriate moment, her heart throbbing. To her mind, the vows were ironclad, and nothing could invalidate the binding agreement. *This is for ever and ever,* she thought.

"I do," Drake answered in turn. He kissed Jennifer long and hard.

The uniformed men rushed out the front door of the small church and lined up beside the walkway, a half dozen on each side. "Present arms!" Sergeant McDonnell barked, and the sabers clinked together over the walkway. Drake led Jennifer under the crossed swords and into the light of the day.

"Well, Mrs. DeSpain, how do you feel?" Drake asked, joy evident in his wide smile and teasing tone of voice.

Jennifer reeled with excitement, her cheeks aglow as she and her husband hurried to board the waiting carriage. She turned to Drake, wrapping her arms around him. "This is the most wonderful moment of my life! We're going to be so happy!" *O God, bring it to pass! I pray that I've done the right thing.*

CHAPTER

~ 2 ~

A New Beginning

A spring rain swept heavily against the windowpanes, and earthy damp smells filled the front room where Jennifer sat on a worn sofa nursing Abby, her youngest. Beside her, Grant lay sleeping. The rain had drummed against the roof of the drab little house in a staccato beat until it lulled him to sleep. Abby looked more like her father, having brown hair and deep blue eyes, while Grant, almost two, had his mother's auburn hair and greenish eyes. He was a healthy little boy with an even temperament.

What concerned Jennifer the most was the New Orleans paper, the *Picayune*, that lay in front of her. The April 10, 1865 headline read: LEE SURRENDERS. She couldn't help but be overcome with thoughts of Drake's return since it had been so hard caring for two babies with her husband away at war. Getting by on the scant money Drake sent made life almost impossible; her days had become long and difficult, her resources limited. *Maybe he can come home now and be a husband and father,* she thought with Abby content at her breast. *Maybe with this stupid war over we can begin a real life—the life we were meant to have.*

Jennifer sadly recalled how little she had seen of Drake and how she had barely gotten to know him during his brief visits. The children didn't know him at all. Jennifer knew that if it hadn't been for her mother's help with the babies and her mother's financial assistance, they would have been unable to survive. Only Salome, her big cat, had managed well since he could fatten himself on whatever he could catch.

Having fed Abby, Jennifer rose from the sofa and went to the window, holding the child on her hip. The dark skies poured out their rain endlessly, the house was sweltering, and the humidity was heavy and hot in the confining room. She ran a hand across her wet brow. She was sweating so profusely that her worn, faded dress was, as always, damp and clammy.

She suddenly heard someone stomp onto the small porch and bang on the door. Grant burst into tears, startled by the loud noise. Jennifer rearranged herself the best she could and approached the door reluctantly. *Who would be calling on a terrible afternoon like this?* she wondered, worried by the urgency of the heavy knocking.

When Jennifer opened the door, the sight so shocked her that she took a deep breath and could not speak. It was Drake, rain-soaked and dripping, bearing a gigantic smile. "The war's over!" he exclaimed jubilantly as he rushed inside. As Jennifer backed away to let Drake make his grand entrance, Abby screamed, frightened by the boisterous stranger.

The returned traveler set his suitcase down, grabbed Jennifer, and began waltzing her around the room. Abby and Grant, unsure what was happening, both began yelling at the top of their lungs.

"You're a beautiful sight!" Drake declared, clinging to Jennifer awkwardly as she tried to pull away to comfort Grant and Abby.

"Drake, you're scaring the children!" Jennifer scolded as she went to her young ones. "Why didn't you send a message? I could have had a nice meal ready, and I would have fixed myself up real pretty for you!"

Drake couldn't help but notice that his wife was much more womanly than the girl he'd married. Her long auburn hair was more beautiful than ever; her skin was fair and smooth and rose-colored. She had alluring lips. She had filled out too, her old tight dress revealing a shapely and mature figure. He could see in her the same alert spirit and the same sense of enjoyment that had first attracted him.

"Drake," she cried as she ran back into his arms, "I'm so glad you're finally home. I've missed you so." She pulled back and put her hands on the sides of his face, as if to hold him steady so she could have a better look. He too had matured. Fine lines showed at the corners of his deep blue eyes, and his face was leaner, sun-darkened, and covered with black whiskers. But the same light, the same fire and love for life, kindled in his eyes as the first time they met. She pulled his face to hers and kissed him long and hard.

Drake reveled in the moment. Her lips were soft, and her kiss left a faint, salty taste. "You're magnificent," he whispered, still holding her close. "You've no idea how much I've missed you. It seems like it's been forever."

"I pray we will never have to be apart again," Jennifer whispered, her eyes moist with tears of joy. The children sat on the couch watching with great curiosity, trying to understand the emotions between their mother and this stranger.

Raising his voice, Drake announced laughingly, "Tonight we'll celebrate! We'll go to Antoine's, the same place we went on our first evening together."

"But what about the children? They're too young to take to Antoine's. Besides, you just returned home. Don't you want to spend some time with your son and daughter? They don't even remember who you are."

"Surely you can find someone to watch them. And I'll renew my acquaintance with them tomorrow." Drake picked up his bag and made his way to the back room so he could get out of his wet clothes. The babies stared at their mother, a helpless expression still on their faces.

The only person I can leave the children with is Mother, and she certainly won't approve of our leaving them with her so unexpectedly, especially since we're going out for an expensive dinner at Antoine's. After helping me with my financial problems so many times, she'll think Drake is wasting our money. She won't like this one bit!

～

It was a cool, refreshing evening as Drake waited outside Mrs. Hamilton's house in an open carriage while Jennifer took the babies inside. He pulled out a long cigar and prepared to light it. The black carriage driver casually held the reins in his hand as the bit jingled in the horse's mouth. "Looks like it's going to be a nice night," Drake commented, blowing a cloud of smoke into the air.

"Yes, suh, it surely do."

Inside, Jennifer timidly tried to explain things to her mother. "We're just going out for a little while, and we won't be late." Jennifer hoped her words and tone would convey her newfound happiness as she unpacked the baby care items her mother would need.

Cora Hamilton had aged prematurely, her hair now a faded gray thanks to the strain of helping her daughter make it through hard times. "Why didn't he come inside with you?" she inquired. "I'll tell you why—because he's the same as he always was and the same he always will be. I just wish you could see that."

"Now, Mother, this is the first time we've been together in a year, and we want to celebrate his homecoming. You certainly can't fault us for that. Besides, now that the war is over, Drake won't be leaving again. He's home to stay, and now we can have a real family."

"The war was a complete waste," Mrs. Hamilton complained bitterly. "I fail to see anything good it accomplished. It'll be hard going here in the South, and believe me, it'll be a long time before the situation improves. I hope your husband can find work. There aren't many jobs available, you know. I don't suppose he's bothered to learn a trade along the way, has he?"

"He's alive and he's home, Mother," Jennifer said evenly. "For now, that's all that matters. We'll manage."

Once Jennifer was back in the carriage, she regained a young-girl enthusiasm. The evening darkened into the quiet of night, and cold drops of lingering rain fell from the oaks overhead as they made their way to the French Quarter.

Drake tugged on his black cigar, confident he had the world at his fingertips now that he was no longer obligated to the army. He wore an expensive gray cotton suit, stylish for the time; he'd bought it after his discharge. It was an enjoyable indulgence after the strict life of a soldier.

"I didn't know you smoked cigars," Jennifer said, a little

offended. "They smell terrible." The irritation reminded her of some of the differences between her and her husband, differences she'd chosen to forget and that she didn't want to face tonight.

Drake replied, "You should get used to it, Jennifer—it's the smell of money and fine living. We're really going to live, sweetheart!" He puffed on the cigar until the end grew bright, then blew a long plume of smoke that trailed behind the carriage.

Once inside Antoine's, Jennifer, seeing the other ladies outfitted in their fine garments, wished she'd had a better dress to wear. Her dress fit rather snugly and was slightly out of style. Determined to enjoy the night to its fullest, she decided that even though she wore a modest dress, it was clean and acceptable. Drake, on the other hand, couldn't have been more in fashion, decked out in his new suit. He was tall and lean and debonair. Jennifer felt proud to be accompanied by such a handsome husband.

Antoine's abounded with the smell of fine food and fragrant flowers. But above all else, excitement hung in the air—the joyous celebration of the war's end. Judging by the way people were indulging in wine and dance with abandon, nobody would have guessed the South had lost.

"I'll have a bottle of your finest champagne," Drake insisted when the waiter appeared. Drake DeSpain was not one to hold back at a time of celebration.

Not wanting to dampen Drake's spirits, Jennifer nevertheless thought about the empty cupboards at home; the money they were spending on champagne could feed their children. She was disappointed too that Drake had not remembered that she didn't drink. But again, this was a once-in-a-lifetime affair—an evening of joy! Her husband was home, her poverty would soon disappear, and she knew that in time she would help him give up drinking completely. Having a more hopeful heart, she watched Drake with genuine interest.

"You look absolutely lovely, Jennifer. I declare you must be the most beautiful lady in New Orleans."

Jennifer indeed glowed with her natural beauty. The lavender dress that she thought fit too tightly enhanced her figure. Her cheeks flushed with color, her full lips were red and enticing, her light green eyes shone with the light of renewed hope, and her flowing, wavy auburn hair reflected the dancing light of the crystal chandeliers.

The waiter popped a cork into a white napkin and poured bubbling champagne into their glasses. Drake quickly drank the sparkling liquid. "That's very good!" he said, bracing himself to contain its effect. "Drink up, darling—the war's over, and I'm home."

"You know I don't drink," Jennifer reminded him.

"But, Jennifer, this is a special occasion. It's a coming home celebration for me."

Ignoring her conscience, wanting her husband's happiness more than anything in the world, Jennifer let go of her fretting. *This is a big night for him. I don't want to spoil it.* For the moment, relishing his presence, her worries were gone. Why not enjoy the experience?

Growing more boisterous with each glass of champagne, Drake soon insisted on buying a round of drinks for the table next to them—four obviously well-to-do people who were also celebrating the end of the war. "We can get back to business now," insisted one gentleman, enjoying the drink Drake had bought him. "I can ship all the cotton I can get once again." He laughed and sipped his drink. "A young man like you with a pretty woman like that," he said, swinging his glazed eyes at Jennifer, "has the world by the horns."

Jennifer smiled at the man and turned to Drake. "Honey, shouldn't we be more careful with our money? We've so many needs at home."

Swaying a little in his chair, Drake opened his coat and removed a wad of bills, his smile growing even larger. "You don't need to worry about money anymore," he blurted, waving the bills in front of her. "I won all this in a big game—and there's more where that came from."

Frowning, Jennifer shifted her attention to her plate and poked at the food with her fork. "You can't depend on gambling to support us, though I'm sure you can find some kind of gainful employment. New Orleans is a big city with many opportunities."

"Don't worry your pretty head," Drake insisted. "I'll find a job around here somewhere."

The evening continued with dancing and dessert and the delightful merrymaking of the French Quarter. Before they knew it, it was well after midnight.

"Oh dear," Jennifer said, hearing a clock strike a single tone for 1 in the morning. "We must go, Drake. Mother will be furious!"

Drake smiled, unworried. "We'll just get the children in the morning. After all, your mother won't be any angrier then than she is now. Besides, if we went to her house tonight, we'd have to wake her and the children up."

Her forehead wrinkled with doubt, Jennifer thought that perhaps Drake was right. He'd been drinking heavily, and she certainly didn't want a confrontation between him and her mother. "All right, but it's still time to leave. It's very late, and I'm exhausted."

She helped Drake stagger outside, where they hailed a carriage in the chilly morning air. Others were leaving as well since the festivities were coming to a close. During the ride home, Drake held his wife close but was uncharacteristically quiet as his head kept nodding.

When they arrived home, Drake made his way to the back room, fumbled in the dark with his clothes, then fell onto the bed. Jennifer undressed, crawled into bed, and cuddled up to Drake. Lying on his back, he held her closely and stared into the darkness. "This is just the beginning," he murmured softly to her. "I'm going to take care of you, Jennifer. You and the children will have the best of everything, just you wait and see." Drake rolled onto his side and pulled her close, squeezing her gently. "You wait and see."

Feeling happy to be in her own bed with her husband, Jennifer kissed Drake softly on the lips. "I'm not worried about the money. I love you, and I'm just happy to have you home."

Jennifer knew their future was uncertain. But as Drake held her in his arms, she put all her worries aside.

~

Striking a match, Jennifer lit the old oven and continued to prepare supper. They had been forced to move to a smaller place with lower rent. There wasn't much in the cupboard right now—flour and lard, some salt and pepper. Their stock of food quickly vanished between paydays. It was April 18, 1866, a year since Drake had returned home from the war. She had decided to fix a meal of biscuits and flour gravy. *It isn't much, but it's all I have*, she thought as she poured out the last of the flour and mixed some of it with water to make biscuit dough.

Sneaking into the room silently, Grant pulled on his mother's skirt. "Grant, you shouldn't sneak up on me like that!" she teased. He always made her smile.

Grinning back, Grant tugged again at his mother's skirt, enjoying her good-natured teasing. He was an obedient boy, was rarely any trouble, and entertained himself well. "Mommy, Mommy, come look," he said pointing.

"Not now, Grant. I'm busy making supper."

Grant continued to point toward the front of the house. Jennifer set her bowl down and wiped her hands on the old apron she was wearing. She followed Grant to the front of the house, his little legs and bare feet carrying him as fast as he could go.

Jennifer saw Abby on the worn sofa, shaking out the last few cigars from Drake's humidor. She had broken them into pieces and was playing happily in the pile of sweet-smelling tobacco. Jennifer quickly grabbed the humidor, set it back on the table, and picked up the cigar pieces. "No, no, Abby. You've ruined Daddy's cigars. He'll be mad at you."

Abby screamed, grabbed handfuls of tobacco, and threw them at her mother. Jennifer roughly pulled her from the sofa and brushed the loose tobacco from Abby's clothes. "You're as stubborn as an ornery mule," Jennifer snapped. Screaming until she turned red in the face, Abby finally calmed down, spent from her emotional outburst. Taking both children into the kitchen, Jennifer sat them down and gave them some bowls and spoons to play with as she returned to her work at the counter.

A frown crossed Jennifer's face. She always felt defeated when she had to deal with Abby's rebellious ways. But that had not been their only problem. It had not been a good year. She glanced around the small, shabby kitchen, which was not even half as nice as the one in the first house they'd rented. She wiped her forehead with the back of her hand, leaving a streak of white flour on her brow. *If Drake could only find a decent job instead of those that require long hours and pay so little. I've lost count of how many jobs he's had—despite the many hours I've prayed for a better life.*

Wandering over to her mother, Abby looked up with big blue eyes and asked, "Daddy coming?"

Picking up the little girl, Jennifer touched Abby's nose with her floured finger, leaving a white mark. "He'll be home soon, honey." Abby giggled as her mother squeezed her.

Drake and Abby had that special relationship often found between fathers and young daughters. At times it was as though they had a special understanding, often ignoring the other family members as they went on walks or sat on the porch, where Abby would sit on her father's lap while he talked to her. It pleased Jennifer to see the two sitting there, for it reminded her of the relationship she'd had with her own father.

The hours passed, and soon it was late evening. Crickets chirped in a chorus, sending their music into the night, as Jennifer sat silently on the front porch waiting for Drake. After eating their biscuits and gravy, the children soon became tired and went to sleep, giving Jennifer a welcome time of solitude. *How nice it would be if Drake would come home right now, just the two of us for a little while,* she mused as she stared at a streetlamp in the distance. But she knew he wouldn't arrive soon, no matter how much she wished he would. He liked to gamble and stay out late every payday, and today was payday.

Late that night, after Jennifer had gone to bed, Drake stumbled up the steps and fumbled with the front door lock for so long that she had to get up to let him in. She opened the door and immediately saw that his eyes were red and smelled the liquor on his breath.

"Hello, my love," he mumbled pleasantly. "What are you doing up?"

Tears rushed to Jennifer's eyes. Had Drake squandered his badly needed paycheck again? "Drake, where have you been? I waited up a long time for you."

"Don't worry about me." Drake laughed a little as his mind seemed to wander, then again focus on Jennifer. He seemed completely unaware that anything could be wrong. Falling into a sitting position on the sofa, he noticed the scattered tobacco. "What's this?"

"Tobacco," Jennifer answered tensely, losing her patience rapidly and wishing she'd remembered to clean up the mess. "Abby got into your humidor and played with your cigars."

Drake shook with laughter. "That little girl has taste, I tell you—those are the finest cigars around."

"Drake!" Jennifer shouted. "We're starving and you waste your pay on selfish pleasures!"

"Calm down, honey," Drake said, calmly reaching into his coat pocket. "You've got the picture all wrong. I won 300 dollars tonight, and all I had to start with was that measly little pay I get. Not bad, if I say so myself."

Sitting down beside him, Jennifer said, "I know you mean well, but we can't afford to have you keep gambling away your pay. What if you had lost it all? I fed the children the last of our food tonight. There's nothing left." She paused a moment as Drake looked at her sheepishly. He had a happy-sad, childlike look about him. "We'd rather have you at home. Abby kept asking for you until she fell asleep. I wish you would stop your gambling."

"Aw, Jennifer—"

"It's not *right*, Drake—you know it's not!" The light in Jennifer's eyes was urgent. "God doesn't honor money made in that way. The Bible says, 'Treasures of wickedness profit nothing.' I—I thought you'd come to church with me when you came back from the war, but you show no interest in the Lord at all. Don't you understand that if we don't build our home around the things of God, we'll be in awful trouble?"

Drake listened with his head down and finally looked up with an ashamed expression on his face. "I'll go to church with you next Sunday, Jennifer," he promised. He took her in his arms and held her, then after a time said, "I have to tell you something, Jennifer. I quit that useless job this afternoon—but don't fret, because I found a much better one!"

Jennifer's new hope shone in her face. "Oh, Drake, that's the best news you've had in a long time! What kind of job is it—working in a government office or something?" she asked, thinking back to his army job on a general's staff.

"Nothing as boring as that," he announced, then gave her a proud glance. "One of the men I was playing cards with tonight told me I was a natural at poker and wants me to work as a dealer on one of his river boats, the *Julie Belle*."

Leaning back, Jennifer sighed, remembering with distaste the stories she'd heard about the evil things that happen on riverboats. It was more than she could bear, and she broke into tears.

"Aw, honey," Drake pleaded in his kindest voice, "don't you worry about me—I can take care of myself. And you and the children won't have to worry about starving anymore; you won't have to worry about a thing. You'll have the best—you wait and see!" Jennifer stiffened with anger. She'd heard those very words before.

She tried to reason with Drake for hours, hoping and praying for a change in her husband's heart, but he finally grew angry. "I'm the one who has to make the living, and I don't want to hear any more of your preaching, Jennifer!"

That night as Jennifer lay beside Drake, she could not sleep. *I thought we'd have a Christian home, but Drake's getting further away from God every day!*

A sense of failure lay over her like a dark cloud, but she wouldn't give up on God now. She prayed with all her might for Drake to give his heart to the Lord. She finally dropped off to sleep, but it was a troubled sleep broken by ominous dreams.

3

A Smoking Gun

Sitting in the shade of the small front porch, Jennifer fanned herself with a newspaper as she watched Grant and Abby play with their old toys in the dirt. Grant was now five years old and Abby four. They giggled with happiness, unaware of their mother's concern. The *Picayune* referred to the hard times the South was going through as "The Reconstruction Period." Louisiana had been readmitted to the Union just the year before, and people were struggling to wrest a normal life out of a war-torn economy.

The huge oak tree in the front yard shaded the children from the sweltering afternoon summer sun. Jennifer glanced again at the paper, hoping to find a job Drake would consider, an unlikely prospect on two counts. *If only Drake would earn a living,* she pondered, *in some way besides working on the riverboat as a card dealer. . .*

For two years now, when he was home, he would work late and sleep late, then rush off in the middle of the afternoon to catch the riverboat before it departed. Oftentimes he'd be gone for days as the boat steamed up the Mississippi, navigating the twisting turns of the busy river. Usually he'd come home too exhausted to do anything with or for his family. Jennifer wasn't sure how much money her husband actually earned, since the money she saw continued to be scarce and undependable.

"Come on, children," Jennifer called. "You've had your fun. It's time for your baths."

"Aw, Mom," Grant pleaded. "Just a little longer—we won't get dirty."

"You already look like two little pigs," Jennifer teased, noting that Grant was muddy from head to toe. All he wore was a pair of short pants. Abby ignored any talk of bathing. Her ragged little dress was filthy as she pushed a toy horse through the dark soil.

"Come on, Abby," Jennifer called. "It's time to go inside."

Abby threw the toy horse across the yard and let out a loud cry, her temper flaring violently.

"All right, you two, just a little longer, then we have to go in and get you cleaned up."

Abby calmed down and went to get the toy she'd just thrown. As usual, Grant took everything in stride and continued his play, smiling pleasantly. A thin little boy, he had the look of a diplomat with his soft green eyes and auburn hair.

Later, after Jennifer had bathed and fed the children and put them to bed, she returned to her comfortable old cane-bottomed rocker on the front porch. The air was heavy as the heat of the day lingered stubbornly. A dog barked somewhere nearby, and in the distance she could hear voices engaged in disagreement. Her evening ritual of sitting on the front porch was invaluable to her. She used these moments to examine the turns of her life, mostly thinking about Drake. She realized that pride made men strong, and that pride also led them to their ruin; it was both their strength and their folly. *Father, I want to talk with You again about Drake . . .* Somehow the words just wouldn't come tonight.

Sitting in her chair, wearing a worn, thin cotton dress, Jennifer DeSpain was the picture of a healthy, beautiful, neglected woman saddened by her circumstances. She had somehow drifted beyond God's care—or so it felt to her at times, though she had not abandoned her duties at church. She delighted to hear God's Word preached and to serve others even more needy than she. She often prayed for something better for her family—for things to change. In her daydreams she wished they could go someplace where there were no gambling riverboats or broken economies.

Wistful thoughts drifted through Jennifer's mind now as her eyes grew weary with the day's duties of caring for two young children, and she slipped into the comfortable and untroubled world of heavy sleep. Salome padded out of the darkness and leaped into her lap. Purring loudly, he made a few circles, then lay his head down and went to sleep.

"Jennifer! Jennifer, wake up," Drake urged, shaking her arm gently. "It's after midnight. What are you doing out on the front porch?"

Startled, Jennifer looked around, glassy-eyed with sleep, not yet realizing where she was. "What . . . Drake?"

"Come inside, honey," Drake whispered, helping her out of the chair.

Striking a match, Drake lit the lantern and illuminated the small, stark room.

"Drake," Jennifer murmured as she came awake, "what time is it?"

"Never mind that," Drake said with his ever-present slight smile and playful eyes. He pulled her to him and kissed her. "You get prettier every day," he whispered in her ear, then kissed her again.

Jennifer responded, wanting to hold on to the precious moment, for at such times she could forget their problems. "Drake, I need you here at home. Why must you be gone for so long?"

Backing away, Drake reached into his jacket pocket and brought out a small box. "Go ahead, open it—it's for you."

Accepting the gift, Jennifer opened the box. It contained a heavy gold necklace with a gold cross. "Why, it's beautiful," she uttered with disbelief. "But you can't afford to buy such gifts for me. We need things like clothes for the children much more."

"You amaze me," Drake responded lightly. "Never thinking of yourself, always putting others first. You're the *best* woman ever, and you deserve this gift. And don't worry, it didn't cost me anything. I won it in a poker game."

Drake had indeed won the necklace in a poker game. Had he *bought* her a necklace, it would have had a ruby or an emerald, but never a cross, for that represented something he didn't believe in. Unknown to Jennifer, he was afraid he wouldn't be able to sell a necklace with a cross on it, so he decided to give it to her.

"I'll never take it off," Jennifer said, slipping it over her thick hair. The gold cross rested brightly against her dress. "It will remind me of my faith. Just tonight I was wondering if God still cared, but now . . ." She looked at Drake. "I've been praying things would get better, but they just stay the same. If only . . . Oh, Drake!" She threw her arms around him. "You just have to get away from the evils of gambling! We *have* to make a better life for ourselves." She began to weep. "I love you so much—and I love our children. If only you could have a job that would let us have a life together as a family, we could all be so happy. We miss you so much." Backing away, she stared into his deep blue eyes, tears rolling down her cheeks.

Drake paused and took a deep breath, the slight smile gone. He stared back, guilt rolling through him like a thunderstorm. "I'll see what I can find," he muttered. "I miss you and the children too."

They embraced, holding each other tightly as Grant watched unseen out of the darkness of the back room.

~

The first time he had a few days off, Drake made an honest effort to find a better job. Intent on pursuing a few leads from friends, he dressed in his best suit and set out to make Jennifer's dreams come true. He carried himself with the bravado of a young man who was about important business. He saw himself as a man who was crafty and resourceful, a man willing to take the risks other men avoided. He felt this so strongly that it became the truth to him, whether or not it agreed with the facts.

At the New Orleans State Bank he addressed a receptionist, a blonde woman. "Good day. I'm Drake DeSpain, and I'm here to see Mr. Bertrand."

She turned toward Drake, irritated until she caught a glimpse of the handsome gentleman. "What did you say your name is?"

"Drake DeSpain. Mr. Bertrand is expecting me."

Rising from her desk, she said, "Just a moment. I'll see if he's busy." She hurried over to a large door and disappeared.

Standing tall and straight and clearing his throat, Drake waited patiently.

The girl returned, a smile on her face. "Mr. Bertrand will see you now."

Inside the office, Mr. Bertrand was standing beside a liquor cabinet pouring himself a drink and holding a cigar gently in his free hand. He was an older man, short and portly with a friendly smile.

"I'm Drake DeSpain, Mr. Bertrand," Drake said, extending his hand. "We've a friend in common—a Mr. Beauchamp, who thought I might talk to you about the possibility of my working here at the bank."

"Oh yes." Mr. Bertrand waved his hand at the liquor cabinet. "Care for a drink?"

"Why, yes, I believe I will," Drake answered as Mr. Bertrand poured the liquor.

"Beauchamp tells me you're a dealer on the *Julie Belle*. Quite impressive! That's one of the finer boats on the Mississippi. My good friend Beauchamp is a gambling fool."

Not knowing whether to laugh or agree, Drake replied, "I'm aware that Mr. Beauchamp frequents the *Julie Belle* quite often."

Mr. Bertrand glanced at Drake as he moved to his big chair behind the cherry wood desk, pleased that Drake had answered carefully. In his quick appraisal, Drake's appearance was impressive. He seemed charming and well-mannered, the kind of man the bank might use to influence investors. "So you were a Union soldier?" the banker questioned.

"Yes, sir, I was," Drake answered nervously, afraid the Southerner would hold it against him.

Mr. Bertrand sported a big smile and took a drink of his bourbon. "I believe in letting bygones be bygones. The war is over, and I refuse to keep fighting it." Of course, that was easy for him to say since he was a wealthy man.

Smiling and taking a sip of his drink, Drake relaxed a little and sat down in front of Mr. Bertrand's desk. "Actually, I never fought a battle. I worked on a general's staff—paperwork mostly."

"We've plenty of paperwork here, that's for sure," Mr. Bertrand stated. "What banking experience do you've?"

"None at a public bank, just the bank on the *Julie Belle*. I'm quite good at handling money, and I'm good with figures," Drake reported. "I'm also very good at being able to tell what people are like, which might come in handy when people ask for a loan." Drake smiled and crossed his legs.

Mr. Bertrand noticed the hole in Drake's shoe and the tattered edges of his old suit. "We go by more than what we can see," Mr. Bertrand explained. "Usually it's a matter of people's assets and personal financial record, their history of performance . . ."

"Of course," Drake interrupted, maintaining his usual slight smile. "I'm familiar with the credit system. What I meant was, I thought my insight might be helpful. I'm a good judge of character, you might say."

His forehead creasing, Mr. Bertrand took another sip of his bourbon. "If I were to hire you, I'd have to start you off as a teller; everybody starts as a teller. You'd have to learn this bank from the ground up."

Drake laughed. "A teller? Mr. Bertrand, I was hoping for a more suitable position, perhaps a loan officer. I assure you, I'm good at what I set out to do. Mr. Beauchamp said that you . . ."

"Mr. Beauchamp owes this bank a lot of money," Mr. Bertrand interrupted hastily, "and Mr. Beauchamp doesn't tell me what to do!"

"My apologies," Drake offered. "I suppose I could lower myself to be a teller for a while. I hope there is opportunity for immediate advancement."

Mr. Bertrand clenched his cigar between his teeth thoughtfully and took a careful draw on it while he stared at the ceiling. "There are no guarantees," he said. "Your performance is what advances you, along with your dependability and your ability to get along with the customers."

Drake shrugged nonchalantly. "I'm most capable. I should be an executive within a matter of weeks." He laughed at his humor, but Mr. Bertrand remained steady and rose from his chair. Obviously the meeting was over.

"I'll be in touch with you, Mr. DeSpain," Mr. Bertrand said coldly, walking toward the door.

"Good," Drake said. He offered his hand but got a limp handshake from the old man before Bertrand closed the door behind him.

To Drake's disappointment, two more job referrals went much the same way. They started off well but dwindled quickly. *I'm overqualified for the meaningless little jobs these people want to give me. They want to take advantage of me, but I'll not be their slave!* he thought to himself as he hurried home.

He arrived home tired and disgusted. "How did it go, Drake?" Jennifer asked cheerfully. "Did you have any luck with your leads?"

Drake collapsed on the old stained sofa. "Those fools! Who do they think I am?" he complained, angered by the day's rejections. "I won't lower myself to take a clerk's job!"

Jennifer sat down beside Drake to comfort him, putting her arms around his neck and bringing her face close to his. The children played on the kitchen floor, unaware that their father was home. "I have a surprise for you," she said sweetly, a pleasant smile on her face. "Mother has a friend who says he can use you at his shipping company. It's practically a sure thing!"

A worried look crossed Drake's face. "What kind of job?"

"I don't really know, " Jennifer answered timidly. "But you're supposed to be there first thing in the morning. Here's the name and address."

Reluctantly Drake read the note in her mother's handwriting. "All right. For your sake I'll check it out."

The next morning Drake went to the shipping company and met the man, Mr. Carlson, a big and jolly man who slapped Drake on the back and laughed heartily. "Indeed I do have a job for you," Mr. Carlson boasted, "and the pay is very good, the best around. Take off that fancy coat; you won't need that here." He took Drake's coat and handed him some large overalls. "Slip into these," he instructed, then afterwards took Drake out to a dock where men were loading and unloading heavy freight wagons pulled by mule teams. "Old Joe will show you what to do, Drake. You might be a little sore the first day or two, but you'll build up those skinny muscles and make a fine-looking man." He slapped Drake on the shoulder again and gave him a genuine smile. "Glad to have you on board!"

The suddenness of it all caught Drake off guard, and the next thing he knew, he was toiling under the weight of eighty-pound feed sacks as the never-ending burden of loading and unloading wagons wore him down. Somehow he made it through the day and rushed home, physically exhausted.

Jennifer comforted him and fed him. "How was it?" she asked, excited about the prospect of a husband who was finally working regular hours and earning good pay.

"It's slave labor!" Drake complained bitterly. "I can't work a job using my back like that! I have a brain, Jennifer! I do better using my head than my muscles."

"But I'm sure Mr. Carlson won't have you working on the dock forever. He's a good Christian man, Drake. He was a good friend of my father's. I'm sure he'll move you up quickly and teach you the shipping trade."

Groaning with the pain of sore muscles, Drake said no more, for he was too tired to argue. Abby came and sat in his lap silently, content to be held by her father. He stroked her head and said, "Abby, I think you are the only person who understands me." She smiled and snuggled closer to the father she so loved.

～

The next morning Jennifer awoke to find that Drake had already left the house. She was delighted that he had taken the initiative to get to work early, until she found his note on the kitchen table.

Jennifer,

I'm going back to my old job on the *Julie Belle*, and I had to leave early to catch her in port. Tell your mother and the family friend that I'm sorry, but I just can't do that kind of hard labor. Please don't be angry with me.

Love,
Drake

Jennifer immediately broke into tears as she stood in the kitchen in her long cotton gown with Grant at her feet.

"Mom, why are you crying?" Grant asked urgently.

"It's nothing you need to worry about, honey," Jennifer answered.

"Is it about Dad working on the gambling boat?" he inquired, having heard his parents argue about that on several earlier occasions.

Jennifer glanced curiously at her son, amazed at his understanding. "Yes," she mumbled.

~

When Mr. Carlson learned that Drake had quit, he quickly sent the one-day paycheck to Jennifer. She couldn't believe that Drake had earned such good money for a single day's work. Silently she lamented over his decision to return to the riverboat and its way of life as she tended the needs of the children for another day.

Jennifer waited many days for Drake's return. Maybe there was a way she could convince him to go back to the job he'd quit. She would show him the fine check he'd earned for just one day's work.

Early one morning a knock sounded at the door. Jennifer quickly put on her robe and left the children eating at the kitchen table as she rushed to the door. When she opened it, she saw a well-dressed gentleman with his hat in his hand and a sorrowful expression on his tired face. "Mrs. DeSpain?"

"Yes," Jennifer answered, a sudden fear gripping her.

"I'm truly sorry to bring bad news, but I thought you might like to know—your husband is in the downtown jail. He's been arrested for murder."

Jennifer covered her mouth with both hands. "Why? . . . What happened?"

The man hesitated, uncomfortable about telling this beautiful woman the awful truth. "It seems he shot a man over a poker game— a prominent man. I'm sorry, but that's all I know. Good day." He walked away, leaving Jennifer in shock as tears rolled down her cheeks.

Quickly gathering the children, Jennifer hurried to her mother's house and left Abby and Grant there. She explained what little she knew to her mother. "I'm so sorry for you, my dear," Mrs. Hamilton said sadly. "I knew it was coming—just a matter of time."

Jennifer rushed off, unable to respond to her mother's comments. Once at the jail, a large police officer spoke with her. "I'm afraid the news is bad, ma'am," the big man said. "He killed an important man, and ain't no court around here will let him get off."

Jennifer was taken to a small room where Drake was waiting. A police officer stood nearby, his hands behind his back as he watched the couple embrace and kiss.

"Drake—what happened?" Jennifer asked. Drake's clothes were torn, and his face was caked with dried blood.

"I'm in terrible trouble, Jennifer," he said, any hint of a smile long since gone. His face was pale, and his eyes were full of fear.

"What happened?" Jennifer asked, fighting back the tears.

"I—I did shoot a man," Drake confessed, "but he had his gun in my face—he accused me of cheating. It was self-defense!"

Jennifer whispered, "What are we going to do? We have no money to fight this."

"The owners of the *Julie Belle* have hired me a good lawyer," Drake informed his wife. "I'll win this in court, don't worry." His words weren't very convincing.

Jennifer saw a sadness in Drake's eyes she'd never seen there before, even in their most desperate times. "I'll be praying for you," she promised. "But I want you to give your heart to Jesus right now, Drake!"

"Not *now*, Jennifer." Drake shook his head. "But I promise that after I get out of this, I'll go to church with you."

"You need more than just going to church, Drake. You need a change in your heart. Can't you see that all this has happened because you're out of God's will? Let me pray with you. It's so easy to be saved!"

But Drake refused to pray, saying, "Later, honey, when I'm out off this place . . ."

∾

Drake's court date came up in only a few weeks. Jennifer sat behind the table where Drake and his attorney were reviewing the written material in front of them. Drake turned and winked at Jennifer. He seemed confident but thinner, as the suit Jennifer had brought for him to wear now fit rather loosely.

Once the proceedings were under way, the jury sat quietly and expressionless in their seats. The prosecution called their first witness—a man who had been sitting at the table when the shooting took place. He explained that the murdered man grew angry, accused Drake of cheating, and came across the table at him. That was when Drake shot him.

Jennifer could see Drake's growing agitation with the man's incomplete story as he shifted constantly in his chair. Drake's lawyer questioned the same man and asked him if the murdered man had pulled out a gun. The man insisted the only gun was Drake's.

"He's a liar!" Drake shouted as he stood and waved his fist at the witness. "He's lying, I tell you!"

"Order!" the judge demanded, rapping his gavel on the table. "One more outburst from you, Mr. DeSpain, and I'll have you taken out of this courtroom!"

"But he's lying, Your Honor!" Drake insisted, still shouting.

The judge signaled the officers to remove the defendant. He fought them as they forced him out of the courtroom. The judge then called for a recess. Jennifer looked at the floor and began to cry, her confidence destroyed. She couldn't even bring herself to pray, not with words anyway.

When court reconvened, Drake sat silently, a defeated man. Jennifer sat behind him, wishing the terrible scene would end or turn out to be merely a nightmare. The witnesses, all prominent men, denied seeing any gun but Drake's. After all testimony and arguments concluded, the jury needed only twenty minutes before returning with a guilty verdict.

A few days later Jennifer attended the sentencing. She prayed they would not hang Drake. To her relief, the judge ruled that the crime was committed in a rage of fury, that perhaps Drake did believe his life was threatened, and thus there was no premeditation.

"However, Mr. DeSpain, you *did* murder a man, and a crime like that cannot go unpunished. I hereby sentence you to twenty-five years in the penitentiary at Angola." The judge rapped his gavel and announced court adjourned as two officers of the court began to lead a despondent Drake away.

When Jennifer rushed toward her husband, the officers stopped, giving her a final moment to speak with him. Drake lifted his weary head, his eyes wet with weeping.

"Drake, my love," she cried through her tears, "I'll wait for you—I'll wait as long as it takes!"

Drake nodded and tried to smile, but he couldn't speak as they took him away.

~

Jennifer didn't know what to do. How would she provide for herself and her children? Without funds to do otherwise, she was forced to abandon her house and move in with her mother, who fortunately had mellowed with age and, sensitive to her daughter's despair, gave herself fully to helping with the children.

Grant had grown inquisitive and would often inquire, "Mother, is Father coming home soon?" On one such occasion Jennifer cried over her son's honest question. Grant clung to her, intent on receiving an answer . "It's all right, Mother, you can tell me."

Finally regaining control, Jennifer held Grant in her arms. "Grant, your father won't be coming home for a long, long time. It's just us now, and we'll have to make do."

"But doesn't he want to be with us?"

"Of course he does, but he *can't* come home."

"Why not, Mother? Why can't he come home? I don't understand."

"He's in prison," Jennifer mumbled, fearing the next question.

"What's prison, Mother?"

Grant seemed determined to find out about his father, and Jennifer knew she'd have to tell him sooner or later. "It's like jail, son, but it's where they keep men who have broken the law in really bad ways, and they keep them there a long time." Jennifer followed

Grant's expression with her eyes as the young boy, trying so hard to be a man, attempted to digest the new information.

"Did Father break the law?"

Jennifer reluctantly admitted, "He was found guilty of shooting a man who he thought was going to shoot him. I miss your father so much!"

Grant stood up and threw his arms around his mother, clinging desperately.

Jennifer broke into tears as she held her son tightly. But Grant remained silent as he hugged his mother.

One day a letter came addressed to Jennifer; it was from Drake.

My Dear Jennifer,

I've reached my wit's end. This is not life! It's intolerable and inhumane. But there is a chance. Please come see me!

Forever your love,
Drake

Jennifer didn't know how she could bear to be away from her children even for a few days, or if the trip could possibly help in any way, but she knew she would have to try. *Lord, You know that I've made many mistakes in my life, and maybe marrying Drake was one of the biggest. But he's my husband, and I believe You want me to love him and do whatever I can for him. If You want me to go where he is, please protect and sustain me along the way. Your will be done!*

∼

The trip was hot and torturous, a long journey through the wilderness and swamps of Louisiana. As the enclosed coach traveled high atop a levee, white egrets below stood nearly motionless in the marsh, like soldiers at attention. Cypress trees draped with Spanish moss towered over the swampland, their bark baked light gray by the blistering sun. The sky overhead was a pale blue, and Jennifer felt as if she were entering a forbidden and foreign land, a land of no return for some.

The coach halted at a gate where guards with sun-darkened faces inspected the two passengers, Jennifer and another woman. The men mumbled something in French, and then the coach lurched on, unconcerned about the comfort of the passengers.

"They don't usually live, ya know," the stern-faced woman in the coach said callously to Jennifer. "It's usually consumption that gets to 'em, living out here in the swamp like this. That's a long and torturous death. You oughta pray that your man, whoever he is, gets something that kills him quickly."

Glaring at the bitter woman, Jennifer let her know with the malice in her eyes that she had heard enough, then turned back to the window. The swamp darkened and thickened as they arrived at a depressing area of unpainted buildings under a shaded canopy of massive trees.

"This way, ladies," the coachman invited, opening the door. "Watch your step, madam," he said to Jennifer. "Them low-top shoes won't give you much protection against the mud and snakes and scorpions."

Jennifer shuddered at the thought but held her head up bravely as she marched forward, stepping on boards laid together as a walkway through the mire. Once inside, she introduced herself, and a pleasant little man recorded her name in a book, then had her sign it. He escorted her to a room with a chair and a barred window in a plain wall. She waited nervously, her stomach turning in knots at the odors and the dim, wet surroundings.

Soon Drake's face appeared, like a ghost, in the barred window, his eyes dark and sunken, his skin sallow, his cheeks hollow. He saw her forced smile, and he moaned involuntarily. "Oh, Jennifer, you are the most wonderful sight a man could see." He clasped the bars with white knuckles. "Come closer, please."

Frightened at Drake's appearance, Jennifer almost wished she hadn't come. "My dear husband, what have they done to you?" She moved closer, then grabbed his hands and squeezed them tightly.

"Jennifer," Drake said with a sigh, "I'm sorry you have to see me this way. And it's not just me—it's all the men. We're like the walking dead. They treat us worse than animals."

Trying to remain strong, Jennifer fought against the tears, but she knew her face revealed her despair. "Drake, we have to get you out of here. This place is killing you."

"There is a chance," he said, a faint spark burning deep in his dark eyes. "There's a lawyer in New Orleans who knows there was a conspiracy at my trial when those men lied on the stand. He's willing to take my case, to *prove* those men lied. There was another witness, a black porter, who saw the whole thing, and he's willing to testify. Contact this lawyer—tell him what you know!"

Averting his gaze, Jennifer hardly knew what to say. "What about money—how much does this lawyer want?"

Drake turned his head and looked the other way, then finally spoke without looking at her. "He's expensive, but he's supposed to be the best." He turned back to her with a look of desperation. "Ask your mother. She has the money, doesn't she? Darling, I'm begging for my life! A man can't last long in here!"

Jennifer could hardly keep from weeping as Drake clasped her small hands through the bars. "Tell me that you'll . . . that you'll give me something to live for."

She watched his face—the face that was always smiling, at least in earlier days. Before, it was the recklessly expressive face of a man who lived for action; but now only ruin glared from his troubled eyes. "I will—I'll do it! Drake, if you only knew how much I love you!"

"I love you too, sweetheart. You're the love of my life! I know I haven't always been the husband you deserved, but . . . ."

Jennifer's heart was breaking, and she whispered, "Drake, I've prayed for you to be saved every day, to turn to Jesus. It's time for you to turn away from everything that brought you here—"

"Time's up!" barked a harsh voice from behind the wall.

Jennifer searched Drake's face, her eyes pleading for a sign that he was ready to hear more about the Gospel. But he grew despondent and stood, then turned to leave. As he limped away, his clothes hung loosely on his frame. She watched him as he turned to give her the saddest look she'd ever seen, as though death was already beckoning him.

4

The Struggle

An angry bolt of lightning split the night sky, startling Jennifer out of a sound sleep. She had been so exhausted from her trip that she had literally collapsed in bed. Now awake, she saw Abby lying on one side and Grant on the other, each clinging to her in response to the booming thunder. A terrified Salome pushed against Jennifer's feet under the cover, whining piteously. Pulling the children closer, Jennifer thought, *My darling children—my treasures—God has given me these special delights. Even Drake in his own way is a gift from God. Drake . . . Poor Drake. How can I possibly persuade mother to give me the money for his defense? She'll have to mortgage the house!* The storm finally gave way to a torrent of water as the thunder moved on. Soon it was just a heavy rain, and Jennifer fell back into a fitful sleep.

The next morning the earth was freshly washed and was being dried with a bright sun. Jennifer eased out of her bed without disturbing the children. She made her way through the house to the kitchen where her mother sat with a cup of coffee and a newspaper. Mrs. Hamilton's hair was almost solid gray, and the weariness of worry revealed its presence in the fine lines around her tired eyes. Jennifer fixed a cup of coffee and sat across the breakfast table from her mother.

Though distressed and anxious, Jennifer remained quiet, wanting her mother to speak first. When Mrs. Hamilton glanced up from the newspaper, she knew from Jennifer's eyes that something was troubling her daughter. "How was your journey?" her mother questioned evenly as she made her way through the paper. "Somewhat of a nightmare, I would suppose."

"That prison is a horrible place, Mother," Jennifer began. "The men look like walking dead men. It was the most pitiful scene I've ever witnessed in my life."

Glancing up from her newspaper, Mrs. Hamilton chided, "You didn't expect prison to be a *nice* place, did you?"

"No, but I didn't expect it to be a place of torture either. It would have been more humane to hang the men than to let them die a slow death." Jennifer hesitated, gathering her courage. "Mother, Drake is a mere shadow. He'll die in there if I don't get him out."

"Get him out? That's impossible," Mrs. Hamilton said, tension marking her face. She closed her eyes and pinched the bridge of her nose. She couldn't bear the thought of prison or war or any other unbearable tragedy. "We had to deal with your father's death and now—"

"There is a way," Jennifer interrupted. "A lawyer in town is aware of the case, and he knows those men lied in court. Another witness saw the whole thing. The lawyer believes he can file an appeal and get Drake released."

Placing her paper on the table, Mrs. Hamilton grew quite serious though suspicious. "Another witness?"

"Yes, Mother. A black porter. He saw everything."

"Jennifer!" Mrs. Hamilton snorted in disgust. "Who would take the word of a black porter? Those rich men will eat him up in court."

"But, Mother," Jennifer pleaded, "it's our only hope—we must try!"

Slowly standing, Mrs. Hamilton shuffled over to the coffeepot and warmed her cup with a splash of coffee. "I told you years ago to expect all of this, and look at all the grief you've suffered. If you had just listened . . ." Her words conveyed refusal, but somehow her facial expression hinted of hope. Jennifer didn't know what to make of the apparent discrepancy.

She bit her lower lip in frustration, but she was a woman of inner strength and would not give up hope. Straightening her back, she said firmly, "Yes, Mother, you—you were right about Drake, but look also at the two wonderful and beautiful children I have!" She lowered her voice and added, "I'll always love Drake. I can't help that."

Mrs. Hamilton hobbled back to her chair, sat down, and waited to hear what she knew was coming.

"Mother, can you hire this lawyer? I realize I'm asking a great deal, much more than I have a right to ask. But it's our only hope," Jennifer begged, clasping her hands together tightly.

"Jennifer, you know I love you. But you also need to understand something else. There was a time, Jennifer, when I would have been glad to see Drake put away so you could go on with your life." Mrs. Hamilton paused, her expression serious. "But I'm not the same woman I was in the past. In the last few years I've grown closer to the Lord, praise His name, and I'm tired of hate and war and hard times. I grieve over the difficulties you've brought on yourself, Jennifer, but I do want to help. If I had the money, I'd give it to you. I know your love is blind, and I know I've been bitter, but no more. I choose to forgive you, and I forgive Drake."

Lowering her head, Jennifer whispered, her shoulders shaking, "Thank you, Mother. Your words mean more than I could ever say. I love you, but I love Drake too, and I'd hoped there was a way to hire that lawyer. To think of Drake dying in that hellhole . . ."

Cora Hamilton was a fighter too, and her stubborn determination made her tough as iron. She knew her time was limited with dwindling health, but once she made up her mind, nothing was impossible! "Perhaps there is a way. This house is paid for. I can get a mortgage on it so we can borrow enough to pay the lawyer."

Jennifer ran around the small table and hugged her mother. "How can I ever repay you? I'm so proud to have you for my mother!"

An expression of dismay softened Mrs. Hamilton's features as she explained, "You'll inherit this house anyway. Maybe the lawyer can get Drake out and someday before long this place will belong to the two of you. It's a fine house, Jennifer, and it'll make a fine home."

≈

Not long after the house was mortgaged and Jennifer hired the lawyer, she found her mother unconscious on the living room floor. Quickly helping her mother to the sofa, she revived her with a damp, cool rag. "Mother, are you all right? Can you hear me?"

Coming around slowly, Mrs. Hamilton waved her hand in front of her as if Jennifer were overreacting. "It's nothing to worry about. I simply grew faint. I'll be all right in a minute."

Worry showed heavily in Jennifer's eyes. "Let me take you to a doctor, Mother. Maybe he can help."

"This happens all the time. It's nothing to be distressed about," Mrs. Hamilton insisted as she sat up with great effort.

Soon afterwards when Jennifer again discovered her mother unconscious, this time with her head on the kitchen table, she had her mother taken to the hospital, where she was diagnosed with a serious heart condition.

Visiting her mother for long hours in the dreary, overcrowded hospital, Jennifer soon grew despondent, fearful her mother was dying. "I've had a good and decent life," Mrs. Hamilton said quietly one day. "The war was hard, but I have a lovely daughter and two wonderful grandchildren. The only advice I have to leave with you is, trust God; He'll always be with you."

"Oh, Mother," Jennifer scolded cheerfully, "you're not going to die. You'll be out of here in a few days."

"I think my life is about done," Mrs. Hamilton said wearily.

"Nonsense!" Jennifer insisted. "Get some rest. Things will look much better tomorrow." She leaned over and kissed her mother's forehead before she left for home. She couldn't bear to consider the alternative. Her mother would recover—Jennifer just knew it.

But the next morning Jennifer was informed that her mother had passed away during the night. At first she found accepting her mother's death impossible. No matter how hard she tried, she couldn't imagine her mother not returning home, not being there when she needed her. Making the funeral arrangements, Jennifer felt a need for her mother's advice, which would never be available to her again. It was only then that the reality hit her: with her husband in prison and her mother dead, Jennifer was alone. Crying heavily, she understood that from now on she would have to trust her own decisions and rely on her own judgment, with God's help. What had her mother said? "Trust God; He'll always be with you." Would He? That was Jennifer's only hope for herself and her children.

As if the grief borne by herself and her children was not enough, Jennifer soon realized that all was not smooth sailing with the lawyer either. James Dennison was a young, soft-spoken man with curly hair and a boy-like face. She wasn't sure she trusted him; it always seemed like he was hiding something from her. His right eye twitched nervously one day as he tried to explain to her, "This is a sensitive case. In time the people involved grow less concerned or move on. It's best to take this thing slow."

"But it's been months!" Jennifer protested. "And nothing's happened!"

"Believe me, that's to our benefit," Dennison continued while fidgeting with a pencil. "The wheels of justice turn slowly, but they do turn."

Dennison had been expensive, his bills frequent. Money had so dwindled that Jennifer knew she had to find a job. Passing a bakery one afternoon, she saw a window advertisement for a woman baker.

When Jennifer entered the small, crowded bakery with its hot air, she saw a round, heavy-set Frenchman with a thick mustache and bushy black eyebrows. He was short and round and wore a tall baker's hat. "I saw your sign," she said, nodding toward the window. "I don't know much about baking, but I'm willing to learn."

The Frenchman, Pierre Dumont, studied Jennifer with black eyes, as if he were sizing up a horse to bet on at a race track. He noted her strong, large-boned figure. "I need a healthy woman who is not afraid of hard work," he said roughly, sweat rolling from his forehead. "My wife was a small woman, and the work here killed her." He took a deep breath, remembering his wife. He was a hard man who believed he could bury his problems in the constant toil of the bakery. "I must have someone to replace her. There is too much work here, and I can't do it all alone."

"I'm not afraid of hard work," Jennifer boasted, throwing her shoulders back.

"Then I'll give you a chance to prove it," Mr. Dumont said. "I'll teach you how to bake. Be here at 4 in the morning." He rudely turned back to his work, obviously wanting no further conversation today with Jennifer.

"Thank you," she said meekly as she left. *What an insensitive man,* she mused, *but I need the money! But who will watch the children?*

Jennifer went to her church and asked the ministers if they knew anyone who would be a capable housekeeper. They referred her to a woman named Lita Jackson, a black woman around fifty years old. Lita had been a house slave most of her life, they said, but she now lived a life of freedom in the poor part of town. Jennifer followed their directions to a ramshackle house with holes in the roof.

"I'm looking for Lita Jackson," Jennifer said to the black lady who opened the door.

"I'm Lita Jackson," she said in a surprised tone. "What you want?"

"I'm looking for a housekeeper," Jennifer explained, trying to be friendly. "I have two children who need looking after."

Lita's face lit up with happiness, her white teeth a noticeable contrast to her dark face. "All I know is how to look after children!"

"I'm afraid all I can pay you is room and board, but I do have a nice house, and you're welcome to share it with us," Jennifer added.

"That suits me just fine!" Lita said happily. "I can cook too—long as it ain't nothin' too fancy. Let me get my things. I been prayin' to get out of this miserable place! And now look what the Lord done— He sent a pretty white lady to rescue me!"

∽

During the silent, early-morning hours as Jennifer prepared for work, she often grieved over her mother's death. It seemed like only yesterday her mother had been present, laughing with the children; but she'd been gone for months now. Sometimes Jennifer imagined Drake being home soon and their enjoying life as a normal family. But the lawyer maintained his flagrant methods and was always quick with excuses and quick with bills for his services.

Looking in on the children just before she left for work one morning, Jennifer found them sleeping peacefully. She could hear Lita snoring in the other bedroom. Lita had been a real blessing, and the children adored her.

Leaving the house silently, Jennifer made her way to the dark street and began her walk to work. She felt a slight smile tug at her lips as she thought about Lita. Nobody could make the children laugh like Lita could. But Jennifer's thoughts soon turned to work and to Mr. Dumont, who had shown no mercy.

~

Arriving at the bakery, Jennifer discovered Mr. Dumont already busy at work, his fat, hairy fingers rolling delicate little pastries on a large table. He gave her a hard glance as she slipped her apron on. "You'll need to get a bucket of hot water and soap—the oven and racks need scrubbing." He motioned with his wide chin at a bucket and brush he had waiting for her.

A lingering cloud of despair due to the never-ending chores hung over Jennifer as she picked up the bucket and brush. *Why is this man so difficult?* she wondered. *All I do is scrub and clean. He hasn't taught me much about baking like he promised.* A few hours later, sweating profusely, she approached Mr. Dumont. "The oven and racks are clean."

"Good," he said, turning from his work at a tabletop. "Bring that sack of flour in here. I'll show you how to make dough."

Going over to the stock room, Jennifer tugged at a heavy sack of flour while Mr. Dumont watched impatiently. "No, no! Bend over and put your shoulder into it! Use your back! Pick it up!"

Straining, Jennifer crouched, lifted the sack onto her shoulder on the third try, and brought it over to where Mr. Dumont stood.

"Don't just stand there, woman! Throw it on the table!" he yelled.

Jennifer tossed the heavy sack onto the table, creating a cloud of white dust. Mr. Dumont tore open the corner of the sack, and flour spilled out. Grabbing a large wooden bowl, he lifted the sack and poured flour into the bowl. "Bring some warm water," he said. "Then you must work a little water at a time into the flour until you have a firm ball of dough."

The more water Jennifer added, the heavier and harder to manage the dough became. She worked it and worked it until her arms and hands were numb with fatigue.

"You must work faster!" Mr. Dumont insisted, his black-haired arms waving, his face angry. "We don't have all day just to make dough!"

Sweat stung Jennifer's eyes as she pushed and pulled at the stubborn dough, working as fast as she possibly could. A strand of her auburn hair escaped her cap and stuck to her face. She brushed it back, leaving a large white smear across her sweaty face.

"That's enough!" Mr. Dumont yelled impatiently. "Now, we take a piece about this size—" He grabbed a wad of dough with his heavy fist and slung it onto a tabletop. "Then we roll it out like this." He picked up a big roller and put all his weight and strength into flattening the dough. "It must be thin, but don't make holes in it."

Handing her the roller, Jennifer tried to imitate him, but she lacked his brute strength. "Push harder, woman! It is not a weakling baby—you won't hurt it!"

The hours ticked away slowly, and by the end of the workday Jennifer's back and arms moaned with pain, just like they did every afternoon. Though her feet and legs throbbed, it was a relief to walk home in the fresh air and escape the heat and hard grind of the cramped bakery.

∼

Jennifer decided to visit Drake again, which would require getting a day off. Mr. Dumont discouraged the visit because he knew about the penitentiary and how men slowly wasted away. A good friend of his had died there. He finally told Jennifer, "Go ahead—you'll see what I mean! The man you used to know is not the same man you'll visit."

The journey to the penitentiary was hard and long, and the coach seemed to hit every bump in the dirt road. The fetid smell of the summer swamp filled the vehicle as it lurched along, carrying a man and a woman besides Jennifer. She was afraid and felt increasingly apprehensive as the time to see Drake drew nearer. It had been months since she'd seen him last, and she had no good news to report from the lawyer, who continued to make excuses. Just thinking about the prison reminded her of death and decay as she remembered its strong odors and the emaciated faces of tormented men.

"You going to visit a relative?" the frail little woman riding opposite Jennifer asked coldly. She had a glass eye that stared wildly to one side, making it impossible to determine where she was looking.

"My husband," Jennifer replied briefly.

"We're going to visit our son—or what's left of him. He's only seventeen, and he's been there six months. Got caught stealing some horses, so now they've made a horse out of him." She was agitated and bitter. Her husband, oppressed with a racking cough, kept a handkerchief pressed to his long, thin face and sparse beard. He had the defeated look of a man worn thin by consumption.

When they arrived at the prison, Jennifer noticed the street wasn't as muddy as before, and the boardwalks that once stretched across the mud were now stacked in a neat pile. As she entered the drab building, she noticed an indifferent little man who wrote in the register, then had her sign her name. He glanced at her with cold, uncaring, colorless eyes. "Follow me, lady." He waddled with a heavy limp, dragging his left foot.

Jennifer followed until she was asked to wait in one of the little visiting rooms with a barred window in the wall. The room of rough, unpainted boards was scarcely four feet wide and was dim and depressing. She sat biting her fingernails, not knowing what to expect. Through the walls she heard the mumbling of low voices. The sour smell of the place nauseated her.

From behind the bars a door squeaked, alerting Jennifer that the time had come. A shadow moved, and a dark face appeared behind the bars—the face of a stranger. *They've sent the wrong man!* Jennifer thought.

Long, greasy dark hair stuck to the man's head, his skull-like face bushy with a ragged beard. His dull, lifeless eyes lay in hollow sockets. Jennifer glanced away, unsure what to say. Not knowing what else to do, her green eyes returned to examine the face. It seemed familiar in some respects, and after many moments of careful contemplation, she realized the awful truth—*it was Drake!* The skin of his face was drawn tight against the bone like an invalid whose strength was gone. She suddenly understood the greater wounds her husband had suffered—his tormented spirit, how deeply his wounds had pained him, how the shock of this hellhole had taken the life out of him.

"No!" Jennifer cried as she rushed closer to the barred window. "Drake, what have they done to you?"

Drake sat like a corpse, his face defeated and pitiful. "You don't want to know," he mumbled, his voice hoarse and deep. "Tell me about Dennison, Jennifer. What is he doing?"

Reaching through the bars, Jennifer grabbed Drake's hand. His pallid skin felt as cold and clammy as wet clay, and his curious eyes waited for an answer. "I've been to see him a dozen times. He says it's best that it's taking awhile because people tend to forget, so they won't be as harsh."

Dropping his head, Drake wallowed helplessly in defeat. He'd been living in overcrowded and unsanitary conditions, but it was the loneliness that had made him an empty shell. The will to live had slowly dwindled, and hope felt out of reach. He lived in the past, in memories of better times, for his present had no joy, no purpose. He spoke in a whisper. "Jennifer, I *can't* last much longer! I *have* to get out of here." He paused, wiping the sweat from his face with a bony hand. "Me and another man have a plan to escape. I have to try while I still can."

The news stunned Jennifer, alarm evident on her face. "But you might be killed! And even if you did make it, you'd be a wanted man—always on the run. How could we ever have a real life together?" Her voice trembled as she fought back the tears. "Think of the children, Drake! What about them?"

"They won't have a father at all if I have to stay here much longer." His beggar's face was heavy with grief as he dropped his head. Jennifer could see his shoulders moving as he cried—a man reduced to almost nothing. She wanted to touch him through the bars but waited a long moment before Drake managed to regain control. He brought his face up to hers, his cheeks wet with tears. "I dreamed I was home with you and the kids, except it wasn't a dream—I was really there." He cleared his throat; his blue eyes, now pale, had a faraway gaze. "We were sitting on the front porch. Abby was sitting in my lap, and Grant was playing under the oak tree. And you—you were sitting next to me—beautiful as always. That was just the other day—do you remember?"

Fear closed around Jennifer's heart. *I'm losing him!* she thought in despair. "Darling," she whispered, moving her face closer to the bars, "we haven't lived in that house for almost a year. You must remain strong, you have to find strength, and there is a way— through faith in God and in His Son, Jesus. Drake, you *must* believe me!"

"What kind of God would allow men to be tortured like this?" Drake spat back. "And you and that lawyer have done *nothing!* The only faith a man can have is in himself. I'll get myself out of here, Jennifer!" His chair raked against the floor as he stood to leave. "You won't have to come to this place again!" He turned and knocked on the door, and a guard let him out of the small room. He didn't even look back.

Still sitting in her small chair, the strain became too much, and Jennifer began crying with frantic sobs. She sat for some time until the uncontrollable crying waned. *He's lost his mind. What can I possibly do? How can I help him?*

The coach rattled over the dusty road, and the trip home was long and painful as Jennifer mourned the weakened and sickened condition of her husband. As much as she hated to admit it, Mr. Dumont had been right. The man she had visited wasn't the man she'd known at all—he had become something else.

～

The stress of the hard work and daily routine left Jennifer thoroughly depleted. Often she had no time or energy left for her children and simply went to bed depressed and discouraged. She had searched for another job, one that would not be so hard on her, only to be laughed at. "A woman working as a silversmith?" a muscular, dark-skinned man had ridiculed. A hawk-beaked nose jutted from his flat, laughing face. "You'd better try something like sewing." Discouraged but stubborn, she had continued to answer job advertisements. One man was so rude that she practically ran from the place. "I advertised for a clerk, not a woman!" The job hunt had led to nothing but misery and despair. Perhaps God really had abandoned her this time.

One of Jennifer's few consolations was reading the newspaper; the stories and advertisements took her to other worlds where people lived and prospered. One day she came across an advertisement for a typesetter at the *Picayune*, New Orleans's largest and most prominent newspaper—a job that consisted of hard work and long night hours. *I can do this as well as any man!* she thought. Something about writing and printing fascinated her—the way the written word could paint a mental picture. *I'd love to work at a newspaper! If I apply for the job, all they can do is tell me no or laugh at me. It couldn't be any worse than what I've already been through.*

The next day, after Jennifer got off work from the bakery, she rushed home, cleaned up, changed clothes, and went down to the *Picayune*. Standing outside the big newspaper building, she reread the advertisement she held in her hand; it said to see a Mr. Walker. Unsure of what to do next, she nervously debated whether to go inside or not. "What's the use?" she mumbled under her breath. "They'll probably just laugh at me." Standing idly for another moment, she finally decided, *I'm already here—I may as well get it over with!*

Inside, Jennifer found a busy office where people moved about like ants on an anthill. She approached a young man sitting at his desk. He appeared to be absorbed in his work, a light film of perspiration covering his face. "Excuse me," Jennifer said.

The man glanced up, his dark hair oily and plastered to his head, his eyes deep brown and friendly. "Yes?" he answered, astonished to see a nice-looking woman at his desk. "May I help you?"

"I'm looking for a Mr. Walker."

The young man smiled kindly. "Oh, you're in the wrong office.

You'll have to take those stairs over there down into the basement to the print shop."

"Thank you," Jennifer said. As she made her way down the wide, dark stairs to the basement, it seemed as if she were moving into the uncertain depths of a new world. The basement was filled with big, noisy machines clanking away in methodical rhythm. Men bustled about, not paying her any attention. Making her way over to an area that looked like a supervisor's office, she peeked in and noticed nobody was at the desk. She waited and waited, feeling out of place and unsure of what to do next.

Finally a small, aging man with thick glasses and a bald head appeared. He smiled at Jennifer and entered the office, where he sat in a worn chair. She stepped forward, "Excuse me, I'm looking for Mr. Walker."

Looking up, he smiled again. "I'm Mr. Walker. What can I do for you?"

"Well," Jennifer began, "I saw this ad in the paper." She lifted the newspaper in her hand slightly. "I'm interested in becoming a typesetter."

Mr. Walker's face broke into a friendly and sympathetic grin that was wide enough to show small, yellowed teeth. "I see," he chuckled. "I've never had a woman working in the basement here before, and I've been here twenty-six years." He gently filled a well-used pipe with tobacco as he appraised Jennifer with friendly eyes. "Typesetting is very dirty work, you know, and the hours aren't particularly desirable."

"I'm more than willing," Jennifer eagerly offered, a hint of a smile in her full lips as she sensed the man's kind heart. "Ink washes off. The dirt from some jobs doesn't."

Mr. Walker liked her answer, and he saw something special in Jennifer—perhaps her determination, or maybe it was her humble and honest approach. He touched a match to his pipe and sucked on it, leaning back in his chair, a smile evident in his eyes. "I may never hear the end of this from my colleagues, but you have the job. We begin at 8 in the evening and leave when the last paper is printed, somewhere around 3 or 4 in the morning. I realize those are hard hours, but the pay is good."

"Mr. Walker . . ." Jennifer sighed with relief. "I'm so happy—I'll be here at 8." As she stood to leave, she turned and smiled at him, a delightful smile Jeb Walker would always remember.

The opportunity to work at the newspaper gave Jennifer a refreshed vigor, for now she hoped she would be able to fulfill a secret ambition. There lay deep within her an affection for the printed word; she had a fascination for the way newspapers conveyed meaning and emotion and reached so many people. She reflected on the romance novels she'd always been so fond of and how the words in them had reached her in a special way. Although the print shop was merely a simple beginning, she had a strong desire to someday write her own thoughts, to state her own mind—a rare achievement for a woman.

∾

After her first long shift at the newspaper, Jennifer felt exhausted, though also mentally renewed with the busy excitement that surrounded the world of news. Her first shift was spent mostly with Mr. Walker as he showed her the general run of things and where to find all of the neatly sorted items she would be using. He had seemed to enjoy her company, a pleasant smile always on his face.

When Jennifer finished her shift, it was 3:30 in the morning, time to report to work at the bakery. In her excitement she hadn't even given any thought to Mr. Dumont or his bakery. *I want to do the right thing—I'll stop by long enough to tell him I quit*, she thought as she walked along in the damp morning air. *He'll probably get angry, but . . .*

Entering the back door of the bakery, Jennifer found Mr. Dumont bent over a huge table of eclairs, each of which he was filling with a creamy custard. He glanced up, his dark eyes puffy with the grind of having to rise so early in the morning. "Take that mop and bucket," he pointed, "and give this entire floor a running over." He turned back to his work, his face still thick and heavy from sleep.

"Mr. Dumont . . . I need to speak with you." Jennifer realized that even though she was about to be free of this intolerable job, she still feared Mr. Dumont.

"What is it?" he barked impatiently. "We haven't time for talk, and I have no interest in hearing about any of your personal problems."

Taking a deep breath, Jennifer steadied herself beside a large wooden table. All of a sudden the exhaustion from working all night hit her, making her feel a bit unsteady. "I'm sorry, Mr. Dumont, but I've found another job. I've worked all night and haven't had any sleep since yesterday at this time. I came by to tell you that I won't be working here any longer."

Glaring at her with sharp contempt, Mr. Dumont picked up an eclair and slammed it onto the table, making an ugly yellow mess. "That's what I get! I give you a chance and you let me down! Who's going to help me today? You can't work one more day?"

Feeling light-headed and dizzy, Jennifer feared she might faint. "No, I can't," she said, placing the back of her hand on her forehead. Steadying herself momentarily, she turned to leave, knowing it would be a mistake to try to deal with this harsh and abrasive man. "I have to go now," she murmured as she slipped out the back door.

Cursing his bad luck, Mr. Dumont gave way to his bitterness. *There is no respect or dedication left!* he thought angrily. *I give and others take! What's the purpose of even trying?*

~

Sitting beside greasy and inky wooden trays of tiny metal letters, Jennifer meticulously gathered the right letters and formed words to match the typewritten page beside her. The place smelled of grease, oil, and ink while the big printing press loudly clattered away, producing newspapers by the hundreds. What made her job more difficult was the fact that the small letters were in reverse, like a mirror image of the actual print. But she'd grown used to that and worked steadily away, often finding and correcting small errors the editors had missed. The black and sticky printer's ink perpetually covered her hands and apron.

"How do you like the dirty work down here?" a handsome young reporter named Messenger asked her, his hair blond and bright above his shiny forehead. He had childlike blue eyes and an eager smile.

"I think it's fascinating the way all of this is so complicated and then comes together to make a newspaper," Jennifer replied. Messenger stared at a big black smear of ink on her cheek as she spoke. "There's still so much to learn—I think it's fun!"

Thinking of the past few months in the hot and stuffy basement with all of the machinery, Jennifer had to admit the work was challenging and interesting and never boring. The hours flew by with the newness of something always to be learned. She'd grown used to the ink and grease and wore it with pride. Mr. Walker had been most patient, careful to show her the correct methods and shortcuts of the trade.

"You have a natural talent for working with words," he'd told her, "even if it's working with one little metal letter at a time. Not many people can easily read in reverse."

"I just think of it backwards," Jennifer admitted. "It's easy."

Mr. Walker shrugged his shoulders and smiled, his small eyes appearing large behind his thick glasses. "You're doing much better than I expected. I'd never have thought a woman would be suited to this kind of work."

"Oh, Mr. Walker, I just *love* it!" Jennifer stated as she proofread a freshly printed section. "It's a challenge—the printing press, the articles in the paper—it's as if I'm making a difference, reaching so many people, like I'm part of history."

Jeb Walker sucked on his pipe thoughtfully. He had been with the paper since his youth; he too had been taken in by the excitement of the printed word. It was something that, once experienced, a person never really got over. "Welcome to the world of news," Jeb offered graciously. "You've been taken in by it, maybe because it's your calling. Answer a question for me—what's worth more than information?"

Rolling her bright green eyes to the ceiling, Jennifer gave the question hard thought. After a moment of pondering, she answered, "Mr. Walker, I can't think of anything."

"Precisely," he agreed. "With the right information, all problems have solutions. The newspaper plays a big part in spreading information, so the information should always be accurate. Always remember that!"

∽

One day Jeb Walker received a visit from the newspaper's editor, C.C. Cromwell, a heavyset man with slicked-down black hair. His stern expression represented his business side, straight and true; but he also had a heart for the people working at the paper and kept a close eye on each and every one. He entered Jeb's office, a fat cigar clenched between his teeth. "Jeb, what's going on down here? I'm hearing a lot of talk about this woman you've hired as a typesetter."

Knowingly, Jeb let a smile crease his aging face. "It's hard to keep a good secret around here. You're asking about Mrs. Jennifer DeSpain, I take it. And you are *right*—she is exceptional, has a knack for the business, C.C."

"Hmm . . ." C.C. sighed, rubbing his rough chin with a meaty palm. "We've been together a long time, Jeb. Is she one of the rare people with ink in her blood, like you and me?"

Jeb nodded. "I'm afraid so, and I hate to lose her, but I know it's for the good of the paper. I'll find someone else. Where do you plan on putting her?"

"Mac Thibeaux is a good writer of editorials and good at teaching others. I think I'll put her with him for a while and see what happens. I'm thinking we need a woman to take care of the articles that female readers would be interested in—fashions, home cooking, things like that." C.C. Cromwell knew his business and was never shy about making a gamble—and his decisions almost always paid off. Nobody would ridicule him for putting a woman on the writing staff, unless they wanted to be recipients of his wrath!

∽

When Jennifer was called to C.C. Cromwell's office, she naturally assumed she'd made some serious error. She removed her ink-stained apron and washed her hands as Jeb Walker stood nearby. "Do you think he has a problem with me—I mean, with a woman working down here?" she asked worriedly.

Jeb didn't want to give away the surprise. "There's no telling what's on C.C.'s mind," he said dryly, knowing she'd be thrilled when she learned of her new opportunity. "He's a stern man but a good Christian man. Whatever decision he makes will be for the good of the paper."

Nervously, Jennifer made her way upstairs, fixing her hair as she climbed. Walking through the office where a few writers were working overtime, she felt the pressure of inquisitive eyes upon her as she approached Mr. Cromwell's door. Knocking softly, she heard a heavy voice invite her to enter.

C.C. Cromwell sat behind his big desk like a king, a cloud of cigar smoke hovering about his head as he stubbed out the cheroot in an ashtray. He came across as cold and calculating with his piercing brown eyes, but he had a heart of gold that he didn't let just anyone see. "Have a seat, Mrs. DeSpain."

Sitting down in front of him, Jennifer couldn't keep the worry from showing in her face.

"Mrs. DeSpain, I'm not a man to beat around the bush," C.C. said with a firm tone. With carefully planned gestures, he knew how to make the most of an opportunity. "I recognize talent, and I don't believe in wasting it. How would you like to work with one of my editorial writers until you can start writing your own? I want you to learn our methods, and I want you to cover the affairs that will appeal to our women readers."

Completely caught by surprise, Jennifer felt excitement run through her like a jolt of electricity. She began to tremble, and when she tried to speak, the words wouldn't come.

Mr. Cromwell could contain his brashness no longer and broke into an amused laughter. "Well, Mrs. DeSpain, I hope you won't have this kind of problem when it comes to writing."

"Oh . . . no, no I won't," Jennifer blurted out. "I mean, I'll do my best. This—this is wonderful!"

"Here, take these books," he said, handing her two volumes. "They're pretty good at telling you how to write a column. You'll find them useful."

Taking the books with nervous hands, Jennifer broke into a gracious smile, gleaming with happiness. "How can I thank you for a golden opportunity like this? Mr. Cromwell, I promise I won't disappoint you!"

"I'm sure you won't," C.C. agreed. "I've only heard good things about you. Now get out of my office and go home. Get some rest and come back tomorrow morning. I'll introduce you to your new supervisor then." He smiled as she left, for he was a man who was thoroughly convinced that all things work together for the best as a result of God having His way in the lives of His followers.

Elated, Jennifer almost fell down the stairs as she rushed back to the basement. When she found Jeb Walker, she teasingly confronted him. "You knew about this, didn't you?" she said, her face red from descending the stairs. The curve of a smile touched her lips, and her eyes sparkled with the light of hope. "You're the one responsible for this, aren't you? You told them about me."

Jeb smiled in his soft way as he held his pipe gently in his hand. "Jennifer, you are very special. You deserve a chance, and the paper needs people like you. I've been here a long time, and I've seen all kinds come and go. I know when a real newspaper person comes along—even if it happens to be a pretty woman."

Jennifer gave Jeb a big hug. "Thank you, Mr. Walker. You've been so kind and decent! Thank you for giving me a chance!"

CHAPTER

~ 5 ~

The Inheritance

Working with Mac Thibeaux at the *Picayune* proved to be a rewarding experience for Jennifer DeSpain. She found him to be humorous and helpful. Mac, a silver-haired gentleman in his fifties, wore a bow tie and wire-rimmed glasses. His hobby was Cajun cooking, and his passion was eating it, as evidenced by his potbelly. Always wearing a friendly smile, his gray eyebrows danced when he spoke. He often likened writing to cooking, an analogy Jennifer could relate to.

"Writing an article is like making a *roux*," Mac said as Jennifer sat next to him while he worked on a new column. "It must have all the right ingredients. You got to stir the *roux* all the time while it cook itself. The same with the column I write. I stir all the time, using different words here and there, until the writing got a shine on it, like the *roux* when it's cooked all the way through. It got to have a shine on it like the shine the sunset make on the Mississippi River when the water ain't too muddy. And it don't make difference to me how you get to desired result—I cook a *roux* a lot of different ways."

Jennifer couldn't help but smile at Mac. His articles were the best in the paper, but one thing intrigued her. "Mac, how do you write in plain English? You talk with such a heavy accent."

Scratching his head as he remembered the past, Mac finally muttered, "I did a little Cajun messing with my writing once. They liked to fired me. But I think of cooking, and the words are like peppers and garlic and onions; if I use them right, it's always good. This way that I just told you has worked for me for more than forty years. Also, too, it sounds more better than the way I talk."

With the use of the books Mr. Cromwell gave her, Jennifer composed her first brief articles for Mac's inspection. She was totally convinced that writing, like musical talent, was a gift someone is born with. She had a burning desire to write and felt that since she wrote with so much heart, her writing would come naturally.

"Hah!" Mac snorted after reading Jennifer's first piece. "Let me tole you dis. The writing has too many adjectives and adverbs, and dose are like bell pepper and celery, and wit' dem you got to be careful. They are taste killers, so don't use too much. You got to mix everything together until it starts to mingle itself real well. You better try it again." He handed her back the piece of paper.

Disappointed, Jennifer rewrote the piece, this time being very careful and studying each sentence time and again, until she felt she had written a decent piece. She presented it to Mac again.

"You got words in here peoples don't know w'at to do wit'!" he criticized. "Use more better words; it a shame to waste dem. Stir 'em in so you can jus' eat dem."

Before long Jennifer knew that writing wasn't simply a talent but a learning process as she spent hours and hours rewriting and rewriting again. It seemed like Mac would never be pleased. But unknown to her, every now and then she would write something he liked. Finally one day he let her know.

"O-o-o boy, it's good! Dis taste real good all its own!" he complimented, a wide smile spreading across his face as his light blue eyes moved from word to word. "I think I let them boys print this, yes. You keep writing like I tole you to cook and it will be good, I garontee!"

Jennifer delighted in finally pleasing Mac. She had discovered that writing was indeed hard work, a skill that would have to be developed over time, but she had the tenacity to pursue it and a genuine love for the business. She cut out her first printed column and placed it in an old picture frame she found in the attic of her house.

It was a brief but finely done article on the many varieties of flowers blooming in Jackson Square. As Mac had said, "It makes my mouth water, yes."

~

Jennifer quickly became a frequent guest columnist on the editorial page. And C.C. Cromwell's office was soon flooded with responses to "the lady columnist." He sent for Jennifer, and when she entered his office, he said, "Please have a seat, Miss Jennifer." Closing the door behind her, he began, "It seems you've generated a very good response from some of our readers." He moved around his desk and sat in his big chair. "Looks like you've learned a lot from Mac."

Realizing C.C. was waiting for a reply, Jennifer said, "He's one of the nicest men I've ever met. Not only has he taught me about writing, but I believe I can cook just about whatever Cajun dish you can think of."

C.C. took a puff on his stub of a cigar, blew a perfect smoke ring, then said abruptly, "I think you're about ready to start writing your own column. I'll be needing three a week—one each for Tuesday, Thursday, and Sunday, with Sunday's being about twice the length of the others."

Astonished, Jennifer had to work at not letting her mouth fall open. "Mr. Cromwell, I can't believe it! I'm *so* grateful. I'd *love* to be a full-time writer for the paper."

"Don't think this doesn't come without its rewards," C.C. continued, his black hair as slicked down as ever while his eyes showed a hint of softness. "No more typesetter pay. I'm ready to put you on a writer's pay, and I think you'll find it fairly attractive."

Jennifer clasped her hands in front of her face, obviously overjoyed. "Mr. Cromwell, you've been so considerate! I'm just . . ."

"You've earned it," C.C. interrupted. He grinned broadly, then swept the air with a heavy hand. "Now get out of here. I'll expect the first copy of your column on an editor's desk Monday morning."

After she left, C.C. smiled and lit one of his fine cigars. *I'm the one who's fortunate*, he thought. *I wonder how many other papers in the country have a good woman writer working for them.* He chuckled. *Not many, I bet. I'm sure it's all in the will of the Lord.*

~

For once, Jennifer's life seemed to reach a time where things were actually trying to work out. She was earning a good living at the *Picayune*, and the lawyer promised her he was finally making headway with Drake's case. He would soon have Drake back in New Orleans for a new trial, he claimed. The children were happy in school and were diligently working at their studies. And Lita cheerfully kept things in order at home. Jennifer was confident that God would soon have her life completely back together.

At the same time, Jennifer did sometimes have disputes with the editors as to how certain things should be stated in her column. One day a junior editor, Bill Wall, a sun-bronzed man in his forties with an eye for detail, explained, "Jennifer, you can't put these abbreviations in a written column; it just isn't done. The article sounds . . . well, colloquial!"

"And that's what I intended it to sound like," Jennifer argued. "I'm supposed to be writing a column that reaches the women of New Orleans, and I'm supposed to write on a level that will reach them. So I do. I write in a friendly style, as if I were speaking to them in person."

Bill shook his head, suddenly remembering that arguing with Jennifer was always a losing battle. "All right!" he said, growing impatient with the dispute. "But if Cromwell complains to me, I've made a note here of all the changes I thought necessary."

"He won't," Jennifer affirmed as she marched out of Bill's office. Her success had given her a confidence she'd never known before and had enabled her to be comfortable with a little boldness.

When she arrived back at her desk, she found a telegram stuck in her typewriter. The messenger had apparently been unable to locate her in the busy building and had stuck the telegram where she couldn't miss it. Snatching it up, she quickly opened it to read the brief and simple message.

August 13, 1868
Mrs. DeSpain:

Your husband has been shot in an escape attempt.
Please come at once if you want to see him—he's not
expected to live.

Druff Beckner
Warden

Numb with disbelief, Jennifer stared blankly at the telegram. She read it again and again, her mind crying out, *This can't be happening! We're so close to getting Drake out!* For a while she sat staring out a window and watching a poor man far down the narrow street scrounge through some garbage cans. She wondered what it would be like to be that man. *He has nothing—and nothing to lose. My life has all been about losses.* For a brief moment she envied the vagrant.

Jennifer closed her eyes and prayed silently. *Father, how much more must I lose? I know You love us, and that Your plan is best. But why must it be so hard? And, Lord, please help my dear husband to come to know You through Your Son Jesus before he dies, whether that is tomorrow or ten years from now. Save Drake's soul, Lord!*

∼

As Jennifer had expected, the journey to the prison was long and hot and miserable. She traveled alone as flying bugs filled the coach when it entered the swamplands. The stinging bites of horseflies and mosquitoes became almost intolerable, and finding an old newspaper on the seat she rolled it up to defend herself against the flying pests. By the time the coach arrived at the prison, she was exhausted from fighting the swarming insects and from urgently praying for her husband's soul.

At the prison, the guard assigned to Jennifer quickly led her to the infirmary, a miserable place of decay and dying men. She found Drake lying motionless on his back, staring blindly at the ceiling. He was soaking wet with sweat and burning up with a fever. His entire chest was wrapped in a heavy white gauze, and his breathing was raspy and strained.

Jennifer gently squeezed his hot and clammy hand as tears welled up in her eyes. "Drake," she whispered softly. "Drake, it's me—Jennifer."

Ever so slowly, Drake turned his head to let his eyes meet hers. A slight smile touched his dry and crusty lips. "You've come, Jennifer," he mumbled. "At least the last thing I'll see is something good."

"What happened?" Jennifer asked in a low tone. Other men lay in their beds either asleep or moaning. She felt it necessary to keep her voice down for their sake.

Drake rolled his pale eyes, recalling the scene. "They chased me with dogs—hunted me down like an animal and shot me in the back!" He returned his eyes to her, his face sunken and his cheeks hollow. "I'm sorry—I'm so sorry for what I've been." He squeezed her hand. "My whole life has been nothing but failure. The only good thing in it has been you and the children. When they're old enough, tell them . . ." He coughed, squinting his eyes with pain. "Tell them their father wasn't . . . all bad."

"Drake . . . !" Jennifer whispered. Hot tears rolled down her cheeks, and her throat hurt. "What did the doctor say? Isn't there something more he can do for you? Maybe he can move you to a hospital. There must be *something* . . . !"

"Too late," Drake responded with hopeless remorse. "Infection has set in—the doctor says it's just a matter of time."

Suddenly Jennifer felt an unexpected surge of courage. "But it's not too late—not for your soul. Drake, there *is* a way! And Jesus Christ *is* that way! Life here is *not* all there is. If you repent and give your life, here and now, to Jesus Christ, you will go on to glorious life in heaven forever."

Letting his tired eyes settle upon her, he took a deep breath. "I know you're right, that I've done a lot of wrong in my life. I know that I didn't want to hear about it before but now . . . tell me about Jesus Christ." As far as he was concerned, Jennifer looked like a beautiful angel, and he knew she was telling him the truth about his soul's needs.

Telling the story of Jesus in her soft voice, Jennifer held his hand tightly as she spoke. For over an hour Jennifer explained the Gospel from the Scriptures, and Drake listened intently. Finally Jennifer read the Bible verse, "All have sinned, and come short of the glory of God." She put her hand on his and asked, "Can you admit to God that you're a sinner, just as all of us are?"

Drake looked at her, his eyes fixed on hers. "Yes. I've been wrong all my life, Jennifer. I don't see how God can forgive me."

"When Jesus died on the cross," Jennifer assured him, "that proved once and for all that God loves us. He gave the most precious thing He had so we could be saved from hell and live in heaven with him." She turned a few pages, then read, "If thou shalt confess with thy mouth the Lord Jesus, and shalt believe in thine heart that God hath raised him from the dead, thou shalt be saved," and then another verse, "For whosoever shall call upon the name of the Lord shall be saved."

"It—it sounds too *easy*!"

Jennifer's eyes were filled with love as she whispered, "Drake, if you were hanging on a cliff and about to fall to your death, and someone offered you a hand to pull you to safety, would you take it?"

"Why, sure, I would!"

"That's what God has done. He sent His Son to die for your sins, and now He's putting His hand out and asking you to take it and let Him keep you from going to hell and death. Can you accept Christ into your life?" Jennifer asked, her face close to his. "Will you pray with me? In your heart, just call on God and tell Him you're a sinner, then ask Him to save you in the name of Jesus."

Drake's face contorted with pain, but he nodded. At once Jennifer began to pray. She wasn't sure how long she prayed or what she said; she just poured her soul out to God. But when she finished, Drake was crying. "Did you call on God, Drake?"

"Y-yes—and something happened!" Drake gasped. His eyes were glowing, and he lifted himself up. "For the first time I feel peace! Oh, Jennifer, God *does* love me! I know it's true!"

Jennifer's eyes filled with tears, and as she leaned down and embraced him, she could only whisper, "Thank God!" over and over.

"I do accept Jesus, and, Jennifer, for the first time, I—I'm not afraid to die!"

Leaning over and kissing him softly, Jennifer said, "With God, we always have hope, even after this life."

For the rest of her visit, Drake listened as Jennifer read many different Scriptures to him and told him about their children. Again and again he begged her to never let them forget him. Finally he grew still, and for one frightening moment Jennifer thought he had died. But then he opened his eyes, and there was a spark of light in them.

"Jennifer, there's one more thing I need to tell you," he whispered hoarsely. He spoke urgently, half lifting himself up, his eyes desperate. "A man named Robert Hutton owed me a lot of money from a poker game on the riverboat. When he couldn't pay, he sent me the deed to a newspaper he owned in Virginia City, Nevada. Do you still have my box of papers?"

Jennifer remembered placing it in the attic at home. "Yes, darling. It's in a safe place."

"The deed's in there. I'm told it was a successful business. It's yours to do with as you please. Maybe you can sell it."

Smiling, Jennifer said nothing but just held his hand. Drake seemed to be feeling better as he talked on and on. "How's my little Abby? I bet she's grown into a fine young girl by now. And Grant— I bet he's a strong boy and likes to get dirty outdoors."

"They're beautiful children," Jennifer told him. She didn't tell him that Abby was the wild one who liked to play outside while Grant loved school and books.

In her final hours with Drake, Jennifer sat beside his bed holding his hand. Not much was said; they just sat there, comforted by each other's presence. When the guard came and told Jennifer the coach would soon be leaving, she turned to Drake. "Oh, darling, I don't know how to say good-bye. I don't want to leave." Tears filled her eyes and ran down her cheeks.

A new Drake, finally free from fear, tried to console her. "There's nothing to cry about. I'm dying, Jennifer, but I'm happy to be leaving all the misery of this prison. I know my sins are forgiven, and

Jesus is with me. I'll see you all again someday." He slowly closed his eyes, exhausted from the visit.

Standing, Jennifer took one last look at the husband she now loved more than ever. His body was defeated, but now he had a new spirit and a new life that would never end. She gave him a lingering kiss, then prayed for strength and walked out of the depressing room. It was the last time she would see Drake on earth.

~

The next few days at the *Picayune* seemed to crawl. Jennifer knew she'd soon be receiving the inevitable news of Drake's death, and finally the dreaded telegram came. She stared blindly at the insignificant-looking piece of paper, but no tears came. She had wept herself out during the long nights, and she knew that now she had to be strong for the children's sake.

"Take all the time off you need, Jennifer," Mr. Cromwell said gently. She left the office shortly thereafter, stunned by the sudden turns her life was taking.

~

"Why do I have to dress up today, Mama? It's not even Sunday!"

"Today is your father's funeral, Abby. We must go and say good-bye to him."

Abby smacked the dresser with her hand, her face contorted with anger. "My father is not dead!"

"I'm sorry, Abby, but we must face facts—he really is gone, and . . ." Jennifer fought back the tears. She was heartbroken at how Abby refused to accept the fact of her father's passing. The child had drawn into her own world, and nothing Jennifer could say seemed to get through to her.

"If some people killed my father, I'll kill them!" Abby shouted angrily. "But he's just gone away for a while! He'll be back—I know he will!" She pouted and stomped into the other room.

Grant watched silently, the perfect little gentleman dressed in a black suit and tie. "Mother, did he die when you were there?"

"No, sweetheart," Jennifer said. "He died in his sleep after I left.

But don't worry, he's with Jesus now. He asked God to forgive him for his sins and to take him to heaven. Meanwhile, those of us who are left behind will just have to do the best we can. And God will help us."

His face stern, Grant came over to his mother and hugged her tightly. "I'll grow up fast!" he said with determination. "I'll take care of you and Abby, Mother."

Jennifer smiled and held her son closely. "I know you'll do your best, Grant. I know you will."

At the service, Jennifer and her children sat in the front pew of her home church while the preacher gave a short eulogy. The *Picayune* had sent an array of fragrant, blooming flowers that now surrounded the plain wooden casket. She choked back her fears, telling herself she had to remain strong. Afterward Drake's casket was moved to the church cemetery, where his body was laid to rest. Only a handful of people attended, mostly for Jennifer's sake since none of them knew Drake.

That evening, after the children went to bed, Jennifer sat on the front porch enjoying the cool summer evening breeze. She allowed herself to reminisce about when she first met Drake, and afterward when the black porter brought her flowers on this very same front porch. The note from Drake asking her out had excited her so. With the memory, her sorrow could no longer be held in check. The first tear rolled down her cheek, and soon her chest was heaving with sobs as she remembered Drake kissing her for the first time only a few feet from where she sat now. Strong and handsome and confident, the only man she'd ever loved had held her softly as he kissed her. For an instant it was like she'd gone back in time, and she could almost feel his warm caress on her lips.

Later that evening, exhausted after hours of crying, Jennifer went inside to go to bed. Drake was gone forever, and nothing she could do would bring him back.

~

To subdue her grief, Jennifer threw all of her effort into her work, writing and rewriting her articles until they "had a shine on dem," just as Mac Thibeaux had described. Letters of commendation poured into C.C. Cromwell's office praising the new woman columnist. "I knew it," he said to Jeb Walker. "Jennifer really has a talent for communicating with words. I don't know where she comes up with some of her ideas, but the readers just love her."

"We miss her down here in the print room too," Jeb responded. "It's not often I get an employee who loves the work like Jennifer did."

"Yeah. That was a shame about her husband," C.C. reflected, thinking of the recent funeral as he clamped his short cigar between his teeth. "She must be a strong person. But she has a good income and a good position with the paper now, so she should be able to support her family without any problem."

Wiping his thick glasses with a clean rag, Jeb placed them thoughtfully back on his face and turned to C.C. "She's part of the *Picayune* family now, and we stick together. We're fortunate to have her."

~

Several months later, looking back, Jennifer realized that her grief had almost consumed her. But thankfully her work had kept her so busy she didn't have time to dwell on Drake and her sorrow over his passing. One day she was working hard on a column about the estate of a prominent local socialite when she suddenly recalled Drake's last comment to her, something about a newspaper he had won and left to her.

At home that evening she went into the attic and began perusing a box containing Drake's papers, mostly court-related records concerning his case. When she opened a plain white envelope, an official-looking document with fancy bordered edges fell to the floor. It was what she'd been looking for—the deed to a Virginia City, Nevada newspaper, including the land and the building and all the equipment. The newspaper was called *The Miner's News*. Because it reminded her of Drake, the discovery both saddened and exhilarated her.

Although Jennifer knew nothing about mining, she pictured a

small newspaper of busy men gathering the production reports of all the mines in the area and summarizing them neatly in their articles. She knew Virginia City was the location of the Comstock Lode, a major gold strike that had received prominent coverage in every paper in the country. *With all that gold and money floating around,* she mused, *perhaps the newspaper has increased in value. I wonder what it's worth these days.* Speculating about a newspaper she now owned yet knew absolutely nothing about was a welcome distraction from the bereavement she'd been carrying.

Curious, Jennifer wrote a brief letter explaining her circumstances and her interest in the newspaper she'd inherited. She addressed the letter to the editor of *The Miner's News*, general delivery, Virginia City, Nevada, figuring the minimal address would be sufficient for the undeveloped West. Having little hope that the inquiry would turn up anything interesting, she busied herself in the following weeks with her column, writing interesting stories that continued to generate public praise. Her love for her work, her children, and her spiritual family made the days pass quickly, and her grief soon became an annoying pest rather than a persistent tyrant.

~

Six weeks later Jennifer received a large envelope with the words *The Miner's News* printed in fancy letters on the corner of the envelope. *Impressive!* she thought as she quickly opened the envelope. The letter was equally arresting, with grand western-style print at the top of the page. *This is professional work*, she thought as she studied the stationery. She eagerly read the letter.

> Dear Mrs. DeSpain:
>
> I'm happy to hear of your new ownership of *The Miner's News*. It's been some time since I've heard from the previous owner, Mr. Robert Hutton.
>
> To answer your inquiry, we publish biweekly mining reports of every known mine in the area—their production, stock values, and the current market on gold prices. We also run advertisements for the sale of mines or mining stock and have a classified section for employment

and the sale of industrial tools and equipment. Also, I write an editorial on the state of affairs of the industry in this area.

Unfortunately, the sale of newspapers only covers our overhead. Profits arise from the advertisements, and in most cases I've had to accept stocks or mining certificates as payment. As the editor, and not the owner, of this paper, I'm not able to cash these certificates. Some have increased in value, while others have depreciated. As a result, our cash flow is currently operating in the red. Any capital you might entrust me with would enable the newspaper to operate with a financial cushion and insure a profitable survival.

Sincerely,
Jason Stone
Editor

Jennifer quickly opened the small newspaper that accompanied the letter. The western-style print used for the paper's name was simply magnificent. *This is a work of art,* Jennifer thought excitedly. The headline read: ANOTHER MOTHER LODE STRIKE! The brief article told about gold and riches and said that soon there wouldn't be a poor man in the entire town! She perused the reports, mostly assayer talk that she didn't understand. She read the editorial with an eagle eye. *Mr. Stone is obviously a skilled and disciplined writer who has undoubtedly had a long career. He must be well educated in journalism.*

Of course, *The Miner's News* was nothing like the *Picayune*. It was just a small western-style newspaper done with extravagant lettering, and yet the quality of the little paper was sharp and clean and crisp. *I'll ask Mr. Cromwell what he thinks of all this business. With his experience I'm sure he'll be helpful!*

～

The next day Jennifer told Mr. Cromwell's staff she wanted to meet with him, and within an hour he sent her a note asking her to come to his office. Aglow with enthusiasm, Jennifer carried the letter and newspaper as she quickly went to the publisher's office. She tapped on the door gently.

"Come in!" C.C. barked, but when he saw it was Jennifer, he lowered his voice. "Oh, Mrs. DeSpain, please come in. You wanted to see me?"

"Yes, Mr. Cromwell. I'd appreciate your advice on something. You see, I've inherited a small newspaper in Virginia City, Nevada. Drake left it to me. I wrote the editor and received this back." She handed him the large brown envelope.

C.C. read the letter first, a heavy frown forming on his face. Then he picked up the newspaper and studied it closely, noting the fine work and excellent writing. He leaned back in his big chair and let his eyes fall on an expectant Jennifer. "Well," he said, giving his words deep consideration, "I'm sure there's something to this small paper. It's in one of the richest places in the country right now. But . . ." He leaned forward and put his elbows on his desk with his arms crossed. "You asked for my advice. First, never invest in something you can't get a look at. There's no telling what is actually going on, although Mr. Stone does seem quite competent. The other thing is, gold towns spring up overnight, but they can disappear just as quickly. Who knows how much gold is really there? It might be gone tomorrow, leaving you with a newspaper in a ghost town.

"If I were you, I'd look into possibly selling the paper to someone who lives there. You could have Mr. Stone run an advertisement in your own paper. Realistically, there's no way you can manage a newspaper from over a thousand miles away! Take your losses early, and above all, don't send him a penny." He saw the disappointment in Jennifer's face. "Those are only my feelings on the subject," he added, trying not to be so discouraging. "It's your newspaper, and you can do whatever you want with it." He handed the paper and letter back to her.

"I appreciate your comments, Mr. Cromwell," Jennifer mumbled, slightly disappointed. "I'm not sure what I'm going to do. I'll have to pray about it."

"Now that's the best advice of all," C.C. nodded. "I can't believe I didn't think of it."

Jennifer stood to leave. "Do you think a small paper like *The Miner's News* would be worth much?"

"I wouldn't know," C.C. said with a shrug. "We do know that it has a printing press, a building, land, and an editor. That should be worth something."

Jennifer smiled faintly, then left Mr. Cromwell's office. Her positive mental picture of the newspaper had been shaken by her employer's realism. What should she do? Late that night she knelt beside her bed and prayed, *Father, I'm so confused. I pray You'll show me the way—and I'll obey, no matter what!*

The Decision

The sweltering summer days mellowed into a cool autumn of vivid colors as Jennifer's life moved along in a stable and dependable routine. But *The Miner's News* troubled her thoughts with increasing persistence. *I wonder what's happening in Virginia City,* she pondered as she took a break from her work and let her eyes wander out the window. *Since Jason Stone knows I'm the new owner, you'd think at least he'd send me a copy of the paper every now and then. But I know how busy they must be—and he said money was tight.*

That evening after the children were in bed, Jennifer sat on the front porch savoring the silence and watching a small whirlwind of leaves spin wildly down the street. The days had grown shorter, and the season had already brought them wrath from one hurricane. Jennifer let worry carry her thoughts where it would as she sat cuddled in a warm sweater. *I wish I could stop thinking about the West, but for some reason I can't!* She remembered what she had told Mr. Cromwell—that she would pray about it.

Using the resources at the *Picayune*, Jennifer had done what she could to learn more about Virginia City, often digging up old newspaper articles about the gold strike known as the Comstock Lode. She'd found the reading so interesting that she'd researched further, learning about the West in general. She found the lifestyle of rugged determination in a new country where there was no postwar oppression absolutely fascinating. *Those people out west are adventurers*, she had concluded. *Bold men and women willing to risk everything for the sake of discovery and the hope of making a fortune. Maybe they don't know it, but they're making history!*

Jennifer waited two more weeks to hear from Stone, then finally decided she could no longer be a silent partner to the excitement taking place in Virginia City. She'd been able to save a tidy sum, so on a clear Friday morning she went by her bank and had them wire the money to a bank in Virginia City.

"I've never sent money like this," she murmured as she signed the paper. "It'll get there all right, won't it, Mr. Tolliver?"

"Why, certainly, Mrs. DeSpain!" Jed Tolliver was a diminutive man of fifty with sharp black eyes and a thatch of salt-and-pepper hair. "It's much safer than the mail or taking it in person. Mr. Stone will get the money today." As she left the bank, Jennifer wore a smile of satisfaction, delighted that she had finally made a decision about the small newspaper.

That night she couldn't sleep for hours, she was so excited at the venture that lay before her. What a spectacular place Virginia City must be. Such an exciting and adventurous life to be a part of! In the still darkness a vivid image of Drake came to her, and with it a sadness. *I wish he was still here—that we were about to start a new life together* . . . Reminding herself of the futility of dwelling on his death, she said her prayers and waited for sleep.

A bright shaft of golden sunlight shone on Jennifer the next morning as she slowly opened her sleepy eyes. She smiled as she recalled the wonderful dream she'd had—a dream so real she could hardly believe she was still in her bed in New Orleans. She'd dreamed she traveled west and became part of the wild and new exciting world of gold towns in the beautiful mountain country. *Could my family and I be part of something as glorious as all of that?* she wondered. The prospect excited her more than anything in a very long time.

With a burst of energy, Jennifer jumped out of bed and got dressed, though doubts began to nudge at her. *I have a good job here that pays well. The children are doing well in school and at home, thanks* to Lita. *I've always lived in New Orleans and have a secure life here—friends, a good home, a church family that loves me and shares the Word with me and my children. Why should I throw this hard-earned and well-established lifestyle away and risk everything?*

There seemed to be plenty of reasons not to disturb their peaceful and meaningful way of life. But then other thoughts came to mind. *This place reminds me of my father and my mother and Drake—and their deaths that have taken such a toll on me. Will those sad memories ever leave me alone?* As she brushed her hair, her mind filled quickly with thoughts of adventure. *It could take forever before the bitterness of the war leaves New Orleans. The dream was so real! Could it have come from God?*

Brushing her hair slowly with the tortoise shell brush and comb Drake had given her for their first anniversary, she studied her reflection in the mirror. *I wonder what the women out west are like?* She laughed, fantasizing about the loud and rowdy mining towns, realizing she would attract the attention of most men, for out there men outnumbered the women twenty to one.

Why not go west? It's always been the brave who have made this country what it is, those who were unafraid to venture into the unknown. The children would probably love it. Why, they'd get an education firsthand instead of having to just read about everything! It would be a new start for us. She moved the brush over her fine, silky hair, and another thought came to her. *I wonder if Lita would consider going?* Jennifer became infatuated with the idea of moving and began thinking about how she would do it.

I've never had a dream like this in my life. God, this must be guidance from You. If it isn't, please slow me down or make it clear to me that I'm going in the wrong direction. Jennifer left for work without saying a word to the children or Lita, her mind churning with thoughts about leaving New Orleans for a grand adventure.

I could sell the house and most of the things in it. We won't need them, especially all this old furniture. After paying off the mortgage I should have enough money to sustain us for quite a while. Besides, our future doesn't depend on how much money we have or where we live. God is our refuge and strength; His love and mercy are untold riches that will provide our every need now and forever! But then again, if I'm wrong, if my dream isn't God's idea, what will happen to us? If only I could be sure . . .

Jennifer walked to work at an enthusiastic pace. *I can't go on like this, always wondering. I'll have to make a choice and live with my decision.* As she moved down the crowded street, she kept praying that God would let her know what He wanted her to do. By the time she reached the *Picayune*, she knew. Somehow God had confirmed His will within her. *We'll go west—I know that's God's will for us.*

~

At work, Jennifer continued to think of the West. She'd made her decision about moving there, but she knew she needed to take the necessary steps slowly to avoid any costly impulsive errors. She glanced at a pile of literature she'd accumulated about the West. *I think I'll write an article on the gold towns—I certainly have enough information!* Without delay, she began working. Writing had become second nature to her, so she let the words flow with energy and emotion, carefully keeping in mind the focus of the intended article.

A week later letters responding to her article formed a huge pile on C.C. Cromwell's desk, mostly letters wanting to know more about the golden West. Suspecting a hidden purpose for Jennifer's articles, the publisher called her to his office.

"Please come in and have a seat," C.C. said when she entered the office. She appeared so young and naive, yet she was bright and ambitious. "You've stirred quite an interest from our readers with this article about the gold towns. If I didn't know better, I'd think you were selling real estate in Virginia City."

"I did some research on the subject since I own a paper there and all. I found it so interesting that I thought it might make a good article."

"Indeed!" Mr. Cromwell exclaimed. "In all my years at this newspaper I've never seen such a response to one article. You've painted a fascinating picture of what things must be like in the West considering you've never been there."

"I must admit, I was curious," Jennifer said truthfully. "It looks like a lot of people are curious."

"I should say so. Many of the people here in the East have little since the war, and times are hard here in New Orleans and elsewhere. I think you've given them a taste of hope in our new frontier, and I'm sure many will actually pick up and go west. You know, of course, that this happened prior to the war too. A fellow named Horace Greeley wrote a book inspiring thousands to venture west. Most of those people were mistakenly led to a sad disappointment and lost everything, including their loved ones. If Horace Greeley had actually *been* west, he might have written a different story."

"What are you saying, Mr. Cromwell?" Jennifer asked, concern on her face. "That I've intentionally misled people with this article?"

"Not at all, not at all!" Mr. Cromwell shook his head vigorously. "It just occurred to me that nobody could write an article like this if they weren't themselves taken with the idea."

Jennifer let her eyes drop. It appeared that Mr. Cromwell had guessed her intentions. "As you apparently realize, sir, " she acknowledged as she raised her eyes to him, "I plan on moving to Virginia City."

Mr. Cromwell's mouth fell open as he stared at Jennifer in disbelief. He had wondered but hadn't quite been able to convince himself it was true. "Are you crazy?" he asked without thinking. "What I mean is, have you thought this through?" He shook his head in dismay. "Why would you quit a stable job earning good pay—a job with all kinds of possibilities for promotion and success? Besides, you own a home here, you have two young children who are comfortable in school . . . This doesn't make sense!"

"It didn't make sense for people to risk an uncharted voyage across the ocean to discover this country either," Jennifer argued with fire in her eyes.

"What are you looking for? Gold? Riches?" Mr. Cromwell demanded impatiently.

"I want to be part of—well, part of history," Jennifer answered firmly. "I want to do something . . . something that *lasts*, Mr. Cromwell! I'll write about it for everyone to read. You can see how much interest there is in the West just by the pile of mail on your desk."

"Yes," Mr. Cromwell said, lowering his voice. He realized he couldn't argue with this young woman. He pulled out one of his expensive cigars and lit it. Leaning back in his chair, he blew a plume of smoke overhead. "When do you plan on leaving?"

"I have to sell my house and get things in order," Jennifer said, repeating what she'd gone over in her mind again and again. "If I can get things settled this winter, hopefully I can leave in early spring."

"I see. What do you plan on doing out there?"

"You said it yourself, Mr. Cromwell. You can't run a paper from a thousand miles away."

"So I did," he agreed, his dark eyes searching Jennifer carefully. "You're a fine writer, Jennifer, but what do you know about running a paper?"

"I'll learn," Jennifer said with moderate confidence.

C.C. Cromwell paused, letting his eyes roam around the room as he gently rotated his cigar between his fingers. Though he wouldn't admit it, he envied the pretty young woman before him. He wished he was still young, so he could go west himself. What he was questioning in her now was actually what had impressed him about her the first time he met her. He hated losing a fine columnist, but he had seen many good writers come and go, and the paper always survived.

"Tell me one thing," he said curiously. "What made you willing to take such a risky adventure?"

Jennifer relaxed, letting her shoulders drop. "I feel God is calling me to it," she answered calmly.

C.C. Cromwell nodded. He knew exactly what she meant, for thirty years earlier God had called him from New York to New Orleans. "Then God will take care of you, Jennifer DeSpain. God will take care of you."

~

Winter rains pelted the roof as Jennifer sat at her desk at home planning their long journey. She had written to Jason Stone inquiring about the paper. He had responded with letters of encouragement, assuring her the paper was doing well and that her money had helped, but that he needed even more money for improvements and supplies in a town where prices had escalated due to the abundance of gold. Sending him another bank draft, she didn't inform him that she was coming. She wanted to walk in on the paper unexpectedly and catch it in its natural state.

Putting down her pen, Jennifer decided she'd waited long enough to tell Lita the news. She walked to the kitchen where Lita stood over a pot of steaming greens. "Lita, I need to talk to you," Jennifer said, sitting down at the kitchen table.

"Yes, ma'am," Lita said, setting her wooden spoon down. She came over to the table and grunted as she let her tired body fall into a groaning wooden chair. "I know'd you been worried 'bout somethin'."

Jennifer began with a pleasant smile. "Lita, how would you like to move with us out west, to Virginia City, Nevada? I know this is kind of sudden, but I've done a lot of praying about this, and I think my children and I need to leave some sad memories behind and get a new start. You've become part of our family, and we'd like you to go along with us if you're willing."

Lita's eyes grew as big as saucers. "What? I don't know nothin' about no west. Does they have any colored folks out there?"

Amused at Lita's animated response, Jennifer said, "I'm sure they do. And you'd still be living with us."

Shaking her head at the huge decision suddenly confronting her, Lita shifted her body in the small chair. "Dis family here is all I got! I couldn't stand the thought of y'all leavin' me here. But den I don't know nothin' about no place like dat. I hear dey have Injuns out yonder. I don't think they'd like no colored folk!"

Taking Lita's black hand in her own, Jennifer went on to explain, "They still have Indians, but you're thinking of the *old* West. Things are different now. There are big towns full of white people, and things have settled down with the Indians. There's peace now."

Putting her other hand to her face, Lita's face showed obvious worry. All she'd ever known her entire life was New Orleans. "Does they have bream?"

Tickled with such a question, Jennifer knew that Lita's favorite pastime was to put on her wide-brimmed straw hat, take a long cane pole, and go down to the bayou to catch bream. "I don't know, but I'm sure they have places to fish."

"You know I love to fish for bream," Lita insisted. After several moments of serious reflection, she added, "Miss Jennifer, if you wants me to go, I'll go, but I surely wish it didn't scare me plumb to death."

"We'll be fine, Lita," Jennifer assured her. "We're in God's hands, and He'll watch over us."

Standing to return to the boiling greens on the stove, Lita added, "I ain't never been nowhere but here, but I reckon folks is alike wherever you go."

～

Jennifer ran an advertisement in the *Picayune* for her house. Speculators came first, northern businessmen with money who wanted to take advantage of those made desperate by the suffering southern economy. But once they met Jennifer and realized she wasn't another poor person at whose expense they could make easy money, they disappeared. "Carpetbaggers!" Jennifer scoffed as she closed the door behind a tall, skinny man with a pointy nose. "Such wicked people *won't* get this house!"

One Saturday morning a young man and his pregnant wife came to look at the house. He was dressed handsomely in a dark suit and wore long sideburns; his wife had a freckled, round face and long, blonde, curly hair. They introduced themselves as Ben and Susan Dailey. After Jennifer showed them around, they sat in the living room to discuss the matter.

"It's a lovely place," Susan said as she held her hands on her round stomach.

"Yes, it is," Ben agreed. "The price is reasonable too. Mrs. DeSpain, we've looked at many places, but we haven't found anything we really like, until now."

"I was born in this house," Jennifer told them, her smile warm and friendly. "I've always loved it."

Ben's eyes roamed the room, inspecting minor details. He looked at his wife, and they nodded at each other as if making a secret agreement. "We want it," he said, his youthful face honest. "I'm fresh out of college and just joined a law firm here." He hesitated, putting his hand to his noble chin. "I can give you a respectable amount of cash to hold it for us, but I'm afraid we can't actually make the deal until early spring. I know this is an unusual request, but if you can hold it for us until then, I'll make it worth your while."

Trying not to show her excitement, Jennifer frowned a little as if in deep thought. "I suppose I could postpone moving until then."

"Where are you moving to?" Susan asked.

"Out west, to Virginia City, Nevada. I own a newspaper there. I need to sell most of this furniture too. Would you like to buy that as well?"

Ben glanced at his wife again, unable to contain his enthusiasm. "We sure would," he said, almost breathless. "You see, my father left me a trust fund, redeemable as soon as I graduated from college. I expect to have it soon."

"Well then," Jennifer said, confident she could trust the young couple, "since you're a lawyer, why don't you draw up the paperwork and we'll come to an agreement."

Standing, Ben shuffled his hands nervously in front of him. "Mrs. DeSpain, we're sure excited about this." He helped his smiling wife up from the sofa, and they moved toward the front door. "I'll get the papers drawn up first thing Monday and bring them by that evening. Will that be all right?"

"Sure. I'll be home after 5," Jennifer said, closing the door behind them. *This is surely God's doing*, she thought.

～

As preparations for Mardi Gras filled the New Orleans streets, C.C. Cromwell made up his mind to give Jennifer the grandest of farewell parties. He told Jeb Walker, "I'm throwing a going-away party for Jennifer on Fat Tuesday, the grandest party day in our fine city. What do you think?"

"I'm all for it," Jeb said, jabbing his thumb into his pipe to pack a fresh wad of tobacco. "What kind of party?"

"Food—tons of good food—and a band!" C.C. said with pride.

"This is no ordinary lady, Jeb. I thought I'd invite the writing staff, the editors, the office heads. I'll let the *Picayune* pick up the bill. We'll spare no expense; we'll have the *best* of everything!"

In late February, the last day of Mardi Gras, C.C. Cromwell rented a suite overlooking Bourbon Street and the parades passing noisily below. People dressed in all sorts of costumes lined the parade route, standing shoulder to shoulder in expectation of catching costume jewelry and bead necklaces tossed from the floats. Jennifer wore a red costume dress she'd found in a trunk her mother had stored away. Resembling a queen's gown, it was covered with glass beads and ruffles.

A three-man band played a tune with a catchy rhythm as Jennifer stood on the balcony watching the parade. Her friends at the *Picayune* were her closest friends ever. Mac Thibeaux came up behind her wearing the biggest smile imaginable. He was dressed like a southern colonel in a white suit. "Let me tole you right now, you gone into full bloom. You sartinly the most beautiful lady here! I want you to know dat!"

"Oh, Mac," she said, overjoyed as she gave him a big hug. "I'm going to miss you. You've taught me so much!"

"Some peoples t'ink that teaching writing is an awful lot of trouble, and I want to tole you—*it sure is!* Dat's why I don't do it! I teach cookin'. You put dat writing in yourself—and you done it too good to put a describe on it." Mac's eyes twinkled as he talked. "Now, why you want to leave New Awlins, I don't know. No one listens to a word of advice I give, so I just wish you well."

"I'll always remember you, Mac. Please write me sometime, let me know how you're doing."

"I'll do that, madam," he said as he turned to C.C. Cromwell who had just walked up.

"Uh-oh. The boss here, and I'm gone," Mac said as he hurried off.

"Nice day for a party," Mr. Cromwell said as he glanced at the sunny blue sky. "Jennifer, we're sure going to miss you at the *Picayune.*"

"I'm going to miss all of my friends there," Jennifer said, noting that Mr. Cromwell's dark blue tuxedo almost made his black hair seem dark blue.

He leaned on the balcony's cast-iron railing and gazed at the busy crowd in the street below. "You know, Jennifer, if I were twenty years younger I'd never let you out of my sight." He turned his head and smiled at her.

"You mean you wouldn't let me go west?" Jennifer asked.

"No, I mean I'd go with you. I admire your determination and your sense of adventure." He glanced back at the street. "I just plain admire you."

Jennifer smiled. The party makeup had enhanced her beauty. Impulsively, she leaned over and gave Mr. Cromwell a kiss on his cheek. "I'm indebted to you and to the *Picayune*, Mr. Cromwell. I'll forever be grateful. Oh, I got makeup on your cheek." She reached to wipe away the smudge.

"Leave it there," he said happily. "It suits me well today."

That day was the most wonderful Jennifer could remember having had in a long time. She breathed in the closeness of friends and the happiness that goes with success. She loved feeling so accepted and needed, an integral part of the group. By going west she couldn't be sure she'd ever experience such deep happiness again.

The party ran late into the evening and ended with everyone wishing Jennifer the best. Mr. Cromwell accompanied her home in a fine black coach. "I want you to remember something very important," he said with his usual I-am-in-charge disposition. "If you get out there and have problems—*any* kind of problems—you get in touch with me. I can help. I have a lot of strings I can pull." He turned to her, expecting an answer.

Jennifer looked hard at Mr. Cromwell—a man who was all newspaper and all heart. "It's good to know I have somebody strong behind me."

"As long as I'm alive you can count on me."

When they arrived at her house, Mr. Cromwell escorted Jennifer up to her front porch. She gave him a sincere hug. "Thank you for everything, Mr. Cromwell."

"From now on, since I'm not your boss anymore and you'll be running your own paper, you can call me C.C." He smiled.

Jennifer laughed. "You're most gracious." She took his wide hand for a moment. "Good night, C.C."

"Good night, Jennifer." C.C. turned and left as Jennifer watched him go, a sadness in his eyes. "I sure do hate to see that girl leave!" he muttered under his breath.

~

Spring arrived, and the irises in the backyard shot up from the ground in all their magnificent colors. Jennifer was checking a list to make sure she'd done everything that needed doing. The four of them—herself, Grant, Abby, and Lita—would be traveling light, bringing only the clothes they'd be needing for their daily routine. The rest of their things she had shipped to Virginia City. The house deal had gone smoothly. Excited with their new baby boy and a new home, the young couple wished Jennifer well, as she did them.

I'm set financially for a while, Jennifer thought, going over the figures again in her head. The house and furniture had brought more than she expected. *I should have enough money to get us settled in somewhere and some to get the newspaper going. I can't worry about all that now. I've made the decision, and we are on our way. Whatever happens, happens, and God's grace won't end for us.*

Soon the shrill call of the steamboat whistle echoed across the river as Jennifer, her children, Lita, and Salome, who simply could not be left behind, boarded the *Cotton Queen,* a luxury side-wheeler bound for St. Louis. As the deckhands slowly pushed the nose of the flat-bottomed, 150-ton steamboat into the Mississippi River, the current caught her and pulled her out. With a full head of steam, she easily made her way upstream with the side-mounted paddle wheels churning a froth in her wake. The captain blew the whistle in long calls to announce his entry onto the river.

Jennifer stood with her children on the upper deck, just outside their room, and watched New Orleans disappear into the humid haze. *There goes my home,* she thought, confident in the Lord's leading but nevertheless feeling slightly afraid of what might come. She turned her head to look upriver. *I can only guess as to what tomorrow will bring. I'm sure it won't be an easy task.*

The *Cotton Queen* picked up speed as black smoke rolled out of the twin stacks. "Mother, do you believe we'll be safe on our journey and when we get out west?" Grant asked as they watched the thick forest on the riverbank pass by. He was a fine-looking young boy, almost seven years old.

"God has always looked after us, Grant," Jennifer assured him. "He won't stop now."

Grant turned back to the amazing view. He'd never ridden on a riverboat before, and he was fascinated by the smooth, swift ride of such a huge boat.

The boat made its way along the curvy Mississippi River. The steamboats heading downriver hailed the *Cotton Queen* with long blasts from their whistles. The thick forest of budding greenery ran deep and heavy along the riverbanks like a solid wall. But there were also fields carved out of the woodlands where farmers took their chances in the fertile Mississippi River delta soil. The blue sky darkened as night fell, and the many kerosene lamps made the *Cotton Queen* into a floating palace. After a fine meal in the dining galley, Jennifer took the children up to their room. Exhausted, she put them to bed, then got ready for bed herself. She checked Lita's room and found her already snoring. "This is going to be a long trip," she mumbled as she crawled into bed. "I hope the children can stand the monotony, and that I can stand the fatigue."

Morning began with a loud whistle as the *Cotton Queen* announced her arrival in Natchez. As the ship docked, the hands hustled to unload and load supplies. Soon they were on their way again, full-speed up the muddy waters of the Mississippi.

On the third day they reached St. Louis. Jennifer and her children were tired of the confines of the riverboat and looked forward to staying in a hotel. Lita had grown slightly ill with the motion of the boat and could only be a little help. "Hold your own, Lita," Jennifer told her. "We still have half a country to cross."

"Yes, ma'am," Lita mumbled. "Who would've thought this was such a big country!"

A night's rest in a lavish hotel helped the weary travelers regain their spirits. "We have to hurry," Jennifer insisted as she roused the children out of bed the next morning. "C'mon, Lita, we have a train to catch."

They caught a coach that rushed them to the Union Pacific railroad station where a locomotive sat puffing steam. Jennifer quickly picked up their tickets from the stationmaster, and they boarded as a black porter helped them with their luggage. "Going to Omaha?" he asked friendly-like.

"And then Virginia City," Jennifer said. "Is it a terribly long trip?"

"Oh no, ma'am," the smiling porter answered. "You take this train to Omaha, where you board the Union Pacific Platte Valley Route. That train is the most powerful there is; it can make the trip to San Francisco in only four days. Virginia City's before that—just a skip and a jump." He tipped his hat. "Have a nice trip."

"All aboard!" the conductor cried as the train lurched and chugged into motion.

The ride to Omaha, Nebraska, was an all-day affair during which the land flattened out and huge trees yielded to the grasslands. Jennifer, Grant, Abby, and Lita pressed their faces to the train window, amazed at the golden-orange sunset that seemed to go on forever.

Late that evening they arrived in Omaha, where they immediately changed trains. They were shown to the Pullman car, where they gladly crawled into bed after a long day of traveling. When Jennifer awoke sometime the next morning, the Union Pacific was already underway with the steel wheels clattering on the tracks.

The train was like a long, rolling hotel. It had luxurious riding cars, dining cars, and Pullman's Palace sleeping cars. About a year before, on May 10, 1869, Union Pacific had made transcontinental travel by railroad a reality. Although Jennifer and her family had to travel a long way around, they would be able to make the entire trip from St. Louis to Virginia City by rail.

Grant and Abby hogged the window as the train clacked along, staring in wonder at the golden grasslands. Lita busied herself with knitting, while Jennifer lost herself in a novel. "Mother, what are those black things? There's lots of them," Grant said, pointing out the window.

Jennifer glanced up and noticed a herd of large, humpbacked animals on the horizon. "I think they're buffalo."

"And buffalo they are," a gentleman in a seat behind them confirmed. He wore a top hat and had a neatly trimmed beard. "Get a good look, son, because they're disappearing fast. Those animals once covered the plains by the thousands."

"What happened to them?" Grant asked curiously.

"Buffalo hunters are killing them off," the gentleman replied.

"Why do they kill them? Are they dangerous?" Grant continued to inquire.

"The federal government put a bounty on them," the man answered. "It's their way of controlling the Indians, by taking their food away."

Jennifer gave the man a stern glance. His story seemed far-fetched. "I thought federal soldiers *fought* the Indians," she said.

"Well, that too," the man agreed.

~

Arrival in Denver brought the Rocky Mountains into view. After only a few brief hours in Union Station, the train began cutting its way through mountain gaps, climbing steep slopes, and speeding along tunnels carved through solid rock. "This is incredible!" Abby commented as she kept her face pressed to the window. Jennifer glanced at Grant in surprise, having never heard five-year-old Abby use the word *incredible* before. Grant gazed at his mother and shrugged his shoulders. Abby never failed to surprise him either.

The trip to Salt Lake City gave them the most beautiful scenery of all, with snowcapped peaks on the horizon and white-foamed, rushing rivers down below. The air was thin and sweet. In some places the train edged along steep cliffs, causing Jennifer to hold her breath. Lita had the good sense not to look out the window.

From Salt Lake City the salt flats spread wide into the Great Salt Lake Desert and slowly changed into an alkaline wasteland of sand

and dust. They passed Promontory Summit, where the Central Pacific and Union Pacific tracks had met each other to finally link the continent with one track. Crossing Nevada by rail, Jennifer couldn't understand how pioneers had made it on horseback, for it seemed to be an endless and merciless desert.

The locomotive continued puffing black clouds of smoke into the still western air. No plains, mountains, or desert seemed able to impede its progress across America. *I can't believe how far we've come in a week,* Jennifer mused. *Things have grown so modern!*

The trip across the West had been a breathtaking view of changing scenes that neither Jennifer nor her children would ever forget. Finally, after a long desert crossing and a journey of cinder-choking air, she prepared to disembark in Virginia City.

Jennifer thought happily, *We've come so far, and things already seem so different out here. I can't wait to surprise Jason Stone!*

PART TWO

THE DEEP WEST

The Arrival

When the train braked to a stop, Jennifer, her children, and Lita, exhausted from the long desert trip, gladly stepped onto the ground. Lita carried a wicker basket containing Salome, and from time to time the nervous cat let out a plaintive squall. They carried their heavy luggage to the side of the station where they could see the town while still standing on the terminal boardwalk.

Jennifer glanced around at the small, rather dingy collection of buildings. "This doesn't look much like the booming gold towns I've read about," she complained. "It looks more like—like a regular town!"

Lita's big brown eyes took in the new surroundings. "Dis place is dry as an old bone—makes me thirsty."

Setting down her luggage, Jennifer went to the stationmaster's window, where a little man with a broom of a mustache sat reading a newspaper. "Could you tell me how to get to the offices of a newspaper called *The Miner's News?*" Jennifer asked.

The little man glanced up, his small, close-set eyes showing beneath the rim of his hat. "I don't reckon I recall no paper here by that name, ma'am."

"Well, it has to be here!" Jennifer insisted, impatient with the dust and the heat and the noisy train.

"Are you plumb sure you're in the right town, ma'am?" the fellow asked casually.

"This is Virginia City, isn't it?"

The little man laughed. "No, ma'am. This here's Reno. The train to Virginia City ain't due in for two hours yet."

Jennifer's shoulders slumped in despair. "How far is it to Virginia City?"

"Not far, ma'am, 'bout two whoops and a holler. Need some tickets?"

"Yes," Jennifer replied, discouraged. The thought of yet another train journey didn't please her at all. "Two adults and two children, please."

Once they had their tickets, Jennifer and Lita sat in rickety wooden chairs on the dusty loading dock waiting for their train, a long two hours of tedious boredom. Grant and Abby ran back and forth on the boardwalk with the abundant energy of healthy children.

"Dis place surely ain't got nothin' growin'," Lita observed. "I don't see how no greens or tomatoes could grow here. It ain't even got no trees."

Weary with travel, Jennifer didn't respond. The long trip had worn her down, and the strangeness of the country made her feel out of place and uncertain of her desires and of the future. She felt like she was covered with cinders, grit, and dust. *Wouldn't a hot bath be lovely?* she thought as she dozed off, only to be awakened by the children's screaming as they played. She didn't have the energy to quiet them down and soon fell asleep, her head nodding. She dreamed about a life in which she had no roots, no family, owned nothing, and was forced to roam endlessly—floating from place to place, unable to find her rightful purpose. Suddenly she was jarred awake by Lita's strong grip.

"Miss Jennifer," Lita said, "wake up—the train's comin'."

The thin, dry air seemed to calm her somewhat. From a crevice in the hills she could see a plume of black smoke ascending above the ridge. The train whistle announced its coming as the engine chugged into sight. Jennifer stood, her joints aching from days of constant sitting. She grabbed a heavy suitcase. "I'm ready to get this train riding over with."

"Me too!" Lita confirmed confidently.

~

The wood-burning engine climbed and twisted and turned and went along more tunnels through solid rock. Heavy black smoke filled the coach, choking the passengers whenever they passed through a tunnel. The steep climbs made it hard to breathe as the air grew thinner. The engine chugged and labored to make each grade, making the cars sway in a sickening motion. Jennifer and Lita grew light-headed as the cars rocked to one side and then the other. Though covering a relatively short distance, the trip took hours as the ascents and curves forced the train to travel at low speed. When they finally arrived in Virginia City, Jennifer had one thing on her mind.

"Where's the nearest hotel?" she demanded from the lanky agent in the ticket office.

One look at Jennifer and the agent knew her patience had worn thin. "Right down there," he said, pointing at a large two-story building. "The Huxley Inn."

Grabbing the suitcases, Jennifer trudged toward the hotel as the children and Lita followed. She barely noticed the sprawling layout of the gold town below Mount Davidson, an eyesore of a mountain barren of forest, but rich with gold and silver ore. The streets were congested with loaded freighters and muleteers cracking whips over protesting animals. Men dressed in fine suits stared in wonder at the good-looking woman carrying heavy baggage. Saloons boiled over with banging piano music and women's laughter as dirty miners relieved themselves of worry with a bottle of whiskey.

Stomping through dry dust and dodging the manure, Jennifer came to the hotel and entered it hurriedly. It was obviously not an average hotel. "I'll need two rooms beside each other," Jennifer told the man behind the counter, noting his large lamb-chop sideburns.

"Yes, indeed," he responded with a smile, a big gold tooth flashing from his mouth. "Sign here."

As she signed in, Jennifer asked, "Can I get a bath here?"

The clerk glanced at her signature. "Why certainly, Mrs. DeSpain. We have the finest Turkish baths right here at the hotel." He clapped his hands loudly, and a young boy appeared. "Take these bags up to rooms 22 and 23." He returned his attention to Jennifer. "That will be ten dollars for tonight."

Reeling, Jennifer couldn't believe the inflated prices, but at the moment she didn't care. She would have paid even more than that just for a bath.

After unpacking and getting situated, Jennifer enjoyed a long and luxurious bath as the day's shadows grew long. Refreshed but weary, she ordered some food and had it delivered to their rooms, where they all ate with the appetite of orphan children. Salome provided her own lunch by capturing a fat mouse, and Jennifer was too exhausted to keep the children from watching with delight as the feline devoured it. Soon afterward, they all went to bed, exhausted from their travels.

~

Renewed by the new day, Jennifer awakened, anxious to meet Jason Stone and eager to see the workings of the newspaper she owned. She quickly dressed, putting on a light tan cotton dress suitable for the warm, dry climate. She arranged her auburn hair carefully, making it appear more businesslike. *I'm sure he's an astute man, and I want to make a good first impression.* Just a touch of makeup added to her natural color, giving her the look of a charming southern belle.

The children lay asleep in the big bed as she went to look in on Lita. Jennifer found her up and dressed and rummaging through a suitcase.

"I'm fit to be tied," Lita exclaimed irritably. "I can't find nothin'! These suitcases got a real shakin' and stirred up ever'thing!"

Smiling, Jennifer informed Lita, "I intend to locate my newspaper business. You can wake the children when you're ready and take them downstairs to eat breakfast. I'll get something to eat later."

"Yes, ma'am," Lita said, not looking up as she continued tossing clothes from a suitcase. "Don't you worry about the children. You go take care of yo' business."

Leaving the hotel, Jennifer found herself on a street already swarming with people and loaded wagons. The busy town sprawled on up the mountainside. Most formidable were the huge mining works with their large buildings and smokestacks that laid a pall of smoke and steam over all of Virginia City. Amidst the mines, homes stood in rows on dirt streets. Houses varied from small to large, each unique in its design, but all having a square, straight-line newness. She smelled acrid dust, dry air, and fresh-cut lumber as trains constantly delivered loads of timber from the north.

Walking seemed to be the most viable form of local transportation as people shuffled noisily down the boardwalks. The sun seemed clearer and more intense than in New Orleans, casting Jennifer's shadow sharply on the ground. She saw all kinds of people—well-dressed men of substance, dirty miners, Chinese, tradesmen, shopkeepers. She saw only a few women, but noticing one lady dressed rather well, she approached her. "Excuse me. Could you tell me where to find a newspaper called *The Miner's News?*"

The proper lady wore a small hat pinned to her dark hair and a long calico dress. She placed a finger to her mouth and rolled her eyes upward, as if searching library shelves for a particular book. After a moment she returned her eyes to Jennifer. "I'm sorry, but I don't believe I've ever heard of a newspaper by that name."

"Thank you," Jennifer said as she continued on her way. *Perhaps she hasn't lived here long, or maybe she doesn't read newspapers*, she thought, amused at the lady's entertaining behavior. She turned up a street lined with retail businesses. *Surely one of these business owners would know.*

Stepping into a dry goods store, Jennifer found the proprietor reaching into a barrel of apples. He turned, his bald head bright red with sunburn, his face tan and smiling. He rubbed his scalp with the palm of his hand.

"Doesn't that hurt?" Jennifer asked with a friendly smile.

"A little," he chuckled. "You may wonder how a store man like me manages to burn the top of his head. Well, I do a little gold panning sometimes, and you have to watch it around here 'cause that wind can pick up in a hurry. It grabbed my hat, and I gave chase after it, but before long it gained too much ground on me and I gave out from the running. I went on back to panning 'cause I was finding a little dust. When I woke up this morning, my whole head looked like one of these red apples." He rubbed his red pate again. "What can I help you with?"

"I'm looking for a small newspaper called *The Miner's News*. Could you tell me where I might find it?"

The man stopped what he was doing and carefully studied Jennifer. His eyes were just slits, as if he'd spent a lifetime in the bright sun. "Well, yes, ma'am, I know where it is." His smile had disappeared, and a cautious light came into his faded blue eyes. "Go on down," he said, pointing through the front window, "to the next cross street and take a left. You'll find it about three businesses down, on the left side."

"Thank you," Jennifer said as she turned to leave. "Have a pleasant day."

"You bet," he said as he watched her curiously.

The newspaper was simple enough to find since it had its name in bold wooden letters across the front. It was a frame building with wooden columns supporting the front porch. Although built from rough-cut lumber, it appeared sturdy, having a single front door bordered by large plate-glass windows. As Jennifer stepped onto the front porch, she noticed the windows were rather dusty, making it hard, if not impossible, to see inside. She grabbed the door handle and pushed, but the door wouldn't budge. Rattling the knob, she shoved harder, putting her shoulder into it, and the door abruptly swung wide open.

Stepping inside, she thought she had walked into a nightmare. Jennifer could see the place had long been out of business. Trash lay stacked on tables and desks, and even the trash was covered with dust and cobwebs. Her heart ached with sickening disappointment. Moving over to the press, she could see it was the rugged, versatile version of the classic flatbed press known as the Washington Hand Press. Looking closer, she could see it still held the type from the last paper it had printed, and with her skill at reading a mirror image, she read the headline: ANOTHER MOTHER LODE STRIKE! It was the same newspaper she'd received from Jason Stone!

Collapsing into a dusty chair, Jennifer felt the rush of approaching tears but refused to allow herself to cry. Her search for security for herself and her children had led to a dark, dank office, and sudden fear began to choke her.

Jennifer walked through the gray shadows to a rear window and abruptly lifted the shade. A shaft of morning sunlight charged through the dust and spilled onto a cot on which a man slept beneath a dirty blanket. Startled, she backed away, staring at him. He groaned, disturbed by the bright light in his face. His hair was long, blonde, and matted, and he had an unshaven young face covered with heavy stubble. Throwing an arm over his eyes to shield them from the unwelcome sunshine, he slowly sat up, swinging his dirty boots to the floor. He groaned again, as if in pain.

"Who *are* you?" Jennifer demanded, standing over him with her hands on her hips.

The man sat with his face in his hands. "We're closed, lady! How'd you get in here anyway?"

"Through the front door!" Jennifer retorted, growing angry.

"Well, get out!" the young man grumbled. "I must've forgotten to lock it."

"I'm Jennifer DeSpain, and I will *not* be ordered out of a newspaper that I own!" Jennifer shrieked.

The young man looked up, his face slightly swollen, his eyes red and puffy. He stared at Jennifer for a long moment, slowly realizing who she was, though at the same time being struck by her beauty. "Oh no!"

Getting a queasy feeling herself, Jennifer asked, "You're not— you're not Jason Stone, are you?"

"Yes," he whispered, too ashamed to look her in the eye.

"What has happened here? Why is everything in such disorder?" Jennifer questioned.

Jason stood and staggered over to a big desk where he opened a drawer. He pulled out a bottle of whiskey, took a big swig, made an awful face, and turned to Jennifer. "This newspaper is defunct—has been for a long time."

"But what about the letters and the newspaper you sent me? The type is still in the press. What did you do with the money I wired to you? Why are you sleeping in here?" The inquiries came fast and furious, and Jennifer was growing hysterical.

"Questions—questions!" Stone said in disgust as he took another long drink from the bottle. He wasn't a big man but an impressive one with square shoulders and an angular frame. His square jaw conveyed firmness, and his eyes were a striking pale blue. "I needed the money," he finally admitted as Jennifer glared at him. "Everything I said was a lie. So what?"

"Why did you cheat me out of my money?" Jennifer demanded, determined to get some answers from this young scoundrel.

Jason helped himself to another generous swallow from the bottle.

"You're a drunkard!"

"That's right. And I gamble too, but unfortunately I never win."

"How dare you . . ." Suddenly hearing the Spirit's urgings within her, remembering how much she'd been forgiven by the Lord, pity overwhelmed Jennifer. She'd stumbled into a derelict's ruins, and though she wanted to be angry with him, she also knew he needed to be shown Christ's compassion. Jason Stone—the man she'd put her hope in—was a helpless drunk, but not a hopeless one. "Stay here," Jennifer ordered. "I'll be back shortly."

Sitting back down on his cot, Jason held his head as it throbbed with the effects of his previous night's drinking. *She's probably going to get the sheriff,* he thought hopelessly. *It won't be the first time I've been thrown in jail. At least they'll feed me there and give me a little time to dry out.* He lay back on the cot, feeling terribly sick and wondering why he didn't just end the whole sorry charade of his life.

～

An hour had passed when Jennifer returned carrying a bundle. Jason was asleep. "Wake up!" she called imperiously. She used the back of her arm to clear a nearby desk, sending burnt candle stubs and papers onto the floor. Jason sat up, trying to focus his blurry eyes. Unwrapping the bundle, Jennifer set two plates and silverware on the desk. She took out some steamy fried chicken and set it on the plates, then spooned out a helping of creamy mashed potatoes. "When was the last time you ate?" she asked stubbornly.

Amazed at seeing food instead of a badge, Jason didn't know what to say. "I don't remember." His stomach growled. "Are you some kind of an angel?" he asked.

"Me? Hardly."

"Then why are you doing this? Why should you care about when I ate last?"

"I'm a Christian," Jennifer stated, "and I believe in taking care of the sick."

Nodding his head, Jason pulled up a chair and tore hungrily into a hot chicken breast. "This is good." He paused a moment. "Aren't you angry at me?"

"Yes indeed!" Jennifer snapped. "You swindled me!"

Jason let his foggy eyes fall to his plate, humiliated and embarrassed. "For what it's worth, I—I'm sorry," he mumbled.

They ate together silently as Jennifer appraised the man before her. He reminded her of Drake. She had seen defeat in that man too, but this man, with God's help, might be salvageable. Behind the beard and dirt and long grubby hair, she could see a handsome young man who still could make a life for himself.

"Why did you send that letter and newspaper to me?" she questioned.

"Like I said, I needed the money," he admitted. "I was desperate for a drink."

"What happened to my newspaper office?" Jennifer queried, casting a glance at the disarray all around them.

Jason shrugged. "Newcomers to Virginia City are tough, single-minded men with one idea: get rich. I was no different, except I didn't dig for gold. I figured I could write what folk wanted to hear and make it big, and it worked for a while. Then Mr. Hutton departed, leaving me in charge of the place. I had enough money for myself, but I couldn't stay out of the saloons and gambling halls. Pretty soon it all disappeared. I don't remember much else."

Jennifer watched Jason, listening intently to his story of failure. It reminded her of Drake's hopes of getting rich quickly—and of the death those desires eventually brought him. *Of all the men in the world, why do I always manage to get stuck with those who are buried in troubles?*

Jason continued, "When you wrote, I didn't think you'd ever come this far just to look in on a small paper. I figured you were some rich woman living the good life down in New Orleans, so what would it hurt if I 'borrowed' your money?"

"Is there any left?" Jennifer asked.

Jason shook his head sadly. "A few dollars maybe."

"But why did you resort to such dishonesty? You write so well," Jennifer said. "Where did you learn to write like that?"

"Back east. I have a degree from Harvard. I studied law there and studied journalism too."

Jennifer stopped eating. She was stunned. A Harvard graduate! "What brought you west?"

"Same as the rest—a lust for riches." Jason grinned mirthlessly as he pushed his plate away. "Let me tell you, this place abounds with greed. And it all began with the four men who discovered the Comstock Lode—T.P. Comstock, Old Virginny Finney, Patrick McLaughlin, and Peter O'Riley. They owned the best-producing mine of all, the Ophir, named after King Solomon's source of gold mentioned in the Old Testament. T.P. Comstock shot himself and was buried without a tombstone. Old Virginny Finney turned into a drunk, fell off his horse, fractured his skull, and died. McLaughlin sold his share, became a miner's cook, and died a pauper. Peter O'Riley sold out for a lot of money but began hearing voices. They sent him to a hospital for the insane, and I heard he died there. So you see, this place isn't exactly what it seems."

Shaking her head at the sad story, Jennifer said, "My goal here isn't to get rich. I decided a long time ago to do something worthwhile, something morally good and significant for mankind."

For the first time Jason let out a slight laugh. "Well, you're in the wrong place then, Mrs. DeSpain. I'd suggest you go back to New Orleans."

"I can't," she said. "You see, I took a gamble too, so to speak. I sold everything. I'm committed to this enterprise, Jason, and I'm not about to give up."

"Good luck then," he mumbled, "for you're in the Devil's Den."

"I believe God led me here, Jason, that He has a purpose for me in Virginia City. And with God on my side, who can be against me?"

"God? What does He care?" Jason asked skeptically.

"He cares a great deal—about Virginia City and about the individuals living there," Jennifer assured him. *Help him see, Father.*

Sensing Jason's disinterest in further conversation about spiritual matters, Jennifer remained silent. Standing, she looked around the office, still amazed that a newspaper office could so resemble a trash dump. "Is there a broom around here?" she asked, eager to get started.

"In the back," Jason muttered.

When Jennifer returned, Jason Stone was gone. She opened all the shades and windows and began the distasteful task of cleaning the place up. *Maybe I scared him away,* she thought as she stirred up a cloud of dust. *He's a lost soul, but underneath all that bitterness and drunkenness I believe there's something special about Jason Stone.*

Back in Business

Jennifer filled a barrel with trash and thoroughly swept the floor, but the place was still a disaster. Discouraged, she left late that afternoon to go back to the hotel and decide what her next steps should be. After having dinner with Lita and the children, she began to formulate plans, discarded several, then finally fell into an exhausted sleep.

Early the next morning Jennifer, Lita, and the children arrived at the newspaper office armed with buckets, rags, mops, and scrub brushes. Thanks to the friendly dry goods store owner, Jennifer had purchased everything she thought she'd need to give the office a real going-over. In Virginia City water was a rare commodity, but fortunately the newspaper had a well just outside the back door.

"Let's move these desks and tables over to one side so we can clean this half of the building," Jennifer suggested to Lita.

Looking around with a scowl on her face, Lita said, "This place ain't fit for a dog to live in! I thought you said you was coming to a business!"

"We're going to make it into a business, Lita," Jennifer insisted as her eyes roamed the premises and her mind dreamed of possibilities. "But first we have to clean it up."

Dressed in her oldest dress, with her hair tied back, Jennifer filled some of the wooden buckets with water and soap. She and Lita began scrubbing floors, while Grant and Abby used rags to wipe dusty chairs.

"Is this really the newspaper Father gave you, Mother?" Grant asked, a puzzled frown on his young face.

"Yes, it is," Jennifer replied as she scrubbed the filthy floor on her hands and knees.

"Then why," Grant asked hesitantly, "does it looks like it's not being used anymore?"

"Yeah!" Abby agreed. "It looks like dirty old tramps have been living in here."

"Children, that's enough!" Jennifer said firmly. "You're right, the newspaper isn't in operation right now, and we have to clean it up before it will be. I don't want to hear any more complaining! Let's just get to work!" She hadn't intended to vent her frustration on her children. *Father, help me handle the situation with greater patience.*

Disheartened, she remembered that friends back in New Orleans had warned her not to come out west, then Jason had told her the paper was no longer functioning, and now even her own young and simpleminded children could see how ridiculous this all was! A sinking feeling of defeat hovered over her. *Have I lost my mind?* she wondered as she scrubbed the floor with renewed vigor. *I can't believe I gave up everything and dragged my family halfway across the country to—to what? This? Once we do get this place cleaned up, I don't know what to do next.* She bit her lip and scrubbed the hopelessly soiled floor even harder.

～

By noon the place was starting to smell clean with the raw, sweet smell of soap mixed with the pungent odor of disinfectant. As Lita swung a big mop over the wooden boards, the renewed deep and rich wood grain brought the office alive. The lacquered chairs shone again, and the children, having forgiven and forgotten their mother's impatience, were proud of their accomplishment.

The front door squeaked open, and Jennifer glanced up to see Jason Stone enter. He looked like a beggar, his clothes dirty and hanging loosely, his hair a tangle as he dropped his head in despair. "I need to get a few of my things," he mumbled at the floor.

Agitated, Jennifer took Jason by the arm. "Come outside," she ordered as she pulled him back out the front door, then pulled it closed. "What do you mean you need to get a few things?" she asked sternly.

"Well, I know you don't want me around here, and I . . ."

"Where would you go?" Jennifer asked firmly.

Jason shrugged his shoulders meekly.

"Let me inform you, Mr. Stone, that you are indebted to me!" Jennifer lectured. Fire blazed in her eyes. "Let me tell you something—I only know one way this paper will get rolling again, and that is with *your assistance!* You're going to help me and show me what to do! You have an obligation, and I intend to see that you fulfill it. Is that understood?"

Jason perked up. "You mean you still want me to work for you?"

"You *will* work for me!" Jennifer was a little surprised at her angry tone of voice, but she had to finish saying what was on her mind. "First things first. As you can see, we're cleaning up your mess, and that will include getting *you* cleaned up as well. I'll give you some money so you can get a bath, a haircut, a shave, and some new clothes—work clothes. You will return here as soon as possible."

Jennifer noticed Jason's perfect white teeth as he smiled. "I'm willing to work," he said, "but where will I live?"

Glancing around at the office, Jennifer suggested, "You were living here before, and you can still live here. There's plenty of space in the back room if you clean it up properly."

Looking over Jennifer's shoulder, Jason could see a black woman and two good-looking children. He let his eyes return to Jennifer's smooth face. He knew just how fortunate he was to be given another opportunity. "I'll do my best," he said honestly.

Relief fell over Jennifer like a fresh rain in an arid desert. She hadn't expected to ever see Jason Stone again, and she was surprised she'd been able to be the firm newspaper boss she needed to be. *Mr. Cromwell would be proud of me,* she thought as she went back inside.

Jason followed. She gave him the money she'd promised. "Hurry back," she insisted, adding sternly, "And no stops at any saloons."

"Yes, ma'am!" Jason responded enthusiastically. He left quickly, a bounce in his step.

Watching him leave, Jennifer wondered if she'd done the right thing. *I wonder if he'll be able to stay away from liquor. If not, I've just hired myself a drunkard!* She shook her head as she watched Jason disappear around the corner. *Or he might just take my money and be gone. Maybe I'm a fool!* Smiling self-consciously, she decided she'd taken an acceptable risk. Although she wasn't always the best judge of character, she felt she should give people a chance to change direction, just as God had done with her. With God's help, if Jason would give his life to Christ, he could be someone special.

∼

By the third day the office was taking shape nicely. Jennifer had given it a personal touch by hanging up photographs of monumental events, famous mines, and prominent people—the sort of pictures one might expect to see in a respectable newspaper office. Dominating the front of the office was a tall counter where customers could obtain service. Behind that sat two heavy wooden desks.

Over to one corner rested the press, oiled and cleaned and ready for business. On the walls in the press area, shelves filled with wooden trays and boxes of type were categorized for easy use. Beside the press was a large table for layout work. Ink and cleaning compounds were labeled. In the other corner stood a potbellied stove with a tin coffeepot sitting on top.

"It's looking like an office again," Jennifer observed with a keen eye as she scanned the large room. "I think we're about ready to get this newspaper going again."

Lita had worked diligently, cleaning every crack and crevice. She was still working, polishing the chairs and desktops with beeswax. "I don't know nothin' about no newspaper business, but I do know dis place is *clean!*"

Strolling over to the front window, Jennifer noticed a man

standing on the boardwalk across the street and looking her way. She thought she remembered him loitering there before but wasn't sure. He had a head of white, unruly hair and a white mustache and was dressed in a fine suit. *Probably one of our competitors spying on us*, she thought as she turned away.

Jason approached, shaved and bathed and wearing some of his new work clothes. Jennifer found it difficult to keep her eyes off of him. "I know I told you this already, Jason, but you do clean up well! Your new appearance is one of the biggest improvements I've ever seen."

Jason smiled awkwardly. His blond hair was cut neatly and was slickly parted in the middle. His face appeared much younger without the light beard that had hidden a small dimple in his chin. His eyes were clearer than ever, and the pale blue color sparkled. "I haven't felt this good in a long time," he admitted as he walked spryly over to one of the big desks.

"You have good taste in your choice of clothes," Jennifer complimented. "What kind of pants are those? I don't believe I've ever seen anything like them."

Jason glanced down at the blue pants that fit him so well. "They were only a little more expensive than most. I bought them because they are supposed to last longer. They're made from tent material by a fellow named Strauss in San Francisco. I think they're called Levi's."

"Well, Jason, we're about ready to get back into the newspaper business," Jennifer said as she picked up an old copy of *The Miner's News*. "Is this the format we'll use?"

Jason took the paper from her and studied it. "Yes, sort of. Now that you're here with all your experience, I thought we might change it a little. Maybe you could write a short article about being the new owner and what Virginia City looks like to a newcomer."

Raising her eyebrows, Jennifer gave it some thought. "That might not be a bad idea," she said. "Let the town know this paper is under new management—maybe attract new readers or win back previous ones."

"I can get the latest mining reports," Jason went on, becoming excited. "I know some of the assayers. One's right around the corner."

"Good," Jennifer added. "Let's get to work." She took a place at her desk and began composing the article Jason had suggested. She grabbed pen, ink, and paper and scratched away, comfortable with her new challenge.

"I'll go round up some information on the mines," Jason said, grabbing a tablet and some pencils. "I shouldn't be gone long."

Jennifer nodded while she wrote, her mind on her work.

Not long after Jason left, an old miner stumbled in and leaned on the counter. He had a grimy, earthy smell about him and wore a toothless grin. "You be the newspaper lady?" he asked friendly-like.

"Why, yes!" Jennifer replied, trying to hide her enthusiasm. This man would be her first customer. "How can I help you?" She came over to the polished counter.

"I got this here mine I want to sell," he began, pulling a legal description from his coat pocket. "It's a good mine, called the Opal, but I can't work it no more—got the croup, ya know." He batted his heavy eyelids in self-pity, sorrowful about having to give up a gold mine for health reasons. "I'd like to ask 2,000 dollars fer it," he continued, "and you might say in the paper that I'll be up there at the mine in case anybody wants to take a look at her. It comes with some good works, ma'am." He leaned over the counter, a bit too close for Jennifer's comfort, as she scribbled down the information. "It's just over the Sugar Loaf," he whispered.

Having no idea what or where the Sugar Loaf was, Jennifer finished copying information from his legal description. "The paper will be coming out tomorrow," she said. "It will carry your advertisement."

"That suits me just fine," he said, grinning happily. He lifted his stained old hat and wiped his forehead with the back of his sleeve. "How much do I owe ya?"

"Uh, two dollars sound all right?" Jennifer asked, having no idea what to charge.

The old miner pulled out a small leather pouch, opened it, and stuck his fingers in. He glanced up. "Ain't you got no scales, ma'am?"

Jennifer didn't understand. "Scales?"

"Why sure! Measurin' scales," he exclaimed. "How ya s'pose to weigh out gold without scales? This here's gold dust in this pouch!"

Wide-eyed, Jennifer didn't know what to say. She'd never seen gold dust in her life.

"I'll tell ya what I'll do," the prospector said, working his fingers in the bag. "I'm purty good at a fair estimation." He slid a piece of white paper in front of him and put two small pinches of gold dust on the paper." "That ought to be right near two dollars," he said, "but I'll throw in another smidgen for good measure." The yellow metal glistened magically on the white surface.

"Fine," Jennifer said, smiling at the beautiful color while she folded the paper over to keep the gold from spilling. For some reason she couldn't explain, even that small amount of gold dust made her heart beat rapidly. She had no idea if it was worth one dollar or ten but just took the miner's word for it.

"Thank ye, ma'am," the old fellow said as he left.

Having finished her short article on being a newcomer to Virginia City, Jennifer went to work on the advertisement for the miner. Besides a legal description of where it was located, she had nothing else. With Jason out gathering up mining reports, she decided to take a trip around the corner, meet the assayer there herself, and see if he had any information to add about the Opal mine.

It was a bright and sunny afternoon as Jennifer left the office. "I'll be back shortly," she said to Lita, who kept finding more things to clean. The children were playing on the front porch in the shade, crouched over a checkerboard they'd found while cleaning the office. Tucking her small purse under her arm, Jennifer walked up the sloping street lined with retail businesses. People milled about in contentment, either enjoying or hoping to soon enjoy an ample amount of spending money.

The assayer's name was Leonard P. Tipton, known to be especially meticulous in his work, she learned later. He had gray hair, a black mustache, and a large round nose ideal for supporting his thick glasses, which he now peered over with curiosity. "You're who?" he asked Jennifer, not having heard her introduction very well.

"I'm the new owner of *The Miner's News*," she repeated a little louder, "Jennifer DeSpain."

"Oh," he said, surprised that a woman would own a newspaper. "Just call me Lenny, everybody else does." He had a constant habit of pulling at his ear, apparently because he was hard of hearing.

"I'm running an ad to sell the Opal mine, but I don't have enough information on it," Jennifer said loudly as she perused all the scientific instruments and chemicals in the dark little office.

"I know that mine," Lenny said as he waddled over to a shelf filled with log books. Jennifer noticed that he had a peg leg. He pulled down a volume and blew the dust off. "Yep, that mine has been sold many times. About all I keep is assayer reports. Will that do?"

"I'm sure it will," Jennifer said, appreciating the man's assistance.

As he flipped through the pages, he explained his personal misfortune with gold mining. "I used to work the mines," he began. "I was the powder man. We used black powder in them days to blast through rock. But then some man named Nobel came up with a new invention called dynamite. That stuff wouldn't have surprised me more if it had brought hail after its thunder, I tell you! Blew my leg off, the flash like to have blinded me, and I still can't hardly hear a thing! So I decided to get into safer work and learned assaying."

Jennifer smiled, her teeth white in the shadows. She'd had no idea mining was so dangerous.

"Here it is," he said as he grabbed a pencil and paper. "I'll write down the most recent entry—about $100 a ton in silver and about $25 a ton in gold."

Curiously, Jennifer asked, "How do they calculate a ton?"

"Pardon? Oh, a ton ain't much," Lenny said. "It's a cube of rock less than two and a half feet on a side."

"I guess rock is heavier than I thought," Jennifer said.

"Indeed," Lenny added. "But the men here are stubborn enough to move mountains of it."

"Thank you for your help," Jennifer said as she left.

"What'd you say? Oh, yeah, anytime," Lenny said as he waved good-bye.

~

The kerosene lamps cast a yellow glow into the night while Jennifer and Jason toiled over the press, churning out newspapers. Her hands stained and her face smudged with ink, Jennifer recalled the exciting days in the basement of the *Picayune* where she'd had her first taste of the newspaper business. In a way she was experiencing the same kind of excitement now, except this time it was a newspaper business that she owned and for which she was responsible. "How many copies do you think we should print?" Jennifer asked, aware that it was getting late.

"Just a few hundred this time," Jason said. "We'll have to peddle them ourselves until we get established again."

Later in the evening, Jennifer admired the stack of fresh newsprint. *My first newspaper production!* she thought proudly. She helped Jason stack the papers on the front counter, ready for delivery first thing in the morning. "I'm dead tired," she said. "I have to get some rest, but I'll see you bright and early."

"Congratulations," Jason said, shaking her hand. "You've just put this paper back in business."

Jennifer smiled. The warmth of Jason's grip felt good in her tired hand.

~

Too excited to sleep late, Jennifer left for the office early in the morning. It was cool out as she walked down the streets, nearly always busy with people. It was like that in mining towns, she'd found out. The town was always awake. When she arrived at the office she awoke Jason, who seemed tired but in good spirits. "C'mon, we have to get these papers distributed."

Yawning, Jason stretched his arms. "It seems like I just fell asleep. Is it morning already?"

"Yes. Hurry!" Jennifer started a small fire in the little stove in the corner and made coffee while Jason got ready for the day.

"This coffee is strong enough to wake a dead man!" Jason complained as he sipped the steaming coffee from a metal cup.

"I wasn't sure how much coffee to use in that little pot," Jennifer explained. "Where should we take these papers first?"

"We'll start with the hotels," Jason said. "They're always interested. We'll leave some with the clerk; he'll collect the money for us, and we can get it later. They each get one free. By then we can sell a few on the streets. We'll also give a few away to business owners; we'll tell them we would like to have them advertise in the paper. As we make our way around town, interest will build."

Hardly able to contain herself, Jennifer began gathering a stack of newspapers. Proudly she stepped toward the door, then turned toward Jason. "Thank you, Jason. I—I couldn't have done this without you."

Jason nodded and dropped his head but said nothing. He watched Jennifer as she moved down the street. *That is one remarkable woman!*

In a short time Jennifer was back at the office, out of papers. The sun was well up in the eastern sky, and Jason had already returned to print more copies. "I found some other places willing to sell our newspapers," he said as he pulled the bar down on the press. "I can't believe how this town keeps growing. Why, there must be 20,000 people here now!"

A little tired from all her walking, Jennifer heated up the coffee and sat down. "People sure seem anxious to read a newspaper," Jennifer said. "I had no problem getting rid of mine."

Jason gave her a big smile as he picked up the stack of papers he'd just printed. He walked around the counter. "I won't be gone long."

Jennifer smiled. It almost seemed too easy.

Just then the front door opened with a bang as the toothless miner who had run an advertisement swaggered up to the counter with a newspaper in his hand. "What kind of advertisement do you call this? How would you know what the production level of the Opal is?" He was clearly upset.

Jennifer took the paper from his hand, eager to solve whatever the problem might be. She studied his advertisement, searching for an error. "I don't see anything wrong with this," she said defensively.

"Why, it says right here," he said pointing to the print, "that my mine only produces $100 a ton in silver and $25 a ton in gold! Where'd you get that from?"

"From assayer reports," Jennifer explained confidently. She knew she'd reported the information truthfully.

"How do you know I ain't hit a vein since this old assayer report?" the miner questioned angrily.

Jennifer noticed the man with unruly white hair loitering outside the front window. He had his face right up to the glass. She turned her attention back to her irate customer. "I'll rerun the advertisement for you and state it differently, but I can't lie about it."

"I ain't asking fer no lies," the miner spouted. "Jest say you got new information that makes these old assayer reports no good. What you got printed here will ruin me! I'll never sell that mine! You got to make it right in the next edition, lady." The miner's fury slowly changed to a plea for sympathy. "I can't go back to Californy all sick and having nothin' to show fer it."

A little embarrassed by the misunderstanding, Jennifer agreed. "I'll get that assayer report out of there," she said calmly. "I'll say it was old information."

"Please do somethin'!" the miner said as he shuffled out mumbling to himself.

About that time the man who had been watching Jennifer through the window came inside. He had a copy of *The Miner's News* rolled up in his hand. "I don't believe I've ever seen a newslady before," he said. His voice was southern, Jennifer thought, but not from Louisiana. "I take it you're new out here."

Jennifer eyed him skeptically. The twinkle in his eye made him appear friendly, as did a slight smile. His fancy suit was dusty, and he was puffing on a fat cigar. "Do you work for a competitor newspaper?" she asked suspiciously.

"I once was the editor of the *Territorial Enterprise*, but that was a few years ago. It seems some people were upset with the way I conducted business, and I was politely escorted out of town." He smiled and took a puff from his cigar. "I couldn't help but overhear the complaints of your disgruntled customer."

"I'm not sure I appreciate the way you've been spying on us," Jennifer said evenly. "What do you want?"

"I spotted a lady in trouble, and I want to help—nothing more," the white-haired man said confidently. "My first piece of advice would be to say that if you're going to write about a gold mine, you'd best know the definition of a gold mine."

"Oh?" Jennifer responded. "And what is your definition of a gold mine?"

"It's merely a hole in the ground owned by a liar," he said dryly. "Once you establish that as fact, you won't have any trouble writing about one."

"I see," Jennifer said. "I suppose you've read this man's advertisement?"

"I have indeed," he admitted.

"Then how would you rewrite it?"

"I'll be glad to show you—no obligation, of course. Eh, excuse me, ma'am, but I believe I recognize a southern accent—New Awlins, most likely."

"I'm from New Awlins," Jennifer said, quite happy to pronounce the city's name with a heavy southern slang. "My name is Jennifer DeSpain. And who might you be?"

"Samuel Clemens, ma'am."

"Are you from the South?"

"Hannibal, Missouri, but I captained a riverboat up and down the Mississippi until the war and spent my share of time in New Awlins." He let his eyes roam as if he were taken away by a memory. "Ah, yes, the Big Muddy . . ."

He took Jennifer's hand and shook it politely. She couldn't help but be taken in by him. His mood was relaxed and infectious. He seemed to possess a brilliance that was essentially western and had the power of a man with the gift of gab. She saw in him a streak of humor that was raw and remarkable, and his ability to see things for what they were led her to believe he might be quite capable with the written word. His manner of expression was natural and his smile contagious.

"There's nothing in the shape of a mining claim that's not salable," Samuel said. "Especially around here. Let me give you an idea of how to write about it."

Now smiling, Jennifer showed Mr. Clemens around the counter

and on to one of the large desks, where he took a seat. He grabbed a quill and dipped it in ink. "Out here in the West, if one wishes to remain a resident, such matters have to be written with a certain amount of care."

Intrigued, Jennifer watched and listened carefully. *Samuel Clemens*, she thought, rather admiring his silvery thatch of hair. *I wonder what he does for a living now?*

Enterprising and Backsliding

Brilliant rays of sunshine brightened the office of *The Miner's News* through the open windows as Jennifer pulled up a chair. Her expression was intent as she stared at the bushy-haired man who punctuated his speech by jabbing the air with a cigar.

"It's very simple," Clemens explained. "The men who advertise mines for sale don't care a fig what you say about the property, so long as you say *something*. Consequently, we generally say a word or two to the effect that the 'indications are good,' or 'the ledge is six feet wide,' or 'the rock resembles the Comstock.'"

Clemens chuckled deep in his throat and punched another hole in the air with his cheroot. "And so it might, though as a general thing the resemblance isn't startling enough to knock you down. If the rock is moderately promising, we follow the custom of the country by using strong adjectives and frothing at the mouth as if a marvel in discoveries has transpired. But if we're advertising a developed mine and it has *no* pay ore to show, we'll praise the tunnel, tell how it's one of the most infatuating tunnels in the land. We can drivel and drivel about the tunnel until we run out of ecstasies but never say a word about the rock! We can squander half a column of adulation on a shaft or a new wire rope or a dressed-pine windlass or a fascinating force pump, and close with a burst of admiration for the gentlemanly and efficient superintendent of the mine, who might also be the owner—but never utter a whisper about the rock!" Clemens leaned back and put his sharp brown eyes on the young woman. "Are you starting to get the picture, Jenny?"

She permitted very few people to call her Jenny, but in this case, she gladly made an exception. Clemens was obviously authoritative and knowledgeable about writing and about the mines; he was the professor and she the student. He even looked like a professor with his white hair and white mustache and eyebrows. *But he's not really that old, judging by his eyes. I bet he isn't over forty.* To answer his question, she said, "I know very little about mining, but I understand what you're saying—only mention the gold and silver if it's a productive mine."

"Not exactly. There's a little more to it," Clemens said as he fiddled with his mustache. "Sometimes the mine owners will ask you to write an attractive article about their mine and the glorious production they're experiencing. You see, they'll be wanting to sell stock in their diggings and may even offer you several stocks for printing a nice word about them. And mining stocks, as you know, may or may not be worth a plugged nickel. Only time will tell."

Finding Clemens fascinating, Jennifer began taking notes. It was becoming increasingly apparent to her that she'd better learn about mining if she was going to run a paper that printed stories on the subject. "How can a person know if a mine is a good one?"

Clemens chuckled as he put his finished cigar in an ashtray. "Why, it wouldn't be for sale otherwise!"

A sudden smile touched Jennifer's lips. Samuel Clemens certainly had a talent for squeezing humor out of blunt truth!

"But I might receive an argument from miners if I were to state that publicly. There are endless high jinks in the mining trade." Clemens paused and leaned back in the wooden chair as he carefully removed a fresh cigar from his coat pocket. As he lit it, Jennifer sensed he was getting ready to spin a tale.

"Invariably, there are always eager bumpkins who are sure they can trust their own judgment when purchasing a mine, but nowadays the more common avenue is to seek professional advice. Of course, that doesn't stop the salting of mines, but it does encourage the sellers to be more creative."

"Salting a mine?"

"Yes. The standard method of hornswoggling a prospective purchaser is to get hold of a few bushels of rich ore from a good mine and scatter it at the bottom of a shaft. The purchaser might say, 'This stuff looks as good as the $500-a-ton rock from the Golden Calf mine' or wherever. Little does he know that it actually *is* from that mine. However, this technique isn't as effective as in the early days, before purchasers became wary and began enlisting professionals to appraise the property, though it is still sometimes used. Some smart operators even do their salting with a shotgun."

Clemens was obviously enjoying sharing his wide knowledge of the subject. He took a big puff from his cigar and blew smoke in the air as Jennifer listened intently. "Old-timers say it was 'the gun that won the West.' A shotgun can be loaded with a charge other than buckshot—fine gold dust or nuggets do nicely. A man in a hard rock mine can stand back from a barren drift and blast the whole face full of particles of gold. However, this method does require decent restraint. A man simply can't blast *any* sort of dust into the face of his drift. It has to be dust that could have reasonably got there in the course of geological events."

"Are people really fooled by such means, Mr. Clemens?"

"Oh, yes! I'm reminded of an engineer who came very close to buying a nice little mine that had at least $80,000 worth of ore in plain sight, with promise of more nearby, of course. The engineer couldn't understand why the owners were anxious to be rid of it. When he ran a bullion assay on the particles, he found they contained exactly 916.66 parts of gold per 1,000, the rest being copper with a trace of silver—precisely the formula the U.S. Mint uses in gold coinage. When he went back and found a larger nugget, he could with some effort read 'ted States of' on it. The engineer refrained from accusing the owners of salting and merely went on his way without buying."

"I can't believe all of this! It sounds as though most of the miners are crooked!"

"As with all other professions, some are, and some aren't. Of course, prospective buyers can insist, if they suspect chicanery, on having the sellers blast out the faces of mine drifts to expose virgin rock instead of artificially improved stone. But even when the interested party watches the holes being drilled and experiences the explosion, he can be fooled. If salters put gold dust in the dynamite sticks, the blast drives the gold into the rock in a most convincing way."

Clemens laughed. "There must be a thousand and one ways to salt a mine, and I know of only 600 or so. Probably the most convincing way to sell a mine is through something written, like in a newspaper. Do you understand how important your paper can be?"

Mesmerized by Clemens's stories, Jennifer was caught off guard by the question. "I'd like to say yes, but I really don't. How could an article in the newspaper be worth more than an actual inspection of a mine?"

"Because," Clemens explained patiently, "a well-written tall tale can arouse and bedazzle a good many otherwise sensible men. Reminds me of a story that I once wrote about the gold-bearing air of Catgut Canyon up near the head of the Auriferous Range. This air, actually kind of a trade wind that blows steadily through 600 miles of the richest quartz croppings you can imagine, is heavily charged with exquisitely fine gold."

"It seems a person must be very discerning when it comes to gold."

"Believe me, Jenny, there isn't much that is stronger than human flesh heated by a passion for gold. In the story I was telling you about, a friend of mine who had experienced unrequited love used to sit outdoors when the wind was blowing. When he came in again, I'd extract a dollar and a half out of every sigh of his broken heart. I went on to say in my tale that several good locations along the course of the Catgut Canyon, complete with gold-bearing trade winds, were for sale. The funny part was, I could've sold them too."

The picture was growing clearer for Jennifer. A passion for gold was powerful and often involved great sums of money, and *nobody* took that lightly. "I see where any talk of mines or gold can be touchy to some people," she said as she sat next to Clemens.

"True," Clemens said. "That poor old miner that you upset is a good example. I suggest you rewrite his ad and make his mine sound like something valuable, but . . ."

"Don't mention the rock," Jennifer finished for him.

Clemens laughed, a contagious and natural laugh that Jennifer enjoyed hearing. "Your newcomer article was sort of . . ." He thought for a moment. "Refreshing. I grow tired of all these hard-talking bamboozlers who write for the papers around here. If you write the article in your style and make the mine sound wonderful, I wouldn't be surprised if it sold tomorrow!"

Inspired, Jennifer moved toward her desk. Clemens stood to leave. "I'll return later to see how you're doing," he promised. Stepping around the counter, he walked out with his cigar stuck firmly in his mouth and his hands in his front pockets.

He's quite a character, Jennifer thought, not for the first time, as she eagerly got under way. *He should write books or something.*

～

When Jason returned, he brought with him several advertisements from store owners. "I'm getting more customers than I had expected," he said eagerly. "We'll have to work even harder to get the next edition out."

Having rewritten the article advertising the mine that was for sale, Jennifer asked Jason, "Do you know a man named Samuel Clemens? He has white hair and a white mustache."

Scratching his head, Jason answered, "No. I don't think I've seen or heard of him."

"Earlier he was loitering across the street, sort of like he was snooping."

"I guess I wasn't paying attention. What about him?" Jason asked.

"Well, he came in here and gave me a lesson on writing about the mining industry," Jennifer explained. "He's really very good."

"Humph! Probably just another freelance looking for a hand-out," Jason warned. "Out here in these parts it's common for a paper to publish something a reader has written, and sometimes, if it's good, other papers will publish it as well. But I'm here to tell you, a writer has to be exceptional before that'll happen."

"We'll see," Jennifer concluded. She liked Samuel Clemens and didn't share Jason's skepticism. "He told me he'd be by later to check in on us."

"Just be careful—you can't trust most of these drifters."

~

Not long afterwards, Lita came into the office with Grant and Abby. "I tell you, Miss Jenny, these children are like chickens in a coop that's too small! I'm afraid if I don't get them out doing some-thin' they's gonna peck each other to death! So I brought 'em on down here."

"That's fine, Lita," Jennifer said. She was at the big table work-ing on the second edition's layout, while Jason was busily digging through some boxes for woodcuts for pictures in advertisements. *Father, I've been so busy with the paper that I sometimes almost forget my own children. Forgive me, and help me to be a better mother to them. I don't know if it's such a good idea to have them here in the office. We've so much to do, and they might interfere . . . Lord, help this to be a good situation for us and for them.*

"I want to draw some pictures," Abby demanded.

"All right, you can sit at my desk and use the paper and pencils there, but don't get into the ink."

Grant walked over to Jason and watched him lining up wooden blocks beside the wooden boxes he was searching through. "What are these?" Grant asked, picking up one of the blocks with intricate carvings on one side.

Stopping his work, Jason flipped the block over so Grant could see there was an ink-blackened picture on one side. "You see that?" Jason asked.

"Yes," Grant answered, "but what is it?"

"If you roll ink on that and then press it onto paper, it'll leave an ink picture," Jason explained. "Can you see a harness if you look real close?"

Studying the dark image, Grant could make out the picture. "Yeah, I see it. Can we stamp it onto a piece of paper?"

"Sure," Jason said as he reached for the ink roller and rolled it across the block. "Lay this paper down flat and press the block against it."

Grant did as he was told and was fascinated to see a perfect picture of a harness on the paper. "Wow! Does it do that every time?"

"Every time, as long as it has ink on it," Jason said enthusiastically. "We print the newspaper the same way. We put everything in this tray your mother and I are working on, then set it in that press over there, slide paper on top, and press it down."

Delighting in Jason's patient explanations, Grant asked, "Can I help you make the paper?"

"Grant, you would just get in the way. We have a deadline to meet, and we don't have time to spare," Jennifer scolded.

"I don't mind at all," Jason quickly asserted. "Actually, I could use some help."

Surprised but rather pleased, Jennifer said no more. Jason seemed to genuinely enjoy helping Grant learn about printing a newspaper. Jennifer thought, *Everyone has talents, and Jason apparently has a gift for teaching children. I sure hope he has left his drinking problem behind him.*

～

After considerable effort and working late into the night, the second edition of the revived *The Miner's News* appeared—and was a tremendous success. Jason returned to the office again and again to print more copies, while Jennifer dealt with an abundance of customers coming through the front door. "Jason, I know of at least two other newspapers in this town—the *Territorial Enterprise* and the *Gold Hill News*. How is it that we're so popular all of a sudden?"

Jason chuckled as he worked over the press. "Several reasons. One, we're new, or at least seem new since the paper was down for so long. People get tired of the same old hogwash from the same old newspapers. Furthermore, folks in these parts have never heard of a woman editor and are curious as to what they might find in your paper. Whatever the reason, we're selling papers and advertising space, and that's good news for us."

Jennifer appreciated their success, but more than that, she wanted to maintain a solid newspaper and not merely be an overnight sensation. "We'll have to keep people's interest," she told Jason.

"That we will," he assured her as he rushed out the door with an armload of papers.

As issue after issue was written, printed, and distributed, Jennifer's newcomer articles were especially popular. Those who had been in Virginia City for some time enjoyed hearing about a novice's misunderstandings and misinterpretations, while fellow newcomers hoped the articles would help them avoid any more personal embarrassment than necessary. But Jennifer was finding it hard to make time to do more writing, because every time she sat down to work, a new customer appeared at the counter.

Jason's work kept him out of the office quite a bit and took much of his writing time too. One day Jennifer complained to Jason, "We can't keep staying up late every night trying to put a new issue together and do our writing too. We need some help."

Jason had to admit Jennifer was right. "What about that friend of yours? What's his name?"

"Clemens," Jennifer answered. "How would we find him?"

"I don't know," Jason said, a bit of a frown on his face.

Two hours later Samuel Clemens walked through the front door carrying something that looked like a large, metal wishbone.

"Mr. Clemens, welcome! You couldn't have come at a better time," Jennifer shouted from the back of the room. "Do you think you could give us a hand? We're really swamped."

Clemens smiled happily. "Timing is everything! Swamped, eh? Anything I can do for good-mannered southern folk, I'd be happy to do!" He came around the counter to look over the workings of the next edition. Jason stood with his mouth open, staring at their visitor. "What's the matter, young man? Your mouth seems to be hanging open precariously. I once knew a man with that ailment, and I know just the cure."

"Jennifer," Jason said, astounded, "do you know who this is?"

"Of course I know who it is—it's Samuel Clemens, the man I told you about!"

"Also known as Mark Twain!" Jason exclaimed. "Exceptional writer, lecturer, and humorist! I'm Jason Stone, and it's my great pleasure to meet you, Mr. Twain." Jason extended his hand.

"Actually I stole that name," Twain said as he shook Jason's hand. "The man that had it before me died, and seeing that he no longer had any need for it, I kindly picked it up."

Jennifer stood beside the two men, bewildered as she stared at Twain. "You're Mark Twain? You wrote a travel book called *The Innocents Abroad*. That was truly a work of art!"

"Why, thank you, Jennifer. It's good to be reminded of who I am on occasion. Keeps me from wandering into being someone else." Twain had a twinkle in his eye.

Jason and Jennifer both laughed at Twain's strange but humorous mannerisms. Any resentful feelings Jason had had about having another writer working at the office were now gone. "Would you be so kind as to write something for this next edition, something funny?" Jason asked.

"If it's *funny* you want, I can't help you. Some find my observations of man humorous, but believe me, I do not intend for it to be merely funny," Twain said, correcting Jason.

Accepting the correction but not especially wanting to admit it, Jason asked, "What's that strange-shaped object in your hand?"

"Oh, this. It's like a water witch or a divining rod, except it's supposedly made of an alloy of precious metals and seeks out the same." He glanced at Jennifer's and Jason's unbelieving expressions. "Of course, I don't believe in any such thing," he amended unconvincingly. "I only purchased it to study its merits. The man I bought it from claims to have located two veins of rich ore with it."

Jennifer and Jason could restrain themselves no longer and burst into laughter at even the great Samuel Clemens being taken in by a gold-town charlatan. Suddenly Twain knew the truth, that his curiosity had gotten the best of him. To take the focus off his hood-winking, he tossed the wishbone-shaped piece of metal aside. "I'll study its scientific properties later. Now, shall we get to work?"

That afternoon Twain puffed smoke like a freight train as he worked hard at his writing. Fascinated by the chronic gambling fever he always found in mining towns, Twain was prone to comment on the subject. But as he began, he found himself sidetracked into writing a short story instead. Jason hurriedly planned the layout of the next edition, while Jennifer wrote another article about being a newcomer in Virginia City.

She often didn't realize until afterwards that much of what she wrote was hilarious to those who were not new to the area. Once she referred to a mine in such a way that it sounded more like a deep well by which miners had their ore lifted to the top in buckets by an ordinary windlass. Such innocent errors helped the laughing miners develop a loving sympathy for the novice newspaper woman.

After a while a delivery boy came into the newspaper office whistling a high-pitched melody. He wore an exceptionally tall hat, resembling a stovepipe. Twain rose from his seat and approached the young man. "Can I help you, son?"

"Yes, sir. I have a letter here for the editor of *The Miner's News.*"

"That would be me," Twain said, reaching for the letter.

The young man snatched his hand back. "But, sir, you don't look like a Jennifer to me."

Straightening, Twain remarked, "This boy has remarkable powers of perception. There may be a spark kindling in his head after all, though I fail to detect any smoke from the smokestack as of yet."

Coming over, Jennifer took the letter. Noticing it was postmarked New Orleans, she opened it and saw it was from C.C. Cromwell.

April 6, 1870
Dear Jennifer,

I trust that your trip was tolerable and that you are sat-isfied with your newspaper business. I continue to receive letters concerning the articles you wrote for the *Picayune*

about the West, Nevada, and the gold mines. It appears
the readers here want more. I've tried having someone
else continue the column, but with little response.

Perhaps you could send me some letters describing
what you've discovered in Virginia City, and I could share
them with the readers of the *Picayune*. I can give you
quality compensation for your time.

As before, if there is ever anything I can do to help
you, contact me without delay.

Sincerely,
C.C. Cromwell

This is amazing, Jennifer thought. *I've already written exactly what
Mr. Cromwell wants in my articles in* The Miner's News. *I'll send him
a few of the papers we have left over. Not only will he be able to read my
articles, but then he can see what a western, mining town newspaper is
like.*

*Father, only You could arrange circumstances so perfectly. Just when
I get so busy that I hardly think about You, You give me another special
gift to remind me of Your loving presence. Thank You, Heavenly Father!*

As soon as they finished the new edition, Jennifer put together
a package for Mr. Cromwell that included a copy of all the editions
printed since she'd been in Virginia City.

∽

The next day people frantically searched to find a copy of the
new edition of *The Miner's News*, primarily so they could read the
new short story Twain had written, titled "The Notorious Jumping
Frog of Calaveras County." At the newspaper, they'd been so busy
that Jennifer had neglected to proofread Twain's story. Besides, with
all his experience, he was certainly qualified to proofread his own
material. Jason set the type and in doing so only read a few words at
a time, and so he did not realize the genius or appeal of the story as
a whole. Jason had to run the press continuously to keep up with the
demand, and Jennifer had already mailed Mr. Cromwell his package,
which included Twain's new tale. Thus a new work of genius was
born unawares.

~

That evening, after Jason had made his rounds selling papers and collecting money from papers sold, he walked back toward the office, overflowing with pride from the sudden success of *The Miner's News*. The paper had never done so well. He jingled his pocket, now full of money, and smiled as he passed a saloon where a man sat out front at a small portable table. The man had a little game going that involved three half walnut shells and a pea. He had a black goatee and top hat and was dressed in a fine suit. "Place your bets right here," he announced loudly. "Is the hand quicker than the eye? The game is very simple—just follow the shell and tell me which one the pea is under."

A dirty miner stepped up and bet five dollars. He easily found the pea and bet another twenty dollars, won again, and went away happy.

"Why, that looks easy," an observer said as he laid down twenty dollars.

"I'm having a bad day and am losing too much money!" complained the man with the goatee. "But it wouldn't be fair to turn anyone away, so I'll take your bet, sir. Just follow the shell with the pea under it."

When the man picked a particular shell, naturally the pea wasn't there. He felt obligated to bet another twenty to win his twenty back, but lost again. Growing angry, he bet twenty again, and lost once more.

Jason jingled the money in his pocket as an idea came to mind. He had no doubt that the first man who had played was working with the game operator to persuade others to get involved. He also knew a trick the operator wouldn't expect. "Will you take a larger bet?" Jason asked.

"No bet is too big for me!" the smiling gentleman obliged.

Counting out the newspaper's money, Jason came up with fifty dollars. A small crowd had gathered as Jason placed the money on the little table. Immediately the man placed the pea under a shell and scooted them around in a clever fashion, then glanced at Jason.

Studying the three shells, Jason quickly reached over and lifted the two shells on the end. "I'd guess it's under the middle one," Jason said confidently.

"But you can't touch the shells!" the man yelled angrily.

"You didn't say anything about that," Jason asserted confidently. "Shall I lift the middle shell and show everyone that's where the pea is?" Jason reached over and put his fingers on the shell.

"No, no, that's not necessary!" The man paid Jason his fifty dollars, folded up his little table, and left hurriedly. The onlookers laughed as the huckster scurried away.

The joy of having fifty dollars of his own made Jason feel like a king. He glanced inside the crowded saloon hesitantly. *Just one drink to celebrate*, he thought as he swung the doors open. The bar ran along one side, extending deep into the narrow building. The smell of raw whiskey permeated a haze of cigar smoke. When Jason asked for a drink, the bartender poured him a small glass and left the bottle sitting nearby, as had been Jason's customary request in the past. Jason gulped down the drink, enjoying the burning pleasure, when a voice boomed from behind him.

"Well, looky who we have here! If it ain't my drunk editor friend!" The speaker, moving closer to Jason, a bushy-haired miner named Big Ned O'Donnell, had a nasty scar across his cheek and arms like tree trunks. His close-set eyes were filled with contempt.

"Leave me alone!" Jason warned.

"What's the matter?" Ned cried in a mimicking voice. "You ain't got enough big-talk whiskey in you yet?" Jason ignored him.

In a flash Ned backhanded Jason across the face, knocking him to the floor. Before Jason could get up, Ned kicked him and sent him sprawling to the middle of the floor. The crowd laughed as Jason crawled timidly back to the bar.

"He's just a spineless whiskeygut!" Big Ned laughed, and the crowd laughed with him.

His nose bloody, Jason paid for the whiskey, then grabbed the bottle and ran out of the saloon.

~

Jennifer couldn't have felt better the next morning. The most recent edition of *The Miner's News* had been a tremendous success thanks to the help of Mark Twain. But she knew she and Jason had contributed to the paper as well. The morning was lovely and still cool from the night before as she walked on the flat boardwalks in front of the stores near the hotel. She could smell bacon frying somewhere, and she heard a rooster crow.

I love it out here in the West, she thought. *It's so uncluttered and open and hardly ever overcast. And everyone seems friendly enough. Thank You, dear God, for all You've done for us.* As she walked by the dry goods store, she saw the owner unlocking his doors. She'd come to know him, having made purchases in his store many times. "Mr. Sutter, good morning to you. How's your sunburn?" Jennifer said with a wide smile.

Turning, Mr. Sutter answered, "Oh, good morning, Jennifer. It's much better now, thank you. That was some paper you put out yesterday!"

"Thank you, Mr. Sutter." Jennifer continued on her way to the office and unlocked the front door. When she stepped in, she noticed Jason wasn't up yet. Slight apprehension disturbed her, but she paid it no mind. She made coffee and began working. But by 9 she began to wonder where Jason was and went in the back room to see if he was there. She found him lying on his cot with a blood-crusted face and an empty bottle clutched to his chest.

"Oh dear!" Jennifer exclaimed as she rushed to get a wet towel. *Father, I don't know what's happened or why, but please help us.* She came back to Jason and shook his shoulder. "Jason! Jason! Wake up!"

Stirring, Jason groaned as he opened his bloodshot eyes. He stared at Jennifer's face for a long time. "I went and did it, didn't I? I went back to what I was."

Jennifer nodded as she sat next to him and applied the damp towel to his face. She didn't want to make him feel any worse about what had occurred, but she did want to be honest with her friend. *Lord, give me the words to say.* "Why did you do this? Who hurt you?"

"A man at the saloon. I don't know why I was drinking," Jason muttered. "I guess I can't help it. I'm weak."

After Jennifer cleaned his face, Jason stood up slowly. He had lost all the animation she'd seen in him since he'd stopped drinking. "Well, now you know what I am—the scum of the earth!" he said bitterly.

"Do you like being like this?" Jennifer asked.

"I hate it! I detest what it does to me and the way it makes me feel."

"Then why don't you quit? Don't you feel better when you're not drinking?" Jennifer's eyes were sad as she observed Jason's suffering.

"I wish I could leave the stuff alone," Jason said, "but I just don't have the strength."

"Only God can give you the strength," Jennifer told him. "Anything is possible if you let God become part of your life."

Jason shrugged. "What does God care about me? I'm only one person in millions. And besides, considering all that I've done . . ."

"He *does* care about you," Jennifer said softly. "He loves each and every one of us. He strongly desires to forgive us for our sins and to give us new life through His Son, Jesus Christ. God can help you, Jason."

Jason turned and gave Jennifer a long look. He thought she was beautiful. "I appreciate what you're trying to tell me, even though I'm not sure I can believe it. I hope you don't mind my being so honest with you. I wouldn't want to do anything that would hurt you, Jennifer. Truth is, I'd do just about anything for you, but . . . well, I didn't want to act improperly. I suppose you have a husband somewhere. I don't understand why he's not with you."

A graceful smile touched Jennifer's lips. "My husband died in a hospital from a deadly infection. That was some time back. That's why he's not with me."

"Oh," Jason mumbled. "I'm sorry."

"Don't be," Jennifer said. "I believe in God, and I know He'll take care of me and my loved ones. That's where I find my strength." She paused. "Jason, you've been honest with me. May I be as honest with you?"

Jason nodded.

"You need to put your faith in God, to trust Him with your entire life. Ask Him to help you with your problem. You can talk to Him just like you're talking to me right now. Will you do that for me, for yourself?" Jennifer placed her hand on Jason's shoulder.

Jason glanced around the room as he held the damp towel to his head, then let his eyes move back to Jennifer's lovely, smiling face. After staring at her for a long moment, sadness came into his face, and his voice trembled as he said, "I can't do it—I can't come to God like that. There's no use putting your faith in me. I'd just let you down—like I've let myself down and everybody else who ever trusted me!" He turned and stumbled out of the room as Jennifer stared at him hopelessly.

He's not beyond salvation, Jennifer thought, *but he'll never find it until he gives up on himself and lets God pull him out of the dark hole he's dug for himself.*

Mining Dangers

The news of the day was generally discussed in the office of *The Miner's News* by several locals who found the homey atmosphere to their liking. It was a place where a man could sit back in comfort over a cup of coffee and express his views without fear of reprisal. Those who were hungry for news and gossip were mostly businessmen who loved to exchange interesting information and sober ideas. Formerly the barber shop had sufficed for this, but now Jennifer's office attracted a covey of curious men, perhaps because it offered a feminine touch and an amusing Mark Twain, who often lured men into intense conversations through his lengthy orations.

"It's my belief that the real mother lode has yet to be found," Twain declared wisely one day. "We've merely scratched the surface."

"What makes you think you're right?" Barney Simmons asked. Barney was a coal oil salesman known for his constant blinking. He had a small peanut-shaped head atop his tall frame. "Nobody knows what's down there."

Pulling at his mustache, Twain paced around the room, obviously engaging in serious contemplation. "The gold ore here is different. Rather than running in clearly defined veins as in most mining zones, it's found scattered, like raisins in a cake. The big raisin, or the big bonanza, I believe is yet to be found."

Pete Twiller chimed in, "That's right! We ain't dug much around here compared to how much there is left to dig." Pete liked to call himself a mule doctor since he'd had experience with all known mule ailments. And an abundant number of mules made their home in Virginia City. He was a short, dumpy little man with dazzling eyes and straight black hair that he kept well greased. He enjoyed the delights of animated conversation almost as much as tending to mule infirmities.

Rarely did Jennifer miss a word of these frequent conversations, for she still had much to learn about the town and the mining there. She kept a pot of fresh coffee on the stove and several cowhide-bottomed chairs handy for these men to sit in comfortably. They admired her generosity and relished the moments of the day spent at the newspaper office where they could freely speak their mind.

Glancing up from her work at the big table, Jennifer noticed a distressed little woman at the front counter. She had a downcast expression as Jennifer moved over to her. "Can I help you with something?" Jennifer asked politely.

"Yes. My name is Milly Potts. You must be the lady who runs this paper."

"That's right," Jennifer said, noticing that Milly had dark circles under her eyes as if she'd been crying.

"I don't trust them other papers," Milly began, her voice troubled. She was a young woman with curly black hair and deep blue eyes, though she appeared to have aged because of grief. "I'm being forced to sell my house since my husband was killed in a mining accident. It seems like all the crooks have been out to swindle me ever since they learned of my husband's death. I thought maybe I could advertise my house in your paper."

"I'm so sorry," Jennifer murmured. "It must be difficult."

"I have three children, and I can't support them. We've so little. I need to sell our house soon so we can afford to move back to St. Louis."

Jennifer suddenly realized her opportunity. "Why, I'm looking for a house! I have two children and a woman who looks after them, and we need a place of our own. The hotel we're staying in is so small—and expensive."

Brightening up immediately, Milly said, "My house is only a few months old and near the school. It's very nice. I'd love to see you get it."

"Well," Jennifer said with her finger on her lip, thinking, "I guess there's no time like the present. Could you show it to me now?"

"Of course," Milly said cheerfully.

"Jason!" Jennifer called toward the back. "Watch the office please. I'm going to look at a house that is for sale."

Jason waved in acknowledgment and turned back to his work. The group of characters hanging around and drinking coffee remained engrossed in their conversation, paying little attention to anything else.

~

When Jennifer came back that afternoon she wore a pleasant smile, yet also seemed concerned.

"Well?" Jason inquired. "Did you like the house?"

"It's perfectly adorable!" Jennifer announced. "It's situated above the Chollar mine near the Fourth Ward School. But I'm worried about Milly Potts. Her husband's body was recovered, but there was little left to bury since he'd fallen down a mining shaft and was dismembered on the way down. Even worse, the mining company hasn't helped her and her children at all."

A caustic smile touched Jason's lips. "It's a cold and hard business, and the companies do little for miners when they are injured—and even less for the families of deceased miners."

"They should do *something*," Jennifer insisted. "It's only right. I didn't realize things were like this."

"To the best of my knowledge, the mining companies don't even keep records of mishaps," Jason informed her sadly. "There's often one man killed a week and at least one injured every day. Falls are the most common form of death. You see, at the end of the shift, as the men come up swiftly from the unbelievably hot shafts into the cool air, they sometimes become faint and fall. As they plummet down the shaft, they are torn apart by the timbers until the dismembered body falls into a pit of hot water at the bottom. Small grappling hooks are kept on hand to recover the pieces, which are rolled in canvas or placed in candle boxes to be taken above to the man's family."

Jennifer held her hand over her mouth in disgust. "That's the most awful thing I've ever heard!" she uttered.

"I apologize for being so candid, but I thought you would want to know the full story of these terrible conditions."

"I appreciate your honesty, Jason, as difficult as it is to hear about such things."

"The 100-degree heat and falling down a shaft aren't the only killers either. Mining bits and heavy tools are sometimes accidentally dropped down the shaft and hit men with a velocity strong enough to drive right through them. Also, when there are cave-ins miners are either killed outright or they die a slow death from lack of oxygen or thirst or starvation. Dynamite mishaps blow miners to bits from time to time too, and of course many die from silicosis, a lung disease caused by breathing the dust in the mine. Other dangers include . . ."

"That's enough!" Jennifer cried. "I can't bear to hear any more!"

"It's a dangerous business, but it pays well," Jason concluded with a shrug. "The miners know the risks."

"That doesn't make the mining companies' negligence right," Jennifer snapped, growing even more agitated. "What about dead miners' families? The mining companies should offer some kind of compensation for their loss."

"Tell them that," Jason said, "and they'll laugh you right out of their office."

"They could take some measures to make the mines a little safer," Jennifer insisted.

"Why should they?" Jason countered. "There are plenty of miners; new people come here all the time. All the companies care about is gold and silver. Miners are expendable."

"Well, I just might have something to say about that!" Jennifer promised angrily. "And it won't be in their office. It will be in *The Miner's News*."

Jason came over to Jennifer, deep concern on his face. "Jennifer, think about the possible consequences. If the miners start demanding better conditions, they could cause big trouble for the mining companies, and the mining companies can cause big trouble for us!"

"True, but we can't just ignore those who need our help," Jennifer said stubbornly, thinking of poor Milly Potts and her fatherless children.

Without another word Jennifer sat down at her desk and began writing an editorial on the dangers of mining.

~

Jason worked all night to print more than a thousand copies of *The Miner's News* to be circulated the next morning. Instead of Jennifer's article of interest on Virginia City and the mining industry, there was a fiery editorial on the dangers of mining and an expressed concern about whether the mining companies should take an interest in safety and should compensate injured miners (or, if killed on the job, their families).

The new edition stirred immediate unrest among the miners and especially in their disgruntled wives, who worried each time their husbands left for work.

"Very interesting," Twain said as he read Jennifer's editorial while he leaned back in a chair with his ever-present smoldering cigar. "But you may have poked a stick into a wasps' nest."

"Good!" Jennifer responded forcefully. "It's about time the mining companies take some responsibility."

"Hmm . . ." Twain uttered as he read further. "This part where you encourage the miners to consider wearing helmets . . . they're not going to fight a medieval war, my dear."

"It was just a suggestion," Jennifer said defensively. "Surely someone could invent protective gear for their type of work."

"It's far too hot to be wearing much down in the steamy pits," Twain informed her. "These miners shed nearly everything but their pants. It has occurred to me that machines could be made to do the work, but it would still take men to run the machines. The fact remains, risk won't keep men away from gold."

"No matter what you or anyone else says," Jennifer argued, her eyes bright green with animosity, "the mining companies can begin by doing something for the widows and families. As a Christian, I can't ask for anything less."

Twain knew better than to argue with an angry woman. "I suppose you're right. After all, they have plenty of money."

～

Moving into the new house was easy for Jennifer and Lita and the children since they had so little to move. The house, set back from the street, was plain and tall and painted white. Salome scouted the new quarters cautiously in hopes of finding a small but plump rodent. Milly Potts had sold Jennifer the furniture too since she had no way to take it with her. Much of it was new, hand-crafted work from San Francisco. It was the kind of furniture that spoke of elegance and appealed to the expensive taste of miners surrounded by dreams of riches and gold.

"Mother, this is nice," Grant said happily as he set his suitcase down. "Is my room upstairs?"

"Yes, Grant. Abby, your room is upstairs next to Grant's. Go take a look, children."

The children raced each other up the stairs as Jennifer turned to Lita. "Your room is right down the hall, in the back, next to mine," Jennifer said, delighted to finally find a place she could call home. The only problem was that by purchasing the house, Jennifer had relieved herself of all her funds. She now had virtually no savings; everything was tied up in the newspaper and the house. Though a little frightened by having almost no operating capital, she believed the newspaper would soon be making a profit, which would allow her to build up some savings once again.

Having to operate on a tight budget for the time being made her feel insecure, but she trusted God to continue to provide and sustain. *God hasn't let me come this far just to fail.*

She thought back to what she'd heard the preacher say at church just the previous Lord's day when he spoke of Jesus' words about our being worth more than sparrows, for whom God continually provides. Presently she had no savings to speak of, but she and her family had untold riches of divine love and care.

Lita rolled her big brown eyes, taking in their new home. "Miss Jenny, it's so dusty out here, I don't think I can keep this nice place clean! There's dust on everythin'!"

"Don't worry, Lita," Jennifer said calmly. "I'm sure you'll take care of things around here just fine. You always do."

"I don't know, Miss Jenny. I'll be sopping wet every day trying to keep all this dust off things," Lita said, a frown on her face.

"After you get things situated here, go down to Kenner's Grocery and get whatever food items we need," Jennifer told Lita. "Tell him to put it on my bill. I need to get back to the office."

As Jennifer turned to leave, she spotted a rag doll lying in a corner. It touched her deeply to realize that in the haste to leave, Milly's young daughter must have overlooked the doll. *How wrong it is for a family to be forced into abandoning their home*, she thought. Knowing what it was like to lose a husband, Jennifer decided, *I'm going to make a difference! I'm going to do something about these poor families who have been forgotten!*

~

Jennifer had barely entered the office when Jason raced around the counter waving a newspaper in his hand. It was a copy of the *Territorial Enterprise*. "You have to read this!" he said, obviously agitated and out of breath. "You won't like it."

Taking the paper from Jason's hand, Jennifer sat down at her desk and read an editorial by Dan DeQuille, the editor of the rival paper. The charges and criticisms she read made her blood pressure rise dramatically. DeQuille accused her of meddling; he called her "a greenhorn do-gooder who is bent on creating disharmony and disturbing the established ways of a mining town." He said her misplaced benevolence was destructive and called her employees "a drunk and a loud-mouthed orator skilled in the art of deception." He left no stone unturned as he condemned everything about *The Miner's News* except the ground it stood on.

At first angry, then heartbroken, Jennifer laid the paper on her desk. She didn't know whether to scream or cry as she felt a sinking feeling in the pit of her stomach. *Why has this man chosen to condemn me publicly?* she wondered. Jason watched her closely, wondering whether she would require consolation or restraint. Turning to him, she asked, "What is this man trying to accomplish?"

Jason shrugged. "Who knows? Maybe he doesn't like the success we've had, or maybe he's tied in with the mining companies. There are many possible reasons for his actions."

"But we've never met. He doesn't even know me!" Jennifer placed a piece of paper in front of her, then dipped a quill into an inkwell and began to write a response. "I'll show him two can play at this game!" she remarked angrily. Deep within herself she knew she should pray about the situation, but at the moment she didn't want to pray—she wanted to strike back!

Shaking his head, Jason could see a newspaper war developing, and he had experienced them before. He could recall no good that ever came out of such a battle. He wished he could stop what was about to happen, but he knew by now that Jennifer was a fighter and that he wouldn't be able to talk her out of her intended course of action.

As Jennifer wrote, she let her emotions take over. She knew she was violating absolutely every rule of sensible writing. But a woman's scorn can be well expressed with the power of the pen, and she was determined to do exactly that.

Twain came into the office leading a man who had an aristocratic nose and a wispy mustache, dressed as high in fashion as his scant means would allow. Talking incessantly, as always, Twain led the man over to the coffeepot and pointed, indicating that was the extent of his hospitality—the man could pour his own cup of coffee.

Jennifer ignored the two men as she feverishly composed her rebuttal to the editor of the *Territorial Enterprise*. Twain gave her a glance and at once saw that she was upset. He looked to Jason for an explanation, and Jason handed Twain the scandalous copy of the competing paper. Twain and his friend read the article together as Twain held the newspaper in front of them. When they finished, Twain addressed Jennifer with the hopefully calming words, "My dear, I hope you're not engaging in a name-calling contest. It's not in your nature."

Frustrated, Jennifer threw the quill down and rubbed her temples with her fingers. "You're right. This is nothing but slanderous rubbish."

Twain smiled. "Jennifer, I'd like to introduce you to a friend of mine. He left San Francisco and is on his way back east. I've persuaded him to stop here in Virginia City—a bit out of the way I suppose, but what are friends for? Jennifer, this is Bret Harte. Bret, this is Jennifer DeSpain, owner of this respectable and increasingly popular newspaper."

"How do you do, ma'am," Harte said, extending his hand in a gentlemanly fashion.

"I wish I could say I was doing better," Jennifer admitted. "But this Dan DeQuille, whoever he is, has ruined my day."

"And mine as well!" Twain said. "I believe I was mentioned in his slander as a 'deceptive loudmouth.'" He turned to Harte. "As my friend here can verify, I'm most proud to be a loudmouth, and I sometimes exaggerate, but I'm *never* deceptive." He turned back to Jennifer. "Bret is a magazine writer, and quite a good one if I do say so myself. Would you kindly allow us to take care of Mr. DeQuille, for I've known the man personally for some time, and I might recall a thing or two to mention about him and his newspaper. With that, along with Bret's satirical abilities, I might be able to give Mr. DeQuille a purgative he won't soon forget." Twain chuckled and champed his cigar.

Bret laughed at the challenge, for he loved being cleverly cynical in a derisive way. "Mark, my friend, I believe we can make an evening of this."

"And so we will," Twain said happily. "Jennifer, why don't you run along. You've let this upset you too much. This is merely part of the newspaper game out here in the West. Since we don't want a war with the *Territorial Enterprise*, Bret and I will send off a bombardment that will end it after the first battle. Dan DeQuille just may have to leave town for a while to avoid the embarrassment of being seen in public."

Jennifer stood and hugged Twain. "I'm sure you and Mr. Harte will handle this professionally and will put a convincing end to it. You're right, I *have* let this overly upset me. I think I'll go help with the house we've just moved into. Thank you so much, Mr. Twain."

Gathering a few things preparatory to her departure, Jennifer left the necessary chore to the two men skilled at writing such challenges. Certainly Dan DeQuille's defamation would not go unanswered.

~

Jennifer spent the next morning with her children, choosing not to go to the office until after the midday meal. The afternoon was hot and the air still as she walked to the newspaper, still somewhat discouraged at her competitor's verbal attack. At the office she found Jason and Twain leaning back in chairs with the smug look of two boys who had been caught with their hands in the cookie jar. They could hardly contain their laughter as they each sat with a cigar clamped between their teeth as they tried, unsuccessfully, to keep from smiling. "And just what are you gentlemen up to?" Jennifer asked.

Jason replied, "We printed a short, special edition of *The Miner's News*. It's all over town by now." He nodded toward several copies on the counter.

Picking it up, Jennifer read the story Twain and Harte had concocted. Dan DeQuille's name was never mentioned, but the article was obviously about him. The clever, witty story about an inept editor and his womanizing ways was so incredibly funny that Jennifer began to laugh so hard, her eyes ran with tears. Twain and Harte had outdone themselves in shaming Dan DeQuille. "Splendid writing," Jennifer said as she caught her breath. "But is any of this true? As you are well aware, DeQuille's article angered me deeply, but at the same time I'd not want to spread lies about the man, no matter how much he has hurt us. Yesterday I felt quite differently, but it's amazing what time spent in Bible reading and prayer can do."

"We've not exaggerated the truth about Dan DeQuille, I assure you. If anything, we've restrained it a bit." Twain added with a chuckle, "It appears that Mr. DeQuille has left town to attend to urgent business in parts unknown. It would be my guess that things will have to settle down considerably before he returns."

Jennifer was confident that Twain and Harte's article would bring new respect to the small newspaper and would certainly prevent a nasty newspaper war. "You've turned a tragedy into a comedy," Jennifer said to Twain. "Where is your friend Mr. Harte?"

"Oh, he caught a train this morning—he had to be on his way." Twain walked across the office. "I'm sure Bret will be pleased with the outcome."

With yet another possible disaster behind her, Jennifer relaxed at her desk and went through her mail. There seemed to be nothing but bills—bills she didn't have the money to pay. *Have I mismanaged my money badly?* She wondered what she should do. She knew that some accounts owed the newspaper money, but she was also aware they wouldn't be paid in time to pay the current bills. *Father, loving Lord, I don't know how things will work out this time, but I'm sure You do.* She opened another envelope, and out fell a letter from C.C. Cromwell.

Dear Jennifer,

I congratulate you on the great success of your newspaper and want you to know that we've reprinted most of it in the *Picayune*. As with any good news correspondent, I'm sending you a well-deserved check. You also might be happy to know that Mark Twain's story about the bullfrog has reached colossal proportions, for many syndicated papers have picked it up. You certainly know how to pick writers!

I'm looking forward to our continuing business relationship.

Sincerely,
C.C. Cromwell

Jennifer took one look at the generous check that fell out of the letter and almost shouted with joy. *I can't believe it!* she mused.

~ 11 ~

Charles Fitzgerald

George Hearst, mining tycoon, believed in maintaining control by intimidating others. Shrewd and ambitious, he thrived on hiring the best lawyers and outmuscling his competitors in court. He had read the latest edition of *The Miner's News* and was clearly upset with its female editor, for her editorial was causing unrest among his miners. As usual, he assumed that anyone who opposed him was guilty of some serious moral lapse, or at best had made himself or herself Hearst's enemy. Such persons had to be silenced, including Jennifer DeSpain. So he called in his top lawyer, Charles Fitzgerald, whose office was in Hearst's building. Charles arrived shortly after being summoned and was let into the office by an armed guard.

As a mining company lawyer, Charles Fitzgerald fit the bill perfectly. Only thirty years old, he had already made a name for himself. The son of a wealthy San Francisco family, he had graduated from university with top honors and was hired immediately to represent Nevada mining companies in sticky litigation. He had been so efficient that his duties quickly expanded to dealing with stocks and shares. The questionable methods mining companies often employed required a capable legal defense, and he excelled at providing it.

Somewhat of a dandy, Fitzgerald enjoyed wearing fine suits. His wavy black hair always lay neatly in place, and his deep blue eyes never missed a single detail. Further, he prided himself on being a lady's man and knew the finer skills of courting. Early in his career, Fitzgerald had made his boss, George Hearst, his model.

"Sit down," Hearst ordered, jutting his chin toward a chair. He had sharp, penetrating eyes set in a colorless face of stone atop a long beard. He held a copy of *The Miner's News* in his hand and shook it angrily as he spoke. "I want you to take care of this hysterical newspaper woman before she causes me serious problems. I'd just ignore her, but she makes so much sense, these stupid miners might come to understand too much of the truth. Do something about the situation!"

"Sir, do you have anything particular in mind?" Charles asked. "Do you want me to file a lawsuit against her or try to scare her off or what?"

"Do whatever it takes!" Hearst snapped. "I don't have time to fool with all this. I want her silenced!"

"I'll see to it, Mr. Hearst." As Fitzgerald walked out, he glanced back at Hearst, who had already given his full attention to some paperwork. He admired Hearst's cunning and his ability to delegate decisively. He knew Hearst was already expanding his operations into the Black Hills of the Dakota Territory. *Someday I'll be as rich as George Hearst—and as powerful, no matter what it takes to accomplish that, no matter how I have to change myself to be that kind of man!*

Back at his own desk, Fitzgerald gazed out his window at the busy streets. Generally patient, he liked to sit back in his chair with his feet on the desk and watch Virginia City's people pause for conversation, then move on. *If only I had Hearst's cold cleverness,* he thought, *I could dominate these people.* But Fitzgerald had what he considered to be a weakness—he had a sympathetic heart that wouldn't quite allow him to treat people like pawns. He knew that most rich men were ruthless—at least those in the mining business, but often he could carry out Hearst's orders only by hardening his heart and forcing himself to step on those unfortunate enough to be in the way. Toward opponents in the courtroom he was arrogant and even malicious, but toward people he encountered in daily life he was fairly friendly.

He was in truth a divided man; he longed to be rich but knew there was more to life than wealth. He didn't quite understand what that something more was or how to find it, or if he really wanted it, but he knew it existed. That ongoing conflict deep in his soul—to achieve the domination of wealth and power, or to show compassion for his fellowman—was taking its toll on him more than he could possibly understand.

Perhaps intimidating legal tactics will be enough to let this woman know what I'm like in court and make her think twice about causing trouble for George Hearst! For a long while he mentally practiced the verbal maneuvers he would make against Jennifer DeSpain. Finally he shrugged, murmuring aloud, "She's only a woman—and a greenhorn at that. It shouldn't be too hard to scare her off."

Leaving his office, Fitzgerald made his way along the dusty streets toward *The Miner's News.* He tipped his hat and bowed graciously to the ladies he passed, and they gave back shy glances and slight smiles. Oblivious to the smells of a crowded mining town, he pictured the pesky newspaper woman as he rehearsed the powerful threats he would use to scare her into writing no more about the mining companies. He would assure her that in the end big money would dominate, as it always does. Turning onto a side street, Fitzgerald went a short distance farther and stepped inside the newspaper office.

As Jennifer watched the well-dressed gentleman enter, she couldn't help but notice that he was most handsome, his eyes a deep blue and his clean-shaven face a healthy tan. As he removed his hat, she admired his black, wavy hair and his tall, trim figure.

Fitzgerald had been expecting an older woman—and a plainer one. In fact, he had anticipated a hardened woman who had gone through many difficult experiences. Instead he found himself facing a charming and beautiful face with green eyes that left him speechless for an instant. He enjoyed looking at her rich auburn hair hanging in sweeping waves.

"Good morning," he said with a smile. "I'm Charles Fitzgerald, an attorney with the Nevada Gold and Silver Mining Company." He bowed slightly, deciding to handle the woman diplomatically rather than by intimidation.

Coming close to the counter, Jennifer smiled in return. "I'm Jennifer DeSpain. Is there a problem?"

"No, not really," Charles responded pleasantly. "It's simply a mining company concern." He rotated his hat in his hands, admiring her clear complexion, for many of the women in Virginia City had complexions like crocodiles. He was a man who admired beauty in women, and he was gallant enough to catch the interest of most of them. Perhaps he was being too gentle with this woman, but he found it impossible to be otherwise.

"I'm more than happy to help," Jennifer offered. "What may I do for you?"

"Well, it seems that your editorial has raised the concern of some mining company owners, and they have asked me to talk to you about it."

"Oh?" Jennifer replied. "I only print what I believe to be the truth. And I don't think it's asking too much for the mining companies to take some responsibility for the welfare of the miners and their families. Do you?"

"Of course not," Charles agreed quickly, "but there is much more to the story. I'd be more than happy to explain it all to you, to inform you of facts of which you probably aren't aware—that is, if you can take some time from your undoubtedly busy schedule." Though he wanted to follow Hearst's orders to the letter and resolve the dilemma, he also wished to come to know Jennifer DeSpain in a personal way.

"Unfortunately," Jennifer said, turning to look over her shoulder at the work piling up behind her, "I do have a new edition to complete."

"I understand," Charles said cordially. "Perhaps I could take you to dinner tonight and explain the mining companies' position—all strictly business, I assure you."

Jennifer felt flattered. *Dinner with a mining company lawyer!* she thought. *He seems so polite and well-educated and sure of himself. And it would only be fair to hear the position of those I've publicly criticized.* "That would be acceptable."

"Fine!" Charles smiled. "I'd like to take you to the International Hotel, a fine dining establishment. Shall we say six o'clock this evening?"

Jennifer had a brief moment of doubt. *I haven't socialized publicly with a man since Drake died.* For an instant she considered refusing Fitzgerald's offer but then thought, *It's only business.* "Please come for me at my home," Jennifer agreed, giving him directions.

"I'll look forward to it," Charles said as he placed his hat neatly on his head and moved toward the door. He turned as he was leaving. "It's certainly been a pleasure meeting you, Mrs. DeSpain."

As he left, Jennifer stood with her elbows on the counter, staring out the front window at nothing. She felt an excitement she couldn't explain. *What has come over me? I haven't felt like this since I met Drake. He's well-spoken, and so intelligent, and very good-looking, but . . .*

She glanced up to see Jason staring strangely at her. He came to stand beside her, his eyes troubled. "Be careful with that one," he said.

"Why should I be?" Jennifer asked, puzzled.

"Because he works for George Hearst, and anyone who is with that bunch can be dangerous."

Jason turned and left abruptly, and Jennifer stared after him, pondering the worried expression she'd seen in his eyes. For a moment she wondered if she'd made the wrong decision, then shrugged and decided that one meeting could do no harm. She was an adult who had experienced enough trouble in her life to be able to recognize more when it came along. If Jason's fears were justified, she would certainly see the truth after meeting with Fitzgerald.

The thing Jennifer forgot to do was to pray.

∽

That afternoon as a piercing summer sun shone through the windows, Mark Twain came strolling into the office with Grant in tow.

"Look what I found," he remarked, "the future newsman of Virginia City. He was headed this way, so I tagged along."

"Grant!" Jennifer exclaimed. "Why aren't you with Lita and Abby? I don't want you wandering through the streets of Virginia City."

"I want to print the newspaper with Jason!" Grant protested. "It's boring at the house, so I walked down here."

Jennifer shook her head, hiding a smile as Grant rushed back to where Jason was working.

"Oh, Mr. Twain, I have a bank draft for you, for your story about the bullfrog," she said as she shuffled through some envelopes to find the check. "I wish I could pay you more, but times are difficult. My old boss in New Orleans sent this—he said your story was picked up by the syndicated newspapers."

Twain took the draft with a smile. "I'm glad to hear the story was prosperous," he said, folding the envelope and slipping it inside his coat pocket.

"Mr. Twain," Jennifer inquired, "how do you get by? I'm certainly not paying you enough to live on."

"Well, Jennifer, I used to be with the *Territorial Enterprise*, and back in those days I bought a trunk full of stock in the mines. When a claim makes a stir in the market, I search through my pile to see if I have any of that stock, and generally I do. That gets me by, though my real reason for returning to Virginia City is to finish a book I'm working on about Nevada in general. I'm thinking about titling it *Roughing It*. But don't think I don't appreciate the added monetary help I receive from you." Twain hurriedly sat down at a desk. Evidently there was something he wanted to write down before the daily crowd of conversationalists arrived.

Meanwhile, in the back of the office Grant watched Jason pick small letters out of the beveled wooden trays and place them in a rack. "You sure do that fast!" Grant said. "You don't even look at the letters."

"That's because they're arranged in a certain way in these small trays," Jason explained. "Look here, this little tray is full of *a*'s, and this little tray is full of the letter *b*. What I'm doing is called hand spiking."

Picking up a letter, Grant examined it seriously. "You can spell faster doing that than most people can write. I know cuz I've watched people write."

Smiling, Jason continued reading from a piece of paper as he formed the small type into words and sentences. Grant watched closely, wishing he could try.

"I have to go do a bit of shopping, " Jennifer announced. "I'm afraid I don't have a dress nice enough for the likes of the International Hotel."

"The International Hotel!" Twain exclaimed, raising his head from his work. "I thought you said you were goin' through tough times. That's no ham and egg restaurant, you know!"

"She's having dinner with a mining lawyer," Jason announced with obvious disapproval.

Twain turned to Jason and then back to Jennifer. "Is this true, Jennifer?"

"It's strictly business," Jennifer told Twain, directing warning eyes at Jason.

"My dear, you must be careful where you tread," Twain cautioned. "The mining companies are a pit of vipers."

"I can take care of myself," Jennifer said evenly. "Mr. Fitzgerald seems like an intelligent, well-mannered man."

"Charles Fitzgerald? He works for George Hearst!" Twain protested. "And George Hearst is the most conniving rascal ever born! Those men are after something, you can bet on that."

"We'll see," Jennifer said as she prepared to leave. "Just remember," she added with a twinkle in her eye, "you have to play in the dragon's backyard if you want to learn about the dragon."

Raising his white eyebrows, Twain watched Jennifer leave. "She has to be the boldest female I've ever known," he muttered.

"Bold or foolhardy?" Jason muttered.

~

Jason brought Grant home around five o'clock but went his way without greeting Jennifer. She was just about ready for her evening and wore a full-length blue dress with white trim. She had her hair up and crowned with a small hat to match her new dress.

"You looks wonderful!" Lita exclaimed as she fussed with the hem on Jennifer's dress. "I surely would like to see the man dat brought all dis on!"

"Now, Lita," Jennifer protested, "it's just a business meeting over dinner."

"Humph! You can't fool no old fool like me!" Lita said. "You gonna have all dem men followin' you."

Jennifer adjusted the small hat and with a careful eye inspected her reflection in the mirror. She knew she was an attractive woman, but rarely did she dress up like this. The experience gave her the kind of confidence that makes a woman feel she's important.

Promptness being one of Charles Fitzgerald's assets, he came early. He stood with his hands behind his back, impatiently waiting for Jennifer, and when she appeared, he blinked with surprise, for he was even more struck with her beauty now than previously. If he hadn't known better, he would have sworn she was part of the San Francisco aristocracy.

"Good evening, Jennifer," Charles said cheerily as he took her hand. "You look absolutely lovely."

"Thank you," Jennifer said. She admired his finely tailored gray suit. He certainly stood out among the roughly dressed miners of Virginia City. He offered his arm, and she took it. As they made their way along the boardwalk, they received the envious attention of all who saw them.

"I trust you're not married," Charles said casually. "We wouldn't want people to get the wrong idea."

"I'm not married," Jennifer assured him. But she left it at that, offering no further personal information.

She's a quick thinker! Charles thought. *I'll have to charm her if I expect her to cooperate with the mining companies.*

Jennifer never had seen anything as eloquent as the International Hotel. It was posh, almost gaudy, with its Nottingham lace curtains on gilt rods and huge walnut tables covered with velvet tablecloths. Their waiter wore a tuxedo. *He looks like he should be conducting an orchestra,* she thought. *This place flaunts its money.*

"Care for something to drink?" Charles asked. "They carry the finest wines from California vineyards."

"I don't drink," Jennifer said.

Charles raised his eyebrows. "Do you mind if I do?"

"Of course not," Jennifer answered. She had a queasy feeling as she remembered saying the exact same thing to Drake. *This is business,* she reminded herself, *not social pleasure like with Drake.* Anxious to get her mind off that subject, she inquired, "So, why are the mining companies interested in me?"

To the point! I like that, Charles thought. "I need to speak with you concerning your editorial on mining safety and the responsibility of the mining companies. While what you said is all true, it's upsetting to the miners and their families. They only see their portion of the picture, and they are easily influenced. They're sort of like a lynch mob—they take to an idea without giving it rational consideration."

"What's wrong with considering a new idea if it's for the better?" Jennifer questioned.

"But you are overlooking how much the mining companies have already done for the miners. You see, before the big companies became involved, prospectors couldn't afford to mine correctly, and thus their conditions were unbelievably dangerous, and yet they continued to mine. The tunnels were small, with barely enough timber to prevent cave-ins. The mining companies brought with them equipment and more efficient mining methods, which enabled men to work together in large groups and eventually become more prosperous." Charles was trying hard to make his point gently.

"But I've heard that a man is injured every day and one killed nearly every week," Jennifer stated with concern.

"That much is true. But although that sounds terrible, that is actually a very low percentage," Charles added, taking a sip of the wine the waiter had just placed on the table. Jennifer noticed he had fine manners. She noted also that he wore a ring on the middle finger of his left hand, the kind that a woman might give to a man.

"Allow me to explain. Did you know that we have almost 3,000 men in the underground labor force alone?"

"I didn't know that," Jennifer said. "You never see them all above ground at the same time. What about the widows and children of those who are killed in the mines? The families of those men are left with nothing. How are they expected to survive?"

The waiter came to take their order, and Charles highly recommended that Jennifer try the leg of lamb, which she did, along with the potato soup for which the hotel was famous. "There must be something the mining companies can do for the families of the deceased," Jennifer insisted. "They could even hold out some of the miner's pay for such emergencies and maybe add a little to it themselves."

Jennifer's suggestions made good sense to Charles. He was impressed with her wisdom. "I could present that idea at a management meeting and see what the company leaders think," he suggested. Inwardly, he knew he would never dare present such an idea to the Nevada Gold and Silver Mining Company—Hearst wouldn't part with a single penny!

I'm glad I met with him, Jennifer thought. *Maybe Charles Fitzgerald isn't as bad as Jason and Twain think.* "The mining companies seem to have so much money—I can't imagine they would be unwilling to make a small sacrifice for their employees," Jennifer suggested.

Charles couldn't help but think that from the mining companies' point of view, the miners were replaceable, expendable. That was sad but true, and he was more concerned with what is than with what should be. He thought of another way to bring Jennifer around to his point of view. "You state correctly that the mining companies have plenty of money, but they also spend plenty. They create the jobs, and they make innumerable sacrifices for the miners. They buy the machinery and build the mills and pay for *everything*. It costs hundreds of thousands of dollars to develop a mine properly. Just to give you an idea of how much effort they have to make, the heaviest sections of the mills were so big that they couldn't economically be shipped here from San Francisco. So the mining companies built a foundry in San Francisco, tore it down, shipped it here, and reconstructed it. That took a huge amount of money, all just so the miners would have decent jobs. If it weren't for the mining companies, the only so-called mines this place would have would be tent-roofed camps with huge open pits full of water."

The waiter delivered the soup, and Jennifer tasted it, glad for a moment's relief from the heavy arguments Charles had presented. "This is wonderful! How do they make potato soup taste so good?"

Charles smiled. He liked to see Jennifer happy. "It's the fine chefs they've brought in—and again, none of this would be possible if it weren't for the mining companies."

Jennifer felt her vehemence gradually lessening. *Father, help me know what to think. I don't want to stop caring about the miners and their families, but am I being unfair to the mining companies in the process?* The contrast between her praying now for wisdom and her not praying about whether she should dine publicly with the mining attorney didn't occur to her.

Fitzgerald knew he was giving Jennifer good answers, answers that would win her over to their cause, but he also realized he was playing a one-note melody that just might offend Jennifer. Perhaps a slight diversion was in order. "Can we take a respite from all this serious discussion about mining issues?" he asked.

Jennifer glanced at his blue eyes, unable to ignore their pleading. "Yes. I'd like to know more, but perhaps we should talk about something else for a while."

"Tell me about yourself. What brings you to Virginia City? I can't place your accent," he said politely.

"I'm from New Orleans," Jennifer answered, flattered by his interest in her. "I worked for the *Picayune*, the largest newspaper there. Then I inherited *The Miner's News*, but I decided I couldn't run it from New Orleans. Besides, the West sounded exciting, so here I am."

Drawn to her ambitious bent, Charles was becoming more impressed with her every minute. "So you packed your bags and came west just like that," he said, snapping his fingers.

"Just like that," Jennifer admitted.

"And you've had no previous experience with the mining industry?"

"All I know is what I've learned here," Jennifer said. "But I'm learning quickly."

Charles let his eyes wander as he pondered all he'd heard tonight. He would definitely have to keep this woman on his side. She would be a formidable opponent. "Jennifer, I appreciate your honesty, and I want to help you understand the mining industry better. How would you like to take a tour of one of the biggest and best mines in the Comstock Lode? I'll take you myself, so you can get a firsthand look at what's really happening."

Though the idea startled her at first, after a moment's consideration Jennifer realized this was an ideal opportunity. The potential gains made the risk worthwhile. Her eyes brightened as she answered, "I accept your gracious invitation. I can't imagine what to expect from this experience, but as a newspaper woman who wants to report the truth, I can't let this offer slide through my fingers."

"I'll show you everything—from the wall where the miners are drilling to the final processing of ingots of gold and silver. The mills will especially fascinate you."

Wiping her mouth with a white linen napkin, she timidly inquired, "When shall we do this?"

"Whenever is most convenient for you. I wouldn't want to interfere with your work at the paper. But you need to know, it's an all-day tour," Charles said, pleased with the prospect of spending an entire day with this beautiful and charming woman. He had successfully pursued many women, and he felt the excitement of the chase as he studied Jennifer with half-closed eyes. To him, women were merely the objects of a hunt, and he eagerly anticipated luring Jennifer DeSpain into his affections. He had no doubt he could accomplish that objective and fulfill George Hearst's directive at the same time.

"Saturday would be best for me," Jennifer decided. She felt an exciting curiosity about what was really going on in the mining business.

"Then Saturday it will be," Charles confirmed.

Father, I believe this is Your doing. Now I'll better understand the matters about which I've been writing. Thank You for arranging this. And thank You for this new friend. I believe this too is Your work. Charles hasn't mentioned You or Your Son, but being such a considerate and gracious man, I suspect that He knows You in the same way I do.

The evening was pleasurable and satisfying as Jennifer learned more about Charles Fitzgerald. He told her his life story, his hopes, his ambitions. Never had she known a man so fully focused. He knew what he wanted and was going after it with all his power. She admired that, though she felt a bit guilty when she realized she was in some ways comparing Fitzgerald with Drake, who had had no such drive. She knew Fitzgerald admired her too, and that pleased her. Unfortunately, having made some incorrect assumptions about the man, she misread the expression in his eyes.

~

From a nearby alley, Jason watched Fitzgerald and Jennifer leave the hotel. It troubled Jason to see his beautiful employer and friend be so taken with the disreputable mining attorney, whom Jason did not trust a lick. As he watched the two disappear down the street, a restless anger that he did not fully understand troubled him. He couldn't quite identify the regret he felt, the wish that he was the one escorting Jennifer home after a delightful dinner in Virginia City's finest hotel.

I was somebody once but not anymore. A sense of worthlessness overcame him, and he took a long swig of whiskey from a brown pint bottle. He stood in the shadows of the crowded buildings until the alcohol deadened his senses, then slowly staggered further into the alley. It would be a long, sad night for Jason Stone, but he was accustomed to that. That was all he deserved, he told himself for the millionth time.

12

The Ophir

On Saturday morning a brilliant sun glared through the windows as Jennifer put on her oldest dress for her trip into the dark caverns of a local mine. Biting her lip, she considered wearing something else, but she had no other dress that would be suitable. Her fear of the unknown and her increasing curiosity about the strange depths below were playing tug-of-war with her mind. *If only I had a clue of what to expect, perhaps I wouldn't be so nervous*, she thought. *I'm sure Charles wouldn't lead me into any danger*, she assured herself as she wound her long hair into a bun, then donned an old bonnet. She turned to inspect herself in a tall mirror. The dress was so old that she now filled it out in a manner that was almost suggestive. Fitzgerald had suggested she wear something old because the mines were so wet and filthy. Finally ready physically and mentally, she left for the newspaper office.

~

Charles Fitzgerald looked forward to his appointment with Jennifer DeSpain. He wore well-used denim pants and a shirt that fit his frame handsomely. He had a hint of a smile as he prepared to leave his rented room. *I'll have Jennifer in my arena today. She'll surely be frightened down in the mines, and in her fear she'll trust me!* he thought with great pleasure. She'd dominated his thoughts since their dinner together a few nights before. She was such a beautiful woman; even more, she was fair-minded and a pleasant companion. She had set something in motion within him that he'd never felt before and that he couldn't quite explain. *What's so different about my feelings for her?* he thought. *I'll have to be cautious with this one. At least today she'll have to rely on me down in those spooky caves.* Relishing the thought, he combed his hair, making sure everything was perfect.

~

Arriving at the newspaper office, Jennifer found Mark Twain crouched over a desk, hard at work scribbling with a quill. One glance at Jennifer, however, and he set the quill aside. "My goodness! You fill out that dress like the wind fills the sails of a schooner."

Jennifer felt her face flush as she glanced down at her old, tight dress. "Charles told me to dress in something I could get dirty," she said defensively. "I didn't know what else to wear."

"I'm sure the miners will enjoy seeing you," Twain informed her, a knowing twinkle in his eyes.

"Where's Jason?" Jennifer asked, suddenly noticing his absence.

Twain turned back to the papers on the desk with a worried look. "I'm afraid the young man is encountering one of his binges and hasn't come in yet. It's such a shame—he has immense talent but has chosen to waste it."

Sighing heavily, Jennifer sat down in a chair. "I've tried to tell him what a good newspaperman he is . . . . If only he'd listen to me," she mumbled.

Twain remarked, "There's more to it—more wood's been added to his fire. I'm surprised you haven't noticed."

"What are you talking about?" Jennifer questioned.

Pulling out one of his cigars, Twain took a long time lighting it, then locked his eyes on Jennifer. "Jason is in love."

Jennifer sat with a long face as she cogitated on what Twain had said. "In love? With whom?"

"With his newspaper woman employer," the old humorist reported, his eyes twinkling as he studied Jennifer's response.

A stunned look quickly came over her face. "With me? I think you are sadly mistaken, Mr. Twain. What Jason *loves* is drinking. What he *needs* is help!"

Nodding, Twain determined he would not say any more. He had stated his mind, and that was enough. "So, where is your dignified escort?"

Glad to change the subject, Jennifer glanced at the clock on the wall. It was five minutes to 8, nearly time for Charles to meet her there at the office. "He should be here any minute," she assured Twain.

Promptly at 8, Charles stepped into the office wearing a wide smile. He carried a small sack and greeted Jennifer cheerfully. "Good morning, Jennifer. And good morning to you, Mr. Twain. Well, Mrs. DeSpain, are you ready for an exciting day?"

Jennifer replied, "I'm a little nervous but nevertheless ready. What's in the sack?"

"Just some ham, cheese, and bread for lunch, and some cold tea too," he answered. "We'll become quite hungry before we're through." He again noticed Jennifer's natural beauty. *It'll be a pleasure to be seen with her*, he thought happily. "Well then, shall we go?"

Watching with great interest, Twain noticed the way the two looked at each other, the kind of look he often called foolish. As a farewell, he warned, "Don't be caught high-grading during your visit."

Glancing at Twain as she pulled the front door closed, Jennifer asked Charles, "High-grading? What does that mean?"

Laughing, Charles explained, "That's when miners can't resist the temptation to let a few pounds of ore find their way into their lunch pails or the deep pockets of their work clothes."

Jennifer shook her head. *Twain has the craziest notions!* she mused as she and Charles walked down the street. She didn't notice the turning heads of curious onlookers.

～

After a shorter walk than Jennifer would have thought, she and Charles arrived at a huge building spread over a mountainside. "This is the Ophir mine," Charles said as he took Jennifer's hand to help her up a long set of wooden steps.

"It was named after King Solomon's mine in the Old Testament, wasn't it?" Jennifer commented.

"Yes," Charles said, slightly amused. "But the men who discovered this mine weren't Bible scholars. Ophir just happens to be a favorite name for mines. T.P. Comstock and his friends discovered this mine, the first big strike here in Virginia City, but now it belongs to my boss, George Hearst, and his partners.

"At first," Charles said as he paused on the stairs and waved his arm across the landscape, "this was just a large pit. As they continued to dig, the sides began to slump, so they tried to construct timbered shafts. Problems arose because of the strange geological formation of the Comstock Lode. As you may have been told, this mine doesn't have a clearly defined vein of ore, and that, Jennifer DeSpain, is a miner's nightmare. Instead, the ore is found scattered here and there amidst walls of barren rock, layers of partly decomposed stone, sheets of clay, and underground reservoirs of hot water. That all makes for quite a challenge."

"Most people don't know anything about this," Jennifer said, peering around at the scene.

"No, they don't. Well, though deposits of gold were wide and could be reached easily, miners feared cave-ins if they chipped the ore with a hammer. An ordinary post-and-cap method of timbering, where timbers resemble a door frame, is no help in an excavation forty or more feet in height. Nor is it possible to use the so-called room-and-pillar system, in which columns of ore are left to hold up the ceiling. Comstock ore can scarcely hold itself up, let alone a cavern. What was needed was a system capable of being extended in any direction. Let's go inside, and I'll show you how they solved the problem."

Listening intently, Jennifer's sense of adventure intensified as she followed Charles into the big, noisy building. *He seems so intelligent, a man who can be trusted to know what he's talking about,* she thought.

Inside, the large building was one enormous room. Jennifer first noticed the mouth of the main shaft, an impressive sight. Great volumes of hissing, hot steam blasted through several square openings in the floor and rushed to the high ceiling. Above the shaft, hoisting works spun as cables wound and unwound from a fifteen-foot spool. She was surprised to see men calmly entering and leaving the very heart of the columns of steam. *I'll be going down there!* she thought and had to quickly put aside her fear.

The most impressive sight was a giant steam engine with a forty-foot, cast-iron flywheel. Jennifer stared in awe as the big wheel spun in rhythm with the deep chug-chug of the steam cylinders.

"That's a 110-ton flywheel," Charles yelled over the noise. "It drives a colossal pump rod made of sixteen-inch timbers strapped together with iron plates that go down the shaft for thousands of feet. That half-mile-long rod can lift two million gallons of water in twenty-four hours. It keeps the mine from filling up with water."

"This is incredible!" Jennifer shouted back. Her awe of the massive machinery had shoved aside her fear, at least for the moment.

"Look over here," Charles yelled, pulling Jennifer along by the hand. "These are the hoisting engines that lift and lower the cages full of men and tools. That's engineer Len Davis at the controls." Davis, a stern-faced man with a tense, muscular jaw, kept his eyes fixed on a large dial that showed the location of the cage in the tunnel as he operated the levers controlling the hoist. A bell beside Davis rang twice, and he applied the brakes, stopping the cables' movement instantly. "That bell connected to a pull rope is the only way the miners below can communicate with the engineer," Charles said.

"Come on, let's get in a cage so Davis can lower us down the main shaft." Charles held Jennifer's hand tightly as they boarded the cage. Her eyes were wide with the fear she could no longer restrain. "Don't worry, Jennifer. Len Davis can be trusted to take us down safely. To say that a man is an engineer is to say that he's an exceptional man—much above average!"

That assurance helped Jennifer only a little as a sense of alarm swept through her. The cage was a simple iron frame with a solid floor and open sides. Feeling her stomach rise to her throat as they rushed downward, she grabbed a side of the cage for support. Just as she moved to look over the edge, Charles pulled her back and held her tightly. "Men who have thrust a foot, elbow, or head outside the cage have hit a timber and suffered serious, even fatal, injuries in an explosion of flesh and bone," he warned.

She began to shake and pulled tighter into the comfort of his half-embrace. She was too frightened to pray. She could only cling to Charles's welcome grasp.

As they sped down the shaft, they passed a tremendous cavern. Through the wet steam Jennifer saw men with candles or lanterns in their hands. She heard busy voices and the clank of machinery. In another instant the two passengers could again see only the upward-fleeing sides of the shaft. Jennifer felt as if she were entering a forbidden and dark land of no return.

The cage stopped at the 1,500-foot level, where a main drift ran north and south along the line of the lode. At intervals were cross-cuts running east or west and short shafts that ran up and down to connect other levels. Along the floor ran narrow gauge tracks that moved carts of ore. Throughout the area were 14-inch beams lacing the large opening together.

As Charles and Jennifer stepped off the cage, she saw that candles and lamps burned everywhere, exposing the network of timbers. The temperature was over 100 degrees, and Jennifer felt faint in the sticky humidity. "I feel so light-headed," she said unsteadily.

Immediately Fitzgerald gently put his hands on her shoulders and eased her into a sitting position on a large rock. "You'll be all right in a minute," he said confidently. "Sometimes the abrupt change is unsettling." She felt comforted by his touch as she strained to regain her equilibrium and confidence.

Pleased with how the situation with Jennifer was developing, Charles thought, *Surely she's coming to trust me more and more. She'll be easy.* He kept a firm but gentle hand on her shoulder.

Ordinarily Jennifer would have moved away, but the attorney's touch had a calming effect upon her.

However, when her head cleared she pulled away from him, uneasy with how much she had enjoyed his care for her. After all, they had not known each other long at all. Wanting to get her mind on something else, she began to observe the pattern formed by the timbers connecting together.

Charles made no move to resume physical contact with Jennifer once he realized she was feeling better. Picking up a lit lantern, not wanting to scare Jennifer away by being too forward, he resumed his description of the mine and its workings. "This masterful creation is the idea of Phillip Deidesheimer, a graduate of the Freiberg School of Mines in Germany. He calls this arrangement 'square sets,' sort of a honeycomb."

Marveling at the timbered structure, Jennifer rose carefully to her feet. "So they can mine in any direction," she suggested. "It's like the frame of a building but underground."

"Yes. It's simple but effective," Charles confirmed. "Let's go where the miners are working."

Wiping the perspiration from her face, Jennifer took Charles's hand as they stepped carefully over the small tracks and debris covering the wet floor. The ceiling dripped water constantly, and the wind from great overhead blowers blew through the mine, making an eerie sound . A strong odor of wet earth and timbers hung heavy in the moist air. They passed through a cavern where the walls glittered as though studded with diamonds. "Is that gold and silver?" Jennifer asked, her heart beating rapidly.

Charles stopped, his pleasant smile showing in the yellow lantern light. It was more quiet here, and their voices echoed down the shaft. "No. That's iron, copper pyrite, and quartz crystal that is mingled with the ore. The silver ore is usually black and gray, and the gold is so light in color that it doesn't look like gold at all."

Running her hand over the cave wall, Jennifer noticed it was almost too hot to touch. She asked Charles why.

"Underground springs," he said knowledgeably. "The Comstock Lode is located in the midst of hot springs, probably caused by volcanic action."

The stuffiness, humidity, and heat made Jennifer feel dirty and hot and weak. *How these poor miners work in such conditions, I'll never understand,* she thought as they cautiously moved along.

Soon they heard the clinking of metal and the sound of men's voices. Candles and lanterns twinkled like stars in the night as Charles and Jennifer approached a crew of miners.

"Ho there!" Charles called out.

"Ho!" a miner called back, his voice echoing as it would in a canyon. The newcomers made their way to the five-man crew. The miners stopped working momentarily to see who the visitors were. With dirty and sweaty faces, they stared at Jennifer in disbelief. To see a beautiful woman deep in the pits of the mine, her face wet with perspiration and her eyes reflecting the lantern light, was a most unusual sight. Such an event made their workday into something special and would be the subject of conversation for a long time to come.

"I'm Charles Fitzgerald." Charles held his hand out to the nearest miner.

The sweaty young man in his early twenties shook the attorney's hand. "You the lawyer fella?" he asked.

"Yes," Charles admitted, "but don't worry, this isn't a legal visit." The miners were clearly relieved. "I'm showing Mrs. Jennifer DeSpain around the place—she runs *The Miner's News*."

The group of miners perked up at that information. "We shore like yore paper, ma'am," said a miner at the back of the group. "Yeah," they all agreed, nodding their heads.

Jennifer felt a sudden pity for this group of working men, isolated far below the surface, trying to make a living for their families in sweltering heat, cramped between imposing walls where danger lurked, much like the darkness just beyond their candles and lanterns. Yet she knew they were proud of their skills, their strength, their ability to tolerate the intolerable.

The appearance of the group would remain sharply etched in Jennifer's mind for the remainder of her life. The men wore only breechcloths or long underwear bottoms cut off at mid-thigh. All were drenched with perspiration, and their bodies glistened in the candlelight as though they had just come up from some subterranean lake. She couldn't help but think that each man's superb muscular form would delight a sculptor. To keep dirt out of their hair they wore narrow-brimmed caps or felt skullcaps cut from ordinary hats. They wore shoes to protect their feet from the sharp quartz. That was the extent of their safety equipment, and she knew instinctively that was not enough. Each dirty face smiled at her, welcoming her presence in their underground world of torment.

Seizing the opportunity to actually talk to the miners in their working habitat, Jennifer asked, "Can you leave your work for a few moments? I'd like to talk to you."

"Why, yes, ma'am," they said almost in unison. Throwing down their tools and working gear, the miners grabbed their lunch pails and sat on the ground.

Charles sat down also and asked, "Do you mind if Mrs. DeSpain asks some questions, boys?"

"Not at all," the first young miner said, eager to be helpful. "My name is Ben Taylor. We'll be glad to help you any way we can." The others grunted in approval, nodding their heads.

"The work down here seems so dangerous," Jennifer said. "So many things can go wrong. Do you ever worry about your safety?"

They all laughed, but Jennifer couldn't tell if it was the laughter of amusement or a laughter to release tension. "Comes with the job, ma'am," Ben finally said with a happy-go-lucky attitude. Apparently he was the leader of this small group, a tall, muscular young man with sparkling brown eyes and a quick smile.

"Do you have a family?" Jennifer asked him.

"I have a wife," Ben said halfheartedly, sounding as if he hardly ever got to see her. "We don't have any kids yet."

"What about her? Do you worry about what would happen to her if something happens to you?" Jennifer asked.

"Ma'am," the young man said, removing his felt cap and wiping the sweat from his brow, "ain't nothing got no guarantees. She's got to play what she's dealt, just like I do, just like everyone does."

A sudden pity for the young man surged within Jennifer. *Such a simple answer to such a complex problem. What a brave young man! I suppose they have to justify their situation in their own minds somehow.*

Charles could see that the tour of the mine wasn't having the effect on Jennifer that he'd hoped for. Instead of being impressed with the mining companies, she was obviously becoming more sympathetic to the plight of the workers. Even her reliance on Charles's strength in this frightening place had given way to her concern for the miners.

The men stared at Jennifer as they sipped lukewarm water from their canteens, happy to have her there even if it was only for a short time. She was a beautiful heroine in their eyes, one who had the courage to buck the rich and powerful mining companies. These men were brave in every way, and they had formed a small union, but they couldn't challenge the mining companies, their only source of lucrative or even livable income. To make much protest to the companies they worked for would be like a dog biting the hand that fed it. But this woman had the nerve to express their needs in her newspaper, to risk her own reputation and social standing for their sake. They admired and respected her for that.

"Do you do any blasting down here?" Jennifer asked.

"Nope," one of the miners said, crumbling some of the rock in his powerful hand. "In this area the stuff just crumbles. We dig it out with picks."

"I guess that's good," Jennifer said. "That makes the work easier, doesn't it?"

"Yeah, but that also means this stuff caves in easy," a toothless miner added.

About that time an eerie, creaking groan came from far back in the shaft. Jennifer jumped. "What was that?"

The miners all laughed . "That's just timber groanin'," Ben said. "There's so much clay in these walls that it expands when the air hits it, and that puts a lot of pressure on the timber. Just like in a house, the wood keeps contracting and expanding."

"Or it might have been a Tommyknocker," one of the men said, smiling mischievously.

Jennifer looked at Charles, who was having fun watching her interview the miners as he ate his bread and cheese. "What's a Tommyknocker?" she asked.

They all hid their laughter. "Well . . ." the toothless fellow said, rolling his eyes upward, trying to think how best to put it. "A Tommyknocker is a little feller that haunts the mines. They get blamed for the spooky things that occur around here. Why, one time I set one of my tools down right beside my boot. When I went to pick it up a minute later, it was plumb gone! I knowed for shore a Tommyknocker borrowed it and forgot to bring it back."

Jennifer smiled. She knew she was being told a tall tale. She wondered if Twain had ever written about the mythical creatures of the mines.

"Ma'am," the youngest of the miners piped up, a young freckle-faced boy of no more than eighteen, "you think he's kidding, but he ain't. Why, I seen a Tommyknocker once! I was trapped in a cave-in for two whole days, and a Tommyknocker visited me and sat with me to keep me company. They're as real as you and me!"

Jennifer smiled knowingly at the young man as she finished her tea. She understood the importance of such superstitions in the mining community, a way to keep the prospect of injury or worse from occupying your thoughts constantly.

At that moment a large rat scurried across her foot. "Ohhhh!" she screamed, grabbing Charles. He saw the rat and wasn't afraid of it, but he let Jennifer hold on to him anyway, enjoying her closeness.

"Don't be afraid, ma'am," Ben said as he fed the friendly rat a piece of bread. "These mines have thousands of rats, and we've taken a likin' to them. This scroungy little varmint just wants some lunch. Besides, these rats can always tell when there's going to be a cave-in. When we see the rats get nervous and head out, that tells us it's time to get to the surface."

"Oh," Jennifer said with a calmness she hoped hid her fear. Standing, she dusted off her dress and wiped her brow with the back of her sleeve. It was so hot and stuffy in the deep tunnel that she was ready to leave. "Thanks for speaking with me," she said to the group of miners. "I appreciate it more than I can say. I wish conditions were better for you all." Her comments brought encouragement to the miners but apprehension to the heart of Charles Fitzgerald.

"You can come back anytime, Miz DeSpain!" Ben told her, his white teeth showing a smile through his dirty face "We surely appreciate all you do for us in your paper."

As Jennifer and Charles walked away from the group, she

thought, *I can leave, but they have to keep working in this awful place.*
The brief visit had touched her deeply, and she knew something very
personal had happened to her. Unknown to her, something personal
had transpired within Charles as well, but the two inner events were
as different as night and day.

After stumbling for 100 yards over a floor covered with loose
rocks, they arrived back at the vertical shaft. Charles held his arm
out to keep Jennifer a safe distance from the edge. "Fall down this
shaft and they'd be lucky to find anything," he cautioned. He pulled
a cord that would ring the bell above, and soon a cage came to a stop
in front of them. They boarded, and as before he clutched her closely
to protect her from the jagged walls that would soon be passing by,
this time actually placing his arms around her. Exhausted from the
steam and heat, she relaxed in his arms. He reached over and pulled
the cord twice, a signal to the engineer to lift them out. The cage
swiftly ascended, leaving the depths behind. For a second she felt
faint because of the rapid change in atmosphere. Feeling a bit overcome, she trusted Charles to hold her safely.

At the top, walking with wobbly legs, Jennifer stepped from the
cage into the large warehouse-sized room. "What an experience that
was!" she exclaimed with a sigh.

"There's more," Charles told her. "Are you feeling up to it?" He
was still hoping to somehow convince her to have more feeling for
the mining companies than for the miners. Though he deeply
admired the way she had shown compassion for the men below, he
had a greater admiration for the power of George Hearst and the
other mining company executives—power he was determined to
make his own. The conflict within him between caring for others
and wanting to build his own empire had not lessened or ceased.

"Yes, I want to see the rest," Jennifer said wearily. "It just takes
me a while to get used to the change." Glancing behind her, she saw
the clouds of steam rising from the shaft she'd just left. *No telling how
many men are down there,* she thought, *working around the clock. I must
do all I can to help them. I so appreciate Charles bringing me here. Though
he works for the mining company, he must care about these men as much
as I do. I'm sure of it.*

~

After Jennifer regained her composure, she felt chilled because of her damp clothes. Charles borrowed a light coat for her as they continued to look at the Ophir's upper works. "These buildings off to the sides are where the blacksmiths, machinists, and carpenters work. You see, there are many more jobs in a mining company than those done by miners. It takes trainloads of timber to make these mines stable and quite a few carpenters to cut and fit the beams." He took her around the adjacent building, showing her the different trades at work.

Charles then took Jennifer to the millworks, just below the tunnel where carts emerged brimming with precious ore. The mill and smelter covered several acres, a giant and noisy building with all of its processes arranged in a downhill fashion in order to let gravity do the work. After climbing a long set of stairs, Charles and Jennifer watched everything from a catwalk high above. At one point he pointed below. "Watch that ore cart dump its load all by itself as it rolls to the end of the track. You see? Gravity at work. Now we'll follow the ore as it flows through those wooden shoots and into the stampers."

Charles led Jennifer as they moved along the walkway. The massive wooden building shuddered in rhythm with the powerful steam engines and the pounding of the massive stampers. A raw and offensive vapor of steam, oil, and chemicals filled the air. Scurrying men below tended and monitored the heavy, pulsing machines.

"I can't believe how big an operation a single mine is," Jennifer said, astounded. "It's simply overwhelming."

"Do you see those giant vats down there?" Charles asked. "The crushed ore goes in there to be spun and pulverized into a paste." He hoped Jennifer was being sufficiently impressed with the power and efficiency of the mining companies, so her admiration for them would overshadow her concerns about the safety of a few insignificant miners.

Jennifer watched the rows of huge vats bubble with a muddy-looking mixture. Many men were shoveling crushed ore into large pots. *If a man fell into one of those, he'd be dead instantly*, she thought gruesomely. *In a way this is all so glorious, and yet so tragic at the same time . . .*

Charles and Jennifer eventually came to some stairs by which they descended to the main floor. Men with shotguns were carefully guarding rows of huge kettles. "Here," said Charles, "as you might guess from the guards' presence, is where they begin to separate the gold and silver from the rock in a process called amalgamation. The muddy juice from the vats is poured into these kettles, where it's mixed with mercury. Both gold and silver dissolve in mercury, but the rock doesn't. Next, they heat the mercury compound in order to separate out the precious metals, which takes place down here." He pulled her along, eager to show her more.

Jennifer noticed that at the last level the area was cleaner and even more protected. "This is where our chemists work," Charles said as a guard opened the door to let them in. "Just over there is where the separation process takes place. They recover the mercury and use it over and over."

"Aren't all of these chemicals dangerous?" Jennifer questioned, wondering if they were in danger just by being in the room.

Charles shrugged and said, "Not really. Like anything else, they have to be handled properly." He directed her attention to another operation. "Lastly, the gold and silver are melted, then poured into these molds to be made into pure ingots."

Approaching a large steel door, Charles asked the guard to open it. When he took Jennifer inside, she almost fainted. Surrounded by large ingots of pure gold and silver she just stared at them. On one side of the small room gold ingots were neatly stacked on the floor. She marveled at the abundance of the beautiful yellow metal that drove men mad. On the other side, another pile of ingots sparkled with white metal that shone like a mirror. The scene practically took her breath away. "It's magnificent!" she said, her eyes wide with utter disbelief. "I could never have imagined seeing so much . . . What will they do with all of this?"

"It'll be taken to San Francisco, under heavy guard, and sold for cash. The United States government buys almost all of it for U.S. coins."

Jennifer turned. "I'll never forget this place, or this day. To think that I was surrounded by a million dollars!"

"Actually a little more," Charles estimated, smiling. His strategy was finally working. He was sure of it. But he was also enjoying the day because he liked being with her. "Having you here is worth more than all of this." He let his eyes fall to her face, and she saw his look of sincere admiration. Seeing a clock on the wall, he noted that it was already late afternoon. "Jennifer," he said hesitantly, placing a hand on her shoulder, "I don't want this day to end. Can I see you again sometime, soon I hope?"

Taking a long, deep look into Charles's dark blue eyes, Jennifer was sure she was in the company of a good man—kind, knowledge-able, and, as far as she could see, God-fearing. He had been every-thing she would expect from a gentleman and more. "Yes, Charles," she said pleasantly, her lips parted in a slight smile, "I'd love to see you again."

He wasn't sure he understood what was happening to him. In fact, he was sure he didn't understand. His goals were still basically the same; he would follow Hearst's orders implicitly. But he was also beginning to care deeply for this courageous newspaper woman.

While walking home, Charles and Jennifer were totally blind to the bewildered glances cast at what appeared to be two dirty miners walking along hand in hand.

When they reached Jennifer's house, Charles walked her up to the front door. "I've enjoyed our outing," he said.

"So have I, Charles," Jennifer said warmly. "I've learned so much today—it was the most exciting thing I can remember doing in a long time."

Taking her hand, Charles slipped his other arm around her and pulled her to him. He kissed her softly on the lips, and she didn't pull away.

For Jennifer, this was her first moment of passion with a man since Drake. Unafraid, hungry for a man's affection, she neverthe-less pulled away, saying, "I—I should go inside. My family . . ."

"Good night," Charles murmured politely as he turned to leave. "I'll talk to you soon."

"Good night, Charles," Jennifer called after him. She stood for a moment and watched him as he walked away, then turned and entered the house.

◦

Jennifer spent considerable time thinking about what she'd seen on the mining tour. Even the sermon she heard at church on Sunday confirmed her desire to help as the preacher spoke about the parable of the good Samaritan. She couldn't stop thinking about the miners' awful working conditions. Although their small union had managed to get their wages up to four dollars an hour, Jennifer felt that the mining companies could do much more in the way of safety for the men.

By Monday morning she was anxious to put her thoughts on paper. As soon as she arrived at the office, she began writing another editorial demanding that the mining companies make the necessary improvements. Jason worked by himself, his eyes cast downward, obviously not wanting to talk to anybody. Twain sat at the big desk he'd made his own, feverishly writing some new piece. When her editorial was half finished, she noticed Twain standing behind her, reading over her shoulder.

"What do you think of it so far?" Jennifer asked.

Twain turned and walked toward the open window. "I hate to tell anybody how to write, but in this case I'll make an exception. These fiery editorials are going to stir up a lot of trouble with the mining companies, and I'm not sure they'll get the reaction you want. Such writing won't win you their cooperation. The madder you make them, the more stubborn they'll become." He paused and turned to face her. It was time for his morning cigar, already in his hand. "Perhaps you could use a story to relate your feelings—show instead of tell."

With a finger on her lip, Jennifer pondered her experienced friend's suggestion. "You mean like in the New Testament, when Jesus used what He called parables. Instead of telling His disciples what He wanted them to know, He showed them with a story. I see it! That's how I can communicate the truth!" She jumped up and gave Twain a big hug. "Oh, I could just kiss you!"

For the first time Jennifer could remember, Twain was embarrassed. Flustered, he cleared his throat and said, "By golly, I . . . well . . . I suppose I'd better get back to my own work."

Hurrying back to her desk, Jennifer sat down, took the editorial she'd been working on, and threw it in the trash. "Perhaps a continuing saga of a fictitious miner and his family . . . I'll call the series 'Miner Tom.'"

Twain lit his cigar carefully and thoughtfully took a deep draw. "I think you're on to something. That would appeal to the miners much more than an editorial, and it shouldn't ruffle the feathers of the mining companies too much. Over time I should think you'd be able to make your point."

Smiling, Jennifer eagerly began writing descriptions of the characters she'd be using. *Miner Tom will be a quiet, strong, and gentle hero,* she thought. She stopped for a minute and stared out the window. *Will this make the difference?*

Over the next few years Jennifer added more and more episodes to her Miner Tom series and in this way let the miners know that she cared about their plight and let the mining companies know that she was determined to prod them into a greater concern and care for their workers. Those years weren't easy as Jennifer wielded the power of the pen, raised her children, and maintained a moderate friendship with only a few people. Her faith continued to be an important element in her life. Though generally content, at times she somehow knew that this portion of her earthly existence was a calm before the storm. She just prayed that she would be ready for whatever was to come.

PART THREE

THE MINES OF VIRGINIA CITY

13

Something in the Wind

As if the storms of work and words weren't enough for Virginia City, a windstorm that bowed to none came out of the Washoe Mountains and assaulted the town. The residents did their best to buckle down anything loose, but they knew the hurricane-like winds would easily demolish roofs and even whole cabins. Those who had lived there for some time couldn't help thinking back to previous storms. One blew the Catholic Church down the slope and two miles across the desert, smashing it into kindling wood. The citizens would store their valuables—their precious metals and money, and especially their ammunition and whiskey—underground. They would even lug pool tables into a cave so they could play a few quiet games while the earth above shook under the blast of the wind.

With her dress whipping around her legs and her hair flying wildly, Jennifer tried to hammer the last nail into the last board across the front windows of the office. A heavy gust caught the wood and ripped it from her hands, sending it end over end in a rolling cloud of dust. Holding her hair away from her eyes, she saw a shanty rolling down the abandoned street. Leaning into the wind, she tried to push through the front door before being carried away herself. Jason opened the door and pulled her inside, slamming the door behind her.

"I haven't seen wind like this since a hurricane blew into New Orleans when I was a child!" Jennifer yelled over the storm's roar.

"It's too dangerous to go outside. We'll just have to ride it out," Jason said, having experienced such windstorms before.

The building seemed to shake back and forth in the tremendous gusts as Jennifer peered through the window into the dark street. The sun was mostly blocked by the dust, and all the rubble flying by made the scene look even darker.

"Don't stand near the window," Jason warned. "Something might crash right through it!"

Moving away, Jennifer muttered nervously, "I'm really worried about Grant and Abby."

"I'm sure Lita is keeping them safe inside the house," Jason assured her. "She may not have much education, but she sure does a fine job of caring for those youngsters."

"I have to be sure. I must go home and . . ."

"Now, Jennifer, you listen to me, it's just too dangerous for you to go out there. If the children were home alone, I'd go check on them myself, but since Lita is there, and with the storm being so powerful, you'd best just settle in here."

Recognizing the wisdom of his words, Jennifer turned toward her desk as she pushed her hair back into place. She tried to concentrate on the work at hand, but it was difficult with the wind howling so loudly through the cracks in the building. A backward glance out the window made it look like they were on a train speeding through a dust storm. "This may sound odd," Jennifer said, "but I have the strangest feeling—like something momentous is about to happen."

Glancing up, Jason said, "These crazy and unpredictable storms make everyone feel that way. It'll blow itself out before long though."

"You don't understand," Jennifer insisted. "I believe something strange is going to happen soon!"

"That's always possible, especially in a town like this," Jason assured her. "Strange things are always happening or are about to happen here."

At times like these Jennifer wished Mark Twain were still around. He had a special way of helping others through the difficult moments that made some days almost intolerable. But a few weeks earlier he had finished his book, *Roughing It*, and said it was time to travel to New Orleans, where he planned on finishing some other books about life on the Mississippi. He had thanked Jennifer for her help, and she had thanked him for all he'd done for her and for the paper. The next morning he boarded the train and was gone. For days Jennifer had regretted his departure, but fortunately the daily work routine soon occupied her mind with other matters.

Jennifer pondered the storm outside and the disturbing premonition she'd just had. The calendar on the wall read 1873 in bold letters across the top. Well into the fourth year of running *The Miner's News*, Jennifer couldn't remember ever having such a strong intuition about anything before. Since she'd come west, Virginia City had expanded almost as far as possible in every direction. To the north, east, and south, the mountain was surrounded by desert; to the west was the barrier of the snowy Sierra mountains. Mining claims, houses, and businesses occupied all the space in between. The place seemed like it was going to bust at the seams, but still more people came—men with hungry eyes and a lust for the yellow dust. What could her strange feeling of foreboding mean?

Just then the front office door flew open, and a heavy cloud of dust blew in along with a young lady wearing a man's hat and overcoat. She pushed the door closed against the wind until it latched securely. When she saw Jason and Jennifer staring at her curiously, she rushed over to Jennifer, her face full of fear. "Are you the lady who runs this paper?" she asked, out of breath.

"Yes, I am. My name is Jennifer DeSpain," Jennifer said sympathetically. *Why would such a pretty girl be coming here during a dangerous storm?* she wondered, surveying the girl with a round face and a freckled, arched nose. Flaxen straight hair fell from beneath the felt hat, and the girl's hazel eyes were almost in tears.

"Mrs. DeSpain, you have to help me! Ben told me many times that if something happened I should come to you. You met him down in a mine one day, when you were on a tour with that lawyer. It was a long time ago—do you remember?"

Immediately the vivid picture of that small group of miners came to mind. *How could I ever forget?* she thought. She pictured the half-naked young leader with a dirty face and a bright smile. "Yes, I remember," she answered.

"I'm Katherine Taylor, Ben's wife. They've had Ben down in the mine almost a week, and nobody will tell me what's going on! For all I know, he might be dead!" She broke into tears.

Jason came around the counter swiftly, took Katherine by the arm, and led her to a chair. "Sit down," he said, gently helping her. "I'll get you a cup of coffee."

Dragging a chair over beside Katherine, Jennifer sat down, instinctively ready to take some notes. "He's in the Ophir mine, correct?"

"No. The Consolidated Virginia. Ben hasn't worked in the Ophir for almost a year."

Jennifer probed her memory as she held a pencil to her lip. "Jason, who owns the Consolidated Virginia?"

Returning with a hot cup of coffee and handing it to Katherine, Jason replied, "I think that's Fair and his gang. They've been known to pull some fast ones."

Katherine took a sip of the hot coffee as she tried to calm down. "I'm worried sick. Why would they keep my husband down in a mine for so long and not let him come up? I've been trying to wait patiently, but finally even this terrible storm couldn't keep me quiet anymore."

"I don't know what the answer is, but I intend to find out," Jennifer answered. "Tell me all you can about the situation."

Katherine related how she and Ben lived modest lives, saving their earnings in hopes of accumulating sufficient funds to eventually move to a better environment, perhaps Colorado, and raise a family there. Since just talking about it seemed to calm her nerves, Jason and Jennifer listened to her dreams, the same kind of dreams expressed by most young mining families in Virginia City and other mining towns of the West.

Jennifer didn't know exactly what she would do, but she knew she would do *something*, as God directed and enabled her. She shared those thoughts with Katherine, and that assurance seemed to relieve most of the woman's fears.

The winds diminished as the afternoon grew brighter, and the heavy dust clouds finally gave way to new sunlight. After Katherine expressed her gratitude and left for home, Jennifer turned to Jason. "I'm going to pay a visit to the offices of the Consolidated Virginia."

"I should come with you. This might not be a situation a woman should face alone."

"Then again, because I'm the owner of this newspaper, they'll have more respect for me than they would for you. And if you were to come with me, they might see that as a sign of weakness on my part."

"Just be careful," Jason said as he stood to face Jennifer. "Those men are shrewd and relentless, and you can't trust them to be truthful. Who knows what this is really all about."

Jennifer's jaw tensed as she left the office. Jason watched her walk down the street strewn with debris. A few others had gone outside to inspect the damage left by the storm. *She certainly has a nose for news—and the courage to face issues head-on,* he thought. *I just hope she doesn't get hurt by some of those wolves—for her sake and for theirs!*

⁓

With her purpose clearly in mind, Jennifer made her way to Charles Fitzgerald's office, ignoring the rubbish the wind had blown everywhere. She had decided it would be advisable to speak with Charles before going to the Consolidated Virginia owners. "There's certainly something strange going on," she remonstrated. "And I'm determined to help Katherine and Ben any way I can."

Shaking his head at her amazing story, Fitzgerald felt compelled to help, though he could not bring himself to do so in a way that would endanger his working relationship with the mining company owners. He'd grown to admire Jennifer greatly, but he admired money even more. If fact, although he'd said nothing to Jennifer, he fancied that he had actually begun to fall in love with her, and he spent a great deal of time dreaming about acquiring a fortune and then asking her to marry him. In reality he had no idea of what love really was or what it took to have a successful marriage, but he held on to his fantasies anyway. As always, he was glad to see her today, happy to have her pretty face brighten his dull office.

"Can you help them?" Jennifer asked, her green eyes pleading for Charles's professional assistance.

"It's not easy to walk into a nest of rattlesnakes and ask what they're up to," Charles said with a shrug. "But I do have ways of finding things out. The Consolidated Virginia is owned by a fellow we call Slippery Jim. His real name is James Fair, and he's a greedy, selfish man not above breaking the law. Ironically, one of his partners, John Mackay, is one of the finest men you'll ever find. Another partner, James Flood, is the real financial brains of the outfit, but also the one most likely to engage in shady business practices. He and Fair are undoubtedly up to something.

"A ways back Mackay, Fair, Flood, and a fellow named O'Brien bought the Hale & Norcross mine just below your house and made a little money with it, mostly by manipulating the value of the stocks. Then they bought the Consolidated Virginia and the California mines adjacent to it. Neither of those mines had ever produced anything, but they've surely dug much deeper by now. I'll see what I can find out tonight. Talk is cheap."

Jennifer smiled. She knew that if anyone could find out what was going on, the attorney could. "Please let me know as soon as you can," she said.

Charles enjoyed being any kind of help to Jennifer. He wished she'd ask more of him, but he figured that before long he'd be a millionaire, and then their relationship would really develop. Women were always impressed with wealth, he felt. "I'll come by in the morning to tell you whatever I've learned."

As Jennifer stood, so did the lawyer. He came around his big desk and took her hand. She responded with a pleasant smile but briskly pulled away. "I must be going. I was so upset about the Taylors' dilemma that I didn't even go check on the house and the children. That windstorm was frightening, but God protected us, didn't He?"

"Sure. I guess He did," Charles replied weakly. "Maybe we can get together for dinner one evening," he suggested, not wanting to talk about God or spiritual matters.

I'm so glad to hear him giving credit to God for our safety despite that terrible storm. Swinging toward the door, Jennifer said, "That sounds fine, but right now my greatest concern is what's going on in the Consolidated Virginia mine. I have a feeling this is big news."

∼

After the windstorm finished its work in Virginia City and moved on, Lita made sure the children were all right and surveyed the house to see what damage had been done. Then, assuming Jennifer would arrive home soon, she sat down to wait. She began to reflect on how much her life had changed since leaving New Orleans. She had become used to the dry Nevada climate, and she didn't complain much, except about how hard it was to prepare meals since not everything was available, especially some of the family's favorites like fresh vegetables, fresh fish, crawfish, and pecans. The main staples had become meat and potatoes, though sometimes fruit would arrive from California. Since Lita did most of the grocery shopping, she was always hoping something more tasty would accidentally find its way to the store, but it rarely did.

She remembered how one day after grocery shopping, trying to be content with the same old regular food, she left the store carrying two large boxes of groceries. From across the street Abe Washington noticed Lita for the first time. He was a blacksmith who mainly shoed mules, an endless task. His arms were as big as most men's legs, and some said he had the strength of five men. Well over six feet tall, Abe generally moved slowly, his huge bulk weighing over 300 pounds. He'd come from Georgia, anxious to exercise his newly acquired freedom, and found his way to a place where mules were plentiful, Virginia City.

When Abe saw Lita struggling with two boxes of groceries, he rushed up to her and easily lifted the weight from her arms.

"What you doin'?" Lita demanded as she swatted at the big black man who now held all her groceries.

With his arms full, Abe couldn't protect himself from Lita's swatting hand. "I'm just tryin' to tote these boxes for ya!"

"I didn't ask for no help," she said, blocking his way. "Give back my groceries and get on along." Abe was trying to smile. Lita could see he was older than she was. He was the first black man she'd seen since she and the DeSpains had moved west of the Mississippi River.

"I just tryin' to help!" Abe protested.

Lita stopped swatting at Abe and gave him a thorough looking-over, noticing his huge, well-toned muscles. He wore a brown derby hat and overalls with suspenders. He had gray hair and big teeth that looked like piano keys when he smiled. She realized he was a find. "So follow me," she ordered, "and put some of dem muscles to work!"

Gratefully, Abe followed her home like a lost dog. After setting the groceries down beside the back porch, he waited patiently.

"Now what you want?" Lita challenged.

Looking at Lita with innocent brown eyes, he shrugged his massive round shoulders, his huge hands hanging loosely. That was his only answer.

Lita stared at him with a long, scornful look. But she was merely playing; she had no intention of cutting him loose just yet. "I suppose you want somethin' to eat."

"Why, yes'm," Abe said, his face brightening with a smile. He was a big man with a powerful appetite.

"Sit in dat chair and wait," Lita ordered as she disappeared into the kitchen. After a short while she returned with a plate of fried grits and salt pork. "Dis all I got right now—it'll have to do."

"It smell right good," Abe said as he dug in.

Lita watched Abe eat heartily. It gave her great pleasure to feed a hungry man, and watching the food flow down his throat reminded her of earlier days, for her father and brothers had been big men, though not as big as Abe. Smiling, she sat down and studied the big man thoughtfully.

For weeks afterwards Abe would often loiter near the back door, hoping to be helpful—and to get some more of Lita's cooking. He was there when the windstorm struck and helped Lita secure the doors and windows. As the wind grew into frightening gusts, Abe noticed the small back porch beginning to sway and creak as if it were about to fly away. He casually opened the back door, stepped out into the gale, and grabbed the two posts supporting the porch, holding them steady. He wrestled with the wind for hours, hugging the posts with his powerful arms, making sure the porch stayed where it belonged. Lita and the children watched him through a window, awestruck with his strength, stamina, and courage.

That afternoon, when the winds subsided, Abe came inside, and Lita gave him a cup of coffee. She brushed straw from his hair and shirt as he slumped in a chair in exhaustion. He was reluctant to leave, enjoying the personal attention.

After a while Lita said, "You better go on home."

Standing slowly, Abe picked up his old derby hat. "I surely wish I didn't have to."

"It's all right," Lita assured him, "you can come back anytime you wants."

Abe went out the back door slowly, shutting it gently behind him.

"He sure is a big man," Abby said, watching him leave.

"Strong too!" Grant added. "Did you see how he held the porch steady against the wind?"

"You children get on out of the kitchen now, so I can fix some supper," Lita said, shooing them away. Later, after all three of them ate, she sat and relaxed and thought about Abe. She had never met a man like him.

When Jennifer arrived home, she was glad to find everything still in its place. "I thought maybe you three had blown away," she said lightly to hide her tension.

"Not us," Abby said as she ran to her mother. "That big man was here. He held the house down when the wind tried to take it away!"

Glancing at Lita, Jennifer said, "She must be talking about Abe."

Bashfully rolling her big brown eyes, Lita replied, "Yes'm. He happened to be here when the wind come, and he helped hold things down. Then we was stuck with him." Secretly Lita was proud of Abe's fascination with her.

"If I didn't know better, Lita, I'd think you're growing sweet on that fellow," Jennifer said playfully.

"Oh mercy, Miss Jenny, why you think of somethin' so crazy!" Lita busied herself with cleaning the house that she'd already cleaned, not wanting to be teased about Abe, though she couldn't stop thinking about him either.

Jennifer went to the front room and sat on the sofa to relax. It had been a long and trying day, and yet she still felt like something momentous was going to happen. *Maybe I'm developing that sixth sense for news that Mr. Cromwell always talked about—"like a hound dog sniffing out a beef steak," as he used to say.* She wondered what kind of information Charles would turn up. Maybe that was what she was anticipating. She reflected on God's goodness in protecting her and her family that day, and asked Him for courage for whatever was still to come.

~

The next day when Jennifer arrived at the office, she found Charles Fitzgerald standing on the front porch dressed in a fine brown suit and waiting for her. Eagerly he reported, "I don't have all the answers, but I did find out some things."

"Come inside," Jennifer said, opening the door.

Over a cup of coffee, Charles poured out his information like a gossip over a fence. Although Jason didn't care much for Fitzgerald, his curiosity made him move closer so he could hear.

The attorney leaned back and locked his hands behind his head, his eyes thoughtful. "It seems that James Fair's partnership has been working the Comstock Lode from both ends. What I mean is, after he bought the Consolidated Virginia and the California mines, reports flooded the market that they were showing great promise and were starting to produce. However, I can't find anybody who can verify that either mine produced anything. But back in San Francisco stocks went up, bringing Fair a lot of money." He shifted positions in his chair and ran a hand through his black hair.

"It wouldn't be the first time such a thing has been done," Charles continued. "But anyway, in the last week or so, reports claimed that what had looked promising now looked hopeless. Of course, this drove stocks in those mines way down. The strange part is that Flood, Fair's partner, has quietly been buying up their own stocks."

Amazed, Jennifer asked, "Then why are the miners being kept locked in the mine?"

"Probably because the owners don't want them to talk too much," the lawyer said. "Might be they've found nothing down there, or Fair and his cronies might just be trying to make a profit by selling high and buying low."

"I think there's more to it than that," Jennifer said. "Maybe they hit a big strike."

"That's possible." Fitzgerald nodded. "And he's holding the miners until he can buy his own stock back."

"I think it's time to bring this to the attention of the public, to print an article about it," Jennifer said, her mind already working. "Thank you, Charles. You've been a great help." She stood and walked toward her desk.

Standing, Fitzgerald smiled at her. "Anytime," he said smoothly. "I'm always glad to help my best girl." Within himself, he felt good about assisting Jennifer like this, but also nervous about uncovering some of the mining companies' sneaky tactics. He cared for the newspaper woman very much, but without men like Fair and Hearst he would never make his fortune.

~

"Here we go," Jennifer said after reviewing the article she'd written. It accused Fair of deliberately lying and said that he had been manipulating stocks through false mining reports, but that worst of all, he was holding men underground against their will.

Jason rolled his pale blue eyes. "You're actually going to *print* this? You're out of your mind, Jennifer! Those men have tons of money, and believe me, they'll retaliate! This is like trying to hold back a windstorm with a bandanna!"

"It's our responsibility as a newspaper to print the truth. I don't care about Fair's stock manipulations really. I just want to pressure him into releasing the men he's keeping captive."

Shaking his head, Jason set her story down on the big table where he would set the type for the paper. "You're sure you want to do this?"

"Absolutely!" Jennifer said without hesitation.

"Well, like you said, here we go. This will surely get their attention."

Jennifer admired Jason's spunk. *He has many good qualities,* she thought. *If only I could convince him that his drinking is holding him hostage just like Fair is doing with those men in the mine. If only I could persuade Jason to allow Jesus to set him free!*

~

The Miner's News caused quite a stir around town the next morning. As far as the stock manipulations, no one held any animosity toward the mining companies for that—they expected it from them. But everyone wanted to know why Fair and his company were holding miners against their will. Like ripples in a pond, the news spread, leading the citizens of Virginia City to want answers *now*.

Unfortunately, James Fair could not be found for comment, and the miners continued to be held against their will. The following day Fair made a statement in the *Territorial Enterprise*. He insisted that the miners had to be held temporarily so they couldn't distort highly important information that might strongly affect the mining market. He insisted the miners were being well taken care of with good food and adequate sleeping arrangements. He denied being guilty of any wrongdoings and said, "What is happening is merely the nature of the business."

Outraged, Jennifer threw the copy of the *Territorial Enterprise* she'd been reading onto the floor. "What a bunch of scoundrels! James Fair is a greedy, selfish, mean man! I thought after our publishing news about the captive miners he'd let them go." She was literally shouting, something she rarely did.

"Calm down," Jason said softly. "It's not over yet. I'm sure there are other avenues . . ." He drew closer. "Maybe some kind of legal action could get those miners out of there."

Jennifer perked up at once, her eyes flashing. "I think you're right. I remember something like this back in New Orleans. When the war was over, the Union army continued to hold some prisoners until they filed something or other." She swiftly grabbed a few things. "I'll be back. I'm going to see Charles. I'm sure he'll want to help." She left quickly, slamming the front door behind her.

Jason didn't like the idea of having Charles Fitzgerald offer help and advice to Jennifer. He just didn't trust an attorney who worked for the mining companies. He slapped his head lightly with the palm of his hand, annoyed at himself for telling Jennifer to seek legal counsel. *I should've known she'd rush straight to Fitzgerald.*

CHAPTER

~ 14 ~

Habeas Corpus

On her hurried way to her attorney friend's office, Jennifer's thoughts ran wild. Frustrated, somewhat angry at herself, she felt that she had let the miners and their families down. For several years now she had looked out for their welfare through *The Miner's News*. She did not believe there was any stronger weapon than the printing press, and yet in this situation her pen had failed to get the miners released. Charles Fitzgerald was her last hope. She hoped his legal prowess could make a difference.

Once inside Fitzgerald's plush office, Jennifer pleaded her case. "There must be some kind of legal document you can file against Fair for holding those men against their will. Their families are worried to death and have no idea what's really going on. Charles, can't you do something to help?"

The attorney sat back in his tall chair with his hands folded in front of his face. He used the appearance of deep thought to hide the fact that he was a bit worried. After long, uncomfortable moments of contemplation, he finally spoke. "Jennifer, please understand. Filing a document like that could cost me my job. It's not that I don't care about the miners, but . . . well, a lawyer who represents one mining company can't make trouble for other mining companies. The situation would have to directly concern the company that employs me before I could get involved."

"Are you saying you won't help?" Jennifer asked, disappointed because her friend's response wasn't what she'd expected.

"I didn't say that," Fitzgerald quickly said in his defense. He would in no way endanger his lucrative position with George Hearst, but neither did he want to harm Jennifer's admiration for him. Trying to preserve both, he chose his words carefully. "I'm just saying I personally can't file anything against Fair. That doesn't mean *you* can't."

Jennifer thought for a moment, then said, "I'm no lawyer. What kind of legal document can *I* file?"

"Well, let me think about this for a minute. It isn't that uncommon to hold men in the mine, and the miners usually don't grumble about it—they're often paid extra wages for that time. It's simply the mine owner's way of preventing any premature disclosures about what's happening down in the tunnels. I don't recall any legal action being filed for such a situation before, but . . ." Fitzgerald picked up a law book and began turning the pages. "I suppose you could get the families to file for unlawful detention, but that would take a while— the miners would already be released by the time the court does anything."

"I heard about some legal tactic . . . I can't quite remember . . . it was a long time ago in New Orleans. A man was required to appear in court or something like that," Jennifer said.

"I know what you're referring to," Charles said, leaning forward. "It would mean coming at things from a different angle, but it just might work. You could file a writ of *habeas corpus*, which would require the miners to appear in court so Fair could formally lodge his complaint against them. Any judge who refused to honor a writ of *habeas corpus* would risk being removed from office."

"Perfect! Can you help me draft the document?" Jennifer asked.

"That I can most certainly do!" Fitzgerald answered, happy that he could please Jennifer without putting his own work or wealth in jeopardy. He removed a quill, took out a piece of paper, and began to write. "You'll have to take this to the courthouse and file it . . ."

~

Just before Jennifer left the attorney's office, Fitzgerald advised her to get Katherine Taylor's name on the writ, since Katherine had a direct interest in the situation because her husband was one of the miners being confined. Jennifer went straight to Bluebell's, a well-established bakery where Katherine worked.

As she hurried through the town, which was quieter than usual, Jennifer could feel the tension and unrest. Various small groups marked by a diversity of dialect and appearance were engaged in conversation about Virginia City's current controversies. An elderly bearded man dressed in a well-worn and dirty suit approached her. "Good afternoon, madam. I'm Henry Abbot. Aren't you the editor of *The Miner's News?*" He touched the brim of his dusty hat politely.

"That's right," Jennifer answered a little impatiently, eager to find Katherine and get the legal documents filed.

"I'm a mine owner," Abbot went on to say. "I own a few mines just north of here. Speaking for my friends and myself, we are most interested in any news about the Consolidated Virginia. What's happening down there? Are they going to release those men anytime soon?"

This poor gentleman has seen better days, Jennifer thought. *Like everyone else here, he keeps himself going by hoping for some good news.* Taking a deep breath, she responded, "We should know something soon."

Abbot smiled, showing his yellow teeth. "Something is going on, isn't it? Something the Consolidated Virginia doesn't want us to know about."

"I'm not sure," Jennifer said harshly. "I just want to see those miners released." She pushed on past him and made her way down the dry, dusty street.

Five minutes later Jennifer entered Bluebell's. The strong yeasty aroma of freshly baked bread caught her off guard as she flashed back to her days working in a bakery in New Orleans. She remembered the long, torturous hours of demanding physical labor with regret. For a moment she thought she saw the glowering face of Mr. Dumont in front of her. She quickly dismissed the unpleasant memory, approached the counter, and tapped a small bell.

Katherine approached from the back, her face lighting up when she saw Jennifer. "Do you have news for me?" she asked excitedly, wiping her flour-covered hands on her apron.

"There is something we can do, but I need your help!"

"Anything!" Katherine said eagerly.

Pulling out the document, Jennifer explained the strategy and finished by saying, "We need to file this at the courthouse right away."

Quickly removing her apron and brushing flour from her dress, Katherine's hazel eyes lit up with joy. Her round face held a pretty smile. She was a farm girl from Virginia who had been lured west by a handsome husband and his promises of striking it rich. She'd grown up on a farm, where she shared all the strenuous responsibilities of farm life, including the physical demands of using heavy tools and handling teams of horses. With her strong arms and wide shoulders, she found kneading a fifteen-pound ball of dough an effortless task.

As soon as Katherine told her boss she would be gone for a little while, she and Jennifer went straight to the courthouse, where they located the clerk and filed their grievance. "Sign here," the little man with a handlebar mustache said, handing Katherine a quill.

"When will we know something?" she asked as she scratched out her name.

With a hint of arrogance, the balding little black-haired man skimmed over the page, reviewing the essential elements of the document. He lifted his droopy eyes and replied evenly, "The judge will have to acknowledge this by tomorrow." He couldn't help but wonder how two women knew how to file a court document. He was of the school that felt women had no business dabbling in men's affairs.

Sensing the clerk's disdain, Jennifer communicated a silent message with her eyes. Katherine understood perfectly, and they quickly left.

Once outside the courthouse, Katherine asked, "How will we know when the judge has made a decision?"

Thinking for a moment, Jennifer said, "I'll ask Jason to keep watch down here. I'm certain they'd be reluctant to tell us lowly women anything."

Nodding in agreement, Katherine understood. "I don't think I'll be able to stand the suspense tomorrow. Can I come over to your office and wait with you?"

Giving her new friend a wide smile, Jennifer placed her hand on Katherine's shoulder. "Why, of course you can. You're most welcome."

"Thank you, Jennifer. I don't know how I would have managed if you hadn't helped."

"It's not over yet," Jennifer warned. "Battling with these tycoons is like handling rattlesnakes—we'll have to be very careful."

~

The next morning brought clear skies and a sun that grew more intense as it rose in the eastern sky. News of the writ had spread, and the air was hot, dry, and still as the townspeople milled about, quietly waiting for word from the courthouse.

Katherine sat at the big desk across from Jennifer's. Jennifer had requested that Jason remain at the courthouse and rush back when he heard some news. Jennifer kept herself busy with some writing, while Katherine idly watched, biting her fingernails agitatedly.

"I don't mean to keep you from your work," Katherine said innocently, "but I'm too nervous to just sit here. How did you learn how to write, and to run a newspaper?"

Jennifer patiently answered, "When I lived in New Orleans, I worked in a bakery for a cruel man, and I needed a better job. A paper in New Orleans hired me, and I started at the bottom, literally—I worked in the basement. Thanks to some good men there, I learned the newspaper business."

"You worked in a bakery?" Katherine said with surprise. "You know how to bake?"

"Oh yes," Jennifer boasted. "My specialty is French pastries."

Katherine smiled. "All we cook here are bread and cakes. These miners wouldn't know a pastry from a dry biscuit." She paused a moment, then curiously asked, "Are pastries hard to make?"

"They're quite time-consuming," Jennifer answered. "I'm afraid

I wasn't strong enough to handle the heavy work of kneading dough. I found journalism much more to my liking."

"I like working in the bakery," Katherine muttered. "I was raised on a farm in Virginia, and we worked hard from daylight to dark. The bakery doesn't seem very difficult compared to that. I'm fortunate because it's hard for a woman to find a decent job out here."

"That's true," Jennifer agreed as she got up from her desk and went to pour them both some coffee. "So what brought you to Virginia City?"

"Ben lived on the farm next to ours, and from our first meeting at a young age we were madly in love." Katherine pulled at her long flaxen hair and had a dreamy look on her face as she told her story. "One day Ben came over and asked my father for my hand, and later we married and everything was fine. But when we told our families we were coming west, they got upset, said we should stay there and inherit the farmland someday. But Ben was convinced we could make a fortune out here, mostly from all the things he'd read. We thought we could practically pick up gold and silver right off the street." Katherine's face quickly changed, her bright smile giving way to a forlorn look.

"When we got here, we were sadly disappointed. There were hundreds of others like us, people who knew nothing about mining or surviving in the West. We had to live in a tent for a while. Ben finally got a job as a mucker, the lowest man on the totem pole in a mine, but we were happy because that paid good money."

"What's a mucker?" Jennifer asked curiously. She thought she'd learned all the mining terms by now.

"He shoveled rock off the floor and shoveled it into an ore cart. It's hard work, but Ben is strong, and he was happy to work so close to the gold ore."

Jennifer served Katherine a hot cup of coffee and walked over to the window. The town was like a passenger train that had rolled to a stop in the middle of nowhere. Everyone had a dubious look that asked, *What's really going on?* Turning back from the window, Jennifer realized that Katherine needed to keep talking.

"Ben is all I have," Katherine continued. "He's a good man, and he takes good care of me. If I lose him . . ."

"Don't worry," Jennifer said, coming closer to Katherine. "God loves us, and He has a way of taking care of us when things are out of our control."

"That sounds like something I'd read about Miner Tom and his family in your paper. Do you know how many people buy your paper just to read the latest chapter in that story?"

"Really?" Jennifer asked. "I know we've been selling a lot of newspapers, but we've made many changes in the paper, so I just figured different people bought our paper for different reasons."

"Ben has told me all the miners love Miner Tom. He sounds like one of them. How do you think up all those situations Tom gets into?"

Jennifer smiled, pleased to hear that the character she'd invented was so popular. "I listen to what happens to miners and their families, then I write something similar."

"It's nice to know someone cares," Katherine said.

"Yes, it is. And remember, most of all, God cares about what is happening to us. That's why He sent His Son Jesus to be our Saviour." She wanted to say more but didn't want to scare Katherine away by being too direct.

Jennifer was glad to visit with Katherine as they awaited news from Jason.

～

The friends Abby had fallen in with at school were a rebellious lot. Her little group consisted of two older boys and another young girl, all of whom loved to defy authority and do whatever they pleased. Drawn to their rebellious ways, Abby quickly became friends and was considered one of the gang. One of their favorite pastimes was missing school as they hid behind one of the mills, where the two older boys would roll cigarettes and throw rocks down the hill at mule teams passing by, trying to spook the animals. Abby adored the two older boys for their daring independence, a quality she couldn't name or verbalize but nevertheless imitated. When a concerned citizen who had appointed himself somewhat of a truancy officer captured the small band and told them he was taking them home so their parents could discipline them, Abby protested wildly, calling the portly man names and kicking at his shins.

"What dis?" Lita exclaimed when she opened the door to see a strange man holding Abby by her thin arm.

"I'm afraid young Abby here has gotten into trouble," John Miller explained. He wore a dark suit and a derby hat. His walrus mustache hid the bottom of his flat face, bringing attention to his beady little eyes. "I caught her and her friends playing hooky. Even worse, they were throwing rocks at mule teams. She needs to be disciplined, or she could get herself into serious trouble." The man didn't elaborate on what kind of trouble he meant, but his tone of voice was frightening.

Her eyes wide with surprise, Lita began pulling Abby into the house. "Yes, suh, we'll take care of it." Closing the front door on the man, Lita turned to Abby, her face evidencing disbelief. "What wrong with you, girl? You know you can't just run away from school!"

"Leave me alone!" Abby yelled as she pulled her arm loose. "You're not my mother!" Abby ran up the stairs to her room and slammed the door behind her.

Turning, Lita muttered to herself, "What am I supposed to do now? That child gonna be trouble."

To some, Lita appeared abrasive, but she was actually easygoing, taking life in stride from day to day. She'd never had any children of her own, but she considered taking care of Abby and Grant the closest thing she'd ever experience to motherhood. It hurt her deeply that Abby had become so rebellious and had now fallen in with the wrong kind of friends, the kind who constantly caused trouble. Unwilling to even think of laying a hand on Abby, she decided she'd better go see Miss Jenny and tell her what had happened.

Donning her large-brimmed straw hat, Lita set out for the newspaper office. She moved slowly down the street, her shadow following in the dust. When she got to *The Miner's News*, she found Jennifer conversing with another woman. Jennifer was surprised by Lita's visit.

Lita shook her head in dismay and waved her hand in the air. "Miss Jenny, I don't know what to do. A man brought Miss Abby home, said she was skippin' school. Then she shouted at me and run off to her room. Dat child's headed for trouble."

"Oh dear," Jennifer moaned as she got up from her desk. "Lita, I'll have to talk to her when I get home. We're expecting some very important news anytime, and I can't leave right now."

"All right, Miss Jenny," Lita said, turning toward the door. "I just wanted you to know, that child's got me worried somethin' awful."

After Lita left, Jennifer looked at Katherine sadly. "Abby is my eight-year-old. She's always been headstrong, especially since she lost her father years ago. Perhaps I've been too lenient with her. Grant, my son, who is a year older, is just the opposite—so studious and responsible. He's actually taken an interest in the newspaper and spends all his spare time working with Jason."

"Ben and I have always wanted children, but we haven't been blessed that way yet," Katherine said, almost apologetically.

Jennifer smiled. She liked Katherine and had a growing respect for her. But the time still passed slowly, like waiting for a long and sluggish train to pass when one is eager to cross the tracks. The afternoon sun remained motionless in the cloudless sky and seemed to yawn like it had nowhere to go or nothing to do.

～

Darkness had almost totally fallen upon Virginia City. The day had been long and draining, but Katherine had eventually lost herself in a book while Jennifer fought to keep her mind on her work. Jennifer wandered over to the coffeepot but decided she couldn't drink any more. Suddenly a shout came from outside, then another.

Katherine threw her book down and rushed over to the window. "Something's happening," she said, her hope rising.

Jennifer and Katherine stepped outside onto the front walkway. Down the street they could see men running and waving their hats. Jason soon approached, running as fast as he could. He jumped onto the front porch, barely able to speak. "The judge . . . has . . . ordered release . . . of the men . . . They should be coming up . . . anytime now."

"What happened?" Jennifer questioned.

Bent over with his hands on his knees, Jason gulped great volumes of air before his breathing finally became nearly normal. "The judge ordered Fair . . . to bring the men before him . . . and to inform him of the charges against them." He took in more air. "Fair took his time but finally agreed to release the men. What are we doing here? Let's get to the mine!"

Grabbing Katherine, who was wavering between shock and tears of relief, Jennifer pulled her along the dusty street as they hurried toward the shaft house of the Consolidated Virginia mine. A multitude of people rushed ahead of them, everyone in a hurry to watch the miners regain their freedom and to find out why they'd been confined. Fighting their way up the steep street, Jennifer and Katherine soon grew out of breath and had to slow down.

The excitement built like a flood as people gathered from all directions. Jennifer and her friends soon found their way to the edge of a waiting crowd and made their way forward until they were at the front. Guards held the crowd at bay, holding up their hands to urge the crowd to remain peaceful.

Soon a torch and kerosene lamps were lit to dispel the increasing darkness. The crowd waited patiently, anxious to see the group of miners emerge from their prison. Katherine took Jennifer's hand and squeezed tightly, her eyes fixed on the shaft house.

Yellow beams of light emerged from the steamed-up windows. A man could be seen holding the door. His attention seemed directed to the inside of the shaft house. He was evidently talking to someone there and ignored the crowd. The man stood this way for several minutes as everyone watched him silently. Another man finally stepped outside just like he might on a typical day, a miner weary from long hours of working in the steamy caverns. More miners followed closely behind and quickly made their way down a slight slope toward those gathered below.

The crowd gave out a huge roar, welcoming the oppressed miners back to the real world of fresh air and roomy space. The miners responded by raising their hands in a sign of victory, their white teeth and eyes contrasting with their darkened and dirty faces. Unable to wait any longer, Katherine ducked under the rope and rushed over to Ben. He picked her up as the two hugged and kissed each other jubilantly. Following her example, other wives did the same, ignoring the guards and rushing to embrace their husbands.

Jennifer enjoyed watching Katherine and Ben's love for each other. But she also felt a pain deep within her as she pictured herself and Drake embracing when he returned after one of his long absences. For a moment she wished with all her heart that she had Drake back, that they could have another opportunity to make the most of their lives and their marriage. Crying out to God with a prayer too deep for words, she put the feelings aside, choosing instead to focus on the joy of the present circumstance.

Pulling Ben along with her, Katherine rushed up to Jennifer. "Ben," she said excitedly, "you remember Jennifer DeSpain, the lady you met down in the mine a long time ago—the lady who runs the paper and writes about Miner Tom. She's the one who got you out."

Ben threw his dirty arm around Jennifer's neck and gave her a grimy and sweaty hug. He was so happy to be breathing open air and to be reunited with his wife, he didn't care what anybody thought. "I knew you'd come to our rescue!" he said loudly. "Anybody who can save Miner Tom can save us!"

Though a little embarrassed, Jennifer let his filthy arm remain around her neck, his other arm around Katherine's neck. "Tell me," Jennifer said, "what happened to cause Fair to keep you down there for so long?"

Ben had a big grin on his face. "We were told not to talk about it right before they let us out. But I can tell you this—it's something *big!* Bigger than you could ever imagine! It's gonna bust this town wide open!"

CHAPTER

~ 15 ~

The Big Bonanza

Although the miners had been warned not to talk, the news was too astounding to keep quiet. Like a kettle that had been boiling too long, the news spilled over the whole town—the miners had hit the big bonanza! As Jennifer had suspected, after striking the top of a wide dome of rich gold ore, the miners were held underground until Fair could manipulate the stocks to his benefit.

Practically overnight, the town of Virginia City went into a frenzy with drunks in the street waving their bottles and shouting, "Gold! Gold! Gold!" Fair's mining company stocks jumped from $24 to $6,000 overnight. But the strike didn't mean riches only for the mining company. The citizens of Virginia City realized that the wealth sure to emanate from the mine would find its way into virtually every clever pocket in the town. Celebrations inside and well outside of town could be heard throughout the night.

Within days Fair's other mine, the California, adjacent to the Consolidated Virginia, also hit the top of the big bonanza. It was now clear to all that the strike was even larger than at first thought. With both mines producing tons of gold ore, the companies hired hundreds of men to work around the clock. Virginia City was thus instantly catapulted into fame and glory.

~

Within days of the strike the news spread nationwide, and the demands on Virginia City's newspapers grew accordingly. When Jennifer and Jason had printed up the first edition to report the strike, it sold out immediately. Returning to press, they worked all night to print hundreds of additional copies.

"I'm delirious," Jennifer complained the next morning as she moved another bundle of newspapers over to the front counter.

Jason's straight blond hair hung in his sweaty face as he worked the press. "We've never sold this many of one edition," he said wearily. "I have to print another hundred copies for a man who's going to buy them to take to San Francisco." Pausing to rest a minute, Jason went over to the potbellied stove and poured another cup of coffee. "This town has gone crazy," he muttered. "A big strike like this means money for everyone, even us! It looks like we'll sell more of this single edition than we normally sell in a month."

Collapsing into a chair, Jennifer moaned with fatigue. It had been a long night, and the day was just starting. "I'm so tired . . . If I don't get some sleep soon, I think I'll faint."

"Go home and rest! Spend some time with your family," Jason encouraged. "I'll keep churning the papers out."

"I think I'll do just that," Jennifer said, rising slowly from her chair. She gathered a few things and left.

Not thirty minutes later, Grant showed up at the office wide-eyed with excitement.

"What are you doing here?" Jason asked. "Aren't you supposed to be in school?"

"They let us out," Grant announced happily. "Half the school didn't show up, and the ones who did were too wild to handle." Grant came around to where Jason was laboring over the press. "Wow! You sure have printed a lot of papers."

"And I have a lot more to go," Jason said matter-of-factly.

"Can I help?" Grant asked, always ready to work at Jason's side.

"Sure. We can make a two-man operation out of this. I'll work the press, and you insert the paper, then remove it after the printing is done."

Grant skillfully did as he was instructed, and the two produced newspapers like a well-oiled machine. The Washington Press squeaked and groaned at producing so many copies, but the two workers kept going without a complaint.

～

After sleeping away the day, Jennifer woke up late in the afternoon. Sleepily, she got up and brushed her hair, wondering if Jason had managed to print enough papers. Still exhausted, she wasn't anxious to return to the office and start working again. A light knock sounded on her bedroom door.

"Miss Jenny?" The voice was Lita's.

"Yes? What is it?"

"'Dat Fitzgerald man here."

"Tell him I'll be down in a moment," Jennifer called. She quickly changed clothes and went downstairs.

Lita met her at the bottom of the steps. "Miss Jenny, don't forget, you need to talk to your little girl about playin' hooky."

"Oh, Lita, I'd completely forgotten. So much has been happening . . . I'll talk to her later today."

Nodding, Lita walked away.

Jennifer found Charles waiting in the front room. He reminded her of a hunting dog that had performed well and now awaited its reward.

"I suppose we have something to celebrate," he said with a gigantic grin. He held a new derby hat in his hand.

A smile adorned Jennifer's face as she gave Charles a brief hug. "I do owe you a great deal of thanks. It might have been a long time before we got those miners out if it hadn't been for your help. I'm so grateful that you allowed God to use you to help the miners."

"Think nothing of it," Charles said with a shrug, embarrassed at the reference to God but not wanting Jennifer to know his true feelings about Him. "How about a buggy ride? I've rented a rather nice carriage."

"Oh?" Jennifer said, peeking through a front window to see a black buggy hitched to a sleek black horse. "That would be a calming change of pace. Too much has been happening all at once." She turned to get a shawl, which Charles helped drape over her shoulders. As they left she called, "Lita, I'm going out for a little while."

Charles drove the team through a boisterously celebrating town and out into the countryside until he directed the horse up a switchback that took them high onto Mount Davidson for a spectacular view overlooking the town. The sunset reddened the sky, while below, in the deep shadow of the mountain, Virginia City sparkled with many lights.

"You were right," Charles complimented after he pulled the horse to a halt. "Something big did happen in connection with the miners being kept confined down in the mine—maybe the biggest thing that will ever happen here." He turned his eyes toward the town "Look at them down there. That's as lively and happy a place as you'll ever find."

Jennifer stared silently at the twinkling town below. She pulled her shawl tighter around her shoulders and turned to Charles. "How long do you think this will last? Surely the gold and silver will run out someday?"

"It's hard to say," Charles commented, thinking of the reports he'd seen about other strikes. "I'd say there's enough ore here to build this place into a permanent city with a prosperous future. I can't think of a better place for a man to find a wife and raise a family." He almost wished he hadn't said those words, but was also glad he had. Though he didn't believe in her God, he was becoming fonder of her. He wasn't sure how he could fit her animosity toward the mining companies and his loyalty to them together, but he would deal with that one step at a time.

When Jennifer heard Charles's hint about matrimony, she threw a quick glimpse at him. Though she greatly admired the man, she wasn't ready to discuss marriage and family. "I don't know, Charles. The big bonanza will bring in all kinds of people, including many undesirables. Life here might get a little rough—not necessarily a great atmosphere for a family."

"Yes, but that won't affect those who have the security of riches, and I'm well on my way." Fitzgerald hesitated and let his eyes wander, then brought them back to Jennifer. He looked at her for a long moment, hesitated, then decided to reveal his recent success. "As soon as I heard about this whole situation, I did a little speculating. I knew old Fair had something up his sleeve when he was holding those miners and silently buying back his own stock. So I took a chance and bought 100 shares of it myself!" He flashed a huge smile.

"Oh, I'm so happy for you!" Jennifer said as she gave him a light, congratulatory hug. "You're a very intelligent man." She didn't realize that she hadn't grasped the full import of the attorney's news, that she hadn't been impressed in the way he'd expected. She also wondered if he understood that material riches cannot guarantee peace of mind.

Charles laughed. He felt truly happy, for not only would he have his fortune, but he was sitting with the most wonderful woman he'd ever known, a woman he felt sure would one day agree to marry him. He whispered, "I plan to share my fortune with someone special."

Jennifer didn't reply, suddenly understanding what Charles had been saying, and the attorney smiled as he pulled her into his arms. Her lips were sweet and soft, and he felt them tremble under his. When he lifted his head, he saw the nobility of her mouth and the glow of her eyes, and for the first time he was a man who understood beauty.

"I apologize if I have been too forward. I guess I've been alone too long," he murmured as he drew back. He placed his arm around her shoulder and gazed again at the town below.

Jennifer had been stirred by his kiss. She was a woman who had known love; and since Drake had died, she'd missed the intimacy of a caring relationship and physical love. Charles's caress had stirred a hunger in her that she'd almost forgotten. He was a successful man who lacked the shrewdness that drove other wealthy men mad, and she knew she could love him. *The difference between them and him is,* she thought, *he has a heart for God.*

A brisk wind made Jennifer shiver.

"We'd better get back," Charles said, noticing Jennifer's chill. "How about a steak dinner?"

"That sounds delicious," Jennifer said. "I can't even remember the last time I ate a good steak."

～

Jason figured he had printed enough copies with the headline BIG BONANZA STRIKE! Grant had gone home just before dark, leaving Jason alone at the office. The whooping and hollering continued outside as he blew out the lantern. "I do believe it's time for a little celebration!" he said to himself. Putting on his coat, he walked outside.

Traveling down the street, Jason felt a sense of jubilation as the revelers carried on as if each and every one of them had struck it rich. He smiled, feeling the excitement of the people around him. Making his way to the saloon district, he watched while people danced in the street to the screech of a fiddle. Fireworks exploded in the night sky, spooking a group of horses. Lifting his eyes to the large facade above, Jason realized he was standing in front of the Golden Fleece, a saloon and dance hall. He was afraid to go into such a place, but he also knew he just had to celebrate—he couldn't hold it in any longer.

Stepping through the swinging doors, Jason saw miners swinging girls across the floor to a tune being played on a well-used piano. Cigar smoke cast a heavy haze across the long room, and whiskey was being poured freely. He approached the long, crowded mahogany bar and watched the celebration in a huge mirror stretched from wall to wall.

"What'll it be, friend?" the slick-haired bartender asked.

"Give me a bottle," Jason yelled above the noise, ignoring the inner voice warning him not to indulge in the troubling intoxicant.

Several drinks later Jason could feel the numbing effect of the alcohol. He slouched at the bar, content with the idea of getting drunk. He watched the girls laugh as they danced with the odd sorts who frequented the saloon.

Suddenly there was a tap on Jason's shoulder. He turned around to see a rather small young woman smiling at him. She wore a low-cut, emerald-green dress with feathered fringes; snow-white feathers accented her black hair. Her light blue eyes were alive in an olive complexion, and she had an effervescent smile that exposed even white teeth. "Care to dance?" she asked, cocking her pretty head to one side.

Smiling back, Jason felt a little too drunk to dance. Besides, he was tired after so many hours of work. "I'm sorry," he muttered. "I'm too exhausted to dance even one step."

"I'm tired myself," the small woman admitted. "I think if I have to dance with another filthy miner and put up with his careless hands, I might fall unconscious. Mind if I have a drink with you?"

"Help yourself," Jason said, sliding the bottle over. Her perfume smelled strong and sweet.

"My name's Molly," the young woman said, her eyes studying Jason carefully. "You don't look like no miner."

"No . . . I work at *The Miner's News*. My name is Jason."

Molly slid Jason's bottle back in front of him and signaled the bartender, who poured her a sarsaparilla. "You must work for that woman then," she said. "I hear she's a brave one, running a newspaper like that. All us girls read Miner Tom—that's a great story she's got going there."

"Yeah, she's one in a million," Jason said with a nod. He tossed down a shot glass full of whiskey in one swift movement and quickly poured another.

"I must have touched a soft spot," Molly said, speculation in her eyes. "You'd better take it easy on that stuff."

"Why should I?" Jason said. He was feeling the effects of the whiskey and, liking it, poured himself another drink.

"You know, you're handsome," Molly said without even thinking about what she was saying. It was what dance hall girls always say to a man, but somehow as she studied Jason's sensitive face, she hated herself for what she was. Life in a dance hall had taken away her innocence, but her eyes revealed a longing that belied the tough set of her painted lips. She was twenty-two years old, but sometimes at night she thought back to a time when she hadn't yet become what she was now.

Jason swung his bloodshot eyes Molly's way and studied her pretty face. "You're handsome too."

"Handsome?" Molly laughed. But she knew what he meant by his drunken statement. "You know, I don't flirt with everyone. I have to be careful—some of these drunken miners are mean."

Several horses raced by outside, and the crack of gunshots filled the air. Jason and Molly both turned to look, but seeing nothing, they turned back to their conversation.

Molly surveyed Jason closer, then pursed her lips before she asked, "Are you married?"

Jason glanced down at her, his eyelids heavy. "No."

The brilliant smile returned, and Molly took a light sip of her sarsaparilla, her eyes remaining on Jason. *He's different from most of the men who come in here*, she thought. *He's nice—not greedy or rude. Of course, he likes his whiskey.*

At that moment, seeing the truth in her eyes, ashamed of what he was doing, overcome by the liquor, Jason suffered the staggering effects of drinking too much too fast.

His vision was suddenly blurry, and the room began to move in circles. As he moaned and swayed, almost falling, Molly caught him and helped him lean on the bar. "Jason, I get off work in a few minutes. Just sit here and rest, and I'll take you home." Unaware she'd left, he held onto the bar as his drunkenness overpowered him.

When she returned shortly, Molly threw Jason's arm over her shoulder and helped him out of the bar. Once on the street, she asked, "Where do you live?"

Jason could hardly lift his head as he mumbled something unintelligible. Molly had no way of knowing that he lived at the newspaper office. "Well," she said, "I can take you to my place—it's just up the street." Though not fully comfortable with her own suggestion, but also not caring if onlookers misunderstood her intentions, she helped Jason down the crowded street where darkness and lamplight battled. A drunkard yelled at her, "Got you a live one, honey? Haw-haw!" Ignoring the remark, she pressed onward until she came to a low-rent hotel that, leaning slightly to one side, looked as if it had survived a mild earthquake.

Getting Jason up the stairs was not easy, but she managed until she got to her room and unlocked the door. As he fell onto the bed, she stared at her unconscious friend. *What on earth am I doing?* she thought. She covered Jason with a blanket, then found one for herself. She curled up in an old, worn-out chair with torn upholstery.

She studied the man she'd brought home, still out cold. *I hope he's not mad in the morning,* she mused. *He'll probably bolt—they usually do the next day anyway.* Exhausted, she quickly fell into a deep sleep.

~

The crow of a rooster awoke Molly. Rubbing her eyes, she saw that Jason was still asleep. Quickly, she got dressed, thinking she should go downstairs and get some hot coffee. She slipped out quietly and eased the door closed. When she returned, she saw that Jason hadn't moved. She gently shook his shoulder, and he roused and glanced around the room. "Where am I?"

"You're at my place," Molly said softly, handing him a cup of scalding black coffee.

Taking the cup, Jason felt the throbbing in his head. He took a sip and groaned as he set the cup on a bedside table. Assuming the worst, he asked, "Did—"

"Nothing happened," Molly interrupted. "You might want to take it easy! You really drank a lot last night."

Lying back on the pillow, Jason let his aching eyes roam. The room had some of her personal effects, in particular a photograph on the dresser, a picture of Molly and a handsome young man, both smiling. "Who's that?" he asked.

Following Jason's eyes to the photograph, Molly jumped up, snatched the picture, and put it in a drawer.

"Sorry," Jason mumbled. "I didn't mean to pry."

The pleasant smile had left Molly's face. She stared at Jason a few minutes, then shrugged her shoulders. "It's all right. That's a picture of me and my husband. He left me a while back."

Even with a headache, it was hard for Jason to imagine a man leaving such a pretty woman. Obviously she was now down on her luck and was getting by however she could. She was not the first woman whose hard times had led her to moral compromise in Virginia City, and she undoubtedly wouldn't be the last. The room looked like a private, personal place, not somewhere she would take a man. He felt pity for this young woman, girlish in her ways, probably lonely and eager to be accepted. He got to his feet, feeling a bit dizzy.

"Are you leaving?" Molly asked, a little disappointed. She didn't like the men she met as a rule, but something about Jason drew her. She couldn't identify the exact feeling, but she knew it was vastly different from the emotion most men stirred in her.

"I guess so," Jason answered, rubbing the back of his neck. "I have to get to work."

Coming over beside him, Molly looked up into Jason's face. "Will I see you again?"

Jason stared down at her, admiring her light blue eyes that seemed to have a smile all their own. He was well aware of her position in life, but there was something in her, a longing for more than this small room, that impressed him. He was a lonely man, and in her expression he read the very same loneliness. "Sure, Molly, why not?"

Molly's contagious smile returned. "I hope it's soon."

"I'll look you up," Jason said. "I promise." He reached for the door handle, then turned back to her. "Thanks for last night," he said awkwardly.

Molly watched with anticipation as Jason disappeared behind the closed door. She thought sadly, *I wonder if I'll ever see him again.*

～

Charles Fitzgerald had been summoned to George Hearst's office. *I wonder what he wants,* he thought as he straightened some paperwork on his desk. *As if he doesn't keep me busy enough!* He made his way to Hearst's office. A tall guard stood outside the door but, recognizing Fitzgerald, opened the door for him. The attorney stepped inside, where Hearst sat behind his huge desk in a plush leather chair. "Sit down!" Hearst ordered gruffly.

Fitzgerald waited patiently while Hearst took his time lighting one of his big, expensive cigars. He didn't bother to offer Charles one. He never did.

"I don't tell another man how to handle his personal affairs," Hearst began in a bitter tone, his glaring, deep-sunk eyes unsympathetic. "Except when it involves my business—then I'll sure say something! This newspaper woman you've been seeing—she has you by the collar, Charley! You haven't done a blasted thing to silence her!" He took an angry puff from his cigar and spewed the smoke into the air. "What's wrong with you, man? Don't you understand that the fortune to be made here is a once-in-a-lifetime opportunity?" He rolled his eyes in disgust. "Women! They can be had by the dozen!" He waited, glaring at Charles. "Well, say something!"

The extreme discomfort Charles felt became pressing heat around his neck. "Well, Mr. Hearst, it's true that I'm on a, well, friendly basis with her, but believe me, that seemed the best way to get what we want. She won't scare easily, and I thought it best to handle it diplomatically."

"You *thought!*" Hearst shouted. "I'll tell you what to think when you need to think. One of her stories condemned my company just because three men died in a cave-in. Doesn't she understand that such risks are part of the business of mining? An occupational hazard. These miners know that! I won't tolerate any more attacks from her newspaper. You either persuade her to shut up about my company or I'll find someone who will!"

"Yes sir, Mr. Hearst," Charles said as he prepared to leave.

"One more thing," Hearst said in a lower but harder tone. "You'd better make up your mind—are you with me or not?"

Thinking of his lucrative position and ever-increasing income, Charles decided he'd better reaffirm his commitment to his hard-nosed boss. "I'm with you all the way, Mr. Hearst. No doubt about it."

"That's smart, Charley," Hearst stated, a cynical slyness in his voice.

As Charles walked back to his office, feeling pulled in two directions, he surmised exactly what he needed to do. *If I can convince her to marry me, she'll have everything she needs. With the extensive funds I'm accumulating, she won't even need that silly newspaper. That way I'll have her and I'll have Hearst too.*

～

Lita saw Abe loitering behind the house late one afternoon. Not that such a sight was so unusual, but the big man was sitting on a small, inverted water bucket and was drawing in the dirt with a stick. She quickly rearranged the pots on the stove so they wouldn't boil over and shuffled to the back door, her loose-fitting house shoes flopping dangerously. Unlatching the door, she stuck her head out and yelled, "What you doin' out there, Abe? Don't you know how to knock?"

When Abe saw Lita's face in the doorway, he slowly stood, then lumbered over to the small back porch. He reached into a pocket in his overalls and pulled out a few rocks that he caressed for a moment, then held them out to Lita. The rocks were dwarfed by his giant hands.

"What are those?" Lita said, her wide brown eyes on the rocks.

"They for you," Abe mumbled. He'd picked up a few pieces of ore that had fallen out of a freight wagon. Although the rocks weren't that pretty, Abe suspected the gold specks were real gold, and he couldn't think of anything he'd rather do with them than give them to Lita.

Grabbing one of the rocks, Lita brought it up to her face and studied it closely. "Dat's a ugly rock!" she concluded.

"But it got gold in it," Abe protested. "You see here?" He pointed with a huge finger. "Dem little specks—why, those are gold!"

Looking again at the rock, Lita could see the small golden flecks of light. "Is dat right?" she mumbled, almost smiling. But then, not wanting to give Abe false hopes, she hid her smile and changed the subject. "I guess you hungry, as always."

"I reckon so," Abe admitted, his eyes wandering off, "if it ain't too much trouble."

Lita went inside and spooned up Abe a bowl of stew she had simmering. She looked closely at the rocks, sparkling with tiny lights. Nobody had ever given her a valuable gift before, and certainly not gold! She wanted to hug the big man, to thank him more than she had, but she didn't want to give him the wrong impression. At the door she said, "Here's some beef stew and potatoes" and handed him a big bowl with a large spoon. As he turned away, she said, "Here" and handed him a large piece of fresh cornbread. Her special-made cornbread was her way of saying thanks.

~

The headline in *The Miner's News* read: BIG BONANZA STILL PRODUCING 1.5 MILLION A MONTH. The date at the top of the page read October 21, 1873. Jennifer studied the new edition with satisfaction. Though it had been going for many months, the strike continued to be the biggest news in Virginia City's history. People from all over the country had moved there hoping to share in the newfound wealth. Many overcrowded trains had steamed into town with men perched on the roofs, while others had arrived on horseback or in covered wagons. An estimated seventy-five to 125 people arrived daily, all searching for gold-strike glory. The city had turned into a swarming mass of people, most of whom slept in tents or stables or hastily built sheds.

The Miner's News had become very prosperous, and Jennifer felt a lighthearted touch of pride in that, though she was also careful to give God the credit for her success. She had surpassed many people's expectations and through stubborn determination and hard work, with God's help, had succeeded. Today Jason had left the office early, eager to be somewhere he didn't care to mention. Except for his occasional drinking binge, he had shown improvement. Judging by his more confident mood, she suspected he might have begun a romantic relationship with some woman he wasn't ready to introduce yet. Jennifer was glad he was over his misplaced affection for her.

Placing the paper on the counter, Jennifer glanced around the office to make sure everything was in order before she left for the day. *I'm famished*, she thought as she glanced out the window. She'd expected Charles to arrive at any minute to take her out to dinner, an occasion for which she had changed into a colorful dress with a fancy design. He had told her he had something special to tell her.

Arriving in a handsome buggy and dressed in his finest dark suit, Charles saw Jennifer come outside to wait for him in front of the office. He helped her into the seat, then climbed back aboard. He drove carefully through the throngs of people in the streets.

"Charles, this reminds me of Mardi Gras," she observed, her head turning in every direction. "So many people out on the streets with such a festive spirit."

Rounding the corner, Charles stopped the buggy in front of The Belleview, an exclusive restaurant with a large facade crafted to resemble an artesian well. He climbed out and threw the reins around a brass hitching post. Walking back to the buggy with a spring in his step, he helped Jennifer down.

"My, you're in a good mood," she said, taking his hand and flashing her familiar full smile. "If I didn't know better, I'd think you were up to something."

Declining to comment, Charles merely smiled mischievously and escorted Jennifer inside. The restaurant had a high pressed-tin ceiling and dark hardwood floors. Red velvet curtains hid the walls, and hand-carved oak dividers topped with brass rails partitioned the room. The well-spaced mahogany tables presented the guests with the luxury of privacy and gave the red-vested waiters plenty of room to serve their customers.

After a dinner of roasted pheasant, with pineapple cake for dessert, the attentive waiter removed the gold-trimmed china from which they'd eaten. Charles took a sip of champagne and set the crystal goblet to the side, leaving the table clear in front of him. He wore a confident smile, and his eyes sparkled with anticipation. "I have something to tell you," he announced, the pride in his voice unmistakable. "I'm now a millionaire!"

Both surprised and happy, Jennifer was shocked at the word *millionaire*, for the word had never applied to anyone close to her. "Charles, I can't believe it! Are you really?"

"Really!" he boasted.

Jennifer found the news astounding. Her success at the newspaper didn't compare with Charles's news. She'd always believed Charles was smart and that he would become wealthy, but this . . . "I don't know what to say. I'm so happy for you."

"This isn't just about me, Jennifer—it's about *us*," he said as he set a small, fancy teakwood box in front of her and flipped it open. A bright diamond sparkled at her from atop a cluster of smaller diamonds, all of which sat on a band of yellow, lustrous gold. It was the most beautiful engagement ring she'd ever seen.

Jennifer had known Charles had a growing interest in her, though she'd never thought of it as affection, let alone love leading to marriage. And she had recognized her own growing feelings for Charles, though she hadn't even once considered that this would lead to a proposal. She'd thought of it only in terms of a close friendship and admiration for a man who, in her eyes, honored God and cared about people in need.

She couldn't remember ever being so confused. She was flattered, embarrassed, nervous, guileless, surprised, frightened, uncertain. "It's lovely," she murmured with a shaky voice.

"I want you to be my wife," Charles said in genuine sincerity. "Jennifer, will you marry me?"

Finding it difficult to regain her composure, Jennifer dabbed at her eyes with a cotton napkin. She didn't want to tell Charles no, but she didn't want to accept either—not just yet. She just wasn't sure what she should do. She knew she should ask for wisdom from above, but at the moment she was too emotionally agitated to put her prayer into words. After a long period of silence she said, "Charles, you've been wonderful to me, but this . . . I don't know what to say." She placed her small hand on top of his and gave a slight squeeze. "I want to say yes, but I'm . . ." She glanced down to avoid looking him in the eye. She wondered if her heart was still beating. "I'm just not sure I should marry again."

Charles assured her, "We don't have to get married right away." The power of his self-confidence was evident in his smile and in his convincing blue eyes. He was a man who excelled at persuasion, a driven man who knew well how to bring others alongside his own goals and aspirations. "Take time to decide, Jennifer. I'll wait as long as you like! I know God will show you what He wants you to do." He cringed inwardly at his own reference to God, but knowing what such a comment would mean to Jennifer, he used it anyway. He took her small hand in his. "Meanwhile, please accept this engagement ring."

Jennifer took a deep breath and gazed deep into his eyes.

Charles took her hand and slipped the ring gently onto her finger. The weight of precious gems and gold—the symbol of a future bond between a man and a woman—gave him a warm feeling of certain success. He savored the moment, then, without saying a word, came around the table and kissed her.

16

The Omens of Winter

Overnight a snowy whiteness fell onto the hillsides and rooftops. Water buckets froze, and barrels burst their contents as frostbitten winds roared in from the Nevadas and over the Washoe Mountains.

This was the first warning of the winter to come in 1874. The more hardy residents sealed their cabins with old newspapers or piled dirt around flimsy tents as they prepared for the long siege. Those who were discouraged or had limited resources prepared for departure.

As shortages seemed imminent, all prices jumped. Virginia City's human driftwood, those who had no place to call home and had to eat scraps and sleep in the open, now began to sneak into livery barns or anyplace else they could hide from the elements. Since cold weather made the days shorter, miners spent more time than usual in the saloons and at the gaming tables. As a result sudden quarrels raged more often, and the cemetery had many fresh mounds of dirt. These were not easy times.

~

Seeing the huge diamond on Jennifer's finger sent Jason back into his private world of lonely despair. This was one more door slammed in his face, another huge letdown. As a result, he'd grown more distant around her, though his feelings for her remained strong. This disappointment had driven him to seek assurance or affirmation elsewhere, a vague sort of security he found in Molly. They had visited several times, and although their relationship was platonic, she'd become an understanding friend.

At the newspaper office one day Jason told Jennifer, "I'll be back later." She glanced up to see him bundling up in his coat and pulling his hat tight over his head and ears. Once outside, he put a shoulder to the icy wind as he trudged through the frozen mud and snow in the street. The once-busy thoroughfares, now in the grip of a winter storm, seemed abandoned by contrast. He pushed his way down the sloping street to the saloon district and made his way quickly up the slick boardwalk to Molly's hotel.

Opening the front door to the hotel, Jason appreciated the blast of heat that originated from the glowing red stove sitting in the sparsely furnished lobby. He glanced up to see the desk clerk, Mr. Moffit, looking at him through thick, heavy glasses and trying to determine who it was that dared to let the bitter cold into the lobby. The old clerk was as nearsighted as a fish. He was old and hunched over and had a long, disappointed face, for he'd once been wealthy but was now in heavy debt. He spent most of his time studying old ledgers and trying to figure out how his riches had disappeared. "It's me, Mr. Moffit—Jason," the newcomer said to ease Mr. Moffit's straining eyes and worried mind.

"Oh, yes. I knew it was you," Mr. Moffit said, though he hadn't known at all. He remembered Jason from his recent visits. "Fine weather we're having, eh?"

"It's miserable," Jason complained. "Is Molly in?"

Thinking a minute, Mr. Moffit answered, "I don't rightly know. You can go up and knock if you like."

Moving up the stairs rapidly, Jason came to Molly's door and eagerly knocked. She opened the door, her smile revealing that she was happy to see Jason. Though wrapped in a blanket, she wore her coat and clothes underneath. The small room was dim, having only the light of a single candle, but her blue eyes were as clear as a mountain stream. "Hello, Jason! I didn't think you'd come see me when the weather's like this," she said, her mood unaffected by the frigid temperature.

"Your hands feel like ice," Jason said as he took her small hands in his. "I want to take you somewhere, but don't ask why."

With an eager look on her face, Molly answered, "That sounds mysterious but fun."

Jason laughed. "Well, let's go right away then," he said.

She threw the blanket onto the bed. "Where are you taking me in such a hurry?"

"You'll see," Jason replied, leading her by the hand.

Molly closed her door and hurried behind Jason down the stairs, through the lobby, and out into the hard wind. He offered her his arm. "Hang on," he said. "I wouldn't want you to blow away."

Molly poked Jason in the ribs with her elbow. She was often teased about being so small.

They made their way through the blowing snow to a general store called The Nevada. They entered the cozy warmth of the wonderfully self-contained world with odd but familiar aromas—the rich fruitiness of plug tobacco, the leather of boots and belts, fresh-ground coffee, cheese, dried and pickled fish, and the subtle fragrances of various new fabrics. On one side of the store stood a counter piled high with groceries, and on the other a counter and shelves filled with dry goods. Hardware, along with the proprietor's high desk stool, took up the rear. From the rafters hung the vague shapes of hams, slabs of bacon, and pots and pans. Once their eyes became accustomed to the dimness, they felt drawn to an island of warmth in the center of the store—the scarlet potbellied stove.

Warming up to the glowing heat, Molly rubbed her hands together and blew on them. Jason stood beside her, holding his hands out to the stove. "What are we doing here?" Molly asked, her cheeks bright red from the bitter wind.

This was the kind of moment Jason had long hoped for, a time when he could be important to someone, if only for a few minutes. Now that he earned good wages, he no longer had any debts and had in fact saved a tidy sum. Since he'd come to know Molly, he'd often helped her with a few dollars here and there, but he wanted to do more. It bothered him to think that she had to work in a dance hall, a young and lovely girl who was down on her luck and had no other options. It made him feel good to think of himself as her benefactor.

The proprietor, a silver-haired man in a well-worn apron and having a pipe clenched between his teeth, greeted them. "It's mighty cold out yonder. If it's warmth you're after, it won't cost you nothin'. Ain't many folks out today."

Jason and Molly had indeed passed few people on the windy street, and there were no other customers in the store. This pleased Jason, for what he wanted to do was personal and not for the public eye. "We'd like to look at your women's coats," he said to the congenial storekeeper. "I'll be needing something for this young lady here."

Molly stared at Jason with astonishment. She'd had few gifts or pleasant surprises come her way, and her hard life generally brought disapproving stares and whispered criticism. Jason's intentions reminded her of a day when she was a child, and her father took her to a store to buy her some nice clothes. She felt the same joy now as she felt then. To think that someone would care enough for her to do such a thing . . . "Jason, why are you doing this?"

"Happy birthday!" Jason replied, his straight teeth forming a perfect smile.

"How'd you know it was my birthday?" Molly asked in disbelief.

"I work for a newspaper, remember? It's my job to know these things." Actually, Jason had overheard some women at the saloon discussing Molly's upcoming birthday.

The store owner returned with several nice coats as he sucked on his pipe. Molly began looking through them as if this was all a dream come true. "We want to see some nice leather boots and warm dresses as well," Jason said, beginning to feel a pleasure he'd seldom experienced. He watched with great pride as she examined and compared the various items. The smiling shopkeeper was able to give them his full attention as Molly tried on the small, lace-up boots, leather coats, and winter dresses.

When she had carefully made her selections, Jason pulled out a wad of bills and paid the cheerful shopkeeper, who clicked his teeth on the pipe stem in delight—not only because he had just made a large sale on a day on which he might not have had any, but especially because he enjoyed seeing Jason's pleasure in helping Molly.

After the shopping spree, Jason walked Molly back to her hotel. As he carried her stack of boxes for her, he barely noticed the aggravating wind. Back in her small room, Jason set the boxes on the floor. He took off his hat and held it idly in his hands while Molly unpacked and spread her new wardrobe on the bed so she could admire the new items. She moved slowly, savoring the moment. She felt a fondness for Jason that she had kept herself from feeling for other men. As she turned toward him, he read her thoughts in her eyes.

Jason's eyes squinted slightly as he looked away self-consciously. "I guess I'd better be going," he said.

Without a word, Molly pulled him closer, then slipped her arms around his neck. Her face was very close to his as he looked down at her. She lifted herself up to him, her breath sweet and soft in his face. "Jason, this is the sweetest thing anyone has done for me since I've come to Virginia City." Without warning, she closed her eyes and kissed him on the lips. Jason stood motionless, overcome with surprise.

He hadn't expected the kiss, for they'd had a relationship of mutual trust and understanding without physical attraction. Both being lonely, they had relied on each other's warm friendship in a time of cold uncertainty. Molly suddenly realized she had violated that trust by crossing an unspoken but nevertheless forbidden line. "I'm sorry," she murmured as she turned away. She took two steps, then turned back to him, sorrow in her eyes. "Jason, I think I'm falling in love with you."

Jason tried to process the varying thoughts racing through his mind but couldn't. He wanted to hold her close, but he didn't trust himself. He pictured himself staggering, drunk, passing out who knows where. *I can't do this to her*, he thought miserably. The gratification he'd felt at buying Molly some winter clothes suddenly vanished, and he saw himself as a foolish dreamer. He hesitantly reached for the door handle. "I'd better be going," he mumbled, then stumbled out.

Watching the door close, Molly felt overwhelming disappointment and rejection rise within her. *I'll never be loved by a decent man*, she thought, *because I'm not decent!* Loss had become a way of life she expected. She deserved it. If only . . . She had offered herself to many men. How could Jason know she was sincere this time? Moving stiffly over to the window, she pulled the curtain aside and glanced down at the empty street—he was nowhere to be seen. *Maybe he'll still be my friend*, she thought hopefully. *I'll never show romantic affection for him again. No man could ever love me.*

⁓

Large flakes of snow drifted quietly in the darkness, floating in gentle swirls to the ground. A white blanket covered the town in a soft and muffled silence. For most, it was a time of sleep, but over 1,500 feet below the town, the night shift toiled in steamy caverns. At the 2,000-foot level in the Bullion mine, timbers creaked and groaned, and then came a loud crash and a rush of dust and debris. Fifteen miners were trapped in the cave-in, and within minutes church bells rang and people began shouting.

The disturbance awoke Abe Washington from a deep sleep. He knew the bells indicated either a fire or a cave-in. He jumped out of his bunk and dressed hurriedly. He glanced at the dying embers in his small tin stove—his house was a simple shed leaning against the side of the mule stables—and knew he'd have to venture out into the night cold if he wished to give any help. Just before he left, he reached under his pillow and rubbed the shiny crystal rock, hoping it would keep bad luck away.

Bundled up against the cold, Abe burst out into the night, swinging a yellow lantern in his huge hand. Making his way toward the loudest sounds, he soon came to the crisis. He pushed his way through a shouting group of men outside the mine. "What happened?" Abe asked, afraid he already knew the answer.

"There's been a cave-in!" a shadowed face shouted. "They need all the men they can get to help!"

Pushing his way forward, Abe stood with a volunteer group waiting for the cage to rise. A foreman recognized Abe. "Stand back," he ordered the group of men loudly. "Let Abe through—we need the strongest men up front."

When the cage came into sight, Abe boarded along with other miners who were determined to do what they could. He squinted his eyes shut, for though he loved to help others, descending into the depths brought out his greatest fears. Rubbing the copper band around his wrist, a charm he believed contained magical powers, he thought about Lita and so got his mind off the cage that was falling quickly toward the bottom of the mine.

~

Jennifer heard about the cave-in as soon as she arrived at the office, but when she heard that Abe was working on the rescue crew, she returned home to tell Lita. Hurrying through the front door, she called, "Lita! Lita!"

Rushing into the room holding a towel in her hand, Lita answered the urgent call. "Yes, Miss Jenny? What's wrong?"

"Lita, there's been a cave-in at the Bullion, and Abe is deep in the mine as part of the rescue crew. I thought you'd want to know," Jennifer said, breathing hard. "I have to get back to the office."

Lita felt like she had just been struck in the stomach. She rushed back to the kitchen, the place where she functioned best, a place where she could think. "How can I help?" she mumbled aloud to herself. "Must be *something* I can do." Shaking her head, she sat down in a chair to calm herself. She pictured big Abe sweating deep down in the mine, working frantically to free the trapped miners, and finally it struck her. *Those hard-working men will get hungry—they got to eat!* Without delay, she leaped up and began cooking biscuits and sausages. Soon she had three dozen biscuits, each stuffed with a thick chunk of spicy sausage.

Lita lined a wooden water bucket with a thick towel and placed the biscuits inside. She laid another towel over the top and poked it down around the sides. After bundling herself up in several layers of clothes and a heavy coat, she pulled a large pair of boots over her shoes. "Abby, Grant, I got to take some food down to the mine. Y'all stay here, and behave yourselves, y' hear?"

Leaving the house, Lita frantically plowed her way through over a foot of snow until she arrived at the Bullion mine where several small groups were huddled around bonfires. Wading through the drifts and up to the white building, she approached a large door, where she was stopped by a slender man wearing a fancy overcoat. "Can't go any further!" he said, holding his arm out in warning. "You'll have to wait out here with everybody else."

Lita shoved the bucket at him, a challenging glare in her eyes. "My man down there working to save those miners. Now dat crew gonna get hungry. You give 'em dis!"

Startled by the fire in her eyes, and realizing the practical wisdom of her words, the thin man wasn't about to argue with Lita. "I'll send it right down," he mumbled nervously as he hurried away with the bucket.

Taking her place beside one of the roaring fires, Lita shifted position every few minutes to keep her whole body as warm as she could. The low gray clouds of winter closed off the valley from the rest of the world. She worried about Abe because she knew about his dread of going down into the mines. But he was a brave man and was willing to overcome his fear in order to help others, and she admired him for that. She couldn't help but wonder what her life would be like if Abe got killed. She had suffered the loss of loved ones and others close to her during the war, and that was a grief she'd hoped never to face again. Lowering her head, she closed her eyes and prayed for Abe's safety.

～

Almost 2,000 feet below the snowy earth, the sweat poured from Abe as he moved rocks and handed them to the man behind him. His strength had placed him at the front, for he was able to pry the big rocks out of the pile by hand. He grunted loudly as he lifted the heavy pieces. A miner beside him kept tapping on the tracks with a hammer, hoping to get a response from the trapped miners.

After many hours of heavy labor, everyone was ordered to be

quiet as the miner tapped again. But this time an ever so slight tapping returned down the ore cart rails. "Did ya hear that? They're alive!" screamed the miner. "Bring me some pipe over here!"

Abe could take a welcome break now—he'd been working for eight hours straight. Now a different kind of crew took over, workers who would hammer pipe through the rock so air could be pumped in for the trapped miners. The constant sound of the sledgehammer hitting the pipe echoed throughout the cave.

Abe leaned back and rested, his overalls turned down to his waist, exposing his muscular and sweaty chest. The temperature was over 100 degrees. A crippled old miner with watery eyes came up to him holding a candle. He held a bucket in front of Abe. "Take some," the miner said.

Abe lifted the towel from the bucket and casually took several of the biscuits. He bit into one and only then discovered that he was ravenous. The food was delicious, so he grabbed a few more.

"Some Negro woman brought them," the miner explained.

Lita brung dese! Ain't nobody else would've thought to put sausage inside the biscuits. Abe realized that Lita must have cared not only about all the men trying to rescue the miners, but about *him* or she wouldn't have come to help. He smiled as he stared at the biscuit in his hand, a biscuit her hands had made. She was so close, yet so far away! Loneliness had long plagued him, but since he first saw Lita, he'd had hope of a better life. He hadn't known the proper way to court her, but he'd made himself available for her convenience, doing chores, and now she'd come to his aid. Just knowing she was waiting above filled him with needed confidence and courage, for just then the shaft rumbled again, reminding him of his present danger.

With renewed strength from Lita's biscuits, Abe powered more huge stones out of the way. They had cleared the tracks by now and were filling the carts instead of using a line brigade of men. The timbers continued to groan and creak, and that worried Abe, because he'd heard the other miners talking about why the tunnel had caved in. The Bullion mine was located at the center of the Comstock Lode, but it was barren. Determined to find underground riches, the desperate owners had tried to save money by putting in fewer timbers, too few to be safe. The rescue effort was a hurried one since they all knew another collapse in the tunnel was almost certain.

It took several more hours before they were able to carve out a narrow tunnel to the trapped miners. Many were hurt and had to be gently laid on a stretcher, then dragged through the tunnel. As Abe worked on the receiving end, timbers shivered and creaked behind him.

It was now late in the day, and up above the silent crowd had swelled. When they saw the first rescued miners being lifted out, they cheered and clapped. Many of the miners had wives waiting there, and the women cried when they saw their rescued husbands walking or being carried out of the mine. Lita watched the miners and rescuers emerging from the building, happy for all of the men but looking for one in particular—a tall black man. An ever-growing affection overwhelmed her as she thought about Abe. She wished she hadn't been hard on him so many times, always taunting him or criticizing his peculiar ways. He was slow of thought and movement but was also deliberate and persistent, a tower of strength. She realized he was a *good* man, though she wasn't sure if he had true faith in the Lord.

Down below, as the last men were pulled through the rescue tunnel, Abe felt a sudden rain of small rocks. Glancing up, he saw the beam above him slowly sag and heard a loud creak. He instinctively raised his huge arms and pushed the beam upward. "Run!" he called out with his deep voice. The other miners scurried past Abe, dragging rescued men on stretchers. The tremendous pressure made the veins pop out of Abe's bulging muscles. "Get out of here!" he gasped again. The last of the miners had escaped the danger, but he was trapped. If he let go of the beam, it would cave in on him. Like a huge oak tree resisting a windstorm, he groaned under the strain. His muscles began to tremble, and his strength was clearly waning. He knew that if he stayed in that position much longer, he would be crushed to death. He released the beam and jumped away from the spot just as the shaft began to crumble with a deafening roar. Desperate, he ran as hard as he could but was soon trapped under falling rock. A loud noise rushed up the vertical shaft, and a rumbling shook the underground passageways.

The crowd above stood in silence and watched with despair. Lita was frantic—Abe had not surfaced yet. She feared something terrible had happened, but she refused to believe it. *No mine is gonna take my man!* she thought angrily.

What seemed to be the last of the men came up through the smoke and steam, but still there was no Abe. Lita rushed into the shaft house, her eyes wide with fear. "Where is he?" she screamed. "What happened to Abe?"

The leader of the rescue party, covered with dirt and dust, heard Lita screaming and came over to her. "Abe saved all of us! He held up the timber so we could get out. I'm sorry, but . . . I don't see how he could have survived." His eyes darted back to the shaft. "As soon as the dust settles, we're going back down." The man's dirty face showed that he was indeed a miner's miner and was thus willing to take the most challenging risks.

A strange calmness came over Lita. She refused to accept the idea that Abe was gone; it simply *couldn't* be true. Stubbornly, she stood and waited, her hands at her sides, her face like black granite. *Father, please watch over my Abe. And help him become Your man if he ain't already.*

At that moment Abe lay trapped, his legs covered with rocks. He ripped off a piece of his shredded shirt and held it over his mouth as he struggled to breathe. The dust was as thick as the pitch blackness around him. More than once he thought that his life was about to end. Unable to move, he could do nothing but wait for help, if help ever came. He thought about Lita and hoped she was still waiting for him. He told himself he'd have to survive or she might get mad at him. He tried to keep hoping and not give up, but that was getting harder and harder.

Nearly an hour later, the rescue team was back down in the mine, fighting the lingering dust and poor visibility. They crept forward cautiously, their lanterns held in front of them. "Abe? Can you hear us, Abe?"

"Over here," came a faint but husky voice.

The miners rushed in that direction, crawling over fallen rock until they located Abe. He was bloody, but at least he was alive. They removed the debris trapping him under a ceiling that still threatened to collapse. The loose clay and ore of the Comstock Lode kept repeating a muffled promise of another cave-in. Two miners crouched on each side of Abe and helped him limp away from the dangerous area. They were soon back in the cage and signaled the hoist operator to bring them up.

Lita heard the bell, but she figured they hadn't been down there long enough to dig anybody out. A greater fear than she'd ever known swept through her. She didn't want to hear that Abe had been lost under tons of rock, but she couldn't leave the scene either.

The wire cable raising the cage slowed, and the vague profiles of men appeared in the steam. Lita stared hard into the cloud as the men stepped off the cage. One was limping, held up by the others. It was Abe!

Lita screamed with joy, ran over to Abe, reached around his dirty and bloody neck, and hugged him with all her might. Though he was hurt, his pains quickly diminished as her cheeks wet with tears pressed against his. He found it easy to smile now—the woman for whom he cared so deeply was hugging him. "It be all right now," he said tiredly, trying to comfort her.

Suddenly overcome with the seriousness of the entire situation, and with how close she had come to losing a man whom she was coming to love, she backed away and glared at poor old Abe. "You big ox!" she whispered. "Ain't you got enough sense to get out of the way?" She sounded irate, but Abe knew exactly what she meant.

By now tears were streaming down Lita's face as she hugged Abe's neck again. She was mighty proud of her man! But she also knew that if the worst had happened, her man might have gone to the wrong place. She would have to talk to him about that, and soon!

∼

No one was surprised when shortly afterward Jennifer wrote a story about Miner Tom working in a mine that was unnecessarily dangerous because the owners tried to save money by not using enough timbers. Naturally, a cave-in occurred, and the miners' families were worried to death. She unashamedly appealed to the emotions of the readers, urging them to be more aggressive with the mining companies and to insist that they be more careful. In the story an independent engineer began to inspect the mines and make sure they were supported properly. As a result of the article, the miners' union put severe pressure on the mining companies to pay independent inspectors to check the safety of the timbers in the mines.

Another brief article appearing in the same edition of *The Miner's News* and in every other paper in town described a new local hero, Big Abe Washington. One paper said, "It's too bad old Abe doesn't drink, for if he did, he'd probably never have to buy another beer, at least not in Virginia City!"

Charles Fitzgerald read *The Miner's News* with a worried frown on his face. *This probably means another lecture from Hearst about how I'm not doing a good enough job of silencing the pen of Jennifer DeSpain! He's out of town right now, but I'm sure he'll get wind of this. Why does Jennifer have to incite the miners like that? I'd better have a talk with her, for her good and mine.*

Having to walk through the snowy streets irritated Charles, for he despised cold weather. The only thing that kept him in Virginia City during the winter months was the prospect of making money. By the time he got to the newspaper office, his feet were numb with cold. He found Jennifer at her desk, crouched over her writing. Unfortunately, Jason was also at his desk, well within hearing distance. Charles glanced at him, but the young newspaperman didn't even acknowledge his presence. Charles would have to keep his voice down.

"Hello, Charles," Jennifer said pleasantly.

"Jennifer . . ." Charles said with a serious look on his face and his voice lowered. He pulled up a chair and drew as close to Jennifer as he could. "I need to talk with you. You must stop being so hard on the mine owners. I know you mean well, but the charges you are making could make my life very difficult. I guess the issues seem straightforward to you, but if you keep this up, the owners will get involved, and the next thing you know there could be legal problems. That could put both of us in a most awkward position." His tone of voice grew increasingly tense as he spoke.

Jennifer's smile faded, and her lips formed a tight line. "Why are you always defending them?"

"I'm sorry," Charles said, holding his hands in front of him with his palms open. "Obviously I'm a little upset. It seems like sometimes you're fighting against *me* with your newspaper, and that makes for a very difficult situation."

"I'm afraid I don't understand." Jennifer was now as irritated as he was, and she made no attempt to hold her voice down. "I'm not sure what you're asking."

Charles ran his hand through his hair in frustration. "I don't know," he said intensely, his temper showing, "why you need to keep doing this. It's like you're on some kind of crusade. I have all the money we'll ever need, so just stop your campaign against the mining companies. Let's enjoy our life together. You won't even need to work."

Jennifer glared back at Charles. "You tell me *you* don't understand? You're a mining lawyer but you don't comprehend the value of the lives of the miners?" Her eyes grew narrow as she faced him. "Do you think I run this paper solely for an income? You think all I want is money? You're sadly mistaken, Charles! To me, my newspaper is a way of showing God's love for the miners and their families, and for all my readers. I thought you felt the same way about your work."

Leaning back, Charles knew instantly that he had misplayed his hand in a game with large stakes. Perhaps a different line of argument was needed. "There is also your safety to consider, Jennifer. I worry about you. Some of the mining company owners don't have clear standards of morality. You could be in danger if you continue to upset them."

"I'll take my chances," Jennifer responded with determination. Hearing Charles say he was worried about her did help, and she knew that sometimes unknown sources representing the mining companies did threaten their critics. "What I really want," she continued, "is for you to understand what I'm doing and why. We both know that life could be safer in the mines. Do you care about the miners and their families, or don't you?"

Frustrated, Charles stood to leave. "We'll talk about this another time," he said, glancing at Jason who kept his head down.

"Good. That should give you time to decide whose side you're on."

Jason grinned as Charles stormed out of the office. *What a shame,* he thought. *A lover's quarrel!*

17

The Threat

As the full wrath of winter set in with a cold Arctic blast, the wind whipped the snow into high drifts against walls, leaving the ground barren and frozen. Bundled up in coats, scarves, and boots, Grant and Abby hurried to school that morning. Grant left Abby near her schoolroom, but shortly afterward she went searching for her group of wayward friends. She found two older boys and another girl her age waiting for her behind the school. She had gotten into trouble with this same mischievous crew before.

"Abby, what took you so long?" asked the leader, a bone-thin ten-year-old boy with unruly hair.

"I got here as fast as I could, Tommy!" Abby protested, pulling her coat collar closer to protect herself against the freezing wind.

"C'mon, let's go," Tommy ordered.

"Where are we going?" Abby asked, not really caring, just as long as she could be with her rebellious friends.

"You'll see," said Stephen, the other boy, who was also ten. He was short and stocky and had front teeth that made him look like a beaver.

Abby followed along with Alice, Stephen's younger sister. She was a bashful and quiet girl, slightly smaller than Abby. She constantly hugged a rag doll.

The group sneaked behind some buildings, then found their

way downhill until they approached the Chollar mine. Just behind the back of the shaft house stood an old toolshed becoming gray with age. Tommy jiggled the door open and entered boldly. "C'mon," he called to the others. The group piled into the dark little building, glad to get out of the blasting wind. "I found this hideout the other day," Tommy bragged as he turned over a bucket and sat on it. The others sat on a long wooden toolbox.

Abby liked being with her reckless friends, even if they did get into trouble sometimes. She hated being at school. Tommy was a smart boy who'd only been caught playing hooky once, and that was because John Miller, a man who volunteered to help out as sort of a truant officer, made a lucky guess as to where Tommy was hiding. He'd never find the group in their new hideout because nobody ever went there.

Tommy pulled out a pouch and started rolling paper around some tobacco. He fumbled with the paper until he finally managed to put together a loose cigarette. Striking a match, he lit the cigarette. The paper began burning at first, but then the flame did its work on the cigarette. The ringleader took a puff and passed the cigarette to Stephen. Hesitantly, the second boy took a puff, but he coughed after he inhaled the smoke.

"Someday you'll be a man," Tommy advised Stephen with knowing authority as he took the cigarette back. "It takes a little practice." He inhaled deeply and stifled a cough of his own. The group sat around watching Tommy smoke while the wind whistled through the cracks between the boards.

"I'm freezing," Abby complained, shaking and pulling her coat tighter around her.

Glancing around, Tommy spotted a few old boards leaning against the wall. He got up and smashed one of them into smaller pieces with his big feet. He then stacked the fragments in the center of the dirt floor. "You'll be warm soon," he promised Abby as he struck a match and set it beneath the boards. But the match quickly burned out without igniting any of the wood. "Crud!" Tommy swore.

"Look what I found," Stephen said, holding a small can of coal oil.

THE THREAT □ 255

"Don't just stand there," Tommy said. "Pour it on."

Resenting being ordered around but nevertheless doing as he was told, Stephen soaked the firewood. Tommy struck another match and tossed it onto the liquid. In an instant the fire stretched toward the ceiling and continued to reach higher and higher. The children moved back from the hungry flames.

"We'd better get out of here!" Tommy yelled as he raced out of the shed. The others hurried after him.

Once they were several yards away, the children looked back and saw black smoke rolling from the small shed as the wind fanned the fire. The entire building was soon engulfed in flames as the children watched in amazement. A firm hand suddenly gripped Tommy's shoulder. The children were shocked to discover two mining company employees standing right behind them.

"You kids hold it right here!" the biggest man ordered, a scowl on his weathered face. "Take these kids back to school—they'll get a beatin' that'll teach 'em a lesson!" he ordered the others.

Soon bells throughout the town began calling men to get the blaze under control before the wind spread the fire. In a place like Virginia City a fire could easily consume much of the town before sufficient deterrents could be used.

～

Jennifer was working at her desk, writing another episode of Miner Tom, when a young boy rushed through the front door. "Mrs. DeSpain," he said, out of breath. He had the look of alertness motivated by fear. "The schoolmaster needs to see you right away— Abby's in trouble!"

Jennifer quickly glanced at Jason. "I'll be back as soon as I can," she said with irritation. "I don't know why that girl can't stay out of trouble!"

Trying to ignore the cold wind, Jennifer and the young messenger rushed to the school. Upon entering the building, she was shown to the office of the schoolmaster, Mr. Powell. He was a portly, completely bald-headed man who had an air of compulsive arrogance.

"Have a chair, Mrs. DeSpain," he said evenly, his small face contorted in a frown. He explained what had happened, taking his time, obviously enjoying the opportunity to exercise his authority. "I have no choice but to suspend Abby from school," he concluded. "In a week we will consider readmittance." He stood up and opened the door for Jennifer. "I think parental discipline is called for, Mrs. DeSpain." His tone of voice suggested he either doubted that she would use such discipline or that it would do any good.

"Thank you for your understanding," Jennifer said stiffly as she left the office.

Abby was standing outside the office waiting. Her face was expressionless as she stared at nothing.

Jennifer glared at her unruly daughter, then took her roughly by the hand as she marched her home, only a few blocks away. "I can't believe this!" Jennifer exclaimed. "You burned down a building? How could a little girl get into so much trouble?" Her words were carried away by the wind. Abby, actually glad to be expelled from school, now had a smug look on her face. Her irate mother didn't notice.

Storming through the front door of their home, Jennifer pushed Abby onto the sofa, where the girl sat stiffly. "Abby, tell me what happened!"

Abby's mouth held a firm and stubborn line. She didn't feel like talking. Seeing herself as an outcast in many ways, she was a little girl with a grudge, though she couldn't verbalize it, even to herself. Her truant friends respected her distaste for authority, and she wasn't about to tattle on them.

Lita had heard her mistress's angry words and came rushing in. "What happened, Miss Jenny?"

"Abby has been suspended from school!" Jennifer snapped.

Lita decided she wasn't needed at that moment and quickly shuffled back to the kitchen where she would be safer.

"What do you have to say for yourself?" Jennifer asked, but not as loudly this time. She had softened a bit when she saw a sorrowful look in Abby's blue eyes that reminded her of Drake.

"I hate school!" Abby finally blurted out. "And I hate my teacher—he's mean to me! I don't want to go back—ever!"

Taking a deep breath, Jennifer tried to make herself calm down. She realized that losing her temper would accomplish nothing with Abby. Taking a seat beside her, she asked, "I'm sorry for shouting at you. Let's talk about this together, all right? How is your teacher mean to you, Abby?"

"He picks on me, and he likes to make me look stupid in front of everybody. If my Papa was here, he'd whip that man good!"

"Listen, honey," Jennifer said softly, "I've spoken with your teacher, and he is strict, but he's only trying to help you learn how to behave properly. Being rebellious is only going to bring you a lot of grief."

"But, Mother, I hear people say that *you're* rebellious, that you get in fights with the mining companies."

Jennifer wanted to tell Abby that was different, but was it really? At that moment she wasn't sure. "Sometimes I have to write angry comments in my newspaper, but I try to proclaim truth, truth that will help the miners and their families." She couldn't tell whether Abby understood what she was trying to say or not, or whether it was helpful to her.

Abby just sat there, wanting the confrontation to end. She didn't know what more to say to her mother; she just knew she didn't want to stop being with her friends.

Sensing her daughter needed affection more than discipline, Jennifer took Abby in her arms and hugged her. "I wish you wouldn't hang around with those other youngsters," Jennifer said softly. "I wish my little girl wouldn't get into trouble."

Hugging her mother, Abby's round, angry eyes couldn't quite hide her deep resentment. In a hushed voice she murmured, "I wish Papa was here."

~

Arriving back at the office, Jennifer found Jason sitting in his chair, looking forlorn. "What happened?" he asked quietly.

"Abby and her friends burned down a building and were suspended from school," Jennifer reported hopelessly. "I don't know what I'm going to do with her. She's had such deep anger ever since her father died."

"Is that all?" Jason asked sarcastically. "I'm afraid we have a lot more trouble than that!" He tossed a piece of paper to Jennifer, but it fell to the floor.

Picking it up, Jennifer read the note, which had been scrawled in a deliberate script.

Either stop your attack on the mining companies or be burned out! This is not a threat, but a promise!

Jennifer nervously set the note on the desk. "Where'd this come from?"

"I found it tacked to the front door when I stepped outside for some fresh air," Jason said, obviously worried.

Jennifer glanced at the front door as if it would offer a clue, then turned back to Jason. "Do you think they're serious?"

"Oh, I think they're *very* serious." He straightened in his chair, as if he was reporting for duty. "Well, you're the boss—what do we do?"

Frowning, Jennifer moved closer to Jason. She had a helpless look in her eyes. "We've come so far, Jason, and we've accomplished so much—I don't see how we can quit now. If we let an anonymous foe tell us how to run this paper, we might as well leave town."

"Of course the place might get burned down too," Jason added soberly. "Then you wouldn't have to worry about whether to keep publishing your newspaper."

Straightening her shoulders, Jennifer's eyes grew dark. "I'll not leave town just because of a few threats!" she announced tensely. "I won't blame you if you decide to leave, but I believe God has me here for a purpose, and until He shows me otherwise, I'm staying!"

Jason jumped to his feet. "I'm no quitter either, and I don't scare easily!" he said angrily. "Sure, we've done a lot of good, and we can do more. If they want a fight, we'll fight 'em! I'm with you all the way on this, Jennifer!"

Seeing the determination in his blue eyes, Jennifer knew Jason meant what he said. *He might have a drinking problem, but he's no cow-*

ard, she thought. *At least I know where he stands, which is more than I can say for Charles.* Though she still had the ring the attorney had given her, she continued to agonize over the decision she would have to make soon. But right now she had even more pressing matters to deal with.

~

They had received threats before, but those had been subtle—somebody said that somebody said. Since this was the first written threat, Jennifer decided to take the matter to Charles.

When she walked into the attorney's office, he thought, *I hope Hearst didn't see her come in. No telling what the old man might think or do.* Trying to please both sides of an ongoing dispute wasn't easy, and her coming to his office, located in Hearst's building, always made him nervous. "What's the problem now?" he asked impatiently.

"I think you should see this, " Jennifer said, handing him the threatening note.

Charles read the note, then laid it on his desk. "I'm sorry this happened," he said. He regretted the friction between *The Miner's News* and the mining companies, and he didn't want Jennifer to be in danger, but he also didn't wish to antagonize those who were making him rich. *Why can't she understand that her little crusade just isn't worth it?* he wondered. *She'll never win against the wealthy mining companies.*

Jennifer asked. "Do you think you could find out who's behind this?"

"That isn't likely," Charles said, running his hand through his black hair in exasperation. "You've offended so many different mining companies, this could have come from any of them."

"But you talk to these people all the time," Jennifer pleaded. "Couldn't you ask some leading questions?"

"But remember," Charles argued, "I represent one of the mining companies. If I start snooping around, they'll think I'm trying to work against them." He walked over to a window overlooking the street. Only a few people ambled about in the cold. "Even if I did find out who was behind the note, what would I do then?"

"You could talk to them, tell them that what they did is against the law!" Jennifer insisted hotly.

"Next thing you know, I'd be blackballed, and then *nobody* would talk to me," Charles said, upset at Jennifer's humanitarian naivete. In his mind there was a simple solution to the troublesome situation—Jennifer should marry him and get out of the newspaper business. She could busy herself with social matters, fraternize with the wealthy, and enjoy the finer things in life. He knew he needed to explain all this to her gently, but patience wasn't his forte.

"Why are you so blind?" Charles blurted out. "Don't you see how easy it would be to avoid all this? Once we're married we could travel, see the world. Instead, you want to bury yourself in your newspaper. There are bigger and better things, Jennifer!"

Jennifer began to respond in anger but held herself back when a deeper question came to mind. *Why is he avoiding the real issue? Doesn't he care what happens to the miners? Earlier he seemed to, but now . . . And what about the danger to me?* Something wasn't adding up. She walked over to the window to stand beside Charles. "Do you love me?" she asked.

Resenting the question, Charles answered tensely, "Of course I love you! Why would you ask such a thing?"

"Well then, why don't you want to find out who's threatening to hurt me?" Jennifer's eyes grew sad. "A man doesn't usually tolerate somebody threatening his fiancée."

"Of course I'm upset about the threats against you," Charles said with a muffled voice. "But you insist on putting yourself in danger by writing things that offend the mine owners. If you aren't willing to sell the newspaper, why can't you just report the news without addressing controversial issues?"

Turning away for a moment, Jennifer decided Charles was due an explanation. Maybe he really didn't understand. "I'm not seeking money or wealth," she began. "I merely want to report truth. Most of the people here in Virginia City are simple people who simply want a good life for themselves and their families. Most of them are poor, but they still have rights. But the mining companies continue to exploit them just because they are poor. All I want to do is something significant, to help others, to do something worthwhile with my life. Being rich isn't what I'm after."

"But money is power," Charles argued with quiet reason. "The more money you have, the more you can help these people. You can support many kinds of philanthropy with wealth. You don't have to dwell among the poor and the filthy to help them."

Jennifer disagreed. She thought about how Christ lived among the sick and the poor, how He got to know them and gained their trust, how He reached out to them and taught them about the heavenly Father. She shared her thoughts with Charles, then stated, "I can't stop doing what God has called me to do. Will you help me find out who is threatening me?"

Charles clenched one fist, then slowly opened it as he let his eyes wander from the window to Jennifer and back again. "I'll see what I can do," he said finally. "I'll speak with the sheriff."

Nodding, Jennifer turned to leave. She was saddened by her new glimpse of Charles's attitude toward her paper and toward the miners. What worried her even more was his love of money, which seemed to be coming between them more and more often. "I'll be at my office," she said as she walked out the door.

"Jennifer . . ." Charles called, but she was already gone.

~

Curiosity had moved Grant to find out how ugly rocks were turned into beautiful ingots of gold or silver. But the books he'd read were disappointing, for they used terms like *smelting* and *amalgamation* and *cyanidation*, and he just couldn't understand those fancy words. He knew men stamped and beat the ore into fine powder, but how on earth did the actual gold become beautiful bars? When he and his family had first arrived in Virginia City, he'd thought the miners merely dug up gold and melted it into whatever shape they wanted, but now he knew better. But how *did* they do it? He decided to ask Jason.

Finding Jason alone at the office, Grant approached him confidently, for Jason never chided Grant for disturbing him. "What can

I do for you, Grant?" Jason inquired, seeing the puzzled expression on the lad's face.

"I want to know how polished gold comes from ugly rocks," Grant said. "I looked in some books, but they just made me more confused."

"Let's check the reference books we have here," Jason suggested. "Maybe they'll be more helpful."

After a while Jason told Grant, "I think we just need to simplify some terms and you'll understand."

"I'm going to write it all down," Grant said. "Then maybe I can figure things out."

The process was slow as Grant carefully wrote down Jason's explanations. "I think I understand now," Grant finally said. "I bet a lot of other people around here have had trouble understanding this too."

Suddenly an idea struck Jason. "Well, what do you say we print it, for the sake of kids your age or even adults who want to know more about the process? I'll name you as the author."

Grant accepted the idea enthusiastically. They set the type and laid out the article together. It would appear on the second page of the next edition. "Don't tell Mother," Grant said as his eyes grew wide with excitement. "I want to surprise her."

Jason laughed. "The only problem is, she usually proofreads the articles before we print the newspaper."

"You do it this time," Grant suggested. "I can't wait to have my own copy of a newspaper article I wrote. Thanks, Jason!" Grant bounded from the office, feeling very proud.

When the next edition came out, Jennifer was indeed surprised, and she too was very, very proud!

～

Winter finally spent its fury and gave way to a few days of golden sunshine, a sight welcomed by all in Virginia City. The warmth of the early-spring days had a rejuvenating effect on the town, and the streets were again busy with activity. Though they knew spring wasn't yet here to stay, people found the break from old man winter exhilarating. The threatened burning of the newspaper office didn't happen, even though Jason and Jennifer continued to print pointed articles shaming the mining companies for severe oversights that often cost the miners life or limb.

One day a delivery man dumped a load of mail on the front counter of *The Miner's News*. His hat sat far back on his head, and a heavy mass of straight hair covered his forehead. He gathered his chewing tobacco to one corner of his cheek so he could talk. "Mornin'," he spouted friendly-like, "got some mail here fer ya."

"Good morning," Jennifer replied as the man hurried out. Noticing a parcel, she opened it. It was a new book—*Roughing It* by Mark Twain. A small note fell out.

March 11, 1874

Jennifer,

I spared you the embarrassment of being a character in this book, but may you enjoy it. Hope all is well in Virginia City.

Mark Twain

Excitedly, Jennifer turned to Jason. "Look what Mark Twain sent us," she said, holding the book up. Jason rushed over and inspected the new volume of Twain's humorous observations.

"Mark Twain is the only published author I've ever known personally," Jason said, encouraged that Twain had remembered them. "I bet there's some good reading here."

Pleased, Jennifer turned back to the mail. There were several letters for Grant. "Looks like Grant has developed a following with his articles on getting riches from rocks. Maybe we'll have our own celebrity here in Virginia City before long."

"Who knows? I might be working for Grant someday," Jason jested.

As she examined the rest of the mail, Jennifer thought about Grant's future. *He does show a sincere interest in journalism*, she thought. *Jason has sure been a great encouragement to Grant*. An uncomfortable contrast again came to mind. *I wonder why Charles hasn't bothered to get close to Grant like Jason has.* That bothered her. Charles kept pestering her to set a wedding date, but for some reason she couldn't verbalize, she hadn't been able to agree to marry him. She felt like something still needed to be settled. Charles's aloofness from her children was certainly part of it, but she somehow knew that wasn't the entire explanation.

Jason went back to his desk, where he fidgeted like a caged alley cat until he finally jumped up and screamed, "I can't stand staying inside anymore! I've got to get outside!" He glanced at Jennifer like an embarrassed child. "Well, I do," he mumbled.

Amused, Jennifer smiled. The nice weather had apparently brought on spring fever. "Take a walk," she suggested. "In fact, take the whole afternoon off—we're all caught up."

Not wasting a minute, Jason grabbed his hat and raced for the front door. "See you later," he called over his shoulder. The street was full of people as the bright sun shared its warmth. Jason had a bounce in his step as he breathed in the cool, springtime air. Deciding to see what Molly was up to, he headed for the saloon district. He had continued to spend time with her, acting as if their embarrassing moment had never happened, though he heard her words again and again in his mind. He kept them to himself like rare coins. She was the only woman who'd ever told Jason she loved him.

As Jason drew near to the Golden Fleece, he heard what he thought was a woman screaming. Ahead on the boardwalk, with a crowd of people in the way, he could catch only glimpses of what was happening. A big miner was apparently dragging a dance hall girl behind him, and she was understandably making a fuss. As Jason came closer, he could see that the girl being pulled along the walk was Molly. Incredibly, the crowd just watched, not offering the assaulted woman any help.

Jason picked up his pace, then shoved people aside with burning anger. Coming closer, he saw the big and burly miner slap Molly across the face. "C'mon, woman!" the big man growled. "You owe me some fun!" Moving even faster now, Jason vented his rage in a loud shout. The big man turned his head just in time to catch Jason's fist squarely on the point of his chin. With a loud smack, the heavy fellow dropped like a sack of potatoes.

Quickly bending over and picking Molly up, Jason asked, "Are you all right? Did he hurt you?"

"I think I'm okay," she said, rubbing the red welt on her face.

As Jason helped her walk away, he deliberately stepped on the miner, grinding his boot into the man's hand. The onlookers laughed.

The two made their way down the street to a cafe with tables under a canopy. Jason pulled a chair out for Molly. Her dress was ripped and dirty and the feathers in her hair in disarray, and she was shaking. He sat close to her, still angry that she'd been treated like that.

Not wanting dance hall girls in his establishment, the proprietor gave Jason a questionable look. But Jason threw him a stiff glance that sent him on his way. Soon a nervous waiter approached, his long and tender nose sniffing something obscure. Jason demanded he bring water right away, and the little man scurried away like a rodent.

"Thanks. You're a hero," Molly said, half-crying and half-laughing. "After such a public act, people might start talking about us."

"Let 'em talk," Jason responded.

"It sounded like you killed that fellow," Molly said. Her face saddened, and her voice fell to a whisper. "He wasn't in the wrong—he just got rough with me."

Their water came, and Jason took pleasure in wetting a napkin and dabbing Molly's face. There wasn't any blood, just plenty of dirt.

"You know," Molly murmured, dropping her eyes, "I'm not so pure, Jason. I do things . . . that aren't right. That man spent a lot of money on me in the bar and probably thought he had a right to me. Maybe he did."

Taking her small hand, Jason looked her in the eye. "Molly, I care about you. I'm going to get you out of that place—it's too dangerous for you to be working there!" *I don't see the two of us ever getting married or anything like that, but I can at least help her find a better life. There's no excuse for anybody being treated like that.*

Taking Jason's statement at face value, Molly dreamed that Jason would take her away like a knight in shining armor and marry her. It was honest hopefulness, a childish wish, but such hope was the only thing that enabled her to keep going. Her happy thoughts brought a light to her face. "That would be a dream come true," she said, expressing her silent wishes.

Jason managed an awkward smile. It felt good to have a pretty girl look up to him, even if it was a dance hall girl.

Fire

Next to *The Miner's News* was a shipping office where Theobold McDoogle worked as the clerk. Theo was a tall, gangly man with a long turkey neck and big eyeballs with heavy lids. A beak of a nose jutted out over the thin lips of a large tobacco-stained mouth. His head often bobbed when he talked, and his straw hat with a brim curled like corn husk bobbed too. An ambitionless man, he seemed like a scarecrow come to life, his gawking face apparently baffled by the dubious people he observed. The only thing that infatuated him more than his own keen observations was to discuss and analyze the strange things he'd seen, which had given him the unholy reputation of being the town gossip.

When Jennifer heard Theo's big footsteps on the walk in front of her office, she ducked down, hoping he was passing by. But he entered the front door, and his big, dull eyes peeked over the counter.

"How do there, Mrs. DeSpain." He had seen Jason leave the newspaper office and knew Jennifer would be there alone. He had a wad of juicy gossip to gnaw on and knew it might pique the newspaper lady's nose for news. "Mighty nice day we're havin'."

"Yes, it is." Jennifer sighed. She knew she was trapped—Theo wouldn't leave until he rambled on for a while and found the precise place in the dry conversation to drop his juicy gossip.

Pulling out a fresh plug of tobacco, Theo took his pocket knife, carved off a chew, and rammed it in his mouth. Now his speech was slurred, and his cheek poked out. "It's mighty dry though. We ain't had no rain—not like last year. Nothin' wants to grow when it don't rain."

Blinking her eyes slowly, Jennifer looked up from her desk to see Theo leaning over the counter and staring at her, his big mouth working the fresh plug of tobacco like a cow works a cud. "Yes, it has been dry," she agreed, wishing he'd get to his point and leave. He wasn't a bad man—he was just annoying.

"It's so dry that just this morning I seen a tree chasing a dog," Theo said with a halfhearted laugh.

"We don't have any trees," Jennifer said, correcting him.

"We used to have a few trees, but the lumber companies chopped 'em all down." Theo knew this to be a fact because he'd seen it happen. He'd been in Virginia City since the beginning, though he'd never had any desire to mine gold or obtain riches—the strange ways of people were enough to keep his interest.

Jennifer continued to scrawl some thoughts for an article on a piece of paper. It was sure hard to concentrate with Theo watching her. Hopefully he'd soon get around to what he'd come to tell her.

"I guess you heard . . ." Theo began, but then he stopped as if an important thought had just occurred to him. Taking his time, he moved over to the front door and opened it. He craned out his long neck and spit a stream of tobacco juice all the way to the street. Jennifer made a face at the disgusting noise when he spit. Then he came back and leaned on his elbows, his long-fingered hands hanging over the counter.

This must be a good one, Jennifer thought. *He's sure taking his time with it!*

"Like I was sayin', I guess you heard . . ." Theo said again.

"No, Theo, I don't guess I did," Jennifer mocked impatiently. She stopped her work, leaned back in her chair, and gave him a cold, indifferent stare.

"Well," he said, rolling his dull, lifeless eyeballs, "that Jason, he has a mean punch. He took out old Claudius Tillman in one blow, and Claudius is one big rooster! Why, I seen it happen—I was right there!" Theo stopped and rearranged the wad in his mouth. "That Jason busted Claudius's jaw with a perfect jab—knocked him out colder than a winter night."

By now Theo had Jennifer's full attention. She stood and approached the counter. "It's not like Jason to get into a fight."

"'Tweren't no fight, ma'am! It was one punch! It embarrassed Claudius so bad, he left town fer good—couldn't stand the other miners making fun of him and all 'cause some little newspaper fella busted his jaw and knocked him out."

"I don't understand," Jennifer said, her voice calm but her thoughts troubled. "Jason doesn't like to fight. Why would he hit someone bigger than him?"

This was the kind of moment Theo savored. She'd asked the right question and was practically begging him for the answer. But of course it wasn't in him to answer right away, so he eased over to the door and opened it. Again he craned his neck out and spat tobacco juice, but this time, maybe because he was excited about hooking Jennifer so skillfully with his news, his aim was off target, and most of the juice landed on the boardwalk. Coming back in, he said, "I'll get that swept up in a minute."

Though disgusted with his vulgar habit, Jennifer was still interested in hearing more. "Why did Jason hit that man?"

Theo lived to see the powerful effect his tidbits of information had on people. "Old Claudius . . . well, he'd done paid fer a girl and was takin' her with him, but the girl got to screamin' at him like she didn't want to go fer some reason. And when old Claudius was draggin' her down the street, along come Jason and knocked him out."

Jennifer was relieved. So it had been a Good Samaritan act. "Good for Jason!" she said. "He helped some poor girl out of trouble. Wait a minute—you said you were there. Why didn't you help the girl who was screaming?"

Bashfully, he turned away, his long neck a little red. "I ain't no fighter, Mrs. DeSpain. Besides, Jason was more than just a little help—he took that girl away with him. It's a known fact—they's secretly sparkin'."

Jennifer dropped her eyes and returned to her desk. She didn't want to talk to Theo anymore. Hard thoughts drew the man's heavy eyelids nearly together and cut a notch in his leathery forehead. Knowing the newspaper lady was an upstanding Christian woman, he figured his story would stir her, Jason taking up with a saloon girl and all. A slight smile tugged at the corners of his long mouth as he straightened his drooping shoulders and headed for the door.

Eventually an anger Jennifer didn't understand gave way to admiration. She'd hoped that Jason would find a woman to care about, but a saloon girl? But then she thought, *Who am I to judge him? Jason's personal life is not my business.* From there she went on to think about him standing up for a girl of ill repute, even fighting a man bigger than himself. *Charles would never be that gallant. He wouldn't even stand up for me!* She suddenly found it difficult to concentrate on her work.

~

With gold and wealth beneath her streets, Virginia City was determined not to be outdone by any city in the West. She prided herself on having some 100 saloons and boasted of having more formal entertainment on the stages of her theaters than anywhere else in the West, even San Francisco. Such greats as Adah Menken graced her stages, and Edwin Booth made frequent appearances. Artemus Ward, well-known humorist, was to appear at Piper's Opera House, and Charles Fitzgerald purchased tickets ahead of time. He was sure that such an entertaining evening would delight Jennifer. He was a man who believed things were best achieved when carefully chosen plans were perfectly executed. Tired of waiting for Jennifer to set a wedding date, he would create the opportunity.

On the night of their special evening, Charles spared no expense, taking Jennifer to a fine dinner and then to Piper's Opera House. "This place is packed," Jennifer said as Charles led her to their seats.

"Yes, but that won't be a problem—we have seats on the front row," Charles announced. He loved being seen with such a fine woman, tonight wearing a green dress that made her eyes dance with color. Her auburn hair was up, and she wore a large-brimmed green hat smartly tilted to one side.

Artemus Ward was clever as he mimicked local politicians and made jokes about the habits of some of the townspeople. "A miner comes home late at night," he said, imitating the walk of a drunken miner to perfection. "And his wife is waiting for him. She says, 'Harry, you work all day and drink all night—no man can stand that kind of life for long!' Old Harry, now he's a reasonable man," Artemus said, his round face alive with the audience's laughter. "Harry thinks about this, then says to his wife, 'You're right, my dear. I guess I'll quit the mine tomorrow.'"

A roar of laughter from the audience rewarded Artemus for his humorous talents. Charles watched Jennifer as much as the act on stage, for she held a certain beauty when she laughed, and the gaiety in her eyes made them sparkle. She applauded the little man on stage and was eager to hear more as he made them all laugh throughout the evening.

After the show, Charles and Jennifer exited the smoke-filled theater and began a leisurely walk home. The evening was pleasant, and the sky was filled with stars. For some reason Virginia City was quieter than usual. *A perfect evening for romance*, Charles thought as he walked with Jennifer hand-in-hand. It was late at night by the time they approached her front door. Charles impulsively pulled her to him and gave her a long, hard kiss. Her lips were soft and sweet. He whispered softly, "You're a wonderful woman, Jenny."

Comfortable in his arms, Jennifer said, "I had a lovely evening. I don't remember ever having laughed so much." She still wore a pleasant smile, the fine dinner and entertainment having made her forget the rest of the world and even her earlier reservations about Charles, though not completely. She yearned for Charles to truly care about the miners and their families, and for her and her family. Most of all, she longed to know for sure where Charles stood with God. Did he have a faith in the Lord, or was it just occasional lip service? And yet, despite all that, there was so much she admired in Charles, and she so enjoyed being with him. She wished she could sort it all out and knew she would have to do exactly that soon.

A lonesome train whistle sounded in the distance. A light fog made the lights in the business side of town below them indistinct. Thanks to the warm spring night air, she was in a vulnerable and relaxed frame of mind.

"I love you, Jennifer. I want to spend my life with you. Can't we set a wedding date? I've been patient, I've given you plenty of time to think it over, but . . ." He watched her closely, delighting in her sincere, firm smile and the way her eyes sparkled in the dim light. He was a man who believed timing was everything, and tonight he had her complete attention.

Jennifer glanced away. But knowing she needed to answer, she swung her eyes back to the man who held her. Finding strength in his closeness, she placed her arms around him. She realized she couldn't put him off forever. *He is in many ways a good man, and God doesn't seem to have brought anyone else along to be my husband or my children's father*, she thought as she gazed into those deep blue eyes that were waiting for an answer.

Suddenly a commotion came from the street below as loud bells rang and voices shouted into the night. Glancing down, Jennifer saw a faint orange glow through the light fog. "That looks like a fire!" she said urgently. "It looks like it's near my newspaper office!"

Turning Jennifer loose, Charles turned to look closely at the flickering light. "It's coming from the business district—it *is* a fire!"

Quickly Jennifer hurried down the walk and onto the street, then made her way downhill toward the scene of the emergency. Charles rushed along beside her.

~

Only hours before, Jason had debated with himself as to whether or not he wanted to go somewhere and have a drink. Since it had been a while since he'd indulged, he figured it would be all right, though he feared the results. *I can't just have a few drinks like other men*, he thought sadly as he fiddled with the doorknob on the front door of the office. *The only way I can drink is to drink until I'm out of my mind.* He turned the knob loose and walked to the small back room of the office. This was his private world.

Lighting a lantern, Jason glanced around. It wasn't much. A simple room about twelve by six feet of rough wooden walls. Along one wall stretched his unmade bunk; opposite it stood a small dresser containing a few personal things and having a water-stained mirror above it. On the dresser sat a washbasin and pitcher full of tepid water from the well out back. Some clothes hung on a clothes rack he'd rigged in the corner. A few sagging shelves held ragged volumes of books and a tintype photograph of him and Robert Hutton, the previous owner of *The Miner's News*, as they stood proudly in front of the new building.

Shaking his head, Jason thought, *I was ready to set the world on fire, to conquer the West with my brilliant writing.* He sadly glanced around the room. *What happened?* A back door set in a blank wall beckoned him into the night. The urge to get drunk was strong, but then he thought about Molly, a girl he viewed as a young woman whose life could've been so different if she hadn't been denied the decent life she deserved. *Who do I think I'm fooling? I'll probably just end up at the Golden Fleece again.* Thinking about talking himself into getting drunk as he watched Molly flirt with the other men sickened him. *I hate seeing her throw her life away. But I'm doing the same thing!*

Jason laid down on his bunk and watched the flickering dark shadows created by the dim light of the lantern. The air was musty and heavy. *I wonder if Jennifer has any idea how hard it is for me to concentrate on my work when she's around. She's so beautiful, so noble and good. She has surely deserved much more than a man like me. And now she's going to marry Fitzgerald—he's a snake!* Jason fluffed the pillow, then placed both hands behind his head as he lay back deep in thought.

Sometimes the newspaper office reminded him of a jail, and right now Jason's little room felt like a cell. He enjoyed the work at the paper, but he also felt trapped there. If he went elsewhere in the evenings, trying to distance himself from the conflicting emotions he felt at the office, he knew he'd turn to drinking. But if he just stayed at the newspaper all the time . . . He liked being near Jennifer, even if she never showed any feelings for him, but he wished . . . *She's the loveliest woman who ever lived*, he thought. *She's been very patient with me and has even tried to help me with my problems.* He found it hard to fall asleep as the urge to go out continued to assault him. *I wish I could just tell Jennifer how I feel about her,* he told himself, trying to be optimistic. *But I can't. I'm just a lousy drunk!*

Jason grabbed the nearest book and tried to read, but he had too much on his mind. *If only I could change, but I can't. There's no way for me to become a different man!* Jason tossed and turned through much of the evening, barely chasing off the temptation to go drink himself into unconsciousness. As it became late evening, the town grew quieter, with little movement outside. The disheartened young man heard a train whistle in the distance, a calming sound, but then came the loud crash of shattering glass at the front of the office. Jumping up quickly, he opened the door of the back room and saw flames racing away from a broken lantern. On the other side of the broken front window Jason saw the shadow of a big man who hesitated for a moment and then disappeared.

Jason's first thought was to run out the back door to escape the consuming fire. But then, thinking about how much the paper meant to Jennifer and himself, he grabbed the blanket from his bunk and rushed over to the fire. Beating the flames, he quickly realized his efforts were useless since the kerosene immediately reignited every time he extinguished part of the fire. Fed by all the paper and ink, the flames spread throughout the office in moments.

Running to the front door, Jason quickly unlatched it and called out, "Fire! Fire!" He turned and looked behind him. *I have to save the press!* he thought. Battling the increasing heat, he ran to the press, grabbed the metal legs, and began dragging it to the front door. He coughed as the thick smoke surrounded him, but he pushed on with desperate determination. He finally pulled the heavy machine onto the boardwalk, then tipped it onto the dirt street.

A crowd of onlookers had gathered and began to form a bucket brigade from a nearby horse trough. In the distance, clanging bells summoned the Young American Fire Company to the scene. Jason tore a long strip off his shirt and wrapped it around his face as he rushed back into the burning building. He grabbed tray after tray of type and threw each through the busted window and into the street.

A thoughtful firefighter threw a bucket of water on Jason when he came near the window, but it was little help as the raging blaze was now climbing the office walls. Continuing his efforts anyway, Jason moved even faster, grabbing anything of importance and throwing it out the window.

When Jennifer and Charles arrived at a full run, she became hysterical. She had hoped it wasn't her newspaper that was burning, and now, even worse, she saw that Jason was inside. "Jason! Get out of there!" she shrieked, advancing toward the flaming building.

Charles grabbed Jennifer and held her back. "No, Jennifer!" he yelled, then said more calmly, "There's nothing you can do."

She turned to Charles, her face panic-stricken. "Charles, do something—get him out of there!"

Holding his hands out helplessly, Charles shrugged. "What can I do?" he pleaded.

Jason, now shirtless, tossed another box through the window just as a portion of the building began to collapse. "Jason!" Jennifer called. "Get out now!"

Hearing her plea, Jason looked up and saw Jennifer not far from the window, her arms extended as she urged him to save himself. His head was spinning, and his lungs ached from the smoke. Knowing there wasn't much more he could do, with his last burst of energy he dove out of the window. Running over to him, Jennifer tried to drag him away from the blaze. "Somebody please help me!" The hand of a strong miner grabbed Jason and dragged him to safety. The young newspaperman gave in to uncontrollable coughing as Jennifer pulled the cloth strip from his blackened face. "Jason!" she cried, holding him close.

Glancing up, Jennifer watched the office of *The Miner's News* cave in. The buildings on both sides were now on fire as well. She and Charles moved Jason across the street to a water trough, where she dipped her shawl in the water and gently patted Jason's blistered skin. He was now unconscious. "You can't die on me!" she cried, holding his head in her lap.

Standing beside Jennifer as she knelt over Jason, Charles watched the fire grow in intensity and consume the shipping company next-door. The Young American Fire Company seemed to be no match for the growing flames. The scene was tragic to most, but to Charles it meant only one thing. *That'll be the end of the newspaper. Now maybe Jennifer will stop her foolishness and give her life to me,* he thought gladly.

~

By dawn over half the business district of Virginia City lay in smoldering ashes as people wandered aimlessly and searched through the debris. In the front room of Jennifer's house, Jason rested in bed. His body was covered with a heavy malodorous grease. Dr. William Coleman, a portly, elderly man with a white beard and small glasses, was a man who had seen death often but who also knew how to bring healing. "He'll be all right," he said, his voice low and husky. "The burns are superficial. I'm mostly concerned about smoke inhalation—it may take him a few days to get over that. Now, if you'll excuse me, I've a full day ahead. The other victims need my attention also."

"Thank you, Dr. Coleman," Jennifer said. "I'll look after him."

"He's in good hands then," Dr. Coleman replied. "Good day, ma'am." He left hurriedly.

Jennifer sat down beside Jason, noticing that his face was blistered wherever the cloth strip hadn't protected it. Her eyes were full of sadness. "Jason, what will we do? A large part of the town is damaged, and the newspaper is burned to the ground," she said softly. "I guess we're through. I wouldn't know how to start over again."

Jason blinked at her, his eyes swollen and red and still burning from the smoke. The blisters on his skin were painful, and his lungs still ached, but he knew he'd be all right. He especially appreciated Jennifer's caring affection. "You give up?" he said hoarsely. "I'd have never guessed it."

Looking away, Jennifer felt a deep depression. "I don't know what to say. I need to talk to God about this, if you don't mind," she murmured. Lowering her head, she prayed aloud for strength and thanked God for sparing Jason while he listened.

Jason felt closer to Jennifer than ever before as he watched her pray. Her pretty, innocent face and the fact that she worried and prayed over him touched him deeply. A concern like that could inspire a man to accomplish the impossible.

When she finished, she glanced at Jason, his blue eyes observing her intently.

"Well, what did He say?"

Pausing for a moment, Jennifer answered, "Sometimes God doesn't answer our prayers right away. I don't know exactly what He wants us to do, but I'm sure He'll show us one step at a time. You see, Jason, God doesn't guarantee that everything will be strawberries and cream in our lives. But He does love us and offers us true spiritual life."

"You mean God didn't tell you more than that? Do you think I risked my life to save that press and that other stuff for nothing?" Jason asked though it hurt to talk. "Get ahold of some canvas and some boards—we'll operate out of a tent until we can rebuild. Soon as I get to feeling a little better, I'll pitch in." Jason smiled. "It'll be just like the old days when Hutton and I first started the paper."

Smiling, Jennifer knew Jason's stubborn courage was the answer to her prayer. "You see, God is already showing us what to do," she said confidently. "We'll rebuild and make *The Miner's News* better than before. God is with us, Jason, and I hope you'll learn more and more about Him." Letting her hand lightly touch the side of Jason's burned face, she leaned over and gave him a small kiss on the cheek. As far as Jason was concerned, that was the best medicine yet.

～

In the weeks to come Virginia City quickly began to take shape again, somewhat grander than before. Trains came in twice as often, bringing needed canvas and lumber, enabling suppliers to make a substantial profit. Facades went up in front of board-floor tents, and buildings quickly rose thereafter. The staccato sound of hammers drove on through the night, while teams pulled freighters full of supplies through the busy streets daily.

The rebuilding of the newspaper progressed well, for Jennifer had wisely put money aside for an emergency. However, the reconstruction was costing more than she would have thought, and when she asked Charles for help, his response was not what she expected.

"You're not going to rebuild!" Charles protested. "That business is going to get you killed!"

"You're always bragging about how much money you have, how you want to help those in need," Jennifer said quietly. "Won't you help me rebuild the paper?"

Studying her, Charles found himself in a dilemma. He couldn't allow his money to be used to build an institution his employers opposed, and yet he cared about Jennifer. "I'm sorry, darling, but I can't do it," he said in a low tone of voice. "Can't you find something else that interests you?"

Her lips tightened, and a hard look came across her face. Jennifer felt uneasy about something she couldn't yet identify, similar to feeling an unknown danger that lurks nearby. In one way she understood why Charles couldn't use his funds in this way, but in another way she didn't understand at all. After all, she was the woman he'd ask to marry him! "I just thought I'd ask," she said, accepting his answer but again wondering what kind of man Charles Fitzgerald really was. She had shared with him how she felt God was directing her steps, and she was sure he would want to be part of God's provision. Now she didn't know what to think.

Fortunately, the rebuilding of the newspaper office kept her mind occupied. Canvas quickly covered a wood frame that was built over the wooden floor, and the facade was built in the street and then lifted into place. The new building would be larger than the previous one.

Despite his injuries and the recuperation that proceeded more slowly than he would have liked, Jason relished the new beginning and sensed that a changed world was at hand. Abe Washington pitched in and proved to be a good carpenter with endless energy as he pounded nail after nail. Once the canvas walls were up, Jason insisted on living in the office just like before. "Somebody has to watch the place," he said happily. "You can't lock a tent."

Jennifer admired the resilient young man's drive. "I owe you a great deal of thanks," Jennifer said. As she left to go home to her family, she turned and looked at Jason. In that instant he saw something in her eyes that made him wonder . . . made him wonder if she was looking at him in that special way a woman looks at a man whom she is beginning to love. He stood stock-still for a long moment, then turned slowly, his jaw set with serious reflection.

PART FOUR

ADVENTURES
OF THE HEART

CHAPTER

～ 19 ～

Disclosure

I can't believe how quickly a town can be put back together,"
Jennifer said, observing the businesses up and down the street from
the newspaper office. "And we've done well ourselves."

Not one to brag, Jason said, "This office is better than the last
one. My room in the back is definitely better." He stood in front of
the new building, proud of its appearance and of the hard work that
had swiftly brought it into being.

The warm breeze carried the smell of freshly cut lumber mixed
with the raw odor of horses and mules. Somewhere down the street
a mule skinner cracked a whip and cursed his mules. The tents had
slowly been replaced by permanent wooden buildings, and the sound
of hammers pounding and saws ripping through lumber could still be
heard.

"Our last order for supplies should be in today," Jennifer commented. "I don't know what we would've done if you hadn't saved
the press and all those other things you rescued."

"Well, we're back in business now," Jason said cheerily. *Though
there is some unfinished business to take care of*, he told himself, his eyes
becoming fine slits. Though he'd told no one else, Jason thought he
knew who the man in the window the night of the fire was. And he'd
soon find out if his hunches were right.

～

Sparkling stars shone brightly in the sky as Jason slipped out the back door of the new office, but he wasn't going somewhere to have a drink. He hoped to verify that the man he had seen through the smashed window as the fire started was Big Ned O'Donnell. One of Big Ned's favorite haunts was the Ore Bucket, a lowly place near the edge of the saloon district. Jason found a good hiding-place across the street, partly behind a stack of wooden kegs, to watch for Big Ned. He waited through the evening hours, his hat brim low over his eyes—just another shadow on the street. Jason had tried this several times before, but he hoped that this time his tactics would produce the desired result.

At ten minutes after 9 Big Ned stepped through the swinging doors, the light casting his long shadow into the street. He paused to roll a cigarette, the flare of the match revealing his bushy face as he glanced slyly up and down the street. Jason kept his hat low and crouched down beside the kegs. Big Ned stepped off the boardwalk and made his way down the street with a long, lumbering gait. Jason followed, keeping his distance, and when O'Donnell slipped into an alley, Jason suspected he would soon have his answers. He was positive when he saw O'Donnell slip through a back door at the Ophir mining office.

Only one window in the building was lit, but it was on the second floor. Searching around in the darkness, Jason found an old section of scaffolding that would serve as a ladder. Carefully leaning it against the building, he began his silent climb. Since the day had been warm, the window was slightly open, and Jason detected the acrid smell of cigar smoke from within.

Jason couldn't see the man in the high-backed leather chair, but he recognized the voice—it was George Hearst. Across from him sat Big Ned, an angry expression burning in his beady eyes.

Hearst complained, "I paid you good money to get rid of that newspaper woman! Now they've rebuilt, and it won't be long before she's provoking the miners again!"

O'Donnell raised his meaty hands. "I burned her business to the ground—and half the town with it!" he growled. "How was I to know she'd rebuild? I figured she'd cash in her chips for sure!"

After a long pause, Hearst said, "I want you to run her out of town—and no excuses this time! If these miners ever really get organized, they could cost me a lot of money. And she's just the kind of person who can plant ideas in their heads with her stupid newspaper. I'll give you 5,000 dollars if you bring this thing to a close!"

Jason almost lost his balance when he heard Hearst's words. The corrupt mining company owner was placing Jennifer in grave danger.

Simpleminded, Big Ned wanted to impress Hearst. "Mr. Hearst, I'll take care of that woman my way! She won't never talk again."

"I don't want any excuses!" Hearst barked. Then his voice became lower and meaner. "How would you like it if the Miner's Union found out that one of their supervisors was working against them?"

Jason decided to risk raising his head to get a better look at Big Ned. Fear shone in the thug's small eyes. "But, Mr. Hearst, we had an agreement."

"If you know what's good for you, you'll get the results you promised me, Ned!" Hearst said menacingly. "Now get out of my office!"

Big Ned got up and slowly lumbered toward the door. He hesitated, then finally mumbled, "I'll take care of it."

Jason quickly scooted down the improvised ladder and stole away in the darkness. *Who can I tell about this? There's no telling who's on Hearst's payroll, maybe even the sheriff,* Jason thought. *I can't let anything happen to Jennifer. I'll have to take care of Ned myself.*

⌇

The clear morning light shone on Molly as she sat by her hotel window having coffee and watching the people walk by. The nights were long and hard for her, but she cherished these private moments in the late morning, a time to think about how she wished things would change and make her life better. *Men strike it rich here all the time,* she reflected, *and not just by striking gold. Some get lucky in business, some at gambling, all sorts of ways. If only something good would happen in my life!*

Her thinking turned to Jason. *He's the nicest man I've met out west.*

Maybe he'll take me away from here, and we can start somewhere else where nobody will know what I was before. But as usual, she became depressed, concluding that her dreams were just that—dreams, wishful fantasies. *Jason treats me more like a little sister than a girlfriend. Considering what I've become, I don't blame him.* Nevertheless, Jason was probably her only chance to escape the daily oppression in which she lived. He was the only man who truly cared about her.

Far down the street Molly spotted Jason's unmistakable gait as he turned into a gun shop. Unable to visit him in the newspaper office, in the respectable part of town, she welcomed the chance to talk with Jason for a while. She quickly dressed and rushed out of the hotel.

Catching Jason as he stepped out of the store, Molly gave him her friendliest smile. "Hello, Jason. Where've you been lately?"

Jason gave her a worried smile. He saw the bright sparkle in her eyes, giving her face a hopeful expression. Jason knew he was generally the only person ever to see that side of Molly.

For her part, Molly was indeed delighted to see Jason. He was like an oasis in the desert of her life. When she noticed the brown paper bundle in his arms and the gunbelt hanging out, her smile changed to a concerned frown. He quickly shoved the belt back into the wrapping.

She immediately sensed something was wrong—Jason was obviously not his usual self. "Why are you buying a gun?" she asked, both inquisitive and afraid.

Jason kept walking as Molly followed along. "There's something I have to do," he said firmly.

"Something you have to do? You're not talking about a gunfight, are you?" Her face paled with deep concern. "What's going on?" She knew men, and she knew when trouble was brewing.

Coming to a standstill, Jason faced Molly. The look on his face was grave and deadly serious. "I have to find Big Ned—he's the one who started the fire."

Molly froze with fear. "But he's a fighter, Jason. You can't face him down—he'll kill you!"

"He's not a gunfighter—he fights with his fists, Molly. Has any-one ever told you he's good with a gun?"

"Are *you* good with a gun?" she asked in response.

"I plan on being good enough," Jason assured her as he began walking again.

She grabbed Jason's arm, stopping him again. "Jason, you can't do this! You're the only good thing in my life. I don't know how I could possibly go on if something happened to you!" The sun made hard shadows on Molly's face. Her blue eyes pleaded helplessly as her black hair glistened in the bright light. She was a young woman whose dreams were about to be taken away.

"I have to do this!" Jason stated flatly. Pulling his arm free, he hurried down the busy street.

Molly helplessly watched Jason walk away. She felt powerless and alone in a cruel world. *He said he has to do something. So do I!*

~

Though he hadn't planned it, Jason was glad he had told Molly about his plans because he knew she would tell others. Talk would spread like an epidemic that Jason was gunning for Big Ned. That way Big Ned would be sure to carry a pistol; even a dumb thug like Big Ned knew his fists were no match for a gun.

Most people assumed Jason was just tired of being bullied by Big Ned and wanted to put an end to it soon. Whatever the reason for the coming confrontation, everyone wanted to be sure not to miss the event. Typical for a town where men would gamble about which bird would take off from a fence first, bets were hastily placed.

Theo McDoogle rushed into the office of *The Miner's News.* "You probably already heard," the eager bearer of bad news said.

"I'm busy," Jennifer snapped, pressured by an approaching dead-line. "If you have something to tell me, Theo, then tell me! I don't have time for games right now."

Almost swallowing his chewing tobacco, Theo straightened up. "I jest wanted to tell you that Jason is gunnin' for Big Ned O'Donnell. He plans on having a shore 'nough shoot-out. The town's got Big Ned at five to one odds."

"I don't believe you! Now please, I'm very busy!"

Theo scurried away, his head hunched between his bony shoulders.

Though Jennifer really didn't believe Theo's alarming announcement, she didn't totally disbelieve it either.

When Jason came into the office, Jennifer cornered him. "What's this I hear about a gunfight?" she demanded.

Afraid to look her in the eye, Jason said, "It's true. I have to stop Big Ned."

"Are you crazy?" Jennifer demanded. "Whatever the problem is, talk to the sheriff about it!"

"Not this time," Jason said evenly. "There's politics in this town. I don't know who I can trust."

"Has it occurred to you that you just might get yourself killed?" Jennifer argued. "You're no gunfighter!"

"That's a chance I'll have to take." He turned away from Jennifer, went back to his room, and shut the door.

Jennifer was so frightened, she couldn't think straight. She tried going about her work, but confusion and fear had their way with her. She realized Jason wasn't about to tell her what was going on. *Why is he doing this? Is it about the newspaper, or something to do with me, or is it some situation I know nothing about?*

Anxiety overwhelmed her as she went back to her desk. She knew it would be useless to plead with her stubborn young friend. Yet she admired his courage in the face of fear, so ironic in a man who had such a great weakness for excessive drinking. She appreciated his strength of character. He held on to strong principles and would do what he felt had to be done. But this worried her, for she knew that could get him killed.

Totally disillusioned and consumed by fear, Jennifer quickly resorted to the comfort of prayer. *Father, please intervene in this situation. I don't know what Jason was referring to or why he has to confront Big Ned. I only know that Jason is in great danger and could get hurt, even killed. Please watch over Jason. He doesn't even know Jesus as his Saviour yet. I know I should have told him more about that before now, but please . . . please, Lord, protect Jason and help him come to know You.*

Since Jason wasn't willing to talk about whatever was going on between him and Big Ned, she didn't know what else to do. She hoped what she'd done was enough.

~

In his stuffy back room, Jason strapped on his gun and practiced for hours that night, drawing the gun from a tied-down holster and shooting with empty chambers. He figured he'd be close enough to Big Ned that he couldn't possibly miss. He drew again and again in front of an old mirror until a bead of sweat formed on his upper lip. *Since Big Ned's not a gunfighter, I doubt that he'll draw any faster than I can. Then again, it's a different matter when two men actually face each other. As long as I don't get too nervous . . . !* He stuffed the gun back in the holster, quickly drew it, and clicked the hammer again. The short-barreled .44 Colt still felt heavy and awkward, but there was nothing he could do about that. He wished he had someone to teach him, but his lack of experience wouldn't make him turn back.

Jason looked at the gun-toting man in the mirror, or was he a man? He would soon know. Was he doing the wise thing, or the good thing, or the honest thing? He knew only one thing for sure—the decision had been made, and now he had to go through with it.

A gentle knock sounded on Jason's door. "Who's there?" he called apprehensively.

"It's me—Grant," came a young voice.

Jason opened the door and stared at the boy. "What are you doing out so late? Does your mother know where you are?"

"No," Grant said as he stepped inside. "I snuck out." He noticed the shiny new gun and fine holster Jason was wearing, then looked at his friend's sweaty face. "Is it true, Jason—you're going to be in a gunfight?"

Nodding, Jason turned away and resumed his position in front of the mirror. He drew the piece, then slid it back into the holster.

"Wow, that was fast!" Grant said, excited by the thought of actual gunplay. "Are you scared?"

"I'd be a fool if I wasn't," Jason replied thinly.

"Then why are you doing it?" Grant asked innocently.

Walking over to Grant, Jason ruffled the boy's wavy hair and gave him a smile. "Sometimes there are things we just have to do—there's no other choice."

Becoming more worried, Grant sat down on Jason's small bunk. He'd never sneaked out of the house at night before, but after hearing the news, he had to find out for himself. After all, Jason was his best friend. It had all sounded like something out of a dime novel until the reality of it hit him. A cold fear ran through him when he realized Jason might be killed. "There's more to it than you getting revenge for Big Ned beating you up, isn't there?"

Cocking his head, Jason glanced over at Grant, wondering how much he should say. "You're a smart boy. Yes, there's a lot more to it."

"Does anybody else know why you're doing this?" Grant asked, trying to piece the puzzle together.

"Not really," Jason replied. "Nobody needs to know."

"Well—" Grant dropped his eyes. "What if you get killed? Then nobody will know what it was you were really fighting about. Don't you think you should tell somebody?"

The boy makes sense, Jason thought. *Nobody knows what I heard through Hearst's window.* Jason sat on the bunk beside Grant. "You're right. There are people in danger, and I need to share what I know with somebody. How about if I tell you?" Jason knew he could trust Grant—he certainly wasn't on Hearst's payroll! Of course, he could have told Jennifer too, but his pride kept him from that. Besides, she might find a way to stop Jason from going through with his plan. Grant couldn't.

Surprised that Jason would be willing to tell him what was going on, Grant's eyes opened wide. Jason liked the resemblance Grant had to his mother when he made certain expressions. Certainly the son would have the right to know that his mother was in danger. Although he was just a boy, he was mature beyond his years; he could handle the news.

"What could *I* do?" Grant asked. "I'm just eleven."

"You can write it down," Jason said encouragingly. "And if Big

Ned kills me, you can put your article in the paper. The people of this town have the right to know what's going on!"

Though at first frightened about everything Jason had told him, Grant decided he could do a good job of writing it all down. Jumping up, he went to the front office and fumbled around in the dark until he found a pencil and some blank paper. When he came back to Jason's room, Jason was unstrapping the gun belt.

The lantern burned steadily, giving off a soft glow. The simple room told nothing about the man who lived there, but Grant was determined to let people know what Jason was really like. His words would portray Jason as the most courageous man he knew. Grant sat on the bunk, the paper in his lap as Jason paced the floor and began to explain, his hands animatedly accompanying his words.

"The night of the fire," Jason began, "when I heard the lantern get thrown into the office and I saw the big man out front, he looked familiar. But with all the effort of trying to put out the fire and save the press, I didn't even think about it any further until weeks later. Then when I thought back to the man I'd seen, I realized it was Big Ned."

Jason shuffled his heels, scuffing the floor as he talked slowly so Grant could write down the main parts of the story. "But why would Big Ned want to burn down our newspaper office? He doesn't care about *The Miner's News*. And I'm just a drunk he picks on. He wouldn't be after me. So I got to thinking, Big Ned had to be working for somebody else." Jason paused while Grant scribbled. "So I started following Big Ned around from time to time, and one night I followed him to George Hearst's office. I climbed up on some old scaffolding so I could listen to them through a window. George Hearst had paid Big Ned to burn down our office, though I don't think he'd wanted Big Ned to burn down half the town."

Grant glanced up, bewildered. Having worked at the newspaper office and being a voracious reader, Grant was well aware of town politics. He knew about the ongoing war between the miners and the mining companies. "Big Ned was working for George Hearst? But isn't Big Ned a mining union leader? Why would he do anything for one of the owners?"

"I'm getting to that," Jason said. "Hearst was upset about our rebuilding the office and staying in business. He thought the fire would scare us off for sure." Jason shook his head. "Maybe I shouldn't have encouraged your mother to start over again. Now Hearst has ordered Big Ned to run your mother out of town, but I don't think Big Ned will stop at anything short of murder."

"Kill her? Big Ned is going to murder my mother? Jason, no!" He was shouting now. "Those men are evil monsters, and somehow we have to stop them!"

"That's why I have to face Big Ned in a gunfight." Jason looked Grant right in the eye.

"Why can't we just expose Big Ned?" Grant asked. "The union needs to know he's a traitor!"

"I don't think anyone would believe me," Jason replied. "Remember, I'm known as a drunk who has had words with Big Ned. Besides, we don't have much time—I don't know how soon Big Ned will go after your mother. I have to do something right away."

Grant set his paper and pencil down and stood up. He was physically and emotionally mature for eleven years old. His face was stern in the lamplight. Though he was nearly in a state of panic because he feared for his mother's life, he understood what it meant when a man had to take care of business, even at the risk of his own life. That burden had been placed on Grant at an early age when his father died. He'd had to be strong then, and he had to be strong now. "When do you plan on calling out Big Ned?"

Jason glanced at the gun lying on the bunk, then turned to Grant. "Tomorrow. The word's already spreading, and in the morning I'll be face to face with Big Ned."

Grant felt a trickle of remorse. He wished he was older and stronger so he could help Jason face Big Ned. He could at least stand by Jason and his mother no matter what happened. "If something happens to you . . . Why do you think people will believe what I write about it?"

"If I get killed," Jason said, "at least they'll know why I did what I did. Don't worry, they'll believe you. Just write it plain and simple—

strictly facts, not your own opinions of anybody, the same way you wrote your other articles."

Grant felt like a heavy burden had just been placed on his shoulders. He knew he might lose his mother and Jason too. "I'll do the best I can," he said weakly.

"That's all I ask," Jason said, forcing a smile and putting a gentle hand on Grant's shoulder. "You'd better get along now. You don't want to upset your mother by being out too late."

Grant went to the door and opened it, then turned back to Jason. "Thanks for everything. I know you can do it!" he said, then eased the door closed as he left.

"I hope you're right, Grant," Jason mumbled. "I hope you're right."

come into her eyes, he said simply, "I'm doing this for you." He reached for his hat and pulled the brim down in a gesture of finality. "If it were anything else . . ."

Confusion marked Jennifer's face, for his reply made no sense to her. Jason tugged at the gunbelt, rearranging the unfamiliar weight on his hip. He gave her one last glance, wanting desperately to tell her how he truly felt about her, but not wanting to make subsequent days harder for her if he should fall to Big Ned's bullets.

"Jason . . . I've already begged you not to meet Big Ned, but . . . if you are determined to do this, at least make your peace with God, in case . . ." She couldn't bear to finish the thought. Jason sent her an unspoken message with his eyes, then left.

She stood motionless, paralyzed by her fear and helplessness. She was also angry. Why was the situation so clear to him but a puzzle to her? She couldn't stop thinking about Jason. She recalled guarded remarks people had made about his drinking—said in jest and quickly dropped, but obviously intended as insults. Yes, he had a drinking problem, but he also had character strengths. If only he would come to have faith in the Lord . . . She pictured his handsome face, his charm; she reflected on his courage and his stubborn will, his ability to commit to something he believed in. A sudden thought struck her like a slap in the face. She had been questioning his reasons for wanting to face Big Ned. But wasn't he the same person now as before? She felt guilty for her quick judgments of the man.

In thinking about Jason, she thought about the other man in her life, one for whom she had for some time now been entertaining thoughts of marriage. The contrast was undeniable. Charles always managed to slide around the issues, to talk his way around things she deemed important, to evade any heated confrontation. He was predictably defensive and clever at finding ways to decline assistance for someone in need, whereas Jason was kind and gentle and caring. How clear, though unsettling, this all was now! Sometimes she wondered if she knew herself at all, being astonished to see things she hadn't known were within her. Bowing her head she prayed, *Father, I can't make sense of all this. I just know I don't want Jason to die, especially without knowing Your Son as his Saviour. Please*

*protect him. Please bring the proper resolution to whatever is going on.
O God, help him—please help him!*

~

Jason made his way steadily down the dusty street, noticing as
the men behind him stepped off the boardwalk and followed.
Storekeepers came out of their buildings and watched silently as
Jason passed, their expressions somber but also eager. The long walk
gave Jason time to think. He was afraid of what might happen, but
he was also afraid the town would detect his fear and see it as weakness. Sometimes when he'd been especially troubled about the
emptiness of his life, he had longed for death; but now that it might
be at hand, he began breathing in shallow gasps. His hands were
sweaty but not shaking, and that pleased him. He remembered
Jennifer's final words about making his peace with God. *I wish I'd settled accounts with You earlier, God. Now that I may be about to die, I
don't know how to get right with You, and I can't turn back from facing
Big Ned, for Jennifer's sake. I'm sorry, God.*

Rounding the corner, an even larger crowd lined the streets in
the saloon district. A hushed silence fell over them all as Jason
appeared. He slowed his walk, the late-morning sun casting a short
shadow in front of him. To his left stood the Silver Dollar. He had
heard that was where Big Ned would be.

He planted his feet and called loudly, "Ned, I'm calling you out."

Anticipation marked every face during the long wait. The men
behind Jason moved to the side, hoping to avoid any stray bullets.
The last few dollars changed hands for late wagers. Finally the saloon
doors swung open, and Big Ned filled the doorway.

Big Ned smiled, his yellow teeth showing through a heavy beard.
He was a man who thrived on hate and loved a challenge. His gun
sat in a well-worn holster. His bushy head of brownish-red hair surrounded a big, dark face; his eyes were close-set, beady, and full of
lust for a kill. "So the newspaper boy is calling me out," he taunted,
his voice rugged and deep. He stepped down into the street, his
malevolent eyes holding Jason in their grip. "It'll be a pleasure
watching you squirm in your own blood," he laughed.

Hearing a commotion in the crowd, Jason turned to see Molly pushing her way forward. "Jason!" she cried as she grabbed him by the arm. "Jason, no!" she cried, tears running down her cheeks. "Please don't do this!"

Not taking his eyes from the big man in front of him, Jason pushed her away. "I must, Molly. There's no other way." Someone took hold of the dance hall girl and dragged her away.

"You'd better tell her good-bye," Big Ned said coldly as he squared off not ten feet in front of Jason.

The next few seconds seemed like an eternity to the young newspaper man. He thought of everything he'd done in his life. He reflected on living back east with a decent family of brothers and sisters, his father, a respectable man of means, and his mother, a gentle and kind woman. He recalled graduating from Harvard, an achievement he thought would secure a bright future. He remembered boldly coming west to make a life for himself in journalism. And he thought of the disappointments and how he'd become a failure. All those thoughts passed in an instant until he came to the challenge at hand. This was the one thing he had to do, like it or not, whatever the cost. His hand remained steady as he waited.

Big Ned glared at him with a viciousness only found in a certain kind of man, his big hand near the pistol on his side. He saw Jason as nothing more than a drunk and a fool and certainly not a threat, but merely a pest to be crushed underfoot.

There was no sound. The sun's rays seemed to brighten around the two men facing each other in the street. It was as if they were on stage, and the bright sun focused on them in their tense drama. The crooked smile on Big Ned's face increased, and his hand jumped. Jason pulled his pistol as fast as he could, but just then an unexpected weight slammed into him.

"No!" Molly screamed as she threw herself against Jason's gun with her face toward him. A shot rang out, and Jason felt the impact upon Molly's small form. She collapsed in Jason's arms, pulling him down to the dust with her. Dropping his gun and holding her tightly, he glanced up at Big Ned.

Big Ned stood dumbfounded, still holding his gun. The onlookers watched in silent shock, a precarious instant in which they would undoubtedly form a verdict. Fear came into Big Ned's eyes as, knowing how easily a crowd can become a lynch mob, he pictured himself hanging from a rope. "I didn't mean to do it," he said uncertainly, slowly holstering his pistol. "She jumped out in front of him—what could I do? It was an accident!"

A low murmur came from the crowd as they reached a decision and eased into the street. Although very few liked Big Ned, they knew he had not shot the woman on purpose. "Get a doctor!" someone yelled.

Slowly retreating back into the saloon, Big Ned quickly demanded a drink to steady his nerves. "It wasn't my fault!" he protested, then swallowed the drink and shoved the glass toward the bartender for a refill.

Kneeling in the dust, Jason held Molly's limp form. "Molly—Molly, can you hear me?" he whispered. Jason felt her warm blood on his hands.

Molly slowly opened her eyes and looked straight at Jason. The familiar and contagious smile came to her lovely face, though her eyes were full of pain. "I can tell . . . you now, Jason," she whispered. "You won't get mad at me, will you?" She sighed. "I . . . I've always loved you . . ."

"Molly, I'm sorry," Jason said with urgency. He had been prepared for his own death, but not hers. He was trembling as he said, "A doctor is coming, Molly. You'll be all right."

"Jason . . ." she whispered so faintly he could scarcely hear her. "Kiss me, Jason."

Without hesitation, Jason bent over and kissed her. Her lips were warm and soft and sweet. When he pulled away, her blue eyes smiled at him, for she had always wanted him to kiss her. At that moment the lively light that made her Molly faded, and her head fell to one side. He held her in total disbelief as a hand touched his shoulder. It was old Dr. Coleman, who put his finger on the side of her neck, then sadly shook his head.

Jason felt like he was descending into some sort of dreamworld. What he'd just witnessed couldn't be happening! He let his hand stroke Molly's silky black hair, her light form unmoving in his arms as they sat together in the dusty street. He glanced down at her simple cotton dress and her small, black boots—the very ones he'd bought her on her birthday.

She loved me. She thought I was someone special. That thought tormented him. Though he hadn't loved her as she'd loved him, he knew he could've done more for her. "Take care of her, God," he pleaded. He stood and picked her up, then gave the light burden to two tall miners who offered to take her. Jason took one last look at her small, still figure, then forced his way through the crowd.

∽

Jason walked without thinking until he came to the far end of the street, darted into an empty bar, and bought a bottle from an inquisitive bartender.

"What happened out there?" the barkeep asked.

Jason scooped up the bottle and slipped out the back door without answering.

Moving into a narrow alley undetected, he took a few generous swigs. *What have I done?* he wondered hopelessly. *I got Molly killed, that's what I've done! All she ever wanted was somebody to care about her. Now she's gone, and Big Ned will still try to kill Jennifer.* He drank some more, trying to silence his feelings of failure. *I'm the sorriest excuse for a man that ever walked the earth!* he lamented. *Now things are worse than ever. Maybe I should just quietly take the train out of here tomorrow morning.* Feeling as low as a man could feel, he emptied the bottle in the next couple of hours as he tried to wash away the horrible picture in his mind of Molly lying dead in the street. Soon he lay unconscious, alone, and forsaken.

∽

Not long before midnight the cold air made Jason's joints ache as he sat cramped in a corner by a water barrel. An empty bottle lay in the darkness beside him. Slowly pulling himself up, he staggered and fell back down. He could barely make out the light from nearby saloons as he got back to his unsteady feet. After considerable effort, he stepped out onto the street and bumped into someone passing by. "Sorry," he mumbled. His vision was blurred and watery.

"Well, well, if it ain't my lucky day! I must be livin' right!" Big Ned O'Donnell said, shoving Jason back into the alley. "You drunken bum, you almost got me strung up this mornin'!" He glanced back to make sure nobody had seen him or Jason enter the alley. This was his opportunity to get rid of Jason for good. "You wanted a fight, well, now you got one!" Big Ned growled as he walloped Jason in the face with his meaty fist.

As pain ripped through Jason's face, there was no fight in him, no hate. He just wanted to die and end the misery that plagued him. The sledgehammer blows continued until Jason fell onto the dirt. Big Ned kept kicking his enemy with brutal cruelty, crushing bones and flesh with his heavy boots. By the time Big Ned grew exhausted, Jason was unconscious. Big Ned, well satisfied, left him for dead.

~

The next morning another drunk stumbled over Jason's bloody body. Thinking he'd found a murdered man, he quickly ran for help. The small group of men who returned rolled the man over and discovered he was alive.

"Why, that's the newspaper feller," a bearded, thickset old man said.

"Shore looks like somebody worked him over good," said another man with blackened teeth. "We'd better get him to the doc."

The men lifted Jason and carried him to the doctor's office, but it was locked, so they carried him to *The Miner's News*. Jason groaned as his broken bones shifted position.

When Jennifer saw the men carrying Jason in, she quickly cleared the way to Jason's bunk in the back room. "We found him in an alley," one of the men said as they laid him down. "He looks pretty bad, ma'am. The doctor ain't in right now, but I'd shore get him to take a look at this here feller."

Lighting a lamp, Jennifer turned to examine Jason. What she saw sickened her. The man she saw didn't even look like Jason, but rather some distorted nightmare. She told one of the men, "Get a bucket of water—right outside the back door." The man hurried away. Jennifer found some scissors and cut off Jason's filthy, bloody shirt. She began praying silently when she saw the heavy gashes and swollen bruises that she knew indicated broken ribs and possibly internal bleeding. "Dear God, help us," she prayed aloud. "Somebody needs to find the doctor and get him here right away." Two of the men stood gawking at her. "Move! Hurry!" The men rushed away.

Jennifer bathed Jason as best she could, wiping away the caked blood and gently cleaning the scrapes and deep wounds, some of which were still bleeding. By the time Dr. Coleman arrived, Jennifer was beginning to doubt that Jason would live. The doctor, well-experienced in treating barroom brawl victims, examined Jason closely. He sewed up the deep cuts, one of which was on Jason's left cheek, then wrapped his chest tightly. Jason moaned, still unconscious.

"It's out of our hands now," Dr. Coleman said in a low whisper. "Somebody wanted him dead, that's for sure. I suspect it was Big Ned, but it could've been someone else too. The way things are here in Virginia City, who knows? You should stay with him, make sure he doesn't thrash around. If he comes to, he'll be in a lot of pain. I'll leave some laudanum. That's all I can do."

Her face tight with anguish, Jennifer asked soberly, "Will he live?" She was afraid of the answer.

"He's young and strong—he has as good a chance as any," the doctor said as he zipped up his little black bag. His gray eyes appeared bigger than they were because of his thick spectacles. "If you need anything, send for me." He left, an old and tired man who was tired of seeing young men die.

The first night Jason suffered from a high fever, groaning and turning all night. But Jennifer saw to it that he got plenty of water and occasionally gave him laudanum, which sent Jason back into a deep sleep.

Jason wandered in a world of darkness and pain. He wasn't sure where he was, though he knew it was unlike life as he'd ever known it. He wondered if he was experiencing death in a black and lonely emptiness where there was no time. Would the agony he felt in this dreamlike fog ever end?

~

Two days passed before Jason returned to consciousness. When he awoke, he saw Jennifer standing over him, her face soft and beautiful in the golden lamplight. "Jennifer?" he croaked. His jaw hurt badly.

"Jason, it's good to have you back with us," she said softly, bringing her face closer to his. "How do you feel?"

He winced when he thought of the racking pain. "I must have been run over by a train," he whispered hoarsely. It was hard to breathe with the tight bandages around his chest.

"Do you remember what happened?"

"Yes," he said, not wanting to talk about it.

Jennifer closed her eyes for a second, choosing her words very carefully. "I'm sorry about what happened in the gunfight," she said. "I heard all about it. Nobody knew where you were afterward, and I was getting worried. I'm sorry about Molly too—so sorry. Was she the girl you'd been seeing?"

A flood of emotion ran through Jason as he remembered the kiss he'd given his dying friend. "She was a good friend, Jennifer, maybe the only one I ever had." He wondered if the look in Jennifer's eyes was compassion or mere pity. "I'm a useless failure, Jennifer. My life isn't worth spit." He swallowed hard. "I just want to die."

"Jason, don't say that. Molly wasn't your only friend—I'm your friend too, and I care very much about you." Jennifer looked into Jason's swollen eyes. "Jason, I'm not the only one who cares about you either. Whether you believe it or not, God loves you. Without God, our lives become empty and we feel useless. But allowing God to become part of our lives gives us purpose and can fill any void we have. I wouldn't tell you this if it weren't so."

Jason stared at her a long time before he spoke. "God only likes good people. What would He want with a bum like me?"

Jennifer pondered what she should say for a moment before going on. "God loves you so much, Jason, that He sent His Son to be punished for your sins on the cross. If you ask Jesus to be your Saviour, He will forgive you for everything and will give you a new life."

"How do you know all this?" Jason asked, tired but curious.

"I read it in the Bible," Jennifer said. "That's God's Word—His message of love to each one of us."

Jason didn't speak for a long time. "Maybe I should read it. I sure need a different life than I've been living."

Her face brightening, Jennifer said, "I think God has big plans for you, Jason. He always does for those who come to Him."

Exhausted from the pain and the strong drug, Jason rolled his head to one side. "I'm at the very bottom, Jennifer," he admitted tiredly. "I have nothing left to lose. Bring me a Bible and I'll read it, I promise."

Jennifer smiled and wiped the sweat from his forehead with a damp towel. "You get some rest," she said, convinced he would recover. *Thank You, Father. Please bring him the rest of the way, physically and spiritually.*

~

As one week turned into two, Jason began sitting up in his bed. He would spend hour after hour eagerly looking through the Bible, reading until he could barely keep his eyes open. After sleeping for a while, he'd start where he'd left off and again read until he could read no longer.

"This is the most incredible collection of stories I've ever read," Jason said one evening as Jennifer brought his supper.

"And the amazing thing is, it's all true. Which part are you reading now?"

"It's a very unusual story," Jason said, turning serious. "About a boy named David and a giant named Goliath. Does that remind you of anybody you know?"

"Oh, yes! Do you understand the lesson from that Bible story? David had tremendous faith in God, and that's where he got his strength, God's strength. If you think that's good, wait until you get to the New Testament."

Nodding, Jason went back to his reading. Jennifer left his dinner and slipped out, rejoicing that she'd been able to share God's Word with her dear friend.

When Grant saw Jason for the first time after the beating, he was taken aback by Jason's scarred, black-and-blue face. "Who did that to you? Big Ned?"

His eyelids half-closed, Jason nodded.

"What will you do now? What about my mother—is she still in danger?" Grant asked. His face showed sincere concern.

"I have to get well before I can even move," Jason answered apologetically. "I'll have to take this one step at a time." He didn't like the risks of doing nothing in the meantime, but he was physically incapable of dealing with the situation, and he still didn't know whom he could trust, and he wasn't ready to tell Jennifer about Big Ned and George Hearst. Besides, he figured that with all that had happened, Big Ned would lie low awhile. Jason hoped desperately that he was right.

Grant nodded, saying, "I've got that story written—it's ready to go. When you were unconscious, we weren't sure you'd live. I almost came down here one night to print it."

Jason thought about this for a moment. "Give me a little more time, Grant. Once I get better, we'll figure out what to do."

Grant seemed satisfied with Jason's answer. "I guess that's all I can do," he had said as he stood to go. "Do you need anything?"

"I'm fine," Jason said, lifting a hand weakly.

~

Three weeks after the terrible beating, Jason finished reading the Bible and was able to stand and get around his small room. He now had a good idea of what God was like and wanted to know more. When Jennifer came in, she found Jason lying on his bed, still weary but looking better. "There'll be a scar on your cheek," she said as she came closer to inspect the cut.

"I know," Jason said calmly. "A reminder of 'the best laid schemes of mice and men.'"

Moving away, Jennifer saw the closed Bible next to Jason's bed. "Aren't you still reading the Bible?"

"I finished it," Jason said proudly.

"What do you think?"

Taking his time, Jason considered his answer. "It gave me a lot to think about. It's like a bunch of fairy tales but much more incredible—so incredible, it has to be true. I don't see how anyone could make up anything like that."

"Yes," Jennifer said, her face softening, "I know what you mean. As you read, you just know deep in your spirit that it's all true. God speaks to us through His Word, calling us to Himself. He doesn't force us to follow Him, but we can if we want, and He rewards us for our faith."

Jason now realized there had to be something more meaningful in a man's existence than simply going along with his weak flesh and its desires. His life so far had led him down a road of hopelessness. The only way he could continue living was to be able to forgive himself, and in order to do that he had to rely on something, or Someone, bigger than he was. The God he'd read about in the Bible was a forgiving and loving God. *If He can forgive me, then maybe I can find a way to forgive myself. Otherwise, my guilt over Molly's death will destroy me.* After a few more moments of silent reflection, he knew it was time to settle his destiny. "How do I get right with God, Jennifer?" he asked.

Jennifer thought a moment, then asked, "Did you read the Gospel of John?"

"Yes, I did."

"In that Gospel Jesus said, 'Ye must be born again.'"

"I remember reading that, but what does it mean?"

"It means something must happen in your heart, Jason. Just as a baby is born into the natural world, we have to be born into the kingdom of God . . ."

Jason listened intently as Jennifer explained the Gospel to him. As she read various Scriptures, something began to change within him. He felt a heaviness as he realized he was lost and bound for hell, but as she read the promises of God's mercy and grace, he began to find hope.

"Will you confess your sins to God and ask Jesus Christ to come into your heart, Jason?" she asked, her eyes warm and assuring.

"I'm not good enough to approach Him!"

"No, you're not, and neither was I. You must take salvation as a *gift*, Jason. It's only by God's grace, His undeserved favor, that we're saved. That's why Jesus died, so He could pay for our sins."

"But don't I have to join the church?"

"After you're saved, you'll want to follow the commands of Jesus and go to church to worship Him and learn more about Him. But you'll do those things *because* you're saved, not in order to be saved. Jason, just ask God to forgive you."

Jason took a deep breath. "All right, Jennifer. I—I don't know how to pray though."

"Just tell God you've sinned, and ask Him to save you by the blood of Jesus." She bowed her head, took his hand, and prayed, "O Lord, let this man come into Your kingdom. Help him see that Jesus died for him, and help him cry out for the salvation of the Lord!"

Jason felt tears burning in his eyes as he choked out the words, "O God, I'm a sinner, but I ask You to save me. Jesus, come into my life, and help me to know You!"

After the two prayed for a while longer, Jason lifted his head, his cheeks damp from his sobbing. "I—I don't cry much, Jennifer, but this time I can't help myself."

"Crying is all right," Jennifer whispered. She wiped the tears from her own cheeks and attempted a weak smile. "I do it myself sometimes."

"I feel—I feel so *clean*," Jason murmured. "Is that what I'm sup-posed to feel?"

"Yes. You're a Christian now."

Jason took a deep breath. "I hope I can *live* like a Christian."

"Jason, it's as impossible for anyone to live for God in his own strength as it is to be saved by his own power."

"So what should I do?"

"Ask for God's help every day, just like you asked Him to come into your heart. And He'll help you, Jason!" Her eyes were bright with happiness. "Getting saved is like a marriage. It only takes a few minutes to *get* married, but it takes *years* to work it out."

"I understand, I think," Jason said softly. He was quiet for a time, then said simply, "I owe you a lot, Jennifer. I don't think I can ever repay you."

Jennifer dropped her eyes for a moment, then said, "We'll help each other, Jason. We're brother and sister now in the Lord!" She reached out and held his face in both her hands. "You'll be amazed at how the power of God will work in your life! As long as you believe in Him and have faith in Him, no challenge will be too great."

Smiling, Jason felt a sensation unlike anything he'd ever experienced. "You know, I believe you're right," he said. He now possessed a confidence and security he'd never known before. He took Jennifer's hand and murmured, "We have a long way to go, haven't we, Jennifer?"

"Yes, but with God's help we can make it, Jason!"

CHAPTER

～ 21 ～

Extra!

The first sign of light trembled over the shadowed horizon as Jason sat in a chair on the boardwalk in front of the newspaper office. The early morning's sweet breeze with its fragrant freshness was gentle and silent. The earth seemed to pause for a moment before it rolled into another sun-scorched day of summer. The deep rumble of mining machinery sounded in the distance, while a brotherhood of crows announced a new day from a faraway rooftop. Special times like these allowed Jason to think of the surprising turn his life had taken. Over a month had passed since his confrontation with Big Ned. Jason's recovery had been slow but sure.

I still have the same problem, Jason thought, turning the facts over in his mind again and again. *I still have to deal with Big Ned. There's no way around it! Once everything settles down again, he'll follow Hearst's orders and go after Jennifer.* How could he deal with Big Ned? The ox of a man was brutal, belligerent, and deadly. Fortunately, just as Jason had hoped, Big Ned's facing Jason and accidentally killing Molly had made him the object of great scrutiny. He had been forced to be careful of his every move. He was disliked by all but was also feared, because everyone knew he liked to manipulate others by making threats or giving a merciless beating. Many suspected Big Ned of bludgeoning Jason, and many thought he could have held his fire when Molly jumped in front of Jason. But no one had proof that could condemn Big Ned, and no one even dared to accuse him. Instead, they watched him like a hawk.

Jason thought about his new life. The old life had a large hole in it that he'd often tried to fill with liquor. Now the hole had been filled by the Gospel of Jesus Christ. Before, Jason had no inner core, no real strength, nothing he could hold on to that offered any security. Now a strong power dwelt within him—the loving presence of God. Jason's mind constantly chewed on all this. *Will God help me when I face Big Ned?* Jason thought. *I remember reading that I shouldn't test God, but how will I know if He'll be with me or not?* As he pondered the spiritual world and God's limitless power, Jason realized it all boiled down to one thing. *I must move forward by faith, asking God to show me what to do and trusting Him to help me. I have to stop Big Ned or something terrible could happen to Jennifer. God, show me Your will, and give me courage!*

Standing, Jason stretched, glad the pain in his ribs was gone. The sky was becoming a light blue and was speckled with small clouds that looked like puffs of smoke from a cannon. Glancing up, he squinted, a slight smile tugging at the corners of his mouth. *You know what I have to do, Lord. I trust You to be with me when the time comes.*

～

When Jennifer arrived later in the morning, she found Jason busy at work recording the mining reports for the next edition. "My! I'm not used to you being up and working so early," she said cheerfully. "You must be feeling pretty good."

Stopping his work, Jason rose from his chair and came around his desk. Folding his arms and sitting on the desk, he replied, "You'd never believe how much better I feel. I watch the sun come up every morning—and every sunrise is beautiful in its own way. I don't recall ever paying any attention to a sunrise before, especially since I was never up to see it."

Jennifer realized Jason was talking about more than just his injuries healing nicely. "You're a changed man. I've never seen you so peaceful and happy."

Remembering how he felt the mornings after his drinking bouts made him cringe. He was indeed thankful that no urge to drink any longer existed; no demon beckoned him to return to that barren, dark wasteland. And a big reason for the change was Jennifer DeSpain. Not only was she a kind and beautiful woman, but she had a warm and loving spirit, and she had helped him come to know Christ. He owed her a great deal.

"I'm happy that my life is whole now and that I don't have to hide behind a bottle anymore." He drew closer to her, his simple expression showing that he had something specific on his mind. "Jennifer, there's something I need to tell you, but you'd better sit down first."

Seating herself slowly, Jennifer became silent, unsure what to expect after Jason's ominous words.

"The reason I went after Big Ned with a gun is because of something I overheard," Jason said, his features indicating that he was about to divulge truth not easily shared. "I followed him one night because I knew he was the one who burned down our office. He went to George Hearst's office, and I listened through a window. Hearst ordered him to run you out of town, but Big Ned indicated he would do something much worse."

The fear Jennifer felt was overwhelming. Her mouth fell open to say something, but nothing came out.

"Big Ned is a traitor, Jennifer. He's part of the miners' union, but he works for Hearst." Jason paused to let the truth sink in. "I still have to stop him. I can't let him do anything to you."

Jennifer began thinking of any possible alternatives. Nervously she said, "Why can't we go to the sheriff? Surely he would take appropriate action."

Stroking his stubbled face, Jason felt the new scar on his cheek. "I have no proof except my own testimony. And besides, who'd believe a drunk like me? You and I know I'm different now, but they don't know that. I also can't be sure the sheriff isn't on Hearst's payroll."

A rush of anger flushed Jennifer's cheeks as she quickly came to her feet, her hands planted on her desk. "Jason, the man is a killer!

You can't get into another fight with Big Ned—he'll kill you. We have to find another way to handle this!"

"If we try to fight this any other way, it'll take too much time," Jason argued. "We can't risk your life, Jennifer. What if Big Ned decides to make his move before whatever we try works? I'm sorry, Jennifer, but something has to be done!"

An overpowering flood of emotions swept' through Jennifer. Dropping her eyes to the desk, she searched desperately for answers. *What will become of Jason if he goes up against that brute? Why is he doing this? God, show us what to do. Protect us all.* Jason's courage impressed her, but Big Ned had already killed one person. "Aren't you afraid, Jason?"

"I was last time, but not anymore," Jason stated. "Maybe I'm fooling myself, but . . . well, I was as low as a man could go—I'd lost my will to live. Then a miracle happened, and now I'm no longer afraid."

Jennifer thought about this, and she understood. Now that he belonged to the Lord, he wasn't afraid to die. But the fact remained that Jason was no match for Big Ned. "Nevertheless, you could get severely beaten, or even killed," she said, desperation in her voice. "Then you would've solved nothing."

Accepting Jennifer's admiration and understanding her concern, Jason knew what he needed to say. "Remember David and Goliath?"

Nodding, Jennifer wasn't comforted by the comparison. "What will you do, carry a slingshot?"

"I'll find another way, something to make things even," Jason said. "I know I can't defeat the man with my fists."

"Not a gun, not again," Jennifer pleaded.

"No, not a gun. Something else. That's all I can say right now," Jason said.

"When?" Jennifer muttered.

"Today's a good day," Jason replied.

The shock of all this news struck Jennifer hard. So much was at risk, with no guarantee of a beneficial outcome. So many questions remained.

"I'm going for a walk so I can think this through," Jason said calmly, noticing the haze of confusion in her eyes, but knowing what he should do.

As Jennifer watched Jason saunter out of the office, a storm of fear raged in her mind. She appreciated his showing her so much respect and concern. His courage was focused on a well-defined goal. But was he being foolhardy?

Walking across the office, she glanced out the front window. People were going about their daily business in a predictable fashion; nothing seemed askew. As she attempted to gather her emotions, she decided there was only one thing she could do. *I'll go see Charles. He can persuade Hearst to put a stop to this!*

~

When she arrived at Charles's office, Jennifer was informed by a one-armed clerk with cloudy eyes that he was in court. "I don't know how long he'll be there, lady. It's not my job to know these things."

Put out, Jennifer asked, "Do you expect him back today?"

"How do I know?" the man snapped arrogantly. "What's so important that it can't wait?"

Ignoring the question, Jennifer marched out of the office. *It seems like the people who work for Hearst are always on edge. It must be a reflection of the man they work for.*

Jennifer decided to go to the courthouse and wait for Charles there. Time was of the utmost importance; there was no way of knowing when things would erupt.

While Jennifer was waiting impatiently in the foyer of the courthouse, Jason was sitting in the newspaper office, having returned just after Jennifer left. *It might be best to confront Big Ned when his shift gets off. That way everyone who witnesses whatever happens will be sober miners—no drunks or gamblers. Plus Big Ned should be a little tired, and that might give me an advantage.* Rising from his chair, Jason strolled around the office, taking a good look at the business they'd built. *This newspaper stands for something—freedom of the printed word. And Jennifer stands for something too. She believes in the Lord and is willing to fight for the rights of the people.* He smiled as he thought about her.

Now it's my turn, he thought confidently. *I have to fight for what I believe in!*

Jason waited for Jennifer but finally felt he could wait no longer. Big Ned's shift would be getting off soon, and he wanted to be there. Grabbing his hat, Jason prepared to lock the office and leave. Footsteps sounded on the boardwalk, and Grant sprang through the front door. "Hello, Jason," Grant said, noticing the odd quietness of the usually busy office. "Where's Mother?"

"I don't know," Jason said soberly. "I was just about to step out for a while."

"Something's wrong," Grant said, seeing the look on Jason's face.

Pausing, Jason reflected on the conversations he and Grant had had in the past. "The time has come, Grant. I have to settle things with Big Ned."

Grant just stood there with wide-open eyes. Although he realized Jason would someday make his word good, he didn't think it would come so soon. "Can I go? Maybe I can help somehow."

Jason placed his hand on Grant's shoulder. "You'd better stay here. Somebody needs to watch the office." Jason knew Grant was too young to manage things at the office all by himself, but he didn't want him at the fight scene where he could get hurt either.

Grant swallowed hard. "All right," he mumbled reluctantly. "But you be careful. Move fast. Don't let him grab you . . ."

"Don't worry, Grant," Jason interrupted. "I'll be careful."

After Jason left, Grant began trying to think of something he could do to help. Suddenly an idea struck him. He removed his now well-worn article from his pocket—the newspaper article he'd planned to print when the time was right. Quickly scanning it, he rushed over to the print table and began selecting the tiny letters.

∼

The afternoon was warm, dry, and dusty as Jason strolled through the business district of Virginia City. He'd never felt calmer or more certain of his duty as he approached the general store. Like a man who had all the time in the world, he carefully inspected a barrel of pick handles that sat out front. He eyed this one for straightness, then checked another for good and consistent grain with no knots. He finally made his selection, finding a piece of white hickory that felt good in his hands. Next he went inside and found a good pair of tight-fitting, black leather gloves that gripped the slick hickory pick handle like sticky pine sap. "I'll take these," he said pleasantly.

Appraising the merchandise through heavy glasses, the elderly storekeeper gave a grunt, then laughed. "Plan on doing some prospecting, do ya?"

"You might say that," Jason admitted agreeably.

"Diggin' for gold?" the elderly man questioned.

"Diggin' for truth," Jason said, smiling.

The old man didn't understand Jason's reply. "I got some mighty fine pick heads over yonder if'n you're needin' one."

"This'll do just fine," Jason said as he paid for the merchandise and left.

It was an enjoyable walk for Jason as he made his way to the Ophir mine where Big Ned worked. He used the pick handle as a walking stick, getting used to its weight and feel. He greeted the people he passed, tipping his hat.

Outside the mining company, Jason found a comfortable keg to sit on in the shade as he watched the shaft house and waited for the five o'clock whistle. Soon the day crew would be emerging from the depths, and among them he would find Big Ned O'Donnell. A confident satisfaction settled over Jason as he patiently waited.

~

Almost livid with impatience, Jennifer approached Charles as he left the courtroom. "Charles, what took you so long? I've been waiting here for hours." She grabbed his free arm and pulled him along. He held a stack of papers in the other. "We must talk right now! Something urgent has come up!"

Giving a brief good-bye to his partners, Charles turned his attention to a panicked Jennifer DeSpain. "Whoa!" he said, tickled at her agitation. "Now calm down! You can tell me what's on your mind while we walk back to the office."

Jennifer did her best to explain the situation as they walked at a quick clip, concluding, "So you see, Charles, my life is in danger! Your boss, Mr. Hearst, has encouraged Big Ned to do away with me!" she said as she finished the story. By this time they were at the office, and Charles opened the door for her. He was smiling and shaking his head. "Come on in and sit down. I think the heat has gotten to you." Ever so friendly, he guided her into his plush office and closed the door. "Make yourself at home, Jennifer. Now, let's go over this again," he said amiably, setting down the paperwork he'd been carrying.

Jennifer repeated the story, including what Hearst had said, the gunfight, and Big Ned's beating up Jason.

Charles laughed. "You don't actually believe any of that, do you? Do you think a man like Mr. Hearst would jeopardize his position in this community by being a partner to such a conspiracy? Jennifer, I'm surprised at you!"

Growing angry, Jennifer retorted, "But Jason heard them with his own ears. Why else do you think he would go up against a man twice as big as him?"

Charles grew indignant. "Jennifer, I've about had enough of these silly games! I want you to stop and think about what you're telling me. Be rational now." He waited for the noisy five o'clock whistle to finish blasting. "You've been taken in by the word of a drunk! Jason is disreputable and undependable. He doesn't even have enough courage to face the pressures of daily life—that's why he drinks so much. Everyone knows he's been consumed with rage ever since Big Ned killed that harlot he was seeing. Jason is no good, and his word is no good!" He slammed his fist on the desk to drive home his point.

Holding her ground, Jennifer defended Jason. "He's different now, Charles. He's become a born-again Christian. Yes, he's had a drinking problem in the past, but he's not a liar, and he's always remained faithful to his job at the paper. I think you're wrong about him."

Throwing his hands up in protest, Charles took a deep breath to calm himself. "Why do we continue to go through all this, Jennifer? You should just sell the paper and free yourself from all these threats and drunks and headaches. I have enough money to last us for the rest of our lives. Let's take a little trip and get married. The newspaper isn't worth all this!"

A sudden wave of indignation swelled in Jennifer as suspicions and reservations about Charles were suddenly unleashed. "Charles, have you *ever* fought for anything important or lasting? All you do is smile and talk. Have you ever really committed yourself to anything besides money? You claim that you are a God-honoring man, but are you? Do you have any understanding or compassion?"

Disturbed by her accusatory statements, grave concern darkened Charles's eyes. He wanted to strike back with words, but he didn't want to lose Jennifer. "I'm sorry, Jennifer, my dear. It's been a long day, and I'm tired. You're right, I should investigate this in case there is something to it. Perhaps I spoke rashly." He came around the desk and let his hand gently touch her arm. "I love you dearly, and I wouldn't allow anything to happen to you. If Hearst is behind this, I'll deal with him through the courts. He doesn't scare me. But, Jennifer, you must understand about Jason—he's a drunk, and you can't count on him."

Before Jennifer could respond, she heard the loud voices of rowdy men from below. Charles looked out to see what was going on. "Looks like some of the miners are settling a dispute," he said condescendingly.

Curious, Jennifer got up from her chair and eased over to see for herself. Suddenly terrified, she realized that Jason was fighting Big Ned!

～

When the five o'clock whistle blew, Jason jumped off the barrel and stretched his muscles. There was no doubt in his mind that today he would bring the truth out into the open and get matters resolved. He watched the dirty miners as they began to pour out of the shaft house. It wasn't long before Big Ned appeared, his woolly head towering over the others. When they saw Jason carrying a pick handle, they knew there was going to be trouble and gave him plenty of room. Soon Jason was face to face with Big Ned, who casually set down his lunch pail.

"It's time for everyone to know who you're really working for, Ned," Jason said, his eyes now narrow slits.

A worried look came over Big Ned's face as he stroked his rusty beard with a meaty palm. He wondered how anyone could know about his arrangement with Hearst. But then, having the anger of a raging bull, he determined to handle the situation in his usual way. "You just can't get enough, can you?" he growled, his voice rough and deep as he rolled up his sleeves to expose his massive arms. "This'll be the last time, whiskeygut!" he said as he moved in closer.

Jason stood poised with the pick handle slightly cocked as Big Ned made a roundhouse swing that would have knocked a bear's head off. But that was just what Jason expected, so he ducked and gave Big Ned's left knee a sharp blow from the pick handle. When Big Ned doubled over grabbing his knee, Jason brought the pick handle down across the back of Big Ned's neck. This sent Big Ned face first onto the dry ground. Like a huge buffalo in a dusty wallow, Big Ned rolled and snorted and climbed back to his feet, towering over Jason.

The crowd thickened as miners and citizens alike rushed to see the brawl. "Get him, Jason," they cried, sensing Big Ned was at least a bit stunned. "You got him now—kill him!" They'd seen Big Ned get away with too many brutal beatings.

Any other man would either have been nearly unconscious or would have surrendered, but Big Ned was a burly brute with bones like a grizzly and ox-like endurance. He cursed as he came to his senses; he was hurt and so more dangerous than ever. Seeing the pick handle coming down toward his head again, he raised his arm in its path. The crack sounded like thunder, and the blow sent the big bully backwards. Jason was on him in an instant and swung the pick handle again, this time catching Big Ned on the side of the head. The new wound bled profusely.

"You got him!" a miner screamed. "He can't win now—beat his brains out!"

Big Ned growled, "I'm not beat yet. Stone, I'll kill you!"

Jason swung at him again, but Big Ned lowered his bushy head, stooped low, and rushed at him. Jason stepped aside and aimed the end of the pick handle at Big Ned's face, smashing his lips and teeth. Big Ned turned and glared at Jason with fiery eyes, crimson gushing from his mouth. Big Ned had taken blows that would have killed most men and remained erect, sustained by sheer willpower. "You can't put me down, Stone. I'm gonna crush your guts out!"

Jason lifted the pick handle and faked a swing. When he saw Big Ned's arm raise up, he swung with all his might and caught the arm with a loud crack that sent the big man reeling. "We can finish this without any more fighting, Ned," Jason said, his pulse rushing. "It's up to you."

Big Ned stared at his broken arm and its unnatural bend below the elbow. Bringing his good hand slowly across his bruised and bleeding face, he threatened, "You think I won't kill you?" He was a bull, primitive and unchanging, his only desire being to attack and destroy. There was no fear in him as he struck out with his good arm, his throat uttering strange sounds. Jason parried the blow and swung hard into Big Ned's stomach. Dull a man as he was, Big Ned had a fighting slyness, for he had not put all his weight into the attack, and now he turned and struck again, catching Jason flush on the mouth and nose with his ham of a fist.

Intense pain stopped Jason in his tracks. His vision temporarily went foggy. Since he couldn't see Big Ned, he moved sideways. He felt fresh blood in his nostrils. Big Ned sensed his opportunity and rushed forward, striking out desperately, but he missed his blow as Jason ducked under him. Jason lifted himself into an upward swing with the pick handle that caught Big Ned in the jaw and sent the bear of a man sprawling. Jason felt the blow register and knew it had found its mark.

Big Ned mumbled something through the blood in his mouth as he slipped his hand down to his boot and produced a long knife. Standing slowly, he waved the knife in front of him with his good arm, his bad arm dangling like a broken tree limb. "I'm gonna carve you up, boy!"

At that instant a huge black hand reached out from the crowd and grabbed the wrist holding the knife in a vise-like grip. Big Ned turned to see Abe Washington glaring at him, Abe's huge arms even larger than Big Ned's. "I'll take that," Abe said in a deep, menacing voice as he forced the knife from Big Ned's hand. He despised the man for his cruelty and envied the little man who was standing up to the bully, something he wished he would've done himself. "No knives in dis fight!"

"I'll take care of you later," Big Ned said, turning his fury back onto Jason and throwing his huge body forward. Jason stepped aside and whacked Big Ned on the back as he passed, once again laying him out on the ground. Again and again this happened until Jason felt the long breaths of exhaustion starting to rack his lungs. *Is this man ever going to stay down?*

∼

Grant quickly printed up a one-page special edition with a headline that read: BIG NED SELLS OUT. The article was brief and to the point, describing how Big Ned was on George Hearst's payroll and had betrayed the miners. The article went on to expose Big Ned as one of Hearst's thugs. As soon as he had printed about twenty-five copies, he ran from the office and down the street toward the Ophir mining office where he knew the action would take place since that was where Ned worked.

When he arrived, he saw that Jason was about to collapse from exhaustion as a bloody Big Ned kept lunging at him. It was apparent that Jason wouldn't be able to hold up much longer. "Extra! Extra!" Grant screamed with all the volume he could. "Big Ned is a traitor—read all about it!"

Although the crowd was thoroughly interested in the fight, hearing Big Ned's name mentioned as a traitor got their attention. "What!" one man said. "Give me that!" He took the paper and quickly read it, as did another man, and another. Soon the whole crowd was yelling, "Stop the fight! Stop the fight!"

Big Ned turned and looked at them curiously, his face a bloody pulp. Jason rested his hands on his knees and bent over, gasping for air.

"Is this true, Ned?" a tall miner screamed. "Are you being paid by Hearst?"

The anger on Big Ned's face turned to guilt. "H-how'd y-you know?" he stammered, a rush of fear gripping him. The fear of facing a large, angry crowd was the only fear he ever felt. "It wasn't my fault," he claimed. "They made me do it."

A rope flew around Big Ned, and instantly the crowd of angry miners pinned his huge hulk to the ground. Others rushed to a nearby supply shed for tar and feathers. Jason could hardly believe his eyes.

Grant approached him, a slight mischievous smile on his young face. "You can't beat the power of the press," Grant said happily.

Still breathing hard, Jason managed to smile. "Can't knock God's timing either. I don't think I could have lasted another minute."

Jason pulled Grant away from the crowd now intent on revenge. They could hear the cries of Big Ned as they applied the hot tar to him.

"Let's get back to the office," Jason said. "It's all over here." He draped his tired arm over Grant's shoulder and walked weakly along.

～

Jennifer watched from up above as they tarred and feathered Big Ned. The crowd of miners disappeared around the corner with the big man in their custody. She turned to Charles, who had given up his position at the window when he couldn't bear to watch any more. "What were you saying about my worthless little drunk, Charles?" A flame burned in Jennifer's eyes as her face reddened. "Maybe you should try looking up the definition of a man—a real man." She glanced back down at the street where the fight had taken place and murmured, "*He* has a lot of heart!"

Jennifer spun and made her way to the door. "I have to go see about Jason," she said, steel in her voice. She gave Charles a thorough going-over with her eyes. "We'll talk tomorrow." She left without another word.

Her tone had been ominous. *Maybe she'll settle down tonight, so we can talk sense tomorrow,* he thought. But it had been a rough afternoon indeed, and it was hard for him to console himself with wishful thinking.

~ 22 ~

Hero

Back at the office, Jason collapsed in a chair, his face dirty, his hair a mess, totally spent from the fight. A throbbing pain assaulted his neck and head.

"I'll get you some water," Grant said, hurrying to find a glass.

Jason felt so good about the outcome that he didn't mind the pain. Grant brought him some water, then stood and watched him gulp it down. "Whew!" Jason said. "I hate to think what would have happened if you hadn't come along. God used you today, Grant, and His timing is perfect!"

"And God used you to save Mother," Grant added, profoundly grateful for all that had happened that day.

When the pain began to subside, enabling Jason to think more clearly, he asked, "When did you print that extra anyway?"

"As soon as you left. I knew what was coming and I knew I had to do something. I've been saving that article—right here in my pocket," Grant explained excitedly.

Shaking his head, Jason had one more point to query. "But the story you printed was based on my word only—there was no other proof that it was true. How'd you know those miners would believe it?"

Dropping his big green eyes, Grant admitted, "I believed you, and that was all I needed. I didn't know if anybody else would believe the story, but I had to try. Besides, you and Mother have told me that people tend to believe what they see in print, whether they're sure it's true or not. Today I just hoped that would be true."

Grant hadn't been able to think the situation through any further than that, and he couldn't really verbalize it all to Jason now. Losing his father at a young age and having a mother whose work didn't allow her to spend as much time with him as either she or he would have preferred had taken its toll on Grant. Though he was often able to comfort his mother and to protect Abby, he'd had no father to mentor him, no male role model to look up to. Consequently, he'd had to rely on his own abilities and often had to fend for himself—until he met Jason.

Grant had admired Jason from the beginning. He saw him as a man who would stick things out when the going got tough. He knew Jason sometimes drank too much and too often, but he didn't think that was the real Jason and assumed, perhaps because he couldn't bear to think otherwise, that his friend would eventually overcome his problem.

Nodding, Jason gave Grant a smile of affirmation. "Thanks for believing in me. But in the future, when you print something, be sure you have more than my word to back it up or you could get in legal trouble. But I don't want to give you a lecture." Jason laughed. "After all, you saved my life!"

Hesitating, Grant tried to work up enough courage to say what he really wanted to say. Deciding to risk sounding like a little kid, he said, "I don't know any man braver than you. I felt like you were out there all alone, and I wanted to help—I had to do what I thought was right."

Realizing Grant was a little embarrassed, Jason came over to him and said softly, "You *did* do the right thing, Grant. That took a lot of courage. I'm proud of you, and I know your mother will be proud of you. We're best friends, right?" He offered a manly handshake.

Grant grasped Jason's hand with a firm grip. "Best friends always!" he agreed, his chest swelling with pride.

About that time Jennifer rushed in, out of breath. "Jason, are you all right?" she asked, worry all over her face.

"Beaten and bruised," Jason answered, smiling, "but, yes, I'm all right. In pain, but so grateful to everyone."

Turning to Grant, Jennifer sensed she was intruding, as if she'd interrupted a private conversation. "Grant, didn't I see you down at the mine? What were you doing there?"

"Just selling papers, Mother," Grant answered with a mischievous smile.

"Papers?" Glancing at the press, she spied a copy of the extra edition and went over and picked it up. Grant watched her eyes dart back and forth as she quickly read the article. Slowly setting it down, she asked, "Who wrote this? Who printed it?"

"I did both, Mother," Grant replied, turning away from Jennifer, suddenly self-conscious.

Jennifer had so many questions, she didn't know where to begin. "So this is why the miners tarred and feathered Big Ned."

"That's right," Jason said casually. "And just in time!"

Jennifer thought she'd better lecture her son about abusing the power of the press but then had second thoughts, and her face softened. "What am I going to do with you two?" she asked teasingly.

"I guess you'll have to keep us on staff here at the paper," Jason taunted. "Besides, Jennifer, it was God who made everything work out today—His perfect timing!"

"Yes, Jason, I can see that. Father, thank You for watching over all of us today, and for giving us the courage to do what needed to be done," she prayed with eyes lifted toward heaven.

Jason couldn't help but think that what had just happened felt like being part of a family, and that felt very good indeed.

∽

The next morning when Charles arrived at work he found an urgent message instructing him to report to Hearst's office immediately. Without delay, he went down the hall and knocked on Hearst's door.

"Come in!" Hearst barked.

As Charles entered, he could see Hearst was busily packing personal items into a trunk. Sweat glistened on his forehead. "Charley,

I want you to sell every holding we have in this town—and do it quickly. Sell lock, stock, and barrel! We should make a large profit. Then I want you to join me in South Dakota at the Grubstake mine. We'll reinvest it all there. I plan on building several mills up there; the ore is rich and shows good promise." Hearst's voice sounded like that of a fugitive.

"But, Mr. Hearst," Charles argued gently, "we can still make a fortune right here."

"Don't argue with me, Charley!" Hearst said angrily, stopping his frantic packing and turning to Charles. "When I say do something, do it! I'm not interested in getting any arguments from you!"

Afraid of pushing Hearst too far, Charles let his eyes wander to the window, which overlooked the area where the fight had occurred. Hearst had undoubtedly been in his office when that took place. And besides, the news from the special edition had run through the town like a flood. *The old man's running,* Charles thought. *He's afraid the miners will come after him next, and maybe he's right.* Charles played along. "I'll need power of attorney in order to liquidate stocks and holdings, Mr. Hearst."

"Get it written up and I'll sign it," Hearst ordered, then went back to his frantic packing.

As Charles turned to go, Hearst called after him, "Oh, Charley, don't even think about trying to make off with my money or I'll have you tracked down like an animal!"

Without replying, Charles pulled the door closed as he left. That thought had crossed his mind, but now he wouldn't dare. What would all this mean for him personally? As usual, that was his only real concern.

～

With no one knowing about his departure and without saying good-bye to anyone, George Hearst made his way to the train station and slipped into a private car he had reserved earlier. Uncomforted by the plush luxury, he sat in a heavily upholstered chair and viewed Virginia City through the window. A shrewd, devious man determined to control others, he now feared for his life in the town where he'd made his fortune, the town he built. Feeling in his pocket, he found the small pistol he'd loaded and placed there earlier. It felt good in his hand, but he owned it only as a last measure of self-preservation; the gun was not his chosen means of control.

Reaching into a vest pocket, he produced a long, expensive cigar and held it under his small nose, savoring the aromatic quality of the fine tobacco. Biting off the tip, he spat it onto the carpet. Methodically, he scratched a match under the cherry wood table beside him and held it to the cheroot. The train gave two short blasts of the whistle and jerked into motion.

I'll not make the same mistakes again! he vowed as the smoke curled above him. *I underestimated two things—the power of a woman and the power of a newspaper.* As the train chugged away from Virginia City, he took one last glance at the town that had made him wealthy. He had no remorse for leaving, for the town had merely been a stepping-stone to bigger and better things—something to be used, then thrown away. He was a man who lived for power, and money was only a tool for obtaining it. Grandiose visions of political prominence enticed him to make as much money as possible, and he planned to eventually return home to his family in San Francisco, then run for the United States Senate.

Having already established his claim in South Dakota—the Grubstake mine—he planned on establishing a much bigger operation than he'd had in Virginia City. This time he would control *everything.* At the moment, though, the thing that intrigued him the most was the power of the newspaper, a useful tool to control people. As a rule he hated newspapers, but recent events had given him an utmost respect for the results they could obtain. *I think I'll purchase a newspaper in San Francisco,* he thought. *Then not only will I have political power but power of the press as well!* He smiled, a rare thing for him. *That might be a good way for Billie Buster to get started. He could run the newspaper for me.* "Billie Buster" was Hearst's twelve-year-old son, William Randolph Hearst.

～

Hearst was gone, and Charles sat in his own office tugging on one of the demagogue's fine cigars hastily left behind. *I'm in charge now*, he thought with self-confident satisfaction. Before him sat the paperwork for the liquidation of Hearst's holdings. *Maybe I can't make off with all of Hearst's money*, he thought, congratulating himself. *But I can make a nice and juicy profit for myself without the old man ever knowing it!* The sensation of power elated him, even if it had only fallen into his lap because of Hearst's departure. The paperwork contained tricky lawyer talk he'd stayed up most of the night preparing. There was no way anyone would know exactly what funds went where. Hearst would get his millions, but there was plenty left over. Charles grinned jubilantly.

A knock sounded at the door, and Charles hurriedly scooped up the paperwork and stuck it in a desk drawer. "Come in, " he called invitingly. He'd been expecting an errand boy to help with the deals he was making, someone he could easily influence and who would be too naive to discern what Charles was up to.

But it was Jennifer who entered, a disturbing somber expression on her face. "Charles," she said quietly, "I heard Hearst is selling out—that he's already gone."

"And I doubt he'll ever be back," Charles said happily.

"But if he's running, he really did tell Big Ned to silence me however he could," she said, fear in her eyes. "Charles, how can you work for somebody like that? Don't you see what kind of man he really is?"

"He has instructed me to liquidate all his holdings, Jennifer. He trusts me with everything." Charles was pleased with himself and had little concern for Jennifer's fears. "It's all over. You can rest easy now, Jennifer."

Jennifer thought about Charles's words. He was right. Big Ned was gone, and so was Hearst. And *The Miner's News* had even more respect than before. "Well," she said, "maybe things *will* settle down now. This whole situation has been so trying, but now . . ."

"Absolutely!" Charles agreed, coming to his feet with newfound energy. "I can see it now," he said, waving his hand in front of his face. "A beautiful mountainside home surrounded by blue spruce."

"Blue spruce?" Jennifer queried. "There are no blue spruce around here."

"But there are in South Dakota, in the Black Hills," Charles responded. "Up there, Jennifer, there's more gold than you could ever imagine."

She suddenly understood what he was telling her. "You're going to South Dakota?"

"*We're* going to South Dakota, Jennifer. You and I and the children."

The fear Jennifer had felt quickly gave way to scorn. "Charles, you're already a millionaire! Don't you have enough? How much do you need?"

Detecting her anger, Charles decided he'd better try to calm her down. "If I can earn just a little more, a few hundred thousand perhaps, we'll be set for life. Then we can travel the world, see things you've never dreamed of. There will be no limits."

"Where does our faith fit into all this, Charles? How does God come into your plans?

"God? What does He have to do with this? Is He the one who's worked so hard to put together my fortune? Don't get me wrong—I believe in God, but it seems to me He helps those who help themselves."

Jennifer was finally seeing the true Charles Fitzgerald. For him trust in God was just lip service, not a personal, growing faith. And as far as the money was concerned, Charles would never be satisfied, he'd never have enough. That wasn't the life she wanted. "Charles, I'm not going to South Dakota with you," she said firmly, wishing she'd seen through his facade earlier. "I won't be a puppet to George Hearst. That man's evil, Charles; he's a criminal! Yet you persist on following him so you can add to your material wealth."

"Jennifer, I'm a mining lawyer—that's my job," Charles pleaded, still wearing his most persuasive smile. "You can't condemn a man for making a living!"

"You don't understand, Charles," Jennifer said sadly. "You just don't see it. You care only about yourself. You have no compassion for others, no moral conviction that will enable you to stand against the wrong all around you. And money can't buy you the courage and power you lack! Jesus said we can't worship God and money, Charles, and you've made the wrong choice—a choice that will ultimately condemn you to an eternity of God's judgment."

The smile left Charles's face, and his tone changed. He didn't believe all that she was saying, but he didn't want to lose her either. He would have to choose his words carefully. "You're such a good woman, Jennifer. I know I'm not good enough for you. I think I understand what you're trying to tell me." He came closer to her, his eyes full of sorrow. "I want to learn about these matters—and you can teach me."

Jennifer wavered, amazed at Charles's admission of weakness. *If he's willing to learn, maybe even to turn away from his sins, I should give him a chance. Perhaps God is changing his heart.* The scorn left her face as she glanced at him. "Charles, if you're serious, then stay in Virginia City so we can talk about this further. You can send Hearst what belongs to him. The choice is up to you." She walked slowly toward the door.

Charles cut her off halfway across the room. "Jennifer, I want you to know that I love you with all my heart. You are and always will be first in my life. I'm tired of being alone. I want to have you with me, close to me. I can't bear to think that you've lost faith in me." Not knowing what other words to use to express his desperation, he kissed her again and again.

"Charles," she murmured, "I didn't realize you felt so deeply for me." Studying his face closely as he held her, Jennifer wondered if he was sincere.

Releasing her and backing away, Charles said, "I do need to go away, but only for a few weeks, to finish business to which I'm already obligated. Can you accept that?"

Jennifer tried to put aside her anxiety. Perhaps she had indeed overreacted. It certainly seemed that Charles loved her. "Charles, I hardly know what to say . . ." She hesitated, then simply added, "I'll be at the office."

After she left, Charles went back to his desk and slid the drawer open. He removed the paperwork and started checking his figures again, counting the money that would soon be his. There was a slight smile at the corners of his mouth.

~

Working contentedly on his story of how corruption in the mining companies had led to all sorts of mayhem, Jason bristled at the interruption of the front office door booming open and the staggering entrance of a young miner, Ben Taylor. He was obviously a little drunk. "Jason!" he called over the front counter as he laid down on it. "They sent me to come get you—you got to come with me!"

"Why? What's going on?"

Ben rolled his eyes as his head bobbed a little. "They're having a party for you, so you got to come."

Turning to Jennifer, Jason could see her disapproval. He turned back to Ben and smiled. "I can't come, Ben. I don't even drink anymore."

Reaching over the counter and slapping Jason on the shoulder, Ben reminded him, "You're a hero, fella! Why, all the boys are down at the Golden Fleece waitin' on you. You can't let 'em down. C'mon, let's get goin'!"

Jennifer stood and straightened her dress. "I don't really think you should, Jason," she said, a hint of fear in her voice.

The very mention of the Golden Fleece brought innumerable memories to Jason's mind, most of them unpleasant, including Molly's troubles and his own drinking habit. He'd known he'd have to deal with those memories someday, and the temptation to drink again as well. It would be a test of his character, though now at least he knew God was on his side. He couldn't hide from the battle forever. He looked at Jennifer. "I don't know when I'll be back," he said as he came around the counter and put on his hat.

Watching him leave, Jennifer felt the strain of not knowing what would happen. She'd realized he'd meet the temptation face to face sometime, and she knew this was one battle she couldn't fight for him.

Jennifer took a deep breath, then whispered a prayer, hope guiding her words. *Father, I know Jason has to face this alone, and yet he's not alone because You're with him. Please help him make right choices and not to allow himself to get into a situation he can't handle. Help, him, Lord, please!*

~

Ben Taylor staggered down the dusty street with Jason in tow. "You ever chop wood?" Ben asked.

"Chop wood?" Jason repeated. "Why do you ask that?"

"The way you swing that pick handle, I bet you could chop a cord of wood in two hours!"

Jason laughed, beginning to share the lighthearted mood of the young miner. When they got to the Golden Fleece, the place was so full that people crowded out into the street.

"Make way! Make way!" Ben shouted as he proudly presented the guest of the party. "Here he is, fellas, the man that whopped Big Ned!"

A loud cheer filled the saloon as miners rushed over to shake Jason's hand and slap him on the back. "Get him a drink, bartender!" a miner shouted. "Give him the best stuff ya got!"

The crowd tightened around Jason, pushing him up to the bar. Pretty girls in fancy dresses hung on his shoulders. "Tell us how ya did it!" a short miner in front of Jason demanded.

"Well," Jason stammered, embarrassed by all the attention, "I knew I couldn't whip him with my fist, so I bought a pick handle."

The men, all of whom had obviously already imbibed a great deal of liquor, screamed with laughter and took heavy swallows of their drinks. "Did ya hear that? He bought a pick handle, har-har!"

Somebody placed a glass of whiskey in Jason's hand. He held it nervously, staring at the amber liquid. He brought it up to his nose and took a whiff. The smell turned his stomach, and he made a sour face and set the glass back on the bar. "Make it a sarsaparilla, bartender," he called, remembering that was Molly's favorite drink. He glanced at the two smiling girls on his arms. They were both pretty in their colorful dresses and wore heavy makeup, but there'd never be another Molly.

"Let's hear a toast for Jason the giant-killer!" one man hollered as all of the miners whooped with joy and the piano banged out jangling tunes. Jason tossed his drink down, enjoying the sweet flavor of the fruity liquid. "Give me another, bartender," Jason called.

The party ran on into the night as the rugged and drunken miners gave Jason their admiration. He was grateful to God for helping him finally find a worthwhile role in life. He felt no dizziness and had no blackouts as he enjoyed nothing but sarsaparilla through the evening. Having the good sense of sober judgment, Jason left while the party was still at its peak. The drunk and happy miners bade him farewell one by one as he slowly made his way out of the Golden Fleece. His shoulders had grown sore with the weight of the girls hanging on him and the constant backslapping. It felt wonderful to be liked, to be treated like a fellow human being, to have a place in the community. It was wonderful to be *somebody*!

Seeing the Light

It was a fresh and cool summer morning in Virginia City as Jason made a pot of coffee on the potbellied stove in the newspaper office. He was thinking of all that had happened and how the town had a new and different attitude now, how the people seemed more content. "I guess we've caused quite a stir," he remarked as he squatted by the stove and rattled the iron door in order to rouse the coals.

Sitting at her desk, Jennifer worked on a new Miner Tom episode. She glanced up and paused, the pencil held against her lips as she gazed into thin air. Thinking of the recent events, she thought again about how Jason had taken on corruption single-handedly. Somewhere within her, shadowy feelings she couldn't identify troubled her. Her heart was trying to tell her something, but the message was obscure. Shaking her head, she replied, "I'd say it was you that caused the stir! But one thing is certain, things will be different around here from now on."

Standing, Jason looked over at Jennifer. She held herself erect, her shoulders back, her auburn hair up except for a few strands that escaped like loose ribbons. A warm glow seemed to surround her as she sat contentedly at her desk, looking like a caring schoolteacher. He wished there was some way to tell her how he felt about her, but the large diamond ring on her finger was a subtle but painful reminder of her attachment to another. "Did you hear the news about the miners?" He didn't wait for her to answer. "They've formed a new union and have even elected new leaders. They're stronger than ever in their protests to the mining companies."

Shoving his hands in his pockets, he walked closer to her as he spoke. "The mining companies didn't hesitate. Seems they want to clear up their bad image and leave all the trouble behind." A slight smile touched the corners of his mouth, and his eyes squinted impishly. "I've heard that the mining company owners have a new respect for our newspaper as well. Seems to have had something to do with the dethroning of Hearst."

Jennifer answered with a small, gentle smile. Jason had touched her with his simple way of speaking, his lively and expressive eyes that danced while he talked. He had a simplicity about him, and yet underneath he was a complex man. He'd risked his life for her! Not once, but twice he had willingly faced impossible odds. These reflections about him were connected somehow to the inner uncertainty that disturbed her. She still couldn't put it into words. She looked at Jason with quiet regard. "We've been through so much together. It's almost like we—" She was amazed at what she'd almost said.

Jason had detected the careless slip, revealing a little of the emotion she kept hidden behind her lovely face. He concluded that it couldn't possibly be what he at first thought, for she loved another. If only . . . Turning away, he cloaked his feelings with impassive words. "I'd better get to work. I have a lot to get done today."

Jennifer detected the ruse in Jason's actions and words. Her expression remained calm, though she felt her face grow warm. She sat silent, feeling strangely alone.

～

In the privacy of her bedroom, Abby plotted her escape. With all that had been happening, with all the dramatic events and changes that had transpired, she felt like she'd been forgotten and misunderstood. Feeling sorry for herself, she was convinced that no one really cared about her. Her mother was too busy to spend much time with her, Grant was spending more and more time with Jason, Lita always had work to do, and her friends from school just got her into trouble. She was alone in a miserable existence. She decided that her only hope of having a happier life was to run away, leave all her troubles behind, forget about the people who kept ignoring her, and make a life of her own. Being only ten years old, she wondered how she would live without the help of others. Glancing in the mirror, she saw a pretty young girl with dark, wavy hair and brilliant blue eyes. A girl with a beautiful face who flirts and teases and makes people like her. She would make her own way; she didn't need anyone else.

She filled a large knapsack with several changes of clothes, a blanket, and a few other personal items, including a rag doll named Sarah, a companion she couldn't do without. She grabbed a candle and matches; she would take some food with her from the kitchen. *Now they'll be sorry they ignored me!* she thought sadly. *If they even miss me.*

Just about everyone in Virginia City had been involved in the recent activities except Abby, who usually sat at home alone, bored, and forgotten. Even Lita, who generally was so meticulous in her care for the children, had been too busy to keep any eye on Abby. Now, with her bottom lip protruding in defiance, the young girl marched down the stairs, determined to be on her way. In the kitchen she found some corn bread and a piece of smoked ham. Wrapping it all in paper, she put the food in her bag and made her way out the back door into the lazy afternoon sun. Nobody saw her leave, and as far as she was concerned, nobody would care.

Abby cautiously walked down various alleys and back streets, unsure of where she was headed or which direction she should take. She soon came to the edge of the city, with only the large millworks and mining shaft houses standing between her and the frontier. She walked alone, unhurried, a slight touch of fear causing her stubborn self-confidence to waver. The late afternoon sun shone red on the mountaintop as the shadows lengthened.

After some time, now well outside of town, Abby noticed sadly that the daylight was beginning to disappear. There were no buildings beside or in front of her as she followed a seldom used trail, until she came to the framed doorway of an abandoned mine. A sign in front warned trespassers to stay out. Reasoning that the mine shaft would be a good place to hide and would offer shelter from the night chill, glancing around to make sure no one was around to see her, she pulled away one of the old gray boards blocking the shaft. As she entered, she felt cool departing winds rush past her and warm winds glide in behind her. She felt like she was walking into the mouth of some huge living beast.

Afraid to stay in the dark mine but definitely not wanting to go back home, her anger drove her further into the mine, its musty and earthy smells filling her nostrils. She lit her candle with a match. She proceeded slowly, often stumbling over rusted tracks. *They'll never find me here!* she thought stubbornly. The mine dripped moisture, and the wind made a soft and low moaning. Fear stretched its long fingers around her, and she began to doubt the wisdom of her venture. *This is far enough,* she decided, setting her candle on a large rock. Unpacking her blanket, she wrapped herself in it and sat down on a dry spot. She leaned against the rock wall and watched the flickering candlelight. She found Sarah and held the doll tightly against her. *I wish somebody loved me*, she thought sadly. *How come nobody loves me?*

~

By late that evening there was no doubt that Abby was missing. Jennifer and Lita were panic-stricken as they looked through Abby's room only to discover that her favorite personal items, including a rag doll named Sarah, were gone. The missing knapsack confirmed their suspicions. "Lita," Jennifer said, breathing heavily, "we have to accept the truth—Abby has run away. We need to ask others to help us find her as quickly as we can."

"Yes'm!" Lita replied, sadness distorting her black face. "That child might be in serious danger. I'll ask Abe to help us!"

Praying the whole way, Jennifer rushed back to the newspaper office in the darkening twilight. She found Jason still working by the light of a lantern. "Jason, Abby has run away! We have to find her before something terrible happens!"

Jason saw that Jennifer was terror-stricken. Jumping up from his chair, he came over and put his arms around her. He'd never seen her look so worried, and he understood and shared her fears. "Of course we have to find her. But we need to calm down and not just dash out and waste time searching in the wrong places. Jennifer, think about it—does she have any friends she could've gone to? Is there anyplace you know of where she might try to hide?"

Jennifer's face went pale, her features tight and drawn. "I don't think she has any friends she would've run to, and I don't have any idea where she might hide. I've spent so much time here at the newspaper that I'm ashamed to say I don't know my own daughter very well." She hugged Jason tightly. "I'm so scared. I haven't given her the attention I should have—so much has been happening . . ."

Holding Jennifer close, Jason prayed for the words that would console her. "God will help us. I'll get some lanterns fired up so we can search around town. And we'll organize a search party." She basked in his gentle words of assurance. "We'll find her!" Jason promised. "We'll find her."

~

Abe showed up after work as usual, hungry for more of Lita's fine cooking. He brought with him a fifty-pound bag of cornmeal, for he wasn't looking for handouts. When he stomped the mud off his big feet on the back porch, Lita jerked the door open. "Get inside!" she ordered, her face wrinkled with worry. "Little Miss Abby done run away, and Miss Jennifer is worried sick. You got to get out and look for her. And I'm comin' along!"

Surprised, Abe set the big bag of meal on the floor. "I got to eat first! I'm tired and needs some nourishment!"

"I done thought of that," Lita replied as she grabbed a greasy sack. "I got some bread and pork chops, so let's get on along!"

Seeing the lantern on the table lit and waiting, Abe picked it up. "Can I have one of dem poke chops now?"

"Get on out the door!" Lita scolded as she pushed the huge man outside.

They made their way into the night, holding the lantern in front of them as they searched under porches, in toolsheds, and in short alleys. As the darkness deepened, Lita walked closer to Abe.

Pressing onward, Abe and Lita's search carried them behind a large mill where they came upon a stack of old lumber. Holding the lantern out, the blacksmith tried to peer beneath the lumber. When something stirred there, he moved closer. "Somethin' in there all right," he mumbled. Holding his arm, Lita knelt beside him, staring into the hole. Again, something inside moved.

"Abby?" Lita called. "Is dat you, child?"

Hearing no answer, Abe and Lita crouched lower, peering into the unknown with wide eyes. A loud screech suddenly sounded as a large raccoon bolted from the hole, knocking Lita on her back and scampering right over her. "Aaah!" she screamed.

Abe pulled Lita to her feet. Trembling with fear, she demanded, "Take me home!" Agreeing that would probably be best, Abe escorted her back to the house. His forehead oily with sweat, he held the lantern in front of them with a nervous big hand. He didn't want to admit it, but the raccoon had scared him too. He considered it a bad omen to be run over by an animal of the night, a sign of bad things to come.

⁓

By the time Jennifer and Jason returned to her house, they found Abe and Lita in the kitchen with milk and cornbread. Jennifer and Jason had entered every business that was open and informed everyone about the runaway little girl. No one had seen her, and now it was late and they were all tired. Going over to the coffeepot on the stove, Jason poured a cup for himself and one for Jennifer. "We can start searching again early in the morning," he said quietly. "We all need to rest."

Everyone nodded in agreement. It had been a long, disappointing night. Abe stood and put on his floppy-brimmed hat. "I be back in the mornin'," he murmured as he slipped out the back door. Lita's big eyes followed him. She hated to see him go because fear still ran through her. She stood and came over to Jennifer, who glanced at her with sorrowful, dark eyes. "We'll find Abby, Miss Jennifer. Don't you worry your pretty head none." Slowly, like a tired old woman, Lita left to turn in for the night.

"You'd better get some rest," Jason said thoughtfully. "There's no more we can do tonight, but tomorrow's a new day."

"But my little girl's out there somewhere," Jennifer fretted, her voice low and dejected. "She's probably all alone, and who knows what danger she might be in! If I had paid more attention to her, maybe she wouldn't have left."

Jason put his arms around her, and she laid her head on his shoulder. No words passed between them, but the warm embrace comforted her. For the moment she didn't care about the mixed and confused emotions she'd struggled with recently.

～

The next morning, bright and early, a group of men gathered at the newspaper office to join in the search. "Don't reckon some Injuns got her, do ya?" a feeble old man asked.

"Herb!" Josh McGregor exclaimed. "There ain't been no Injuns around here in over ten years. You're scarin' the lady, so just pipe down. Why, that little girl's probably holed up someplace safe. When she gets hungry, she'll come on out." Josh was a harness maker and an expert on children, having twelve children of his own, all with red hair just like him.

"I appreciate you men coming," Jennifer said, trying to be pleasant, though worry gripped her features. "If we split up in an organized fashion, we can cover more ground."

Jason came over to the group holding a piece of paper. "I've drawn it out. One group can cover the south side and the other group the north side."

As the men mumbled over hot coffee, Grant kept busy at the press. He'd had the idea to print up flyers and would soon have them ready. His job would be to post and distribute the flyers around the busiest parts of town.

"Well," Jason said, putting on a light coat to fight the morning chill, "we'd best get going. Jennifer, I think you should stay here. The office will be the hub of operations."

Not saying a word, Jennifer came close to Jason as the rest of the men left. Her eyes pleaded as her hand slowly gripped Jason's arm. With a look of confidence, Jason said, "We'll find her, Jennifer, or I'll die trying."

Before Jason went on his way, the two prayed together for Abby's safe return.

~

Back at the house, Lita let Abe in the back door and served the big man a hot breakfast of eggs and grits. After he was finished, he reached into the front pocket of his suspendered overalls. Pulling out his piece of clear crystal quartz, he rubbed it with his wide thumb. Lita came up behind him and brushed bits of lint from his silvering short hair. She spied the stone, something that always worried her. "You just might be conjuring up evil with that rock," she informed him confidently. "You need to believe in Jesus! I'm tired of your old superstitions."

Turning in his chair, Abe glanced at Lita with apologetic eyes. "But dis here's a magic stone," he argued weakly.

"It's from the dark side," Lita said with certainty. "Let me give you somethin' you can trust in." She slowly removed a silver-chained necklace from around her neck. A silver cross dangled delicately from it as she slipped it around Abe's heavy neck. His big hands moved over warm bright metal as he studied the little cross. "What dis?" he asked.

"Dat's the cross of Jesus," Lita informed him. "He was the Son of God, and He came to earth to help us. When the Romans nailed him to the cross, he died for all our sins. If you want to rub on somethin' you rub on dat! You ask God for *His* help!"

Abe liked Lita's giving him something so personal. He let the cross fall to the front of his neck. Lita quickly picked up the crystal lying on the table and tossed it into a nearby wastebasket, causing Abe to jump. "You don't have to throw it away!" he protested. "It's got healin' power."

"You got all the healin' power you need already. You jus' do like I say. Have faith in the Jesus who died on dat cross and you'll see what God can do! Now, here's some lunch," she said, handing him a small sack. "You get on out there and find dat little girl." Abe had never seen such strong trust in God as Lita had just manifested. Not knowing what to believe for himself, but wanting to ask Lita questions later about that Jesus she'd been talking about, he rose from his chair and grabbed his old hat.

"I'll do whatever I can," he said as he walked out the back door. He turned to give Lita another going-over with his aged eyes. He adored her and would do whatever she asked.

~

Nervously trying to find something to do at the office, Jennifer couldn't keep herself from worrying about Abby. *I can't just sit around here and wait*, she thought. *I think I'll go see Charles. Maybe he can help somehow.* She slammed the door behind her as her gingham dress rustled with her fast pace.

Finding Charles sitting comfortably at his big desk, she explained her dilemma. "Half the town is looking for her, and Grant is nailing up flyers. Charles, I'm so worried. Where could she have gone? What if something tragic has happened?"

With his ever-confident smile, Charles came around to Jennifer. "She'll turn up," he said easily, no hint of concern on his face. With all the work he had to do to sell Hearst's holdings—and make a new fortune for himself, he couldn't be bothered with worrying about a misbehaved child.

"Would you help us look for her?" Jennifer pleaded.

"I wouldn't know where to begin," Charles protested "Besides, I have sales pending on Hearst's properties. The money is accumulating nicely."

Jennifer's expression went cold. The fog was lifting, and she was finally beginning to see things more clearly. *Father, have I wanted to believe in Charles so badly that I didn't see what kind of man he really is? Have I been blind to the spiritual issues involved? Help me now to do and say the right thing.* "Charles, I'm not wanting to be your judge, but don't you care about anything besides money and deals? Are these things so precious to you that you can overlook everything else? Do you consider financial profit more valuable than the life of my daughter?"

Charles Fitzgerald was a man who grew humble whenever trouble came, but as soon as his life grew calm again, his deceptive, ever-present smile and easygoing attitude would return. He now gave Jennifer his close attention, attempting to measure both her and the response that would serve his purposes best. An hour earlier he'd been a man who was content with his life. Why was she so set against financial success? Yet his ego wouldn't admit that he couldn't have her. Shaking his head with bewilderment, he said, "Jennifer, can't you see what Virginia City is doing to you and your family? Your own child has run away! Let's put this place behind us—come with me to South Dakota. It would be better for everyone."

While recognizing Charles's general statement of concern about her family's welfare, Jennifer also saw that he had refused to directly address her problems, especially the importance of finding Abby before harm came to her. Her eyes turned to slits, and her face tightened. "Charles, you say the right words sometimes," she said evenly, "but you really only care about yourself. I don't know for sure if Abby is dead or alive, and all you can do is talk about money and tell me I need to move to South Dakota with you. You've told me you love me, but I don't believe you even understand the meaning of the word."

"How can you say such a thing?" Charles protested. "I've worked hard to make a future for us, but you seem to fight me every inch of the way. Can't you see why I'm doing all this?"

"Yes, Charles, I see. I finally see," Jennifer added.

Charles went on, "Nobody trusts anyone else, and there is no loyalty really. But monetary wealth is respected." His smile had disappeared. "Jennifer, like poker, life is a game, and whoever has the most money wins."

"A very gallant sentiment," said Jennifer mockingly. "Most noble."

Charles stood stiffly with a tense look and no smile. "I thought we were in agreement on this."

Jennifer looked at him critically, perceiving his faults more clearly than ever before. "I'd thought you had a deep respect for God, a personal trust in Him. But now . . ."

"I don't believe in whims and dreams. And I don't choose to have faith in a far-off deity rather than in my own abilities. I'm sorry if that doesn't meet your approval, but that is my faith, my religion. I'm sure you're willing to grant me the right to choose my own way." Charles was confident he could once again make others believe in the wisdom of his words. "I'm a man who selects the path that seems most sensible to the God who made him. That path has made me rich. Would you rather that I be a drunkard or a beggar?"

Staring at him coldly, Jennifer realized that once she had admired this man, but he'd destroyed her trust in him by his careless speech and self-centered behavior, and now she saw him simply as a foolish man with no admirable qualities. Remembering how she'd felt about him and reflecting on how mistaken she'd been made her feel ashamed. *Father, if only I had sought your mind on all this along the way, instead of trusting my own discernment . . . I've made so many mistakes—with Charles, with Abby. With Jason too? Give me the strength, the wisdom I need now!*

"I'm going to South Dakota," Charles said, still hoping to achieve the intended effect with this conversation. "If I send for you, will you come?"

"No, I won't. Certainly you know that."

He shook his head in dismay, not understanding how such an intelligent, beautiful woman could refuse his gracious offer. After all, he was offering to forgive her misunderstandings of him and to give her a prosperous financial future. "I'll come back for you then."

Amazed both at the man's persistence and his lack of understanding, Jennifer shook her head. "In the beginning I trusted and admired you completely, and I was so happy. But you gradually destroyed that by the way you talked, the way you valued the wrong things and neglected everything important, the way you manipulated my emotions and took charge of me like you were some kind of deity. Worst of all, it has become clear to me that you have no relationship with God. I think deep inside I knew our relationship was wrong, but I wouldn't admit it to myself. I prayed you were really not what I was beginning to think you were. It's a terrible thing for a woman to fall in love, then see she was wrong. It makes her doubt that love exists between a man and a woman at all."

The weight of what Jennifer was saying suddenly registered with Charles. He looked at her long and hard, but she held his stare, her eyes ablaze. "You're mistaken about me, about what I can do for you," he uttered weakly.

"Take your money and follow Hearst," Jennifer said firmly. "You're good with words, Charles, but you're a weak man. You can fool a lot of people—you had me fooled—but you are a man who worships himself, cares hardly at all for others, and has no respect for God." Jennifer felt new strength surge through her. Stepping up to the attorney's desk, she removed the glinting diamond ring from her finger and set it on the fine mahogany top. "I believe this is yours," she said forcefully. "It has me taken a long time, but now I see clearly who you really are. Charles, our relationship has come to an end." Turning, she walked out the door.

Jennifer returned to the office with new life in her step. She felt as if she'd been washed clean, as if she'd been blind but had been given sight again. She would return to the task of finding Abby with a renewed spirit and a clearer mind.

∽

The day grew long and tedious as searchers frequently ran into each other in alleys, barns, and haylofts.

Deciding to look where others weren't looking, Abe walked to the edge of town, where he meandered down a seldom-used road. *Maybe she wandered dis way*, he thought, not really believing it. Soon not much was left of the day, and he was sure his luck was running out. Hesitantly, he pulled the little cross from beneath his sweat-soaked cotton shirt and looked at it. He was proud of it because Lita had given it to him. His old stone hadn't done much good, but the cross represented a God he'd always suspected might exist but knew nothing about. He rubbed the cross gently as he turned a corner. Up ahead and to the right he saw an abandoned mine shaft. Coming closer, he saw that one of the boards blocking the entrance had been removed. On the ground the big man saw small footprints the size a child like Abby would make. Fearing the dark, confined spaces in the shaft, he thought, *I don't need to go in dere. I can go get help.* But he knew it would soon be dark. If she was in there and they didn't get her out by nightfall, she would be there another night. And if she was injured . . .

Abe knew what he had to do. Taking a deep breath, he tore off more of the boards so he could proceed. Stepping into the eerie, moaning mine shaft, he felt the fear he'd always had of mines; he remembered the cave-in that had almost cost him his life. And as if mines weren't bad enough, an abandoned shaft was even more dangerous. But recognizing that Abby might be in there, he put aside his fear. Taking a small candle from his overalls pocket, he lit it, swallowed hard, and forced himself onward. Rubbing the silver cross, he hoped the power of Lita's God would help him.

∾

After Abby had curled up in her blanket, she'd felt secure in her hiding-place even if it was a little scary there. As the hours passed, she grew damp and cold. The warm light from her fat little candle cast a faint glow as she dug something out of her knapsack to eat. After she finished, she held Sarah tightly and soon fell asleep.

Sometime during the night, though she had little concept of the passage of time because of the constant darkness, Abby had awakened cold and thirsty, her candle having burned out, leaving no light to dispel the darkness. Shivering, she stood and felt around for her things. Finding her knapsack, she picked it up along with her blanket and rag doll and chose her steps cautiously, hoping to find her way back out of the shaft. But she had become disoriented, went the wrong way, and ventured further into the mine. The damp cold made her bones ache, and a constant dripping echoed through the windy shaft. The blackness was thick and the musty odors rank. She became scared for her life, sure nobody would ever find her alive. Wishing she hadn't run away, she'd longed for the warmth of a loving and understanding hug from her mother.

Uncertainty and fear had made Abby cower in defeat as she collapsed next to a cold rock wall. She shivered in her damp blanket and trembled in a darkness as black as coal, trying to hope for rescue, but realizing all hope might be gone. *If God loves us like Mother keeps saying He does, why did He let my father die? Maybe He'll let me die too.* No one heard her weeping in that place of heavy darkness.

CHAPTER

~ 24 ~

New Hopes

Abe was a brave man who would fight a mountain lion or face a deadly fire or wrestle a bear, but entering an abandoned mine shaft put terror within him. The confinement, the darkness, the danger of a cave-in or stepping off into some bottomless pit—all of these things nearly paralyzed him with fear. Some had told him that the mountains were living things that grew angry with those who disrespected them by boring holes into their sides, and his superstitious nature made him wonder if those stories might be true. *Who knows what's in there*, he thought as he cautiously entered the shaft. His small candle was dwarfed by the darkness that surrounded him. *I could get buried alive in here*, he continued to worry. *But dat little girl might be in here. I got to see if she is. I can't just walk away.* He rubbed the tiny cross with one hand and held out the candle with the other.

The jumping shadows and slimy rock walls seemed to be closing in on him. His eyes grew wide at the strange sounds coming from far ahead, and his hands began to shake. Then he heard what sounded like a tiny whimper, something like a rabbit in a trap. "Abby?" he called, his heavy voice breaking the silence. "Abby? Dat you?"

At first Abby thought she was dreaming when she heard someone call her name. Numb with cold, she thought maybe she had died and it was God calling her. Afraid, she didn't answer. But then her name again echoed along the cavern walls. She was frightened, cold, wet, and hungry—and anxious to be found. "Here!" she called. "I'm over here!"

Abe was never so glad to hear a voice in his entire life. Not only was he thankful to find Abby, but it felt good knowing he wasn't alone in the darkness. "I'm comin', child!" He quickened his pace, disregarding the fears that just minutes before had almost made his heart stop.

Spotting the dim flicker of a candle, Abby called out again. When Abe approached, she was trying to stand, but her legs had gone to sleep. He set the candle down and gently picked her up, then grabbed her bag. "Get Sarah too," Abby said, pointing to the limp doll.

"I sure enough will," Abe said happily. "We wouldn't want to leave her in dis place—no, ma'am!"

Abby held the candle while Abe carried her through the wet, rock-strewn mine shaft. "You sure got some people worried," Abe said.

Abby didn't comment. She felt comfortable in the big man's arms as he carried her out of the shaft and into the twinkling starlight. Abe paused and took a deep breath of the sweet and fresh evening air. Anxious as he was to get back to town, he took his time, wanting to carry Abby gently. The night was still and quiet; there was no one else on the old road.

"Were you scared?" Abby asked.

"Yes'm, I surely was," Abe admitted.

"I was too," Abby confessed. "I thought I was going to die in there."

"Well, you be safe now," Abe said. He realized that the chances of his finding Abby in the abandoned mine had been extremely slim. *Maybe the God Lita told me about was lookin' out for us*, he thought. He would definitely be asking Lita some questions.

When they entered town at the end of a busy street, a man saw Abe carrying the little girl and rushed over. "You found her! Is she all right?"

"Of course I'm all right!" Abby answered quickly. "Abe saved me."

"He's found her!" the man yelled at the top of his lungs. "Abe found the little girl!"

A small crowd quickly gathered and followed Abe down the street, lit with lanterns. "Where'd you find her?" they asked over and over.

"An old mine up the last road yonder," Abe said, swinging his head back to indicate the direction from which they'd come.

"That boarded-up mine?" a skimpy fellow with a heavy beard asked.

"Yes, suh," Abe replied.

"Why, that's old Sutter's mine," the man said in astonishment. "Did you know it has a 400-foot drop about a hundred feet back in the shaft?"

"Naw, suh," Abe said, not wanting to think about it. He trudged on until he rounded the corner near the newspaper office. The crowd following him had grown considerably.

Jennifer, Jason, and Grant had been waiting impatiently, figuring there was nothing else they could do that day, when they heard the noise of the crowd's approach. They jumped up and rushed through the front door. Standing on the boardwalk, Jennifer watched the group draw near, Abe at the front. Was that Abby he was carrying? For a second her heart felt as if it had stopped beating, for in the dim light it appeared that whatever he carried was limp. What if Abby was . . . She bounded from the walk and ran to Abe, her arms extended. "Abby! Abby!" she cried.

"Mother!" Abby said, extending her little arms.

Quickly, Jennifer took her beloved daughter into her arms. "Oh, Abby! You're alive! We've been so worried. I was afraid something had happened to you." She hugged Abby tightly, giving her all of the love she possibly could. *Father, thank You for watching over my Abby, for watching over all of us.*

This was exactly what Abby had so longed for—to be accepted and loved. She hugged her mother with all her might. Now that the perpetual anxiety had ceased to torment her, she came alive with all the attention and love.

Jason spoke up. "Abe, where'd you find her?"

The bearded skimpy man answered for the big black man. "He found her in the old Sutter mine. It's a wonder Abe and that little girl weren't killed—that's a dangerous place even for an experienced miner."

Turning to Abe, Jason took the big man's arm. "Come on, I've got some hot coffee in the office." They followed Jennifer, carrying Abby, into the office. For hours a large group of people hung around to get the entire story while Jennifer tended Abby, cleaning her up and giving her something to eat and drink. The generous amounts of food that had been brought in for the volunteers were enjoyed by all as they celebrated Abby's safe return. Once summoned, Lita came there too, so proud of her Abe.

As people love to do, they told the story over and over of how Abe had fought his fears and rescued Abby. Abe was again the hero of Virginia City!

~

A few days later Jennifer and Jason sat in the newspaper office. The last edition of the paper had sold well with the exciting story of Abe and Abby. Jason noticed that Jennifer hadn't worn the gaudy diamond ring in days. He'd wondered about that but had been hesitant to ask about it. "I hope you didn't lose that expensive ring in all the excitement," he said casually, hoping his curiosity wasn't too apparent.

Glancing at her hand, conflicting thoughts stormed through Jennifer's mind. It had been an ordeal with Charles, but she was glad it was over. "I did lose it in a sense," she said calmly. "I gave it back to him."

The news so shocked Jason that he dropped the mining report he was working on and turned his eyes to Jennifer. "You broke off the engagement?"

"Yes."

This was the best news Jason had heard since Abby was found. For a moment he was at a loss for words, because this information opened doors he'd never dreamed would open. "I'm sorry to hear that," he said sadly, not really sorry at all.

"Don't be," Jennifer said with a shrug. "I'm fortunate that things happened the way they did. Charles wasn't the man I thought he was, nor the man he pretended to be."

I could have told you that, Jason thought. "You seem relieved," he observed.

A pleasant but mysterious smile appeared on Jennifer's face. "I'm so foolish," she admitted. "I'm embarrassed by how naive I was about that man. All Charles cares about is how much money he can accumulate. He has no genuine concern for others and no genuine respect for God."

Nibbling on a pencil, Jason felt deeply happy for Jennifer. Though he didn't know if she'd ever become interested in him, he cared enough for her to be content with seeing her happy. And he knew she would have never been happy with Charles. "I guess sometimes things work out for the best," he said, trying to sound optimistic.

Standing, Jennifer walked over to the front window and looked out, holding her hands on her hips. "So many things," she said as if she were talking to herself, "so many things that seemed totally impossible have worked out." She paused a moment as if recalling the past. "I've been so fortunate to have made it this far even though my faith was sometimes weak. I know God has guided me and watched over me. It's all too incredible to be coincidence. He's a patient, loving, all-wise God!"

Nodding, Jason agreed, for his life had been in ruins before he came to know Christ as his Saviour and Lord. He walked over to the window to stand beside Jennifer. Up and down the street people rambled on their happy way—just another sunny day in Virginia City. "You've helped me turn my life around too," he said. "I was headed for certain destruction."

Jennifer turned her attention to Jason, her eyes full of compassion. "Giving your life to God was the best thing you could ever do, and you are doing well at following His ways," she affirmed. Studying his face, she realized even more than before the depth of the feelings between the two of them. She knew now without doubt that she was attracted to Jason. This man before her had stuck with her and had risked his life for her; he was dedicated and true, something she knew to be rare. But for the moment she concealed her feelings, unsure of how to express herself.

An observant man, he detected a subtle hint of admiration in her eyes, the kind of admiration that a woman sees in a man. But considering what he'd been, he couldn't let himself believe it was true. He'd seen this look before, and nothing had come of it. He shrugged his shoulders. "Things are settling down around here," he said to break the silence. "Virginia City is growing tame."

Turning back to the window and glancing down the street, Jennifer had the same feeling. Virginia City was finally becoming civilized.

~

Alone in his hotel room, Charles Fitzgerald packed his things with short and quick motions. He was thoroughly disgusted. *Jennifer DeSpain isn't worth my attention anyway,* he thought reproachfully. *If she doesn't understand the value of being rich, then she's not the woman for me.* He slung a wad of bills into his valise. The money he'd kept for himself from Hearst's holdings amounted to a tidy profit. *If I could just convince her to come with me . . .* But he knew it was no use. Jennifer was a strong-minded woman. Of course, he could stay in Virginia City and keep fighting for her affections, let her know he wouldn't give up. He shook his head. Angrily, he accepted the fact that he wasn't that kind of fighter. He had to follow the money. He poured a glass of whiskey, then angrily threw it against the wall.

It could've been different, he mused, saddened by the way his circumstances had changed. Not only had he lost Jennifer DeSpain, but he'd lost a battle of words and reason. And for what? Glancing at the bag that held his money, he relished the thought of accumulating great amounts of it. A slight smile crept onto his sweaty face. *I haven't lost everything,* he thought with great satisfaction. *Someday she'll be sorry she refused me, for I'll be one of the wealthiest men in the West!* He set his luggage by the door for the porter to take to the station; his train would be leaving soon.

Reaffirming his decision to pursue great personal wealth, he held his head high. *I might even go into politics,* he thought, hoping to soothe his ego. *Then she'll rue her decision. I'll make her sorry!* Later that morning Charles Fitzgerald left Virginia City forever.

～

Lita was determined to give Abe a fine reward for his heroic work. She spent all morning the day after he returned with little Abby baking her finest apple pie, and nobody else was allowed to touch it—it was strictly for Abe. She was so proud of the big man that she couldn't find words to express herself. When he came to the back door late that afternoon, she scolded him playfully. "Where you been? I been waitin' all day for you!"

"Been workin'," Abe said meekly.

Lita pulled him inside the kitchen and sat him at the table. She turned to the stove and removed an apple pie she had warming under a cloth. "Here," she said, placing the fragrant pie before him. "You saved my little Abby, and I cooked this special for you. Now you dig in." She handed him a fork.

"Uhm-uhm, that surely smells good," Abe said. He liked being a hero in Lita's eyes, for as far as he was concerned, the sun rose and set on her. Her delightful way of scorning him tickled him, though he wouldn't laugh aloud. Sometimes she fussed and fretted over everything he did, but that was all right too because he knew that deep down she cared for him. But he wasn't sure how to return the affection, being a quiet and solitary man. So he had done the best thing he could think of and made her a new cross to hang around her neck. Then they'd both have one. But the one he made for her was even better, because it was made from solid gold.

After he had his fill of the delicious pie, he shoved the plate away. When Lita passed by, he grabbed her wrist and pulled her to the chair beside him. "Sit down here a minute," he said softly.

Surprise in her eyes, Lita slowly sat down, wiping her hands on her apron. She'd never seen Abe act this way, and it left her speechless, a rare state for Lita.

"That cross you give me," he began, "I believe it really works, 'cause I'd've never found dat girl on my own."

An uncontrollable smile came to Lita's round face. "I know God is real," she confessed. "He be the most real thing in the world. He made the whole world and the stars and the sun and the moon and— and everything that was made."

Abe nodded, his calm old eyes on Lita's smooth face. What she said made sense, for he thought it was a complete miracle that she'd come all the way from New Orleans to be part of his life. Thinking about that made him very happy. "I got somethin' for you," he said, reaching into his overalls chest pocket. He pulled out a delicate cross and placed it in her hand. "You gave me yours, so I got you another one."

Closely examining the cross, Lita knew without a doubt that it was fine gold. And she knew by its rugged construction that Abe had made it. It was the most beautiful sight she'd ever seen. Her big eyes welled up as she tried to speak; she was so choked up, nothing would come out for a long time.

"Thank you, Abe. It's beautiful. And does you know why I think it's so beautiful? Because you made it for me. But I also likes it 'cause it reminds me of Jesus, God's Son who came to this here world to die for our sins. If we asks Him to save us from God's bein' angry against us because we've done wrong things, He forgives us!"

As Lita continued to explain the Gospel to Abe, the big man listened intently, and not just because it was Lita who was doing the talking. He knew this was what he'd been searching for so long in his superstitions and charms. He knew He needed God in his life, and before long he asked Lita to help him pray to Jesus to ask Him to be his Saviour.

Afterward, Abe placed his huge arms around Lita and pulled her to him. He hugged her tightly, and she loved every second of it. *Now that we both belongs to Jesus, I ain't gonna never let this man get away,* she promised herself.

～

Over the next year Virginia City settled down and became a stable mining production town producing great riches. The heyday of wild fortune seeking had mellowed to a constant, predictable profit and steady routines. Virginia City was a mild town now, compared to what it had been when Jennifer had arrived. The arrival of more women and the construction of a permanent church, rather than church happening only when a preacher came through, were signs of the changing times. *The Miner's News* was a solid newspaper selling more papers than ever.

One day Jennifer was proofing the next edition, dated August 9, 1875. "Grant does quite well with his articles," she said as her eyes skimmed the page. "He's going to make a good newspaper man."

"He had good teachers," Jason reminded her.

"But he's still only twelve. Not many twelve-year-olds write newspaper articles," Jennifer reminded him. She wore an easy smile, pleased by the development of the newspaper and by many other things.

It was late in the afternoon, another day of dry dust and sun-scorched ground. The office had its own aromas of coffee, newspaper ink, and sweat. What had once been loosely defined as a struggling newspaper had proved to be a business able to survive the most difficult challenges, a newspaper that had touched the hearts of many readers. The sun swung lazily over the western slope and dropped quietly behind the mountain range, leaving its red hue as a reminder of the day's heat.

Picking up some mail, Jennifer read a one-page advertisement about a small mining town in Colorado, a town the ad promised would be the new El Dorado with its great riches in gold and silver. "Did you read this?" she asked Jason, holding up the copy.

Glancing over, Jason replied, "Oh, we get stuff like that all the time. It seems Colorado is the new great wild mining frontier, and every town is the new El Dorado. I'm sure they're exaggerating just to get people to come to their towns."

"But with so many towns making the same claim," Jennifer responded, "there must be some truth to some of it. I read something the other day about a place called Central City, not too far from Denver. Evidently people are pouring into these places."

Jason stroked the stubble on his face and said, "That's the way it was here in the beginning."

"I remember riding the train through Colorado," Jennifer said, rolling her eyes as she recalled the huge mountains and wild forests. "It was the most beautiful country I'd ever seen."

"Unlike this dried-up buffalo wallow," Jason teased. "I don't think we have a tree left around here—just rocks and mountains on one side and desert on the other."

Jennifer got a dreamy look on her face. "I wonder how hard it would be to establish a newspaper in one of those rapidly growing new towns in Colorado? The air there is so wonderful to breathe—it has a pure, sweet, fragrant quality that seems to encourage the happiest and healthiest of moods."

Jason glanced up quickly, surprised. "You mean after all we've been through here to establish this newspaper, you'd be willing to sell out and travel to new and unknown frontiers? It could be very difficult in those undeveloped towns and mining camps—bad winters, snowstorms, a shortage of supplies."

Shrugging her shoulders, Jennifer cocked her head to one side as if flirting with the idea. "You never know," she said, "it could be exciting—an ideal opportunity for a new newspaper."

"What about *The Miner's News?*" Jason asked.

"Oh, I'm sure I could make a fine profit on it," Jennifer assured him. "Dan DeQuille has been trying to buy me out for some time. I'm not sure if it's the newspaper he likes or if he just wants to eliminate any competition with the *Territorial Enterprise*, but either way . . ."

On one hand, Jason was reluctant to accept the idea. However, the prospect of adventure did stir his imagination. Gazing outside, he could see the shadowy blanket of dusk covering the town. "Care to take a walk?" he asked innocently.

Raising her eyebrows in mock suspicion, Jennifer welcomed the chance to get out of the office and take a stroll on a pleasant evening. "That sounds nice," she said appreciatively.

After locking up the building, Jason took Jennifer's hand and led her down the street. Lanterns were coming on behind windows that threw their yellow squares of light onto the dusty street. The lamp

lighter who lit the streetlamps scrambled up and down his short ladder at every stop. "It's a fine evening," Jason said, his feelings lifting.

"Yes, it is," Jennifer agreed as she and Jason swung their hands
in rhythm with their stride.

The new Jason had more confidence than the man he'd been
before. Now that Charles was gone, Jason felt it was his duty to tell
Jennifer how he felt about her. They noticed various businesses closing their doors, while the saloons' and dance halls' busyness were
marked with bright light and loud laughter. The heavy odor of grain
and hops emanated from the Nevada Brewery, and high above stood
the shadows of the grim and grand mining works of Mount Davidson.
At one point, under a roof covering the boardwalk, he pulled her to
a stop. "Jennifer, there is something I must tell you."

Jennifer's face looked surprised. "What is it, Jason?"

He paused, his eyes holding hers, though he was still a little nervous. "I've waited a long time to tell you this, Jennifer, but . . . I love
you. I always have, though now I love you more than ever. I'll stand
by you always, no matter what."

Thrilled at what she was hearing, but nevertheless stunned,
Jennifer hardly knew how to respond. After so much inner turmoil,
she had come to recognize her affection for Jason, but now that the
moment was here . . . Gazing at him, she realized he had become a
very handsome and worthy man and, most important, a man of God.
He had stood up for her and fought for her, even at personal risk. Yet,
so soon after her final confrontation with Charles, she was hesitant
to acknowledge her feelings for any man. Before she could think any
further, Jason put his arms around her and pulled her to him. He gave
her a long, affectionate kiss.

Though caught off guard, Jennifer responded. She had been
lonely for a long time, and now as Jason held her, she found herself
surrendering to his love. There was something special about Jason;
he was all she'd hoped to find in Charles. Suddenly apprehensive,
wanting to be sure she wasn't again making the mistake of rushing
into a relationship without having God's guidance on the matter, she
pulled away.

"I'm sorry," Jason mumbled. "I shouldn't have done that."

"No," Jennifer said. "Jason, I wish . . . I wish I knew my own heart better than I do. I thought I loved Charles, but God wasn't in it. And now . . . I just don't want to run ahead of God again. I hope you understand." She gently took his hand, inviting him to continue their evening stroll. He gave her a smile of acceptance.

She'd been honest with Jason—she truly didn't trust herself anymore. She didn't understand her own feelings. In a way she felt lost, not sure which way to turn. But one fact was clear in her mind: she could not remember a kiss ever being so satisfying.

Shaken, Jennifer gave a half laugh and reached up to touch her hair. "I'm not refusing you, Jason. We'll talk about it," she said, her eyes sparkling, "after we get to Colorado."

Jason grinned as he felt a sudden rush of excitement. "We'll do that, Jennifer! We truly will!" he exclaimed.

As they walked along, they spoke of the future—and they both knew that the best was yet to come.